HUNTED

HUNTED

REBECCA ZANETTI

BRAVA

KENSINGTON PUBLISHING CORP.
www.kensingtonbooks.com

BRAVA BOOKS are published by

Kensington Publishing Corp.
119 West 40th Street
New York, NY 10018

All Kensington titles, imprints, and distributed lines are available at special quantity discounts for bulk purchases for sales promotions, premiums, fund-raising, educational, or institutional use.

Special book excerpts or customized printings can also be created to fit specific needs. For details, write or phone the office of the Kensington special sales manager: Kensington Publishing Corp., 119 West 40th Street, New York, NY 10018, attn: Special Sales Department; phone: 1-800-221-2647.

Brava and the B logo are Reg. U.S. Pat. & TM Off.

ISBN-13: 978-0-7582-5927-1
ISBN-10: 0-7582-5927-1

First Kensington Trade Paperback Printing: May 2012

10 9 8 7 6 5 4 3 2 1

Printed in the United States of America

To Tony Zanetti for doing more than his fair share with the kids, dogs, and house so I have time to write—the heroes in my books have nothing on you. I will remember this and not say a word next time I break a toe stumbling over the size fourteens you've left by the door.

To Gabe Zanetti, who rises to every challenge with strength and determination as well as an excellent sense of humor;

To Karly Zanetti, whose kindness and great intelligence will come in very handy when she takes over the world someday;

I love you.

ACKNOWLEDGMENTS

Thank you to my agent, Caitlin Blasdell, for the time, effort, and incredible insight she brings to my writing;

Thank you to my editor, Megan Records, who works so very hard for each of her authors while still keeping an incredible sense of humor;

Thank you to all the folks at Liza Dawson Associates and Kensington Publishing for the support;

Thank you to my critique partners, Jennifer Dorough and Sayde Grace—you're both brilliant;

Thank you to my Beta Readers, family, and friends: Jessica Namson, Gail English, Jim English, Debbie Smith, Stephanie West, Brandie Chapman, Kathy Zanetti, Herb Zanetti, Augustina VanHoven, and Bonnie Paulson;

Thank you to my colleagues and friends: Cynthia Eden, Kate Douglas, Lynn Rush, Lethal Ladies, FF&P Mudpuddlers, and the IECRWA group.

Chapter 1

"She's going to kill you," his old friend muttered.

Conn Kayrs raised an eyebrow, cutting his eyes to Kellach from across the scarred table. He hadn't been in Shea's tavern in a century, yet the tables were the same. Beaten and solid. "She can try." Damn, he hoped she tried. For no other reason than the excuse it gave him to put his hands on her. Finally. After all this time.

Kell tipped his ale back, his dark gaze remaining steady on the tavern door. "She's coming."

That she was. The air thickened as if in anticipation of a lightning strike—or a witch's temper. Conn relaxed in his chair, stretching his long legs to cross at the ankles. His boots caught on worn grooves in the wood. "You might want to make yourself scarce."

Kell tied his dark hair back at the nape, his shoulders tensing. "You may need backup." He glanced at the row of patrons lining the bar on hand-carved wooden stools centuries old. Mostly witches, maybe a couple humans. People who lived on the northern coast of Ireland, happy in the knowledge most of the world didn't know they existed. "Though we should clear everyone else out."

Conn fought a grin. His friend sounded almost . . . concerned.

As a fierce witch and a dangerous warrior, the enforcer

for the council was trained in witchcraft and traditional war. Kellach's main job was to protect the leading council, the Coven Nine. He feared no man. But a woman? Well now, that was another story.

"Your cousin isn't that dangerous, Kell." Though what did Conn know? Moira had been training for a century. Her skill set might be deadly. If so, they needed to get a couple things straight.

Several folks lining the bar cast wary glances over their shoulders. Even in this day and age, vampires were a scarcity in the north, so Conn kept his fangs hidden. He didn't want to spook them—although his metallic eyes probably gave him away.

Watching carefully, he wondered if anyone would challenge him. He'd never battled a witch. They'd been allies of the Realm for centuries, though he often wondered about that. Witches kept their powers shrouded in secrecy. Not even his king knew the full extent of what magic allowed them to create.

Kell's lips tightened in his rugged face. "Moira is the seventh sister of the seventh sister. All power. You have no idea what you're doing, my friend. She told you not to come to Ireland, and you should've listened. You shouldn't be—"

The door swept open on a gust of wind. Electricity crackled through the room. Moira stepped inside, her green gaze hard on Conn. His heart seized. How had he forgotten her beauty? Her power? Her tiny size?

Conn scraped back his chair and stood. "Hello, mate."

Her focus remained on him. "Get out."

Stools toppled, chairs clattered, and patrons stumbled in a mass exodus. He couldn't help his grin as the door slammed shut behind her. Even from across the room her scent of lilacs whispered toward him. Tempted him. "Feeling dramatic, *Dailtín*?"

"I believe I've asked you not to call me a brat." She stepped into the empty tavern, all grace, all intent. "Kellach, please leave."

"Yes, Kell. Get the hell out," Conn said cheerfully, his gaze on his mate. He'd missed those rioting red curls and that translucent skin—almost as much as he'd missed the fire in her eyes and the spirit in her tiny form. Almost. her lilting voice grabbed him around the throat and squeezed.

With a muttered, "It's your funeral," Kellach stalked outside. The air relaxed as his power dissipated.

Silence. Alone in the bar, Moira and Conn stared at each other for a moment.

Finally, she sighed and tugged a hand through her wild curls. "You need to go home, Connlan."

He ran his gaze to her toes and back up, truly appreciating the faded jeans and tight white shirt decorated with Celtic knots. The sight of the dainty witch in modern clothing reached deep in his gut and twisted. The need to take her to the floor nearly had him lunging. "Or what?"

Fire flashed in her emerald eyes. "Or I'll destroy you." Power all but danced on her skin with the threat.

Damn. That voice, that spirit. His heart leaped to life and his cock jumped to attention. "Think so?"

She sucked in air, her hands fisting and then relaxing at her sides.

That's right, sweetheart. Center yourself. He gesture toward Kell's vacated chair. "Have a seat."

"No. You need to leave, Conn. Please." Determination and a hint of desperation broke through her calm façade.

He cocked his head to the side, unease tickling his nape. "Did you just say *please*?" Every instinct he owned flared to life. "What the hell's going on, Moira?"

Her eyes widened just enough for him to doubt her intent. "I need time, Conn."

"I've given you a hundred years." Why the hell was she

trying the innocent approach with him? He knew her better. "I told you eight months ago I was coming." He'd meant to fly across the ocean the next day, but war had intruded. Being commander of the Realm's soldiers often took a heavy toll.

"I need more. Just a bit, to prepare to, uh—"

"Prepare for what?"

The morning after he'd marked her, when her father wanted his head on a spike, he'd tried to make peace. One moonlit night he'd taken her virginity and she'd taken his heart. Fate had made an appearance, forming the Kayrs marking on his palm that he'd transferred to her hip during sex. Even so, he'd signed the treaty promising to leave her be for a century—to train as the Seventh. Time was up.

"We had a one-night stand and ended up mated. That's all." She sighed. "You want to solidify our alliance. But I'm not ready to, um, concentrate on us."

He waited.

She clasped her hands together. "I'm asking for more time. Just a little."

"Why?"

"Do you trust me?"

"No." Not in a million years. "Try to play me and you'll regret it, *céadsearc*." Sweetheart. He'd learned the endearment the night she sighed it in his ear, her body wrapped around his, her darkening eyes stealing his heart forever.

"I'm asking you. Go home."

Studying her guileless expression, he stepped out from behind the table so nothing separated them but highly charged air. He'd trained as a soldier, the best in the world, and his instincts were finely honed. Drawing on those, drawing on his gut, he lowered his chin. "No."

Fiery temper swirled in her belly and it took every ounce of Moira's control to keep from lighting the jackass on fire. She'd tried to be reasonable with him. A soldier, the best, the only thing he understood was battle strategy and bullets. Fine. "I've asked you nicely."

He smiled. Slow. Dangerous—a warning from a true predator. "Don't get me wrong, *Dailtín*. I like you soft and pleading."

His rumbling voice heated the fire already burning in her. Memories of her pleading for his touch, for his claim, escaped the box she usually shut them in. One night. One long, delicious night with him so many years ago. Her nipples peaked along with her anger. Her gaze swept him. Well over six feet, eyes the color of the deepest riverbed— dark and green and too knowing. Thick shoulders, powerful thighs, and his handsome face proved the Creator was a woman. A goddess. Only a goddess would've spent time ensuring each sharp hollow and rugged peak somehow combined into lethal masculine beauty.

She avoided looking at his broad hands. Too many memories of those clever fingers that had brought pleasure . . . while his leaving had brought pain. He hadn't wanted to keep her a century ago. An emotional shove down took care of the ding in her heart. He sure as hell wasn't going to claim her now just because of Realm politics. "I don't want to hurt you, Connlan." Her voice softened as she spoke the absolute truth. "But I will."

He reached for a band from his pocket and tied back the thick mass of dark hair whispering for her touch. When had he grown it to his shoulders? "Let's get to it then." His stance widened, his gaze narrowed. "Show me what you've got, baby."

She centered all thoughts, her hands opening palms up at her sides. "I hoped you'd be reasonable." Bollocks. She'd hoped he'd come to get her before now . . . before he had to. Because he wanted her. Air began to stir, tempting her nostrils with the scent of gunpowder and sage. Connlan.

He raised an eyebrow, peering down at her. "Why don't you tell me what's going on?" While he phrased it as a question, command tinged each word. "You're scared . . . and I find I don't like that. At all." He measured her, his gaze roaming her body and leaving tingles in its wake. "Are you frightened of me?" His brows furrowed.

"Not even a little bit." She allowed her voice to quiet to keep from cracking.

His face smoothed out, a dark eyebrow rising. "There's someone more dangerous than me?" His full lips quirked and a dimple winked in his left cheek.

That damn dimple.

"No." Not a being existed on earth more dangerous than Connlan Kayrs. She saw no reason to lie to him. He even dressed as a soldier in black cargo pants and a dark long-sleeved shirt, no doubt hiding weapons. "I'm busy right now, Conn. Events are taking place and I need to be involved. I have work to do."

"Let me help."

Moira shut her eyes. Such an offer—the temptation to accept warred with common sense. With reality. She opened them. "I wish you could." Regret flushed through her. "We mated a century ago. Another decade won't matter." Bitterness tinged her words.

Conn's eyes darkened. "It takes a century for a witch to come into power, to study and learn. So I gave you the time. Because you asked nicely." He took a step forward. "I'm done."

The threat and determination in his gaze washed sadness through her. This was about duty and power, not love or passion. "We shagged once, Conn. One night isn't going to determine my fate, marking or not." She'd never forget the heated pain of him marking the front of her left hip bone as her orgasm exploded—right before his did. He'd left her the next day to deal with the aftermath, with the anger of her people that their Seventh had mated for all time with a *vampire.*

He held his right palm toward her, showcasing the intricate design with the raised *K* in the middle. "You're not the only one with a brand, darlin'. I wear the mark, too."

The Kayrs marking. Legend declared the brand appeared when a Kayrs met his mate, transferring during sex. "I've read of your family, Conn. Some matings were arranged."

"So?" His voice rumbled lower with anger and warning.

The wind outside increased in power, beating against the high row of windows to get in. A storm threatened. Moira lifted her chin, meeting his gaze. "Did you mark me on purpose?"

Conn took another step toward her, his jaw firming. "Are you asking if I forced the mark on my hand and then on your flesh?"

She fought the urge to retreat. "Yes." Enough with fate and destiny. She was sick of the pressure. "You know what I am—the line I hold."

"I do. You have the potential to be the most powerful ruler the Council of the Coven Nine has ever claimed."

"Yes." Fire ripped through her. His family ruled the vampire world and thus the Realm, a coalition of powerful allies including shifters and witches. "Quite the allegiance our mating might make for the Realm."

"But our mating didn't cement anything, now did it?" Tension spiraled from him. "Because you needed space—because you haven't declared your intention to be mine." Something in his tone promised she'd be making such a declaration soon.

He didn't know her or what she could do. She'd disappear before allowing herself to be used as a political pawn in his war. "You'd do anything for the Realm."

"Ah, Moira," his voice softened to a deadly tone, "you're miscalculating here."

She suppressed a shiver. "Why's that?"

"The second I marked you, the second you became mine . . ." Something flashed in his eyes. Regret? Anger?

She doubted being forced to wait a century had been difficult for him, and wishing for such a thing was just silly. A century ago he'd agreed to leave way too easily. And now he showed up when the Realm was at war with the Kurjans? The Realm needed the Coven Nine to continue the alliance—especially since the demons had declared war as well. "Your family, the Realm is everything to you. You would've mated for political reasons." He probably had. Duty was all but stamped on his handsome face.

Not by one twitch of an eyelash did his expression alter. "Possibly."

"Did you?" Her voice dropped to a hush. Her body steeled for the emotional blow.

"No." Silver began to thread through the green of his eyes—true proof of a vampire's anger. "I didn't consciously mark you, Moira." Conn blew out a breath. "But I felt the rightness of it. The belonging when the marking appeared." His stance settled again. "You were meant to be mine, and I'm taking you home."

The certainty of his vow convinced her as nothing else could have. He'd told her once he didn't lie or threaten. A vampire like him didn't need to do either. He wouldn't leave easily.

She sighed. "I'm staying here." She drew her fingers in, allowing molecules to reshape from her energy. Quantum physics at its finest. "You're leaving."

He flashed his teeth. "Get to it."

With a nod, she concentrated on the invisible molecules in the air, throwing subatomic particles through them to alter the matter into pure, dangerous burning energy. She'd been coming to Shea's for decades and had taken her first drink at the bar. Damaging the tavern would not only bother her, it would totally tick off Danny Shea, and the old witch would tell her parents. As well as charge her triple for any repairs. She needed to be careful and aim just for Conn.

Electric blue plasma wavered and then formed into the size of a cantaloupe in her right hand, which she pulled back and threw at his torso.

The mass flashed through the air. She felt a quick moment of regret. The energy wouldn't kill him, but oh man would it hurt. The ball would singe his skin like a very bad sunburn. Of course, vampires had no more problem with the sun than did humans. Legends were bunk. This strike was merely the beginning.

She expected him to evade the energy weapon. Order her to stop its movement. Instead, his lips tipped ever so slightly. He held out a hand. The plasma ball halted mid-flight, then swept forward until it hovered above his palm. Captured.

Moira stepped back. Her breath caught in her throat. "That's impossible." She'd focused her own energy into the matter to create the force. No one else could control her creation. Fear slithered down her spine.

He shrugged, shifted, and threw the orb at her with an impressive push-off.

She leaped to the side, the ball rushing past her to collide with a bar stool, sending the worn seat into the air to land back with a crash. The scent of ozone whipped through the space. Her knees gave, and she clutched the edge of the bar, digging her nails into the wood, her eyes wide on Conn.

"How?" Her voice trembled, but she was beyond caring. Straightening, she unclenched her fingers and pivoted to face him. How could anyone not only take her energy but use it against her? Impossible.

He shrugged. "What exactly do you think I've been doing this last century?"

Adrenaline flowed down her back through tissue and muscle, causing her to feel a bit light-headed. "Training the Realm's soldiers for the war we all knew was coming." The war with the Kurjans, the pasty-white bloodsucking monsters who were afraid of the sun since it fried them.

Conn nearly grinned. "Yes. The vampires and shifters are prepared. But I multitasked."

"Multitasked?" Her voice wavered while dread ripped through her. The deadliest soldier ever born to the vampires multitasked? He was shagging kidding her. "Meaning what?" Only force of will kept her knees from buckling. Again.

"You know exactly what I mean. Rumor has it you've been training—swords, guns, knives . . . even hand to hand." Two long strides had him a foot away from her. "Now darlin', where do you suppose you gained those skills?" A dark flush whirled over his high cheekbones.

She angled her head to meet his eyes square on. "I worked damn hard on them, Connlan."

His thumb and forefinger grasped her chin and his eyes darkened. "I'm sure you did. When we mated, Moira, my skills became yours." Leaning down, he brushed his lips across hers before straightening back up. "And yours became mine."

Her breath hitched. Her heart swelled. Her thighs softened. All from one small kiss. She jerked out of his grasp. "Bollocks. You lead the soldiers of the Realm. You don't study."

Genuine amusement lit his eyes. "You think I merely hit things?"

Well, yeah. "I assume you play chess once in a while with the king, but other than that . . ."

He laughed— a true throw-your-head-back deep masculine chuckle. "While my brother and I do enjoy games of strategy, some studying is often involved."

Military strategy, maybe. "You're telling me you've spent the last century studying quantum physics, string theory, and the other applications of magic?"

"Of course." His gaze dropped to her lips, making them throb in response. "I mated a witch. A basic understanding of all scientific principles, most notably quantum physics, is necessary to manipulate energy and matter."

To practice magic. True magic. Her mind spun. On all that was holy. "So you can manipulate my energy. Since we've mated." Son of a bitch. How the hell was she going to keep him out of her life now?

He cocked his head. "Now's the time to tell me what has you so frightened."

"I can handle my own problems, Conn."

Irritation curled his lip, hinting at a temper she really didn't want to see. "Did you truly think I'd leave you alone, Moira? With Virus-27 on the loose? With witchcraft being used to harm people?"

She closed her eyes briefly. The virus created by the Kurjans to attack vampire mates—to take them genetically down to human form and maybe beyond—by using genetic science combined with quantum physics and true magic. "Yes."

Her gaze focused on him. Virus-27 was the absolute least of her worries right now. Her mind scrambled for something, anything to get him to leave.

He exhaled, taking a step forward into her space again.

Sage and power swirled around her in the scent of male. "I'm done waiting, Moira." One large hand smoothed through her curls, clenching to tangle at the nape of her neck and tugging back.

Her neck stretched and her hands reached out for balance, grabbing the shirt covering his broad chest. She opened her mouth to protest.

His descended.

Firm lips slid against hers. Heat seared her, shooting down from her mouth to her core. She swayed toward him, opening her mouth to allow entrance. Like the soldier he was, he dove in, all purpose, all blazing fire, his lips capturing hers as his tongue took control. The brand on her hip began to burn with desperate need.

He growled low, grasping her waist and tugging her flat against him. His mouth devoured hers, his tongue claiming every inch, the hand on her hip clenching with restrained power. The erection against her belly jumped with demand.

Her knees weakened. Her heart pounded. Desire for him lit her on fire. Need spiraled deep into her womb. She *craved*.

Releasing her, he lifted his head, his fingers spreading out to cup her scalp. Desire shot silver through the green of his eyes. A muscle ticced in his jaw. "Let's go to your cottage, Moira."

She sucked in a breath, her eyes widening on him. Was there anything more intriguing to a woman than a strong man who wanted her? Memories of what this man could do with his hands, with his mouth, flushed through her mind until her body ached. She ran her hands down his flat stomach to curl around his leather belt. They'd had one night. It wasn't like she'd practiced sex this last century. "Not a good idea, Conn."

"Why not?"

Because she didn't know what to do. "I don't want you." She lowered her chin.

"Liar." His eyes softened in what had better not be understanding.

Then he cut his gaze behind her, a frown settling between his masculine brows.

"What?" She released his belt, an odd tingling running over her neck. The air changed. Her skin heated. Matter shifted and energy zapped. Oxygen swirled. A passage opened. "Conn—"

Invisible claws dug into her flesh and ripped her away from him.

Chapter 2

What the hell? Conn leaped forward and grabbed Moira's arms, settling his stance on the tavern's wooden floor. Wind twirled behind Moira in a circular pattern with the force of gravity, fighting to draw her in. A swirling white mass of a tornado concealed the other side. She cried out, her green eyes wide with fright, her hands digging into his forearms until she drew blood. Her hair whipped behind her, yanking her head back.

A high-pitched squall emerged from the abyss. Bar glasses shattered, sending shards spinning. One sliced into his neck. Electricity sizzled through the air, sparking against polished surfaces.

The energy pulled Moira's head back farther, the cords in her neck stretching. Her hold loosened on his arms. She half fell in the swirling mass, tugging him with her. Ice, fire, liquids, and gels, all commingled against his skin. Dimensions?

Enough. With a growl, Conn stepped forward, manacling an arm around Moira's waist. So many sensations ripped across his flesh he couldn't discern between heat and cold. Yanking her to the side, he pulled his gun and fired. The green laser from the weapon exploded across the dimensions, sending sparks of pure, white light in return.

A furious bellow echoed.

A clash of thunder sounded.

The abyss released them with a loud crash.

The force sent them flying. Conn landed on his back, clutching Moira to his chest. Her forehead knocked into his chin. Paper napkins scattered to land on every surface. Then silence.

The outside door burst open, and Kell ran inside. "I heard an explosion." He surveyed the destroyed tavern. "What the holy hell?"

Conn took a deep breath, dropping his head to the floor. His entire body ached as if put through a cement mixer. "Moira." He needed to make sure she hadn't bruised her head. She trembled against him, her breath coming in shallow gasps. Anger simmered beneath his skin. His mate was terrified.

Then she lifted her head.

He'd misjudged her.

Pure, raw fury lit her expression. Shoving against his chest, she leaped to her feet. "Son of a bitch." Shaking hands pushed back rioting curls as she rounded on her cousin. "Some sort of pull, out of nowhere. Out of the air." She stalked over to the bar and back, her gaze on the glass littering the floor, thoughts scattering across her face. "Finally, an explanation. This is *how*, Kell."

Conn stretched to his feet. "How what, Moira?" Fury began to bubble anew through his veins. He was a soldier and more than adapt at quashing his emotions, but the heat ripping along his muscles hinted he might not be able to contain his temper.

She whirled around. "Oh, ah . . . nothing."

He saw red. Two strides had her biceps in his hands as he lifted her; two more had her ass slapping the bar. Surprise lit her face and she stilled. He leaned in, allowing every ounce of pissed-off power to show on his face. "How what?"

The surprise waned and she flared to life. Temper flashed bright green in her eyes, sparks danced on her skin. "Manhandle me again, Kayrs, and you'll end up on all fours baying at the moon." She tried to find leverage with her legs, but his hips kept them immobile on either side of his.

Oh, he'd made a mistake. No way in hell should he have allowed her a century. "Let's go pack your bags, Moira. We're heading home." The sooner he got her safely ensconced at headquarters, the sooner he could hunt for whoever was trying to take her.

She took a deep breath, making an obvious effort to keep from screaming. Color washed her porcelain skin a blazing pink. Perfect teeth clenched as she pushed sound out. "I am home."

"No. Home just became an underground fortress guarded at every turn."

Kell cleared his throat. "Ah, as much as I'd like to leave you to vampire foreplay, we need to get going."

Conn pressed his hands into the rough wood on either side of Moira's hips. She wasn't going anywhere. Turning only his head, he pinned his friend with a look promising retribution. "Apparently you haven't been forthcoming with news about my mate, Kell."

Fire flashed in Kell's black eyes. "I told you thirty years ago to get your ass to Ireland, and you didn't listen."

Conn ignored Moira's gasp of outrage. "I spoke with my mate," he pivoted to concentrate on the stubborn woman, "who informed me she needed more time to perfect her art and prepare to take her place on the Nine." What in the hellfire had he missed?

As the seventh daughter of a seventh daughter, Moira was pretty much guaranteed a place on the Council of the Coven Nine, the group that led the Wiccan world. He'd understood her need to prepare. Not only did the members rule their world, they did so using quantum physics, or elements that could blow up the universe. Harnessing those elements took training. As well as luck, as far as he was concerned.

Kell huffed out a loud breath. "I'll arrange transport." His boots clomped across the floor until the sound of the door closing echoed like an omen through the silent bar. Conn slid his gaze to Moira.

She shifted her weight. Cold metal instantly pressed against his jugular. "Back off, Kayrs." Her gaze met his as she held a knife to his throat.

He smiled. The hellion could move and fast. Deviant that he was, his cock flared to life again. So did his temper. He leaned further into the blade. "You think you can cut me, Dailtín?"

Her eyes narrowed. "You think I won't?" The hoarse tenor of her voice belonged in a smoky bar, singing the blues. "I have things to do, Conn. If I need to put you out of commission to do them, prepare to bleed."

His fangs lengthened. That hadn't happened unconsciously since puberty. Centuries ago. The woman would actually cut him. The strategist within him calculated the situation and how to reason with her.

Moira's eyes glowed a mystical hue; her wild red curls screamed passion. Defiance was stamped on every angle of her face, challenging him. But something else glittering in those eyes caused his blood to thrum. A knowledge, a confidence to be found in only the most elite warriors he'd ever trained; those whose confidence had been forged in fire and blood.

She had it.

The warrior in him roared to life, overtaking any rational thought. He shot his arm up to grab her wrist and force the blade from his throat. "Let go of the knife, Moira." Soft skin covered toned muscle under his hand.

He could tighten his hold and make her drop the weapon, but that's not how this was going down.

"No." She took advantage of his movement and dug her heel into his thigh, clapping his ear with her free hand.

Pain exploded in his skull. His temper howled. Clutching his fingers into her hair, he jerked her head back. The white column of her throat stretched. She yelped in protest. He lowered his head, his fangs elongating completely. His lips enclosed her skin.

He struck.

Her entire body went rigid. The knife clattered to the floor.

He drank. Honey and spice exploded across his taste buds followed by a punch of raw power. His mind swirled. Arousal, lust, fire whipped through him until the need to get inside her pushed all other thoughts away. Quick swipes of his tongue sealed the wound and then his mouth was on hers, delving deep.

She moaned low in her throat, pulling him toward her. Heat cascaded from her.

He released her arm, encircling her waist and tugging her forward until his cock met her core. He wanted her naked. His tongue tangled with hers, the little whimpers gasping from her boiling his lust even higher.

The boom of a gun jerked him away. He jumped around, using his body as a shield. Kell stood in the entryway, calmly placing a Beretta in his belt. Plaster dropped from the ceiling, which was marred by a large bullet hole.

Conn snarled.

Kell held both hands out. At six and a half feet with midnight dark eyes and hair, the witch took a placating stance that had to be unfamiliar. He wiped plaster off his shoulder. "I know it's deadly to mess with a vamp and his mate, but we really have to go."

The whir of a helicopter startled Conn. He hadn't heard it arrive. "Where?"

"We've been summoned by the council," Kell said. "Now."

Moira leaped off the counter to land next to Conn. She ran a trembling hand through her curls. "We're already late."

He grabbed her arm. "I'm going with you or you don't go." He needed answers. If the stubborn witches in the room wouldn't provide them, he'd go to the top.

"While he can't see the council," Kell dropped his gaze to his cousin, "we could use his help. At least until Daire and Adam return."

Conn stilled. "Daire and Adam?"

Kell and his two brothers served as the chief enforcers for the Nine. Something huge must be going down if they all had been summoned at once. Suspicion tightened Conn's shoulders.

"Why are you with Moira, Kell?" Conn's voice dropped to an octave that should've warned his friend. He'd assumed Kell was with Moira to perform his duty as liaison and enforcer and perhaps to provide protection. But if his mate needed protection, someone should've called him.

Kell cut his gaze to Moira. "I believe that's a conversation between you and the Seventh, Kayrs."

"Don't call me that." Moira stiffened. "You've no right to be pissed, Kell."

Kell stepped forward, his eyes blazing. "No right to be pissed? Are you kidding?" He swept his hand toward Conn. "There's a good chance I'm going to end up in a fistfight with one of my best friends because you've refused to get your life in order. And now it might be too late to fix our world."

One step had Conn in front of Moira. "Don't yell at

her." A brawl was guaranteed—though the first punch came from the brat behind him. Two-fisted and right to his kidneys.

"That's it." Conn swirled around and ducked, tossing his witch over his shoulder. She bellowed in surprise. He pivoted, heading for the exit. "Since I'm under strict orders from my king not to piss off the council, we'll go meet with them now. You can explain what the hell's going on during the flight." He strode through the door and into the sun, not caring whether or not Kell followed. Moira struggled, smashing her hands into his back. "Then, mate, we're going home."

Rage burned in his gut. Moira's family had power and knew how to wield it. The second he forced her from Ireland, they'd declare war.

So be it.

Chapter 3

Moira settled back against the plush seat in the helicopter, for once not appreciating the luxury of the well-built machine. She longed for the sound of rushing wind to drown out the testosterone-filled silence of the two men currently ignoring her. Kell sat across the aisle with his legs extended, head back, eyes closed. Conn dominated the seat next to her, punching laptop keys until his computer flared to life. Maybe she should go visit with the pilots. She pushed up on the armrests, only to still when Conn swiveled his head.

Green eyes pierced her. "Sit. Back. Down."

Warning filled his tone and should've pissed her off. The energy needed to get truly angry escaped her. Tired. She was so damn tired. Leather hissed out air when she flopped back down.

A rugged face took shape on the screen. Bugger. He'd called the king.

"I've walked into a shitload of trouble," Conn said as a greeting.

Dage Kayrs lifted an eyebrow. "Good to see you, too, brother." Tight and packed hard, the king filled the screen dressed in jeans and a black silk shirt. The background appeared to be a filmy screen . . . not giving a hint as to his whereabouts. He cut his silver gaze to the side. "Hi, Moira."

"Hi." Pride filled her at the steadiness of her voice. Calm. She'd stay calm.

"Sorry." Conn rubbed his chin. "How is your mate?"

Dage frowned. "Emma's working around the clock to find a cure for the virus." He sighed. "Her sister is due in less than a month, and Talen's driving me crazy."

Cara had been infected with Virus-27 while pregnant, and nobody knew what the chromosome-altering disease would do to the baby. But Moira had assisted with defeating the catalyst in Cara's blood that would've sped up the process in changing her from a vampire mate with twenty-seven chromosomal pairs back down to a human with twenty-three. Of course, no one knew if the virus would stop there or keep deleting until death. For now, they'd slowed the damn bug down.

Dread filled Moira. "Cara is strong, Dage. She'll be all right."

The king nodded. "I hope so." He shifted back to his brother. "So? How angry is the Council of the Coven Nine?"

Conn shrugged. "I don't know yet. My guess is pretty pissed."

Moira nodded. "Good guess."

Dage lifted an eyebrow. "I didn't think my request was unreasonable."

The arrogance of the Kayrs men should be bottled and sold. "Not once in the history of the Realm has a king requested our soldiers train under his direction." In fact, if you asked her, the coven's soldiers could kick the vampires' asses. She smiled.

An answering smile flirted with Dage's full lips. "You've been working on diplomacy, haven't you?"

"Yes." Someday she'd have to use it all the time on the council. Unfortunately.

"Keep working on it." Conn leaned closer to the computer screen. "I'll explain the danger of the new breed of werewolf, and our training schedule."

"It's about control," Moira muttered. "Our people ally with yours. We don't answer to you." So much for diplomacy.

"No. The stakes are so high, we all need the right training." Dage frowned. "Who's spinning my request in such a manner?"

The entire council. Moira eyed Kell across the aisle. Damn man should wake up and help her out. "We train our own soldiers, King."

"We'll see about that." Dage cut his gaze to his brother. "Why am I getting the feeling more is at play here?"

"Your instincts are spot on. What I understand so far"— Conn aimed a glare her way—"is that somebody has learned to transport people against their will."

"Excuse me?" The king stepped closer to the camera.

"A portal of sorts opened up and tried to yank Moira through. I figure it's close to teleporting."

Dage frowned. "Only a few of us in the world have the ability to transport through dimensions and arrive somewhere else, Conn."

"I know. Could you transport someone if they weren't doing it with you?"

"No." Dage gazed into the distance. "Transporting is jumping between dimensions." He focused back on them. "Moira, the specialty of quantum physics the witches master is similar. Have your people been experimenting?"

Conn stiffened, and Moira kept her focus on the king. "No. We use energy to alter the state of matter on a subatomic level. Pure science, Dage. You manipulate time more in line with string theory. The two are totally different." But, well . . . science was science.

"What if both happened at once?" Conn asked.

Moira shrugged. "Then an incredible amount of power might be released. Perhaps enough to yank someone through dimensions from a remote location." The person doing the transporting would be drained of energy for long afterward. The idea explained the gap in time between disappearances of council members. A fact she was under strict orders not to reveal.

"Anything you want to tell us, Moira?" the king asked softly.

Even across the distance, a prickle set up at the base of her skull. She slammed shields shut and smiled. "I'm a well-trained witch, King. Stay out of my head." While she considered Dage a friend, akin to family, her head stayed closed.

Dage glanced at Conn.

"He can't get in, either," Moira said. As her mate, he had a good chance of getting past her mental shields soon. They'd only been in the same vicinity for about two hours, and already she sensed his feelings. Pure, pissed-off male. That was nothing compared to the fury she'd meet if he breached her shields and read her thoughts.

"Yet." Conn's threat hung in the air. "Though I can tell you the council is circling the wagons and has recalled the enforcers. In fact"—he frowned, his gaze on her—"Moira here isn't nearly as surprised as she should be that someone tried to take her. I'm thinking this isn't the first attempt."

"Is it the Kurjans, Moira?" Dage asked, his jaw hard. A white-faced, red-haired vampire race afraid of the sun, they had created the virus in order to steal vampire mates.

"I don't know who it is." She truly didn't. The Kurjans were more likely to show up with an armored tank than manipulate time and dimensions. Too subtle.

"This is the first I've heard of the ability to open dimensions in such a manner." Her jaw firmed as she glanced at Conn. "In addition, it's the first time someone has tried to transport me."

"What about others? Has anyone else been taken?" Conn went for the jugular.

The damn man should've been a barrister. "Not to my knowledge." The lie rolled smoothly off her tongue.

"You're a terrible liar, Dailtín." Conn turned back toward his brother. "Anything new on the demon front?"

Dage exhaled. "No. While they declared war eight months ago, they have yet to make a move . . . unless this new transport business is their first strike." He rubbed a finger in the cleft of his chin. "The demons fight by messing with images in the brain . . . as well as traditional weapons. I'm not sure I envision them playing with physics."

Conn angled the monitor. "My guess is it's witches or . . . well . . . us. Maybe a vampire with the ability. But if you think about it, the Kurjans studied biology the last three hundred years, preparing the virus. Maybe they've branched out to quantum physics."

His frown bracketed hard lines at the sides of his mouth. "Moira has been summoned by the council. Then I'll get the truth about other disappearances from my mate." He cleared his throat. "I need you to make a phone call, Dage."

Dage's expression remained like stone, yet blue shot through the silver of his eyes. "Are you sure?"

"Yes."

"Consider it done." The king clicked off.

What in the blazes was that about? Moira turned toward Conn. "Care to explain?"

Arrogance stamped into every line of his chiseled face. "No." He snapped the laptop closed, glancing out the window. "Dublin looks stunning."

"Yes." Dublin stood as the cleanest city in the world with a mixture of ancient and modern architecture. Yet the economy of Ireland as a whole kept spiraling downward. True proof the council was in trouble. "You haven't been here for a century, Conn." A tiny bit of irritation crept into her voice.

He clasped his hand over hers, tugging until her palm rested against his hard thigh. Heat flared right to her heart. "I needed an ocean between us to keep from taking you, Moira."

Baloney. He'd walked away and hadn't looked back. Maybe if she'd had some experience or something, he'd have stayed. But he'd been her first and only. She shook her head. "We don't even know each other." They'd had sex one night and had ended up mated for life. In fact, it wasn't until the last ten years that he'd contacted her. Formally at first, then with some ease.

He sighed. "You were so young. I understood you needed to grow into the leader you're meant to become." His hand tightened over hers. "But time's up."

The man wasn't getting it. Her nails clutched into his leg. "You don't need to do this. Fate can't force us into anything." He had to stop touching her. It'd been a century since she'd had sex, and her body was on fire. The second he'd marked her, he'd ruined her for all other men. Literally. Vampires were male only. Once mated to a vampire, the woman became untouchable by any other male. An allergy of sorts.

"I want to take you home."

"You do not." The words slipped out before she could bite them back. Heat climbed into her face. She kept her gaze straight ahead.

He grasped her chin between his thumb and forefinger, tugging her to face him. A puzzled frown settled between his dark eyebrows. "You can't possibly believe I wanted to stay away from you for an entire century."

She blinked. Twice. Vulnerability tightened her stomach. Pure stubborn pride tightened her shoulders. His expression smoothed out, his hold firm on her jaw. "Well, now."

"You can't tell me you weren't relieved the council forced you to your own continent." Maybe he'd deny it. A stupid, soft voice echoed the plea in her head.

He exhaled, blowing out air and glancing to the side. "Maybe a little. At first." He focused back on her. "The marking caught me off guard. The night we shared . . . I don't usually lose control. Ever, actually."

She knew he'd been relieved and even understood it a little bit. Yet, something ached deep inside. The marking. "Me either. So let's ignore the marking and tell fate to bugger off."

"Moira." The softness of his tone provided warning and set goose bumps jumping on her skin. "Forget fate." His gaze held hers. "I made you mine and I'm taking you home."

Irritation and dread comingled in her gut. "You don't really mean that. I need to stay here."

"No, you don't." He released her face to glance at his wristwatch. "The nine members of the council are spread across the globe. You can work from anywhere."

She bit back a sharp retort. He needed something she couldn't give. "What do you see happening here, Conn? We head back to your home, I work via the net and you go off and fight wars?"

"Yes." He slipped the laptop into a dark sleeve, perching it on the floor. "I understand you'll need to travel sometimes for work, and that's okay. But I also envision children, and you staying safe and protected." His shoulder took up half of her seat when he relaxed back in the chair. "Of course, kids are a long way off. After we win the war. For now, I thought you'd want to settle in."

Oh, if he only knew. She struggled to keep from smacking him on the head. How could a being with advanced intelligence be such a moron? Her shoulders shrugged against the walls closing in.

The helicopter rushed over the streets of Dublin. Soon the setting sun sparkled off the Liffey River as they maneuvered, hovered, and finally touched down on the roof of one of the new buildings. Conn raised an eyebrow. "We're going to Kell's place?"

Moira shifted in her seat as the pilot cut the engine. "Not exactly." Well, kind of. Kell lived there, too. She unbuckled her belt. "You haven't been here, have you?" If the vampire had been on her continent, she would've sensed him.

Conn slid the door open. "No. I've mailed information to Kell here before. As well as new weapons for the enforcers." He jumped out.

She'd used a couple of those. Accepting his outstretched palm, she leaped to the ground, ignoring the strength in the vampire's broad hand. Tingles cascaded up her arm. She jerked back, barely refraining from rubbing her palm on her jeans. The natural musty smell from the river wafted in on a light breeze, and she ducked her head to run across the gravel to the blue metal door.

Kell beat her there, opening it and gesturing her inside. The rubber soles of her tennis shoes beat silently down the five steps to the interior door, which she pushed open to reveal a large, rather empty foyer for three penthouse apartments.

"Be ready in fifteen minutes, Moira. We need to stop by The Squid on the way," Kell said, striding toward the east apartment and shoving open the door without looking back. The click of the bulletproof door shutting echoed against the marble tiles.

Should she turn? Or just act casual? Kayrs was about to be in her apartment, her private domain. He stood behind her, his silence heavy with question. She understood enough about him to know he wasn't going to like the answers. Steeling her shoulders, she loped to the west apartment and opened the door.

He followed her inside, bringing the masculine scent of gunpowder and sage into her space. A low whistle escaped him at the sun setting over the sparkling view of the Liffey. "Beautiful." The door shut behind him, and she held back a nervous hop.

The scent of lemon hung in the living room, the tables polished a deep brown. Plush pillows she'd spent days choosing with her sisters were scattered across the room. With a sweep of her hand, they lifted to line up perfectly on the leather sofa and matching seats. Moira cleared her throat. "Ah, make yourself at home, Connlan. I'll be a minute."

How she'd get him to stay in the apartment and not follow her to the meeting was beyond her. She'd need to knock him out. Quantum physics and magic wouldn't work—she needed a brick.

"Moira." Low and soft, his voice caressed nerves across her skin.

Her shoes squeaked when she pivoted to face him. "Yes?"

He more than overwhelmed the small entryway, his combat boots looking lethal on the white marble. Cocking his head to the side, he took in the tumbled stone fireplace with the northern seascape painted by her sister Brenna perched above the mantel. "You live here?"

"Sometimes. It's easier to stay here when I'm teaching at the college than go home to the cottage." Though teaching wasn't why she owned a condo in Dublin. "I'll hurry, Conn. Grab a beer from the fridge." She needed to get a move on. The man would have to fend for himself.

Scurrying to her bedroom, she closed the door, wasting precious moments to lean back and sigh. The deep maroon comforter her sisters had given her as a housewarming present beckoned her to jump inside and hide—like they let her do when she was four. Her light scent of lilac perfume, specially made by her sister Molly, hung in the air and propelled her to action. Quick movements had her at the closet, tearing out the appropriate clothing. She hurried to change.

The laptop dinged on Darcy's hand-me-down desk in the corner.

Dread wound down her spine. Tugging her top into place, she crept across the room and answered the call. "Hello, Vivienne."

Vivienne Northcutt, head of the Coven Nine, gave a curt nod. "Moira."

"Kell and I are on our way, ma'am." Moira glanced at the antique clock ticking away the minutes on her bedside table. She'd found it at old Malley's garage sale the year before, and the darn thing was always five minutes slow.

"I'm issuing a formal order for you to bring Connlan Kayrs to the meeting today." Not by one flick of an eyelash or catch in her voice did the leader let on this was anything but astounding news.

Moira gasped. Her heart thumped hard. "That's impossible." The security developed by the witches in protecting their leaders was unbeatable—even by the ultimate vampire soldier. "I don't understand." But she did. The ramifications all but slapped her across the face.

Vivienne pursed thin lips in a parchment white face. "I think you do."

Temper threatened to flare and Moira shoved anger down. "Then why would you ask this?"

Fire flashed in the witch's coal black eyes. "The king requested his brother's presence at our meeting today. I am acquiescing to the king's wishes."

Ah. The phone call Conn had asked Dage to make. Moira shook her head. Absolute panic ripped through her system. "He'll die." While vampires were difficult to kill, even Conn wouldn't survive trying to reach the council.

"Maybe." Viv drew air into her lungs loudly. "I explained that fact to Dage, but he insisted Conn would survive our security because of the mating . . . which he might."

Moira smoothed out her expression. Did the Nine know of Conn's abilities? "Do you believe our mating has given Conn powers vampires don't usually possess?"

Viv could give lessons in donning smooth expressions. "We've considered the possibility since your mating. But, well, no. Not unless he's spent the last century studying our ways." She sniffed.

It was exactly what Conn had done.

"I see." Realization settled heavily on Moira's shoulders. "So you expect him to die today." It was certainly a possibility. Being able to harness her energy didn't mean he could pass through the veil. "Quite the strategy, Aunt Viv." Moira shook her head. Even more than usual, she dreaded the day she'd sit on the council.

"Strategy?" Viv lifted her eyebrows.

"Conn dies and it's the king's fault." Moira grabbed a moonstone bracelet off the table, clasping the silver around her wrist. "The Nine withdraws from the Realm . . . or the Realm kicks us out. Either way . . . it's smooth for you." They couldn't withdraw from the Realm. What was the council thinking?

Viv's eyes darkened. "Quite the strategic thinker, aren't you, Seventh?"

Oh, her aunt had no idea. Fear forced Moira to lower her voice to keep from stuttering. "We don't want the Kayrs family as enemies, Viv. You should've told Dage no."

"Refusing the king's request would've been tantamount to withdrawal, and we're not ready to take that step." A dark flush slid up Vivienne's face. "We shall worry about the consequences later."

"Consequences?" Fire rushed through Moira's veins. "Aunt Viv—"

"Enough." Electric green energy crackled on Vivienne's skin. "Moira, you are the seventh sister of the seventh sister. You were born to lead this council, and you've taken an oath to obey our laws." Her narrow nostrils flared as she settled her face into firm lines. "These type of difficult decisions will face you every day."

The weight of destiny almost knocked Moira to the ground. The rush of anger kept her standing. "If Conn doesn't make it through the veil, the vampires will be the least of the coven's worries." Reaching out, she cut the line. An empty threat, unfortunately.

She considered calling Dage and quickly discarded the thought. The king would back up his brother. Her only choice was to deal directly with Conn.

Chapter 4

Conn swallowed another gulp of Guinness, his gaze on the inside of Moira's refrigerator. Everything was lined up neatly and by color. Beer to the left, limes to the right. Sodas on the second shelf, condiments, lined up by size, on the first. Weird. Shouldn't he know this about her? They'd been mated for nearly a century. He knew what kinds of food she liked because she'd told him in a recent conversation, though he had no clue she was nutty with her food organization.

Nutty and far too vulnerable for his peace of mind. He'd hurt her by agreeing to the coven's demands a century ago. How had he missed that? Maybe because the relief in being given time to deal with the overwhelming feelings of possession and need that had clawed at him.

When he'd left Ireland, his heart had firmly stayed in her delicate hands. She owned him—body and soul. Distance had assisted him in finding peace. Time had given him a chance to plan. He was older and wiser . . . and was not letting go of her, so the woman had better find peace with that.

He closed the door, leaving the peaceful kitchen with its ocean fresh walls and burnished oak cabinets—original Jono Dungs, a master craftsman for the last two hundred years. Wide steps had Conn in the living room. The jewel tones she'd chosen spoke of sensuality and sex. It was much different than her sweet cottage with the homemade quilt he'd visited so many years ago. The cottage belonged to a girl. This room, well now. It belonged to a woman.

A movement near the hallway caught his eye, and he turned, stopping short.

Moira had emerged from the bedroom dressed in a tea-length black skirt and scarlet buckled jacket. Long, calfskin black boots covered her calves to the knee. Rioting curls had been tamed with a clip at her nape, and dark makeup enhanced otherworldly green eyes. She was stunning.

Conn's mouth went dry. His tongue swelled. He'd felt lust before, but this landed far beyond mere lust. A wanting, a craving set his blood on fire. A primitive need to claim had his nostrils flaring and his lids half lowering.

She took a step back. Smart girl. Her pale hands clasped together. "You need to stay here, Conn."

The conviction in her words, the plea in her pretty eyes grounded him. "No."

Air swooshed into her lungs as her chest expanded. "You don't understand the risk you're facing."

Was that a fact? "If we're allies, Moira, and I believe we are, then the council won't do anything to harm me." So the rumors were true. The damn Nine might actually withdraw from the Realm.

He'd need to get Moira to safety before anyone else declared war against the Realm. As if the Kurjans and now the Demons weren't enough to battle.

"We're allies, Connlan." Her gaze remained steady on his.

Impressive. "For how long?"

She opened her mouth to answer as the door flew open. Conn dropped into a crouch to defend, then slowly straightened as a small female barreled into his arms.

"Connlan Kayrs. Well, it's about darn time." Brenna

Dunne patted his back, stepping away to smile with a twinkle in her gray eyes. "Thank you so much for the souped-up computer you sent for my birthday. I love it."

Conn returned the smile of the unexpected eighth daughter of Doctor Patrick Dunne, probably the smartest man on the planet. Well, after Conn's bother, Kane. Conn smiled at the miracle bouncing on her heels before him. In the entire history of the witches, never had an eighth daughter been created. Seven was truly the magical number. "I thought you'd enjoy playing with human satellites."

Brenna nodded, sending mahogany brown hair flying. Unlike her seven elder sisters, she'd inherited neither the green eyes nor the red hair. Truly unexpected. "Yes. I tapped into some governmental databases last month and transferred war funds to humanitarian efforts in the middle east."

Conn's heart warmed at the woman born eighty years after he'd claimed Moira. She was family. "Still trying to save the world, are you?"

"Of course." She glanced at her sister. "We need to fix the Irish economy and fast, Moira. I created a plan."

"You always form a plan." Moira swept toward the door. Turning the gold knob, she tossed a smile over her shoulder. "And they always work, which is impressive. We'll go over it later, okay? For now, I need you to entertain Conn."

Amusement warred with irritation down Conn's spine. Two strides had him at the door. "I'm going to meet the Nine with you, Dailtín."

Brenna gasped from behind him. "You can't, Conn. You'll never make it past the security."

He pivoted and winked. "I've been invited, Bren." A gentle nudge had his mate out the door, which he closed with a soft click. "Let's go."

"No. The security isn't men with sticks or guns." His

mate turned, shoving him against the wall. He allowed her to move him. Tension radiated from her. "Only witches pass through the veil to the chamber. You'll die."

He grasped her elbows. "What veil?"

"The veil." Exasperation filtered a soft peach under Moira's skin. "We're witches, Connlan. Do you really think we protect the sanctity of our headquarters with shooting plasma balls?"

Well, yeah. "I've never thought about it."

A veil. Maybe he could learn to drum one up to protect the women at his headquarters. He'd like to see his family better protected. "Considering I have your powers, I should be fine." Maybe. Who knew? Damn witches kept everything secret.

"No. The forces in the veil will rip off your head." She shoved away from him, striding down the hallway to punch the DOWN button for the elevator. "The veil consists of perfectly chosen subatomic particles that identify my species. Even more than that, the particles identify *power* within my people. You have to own a certain amount to survive." The door slid open and she glided inside.

"I have power. You've seen it." But did he have enough? His life was just getting interesting, and he'd hate to lose his head.

An indelicate snort emerged from his mate. "Yeah. You can throw plasma. So can my two-year-old nephew." She stabbed the button for the garage level. "Have you even considered that your death will guarantee the Realm splinters?"

"Then I'd better not die."

The woman was seriously underestimating him. Apparently, the Coven Nine wanted him dead. Either they'd discovered his new abilities, or were planning on making quite the statement with their withdrawal from the Realm.

He'd had enough of dancing around with his mate. "If

the Nine truly ordered my death, would you allow it, Moira?" Long ago he'd stopped worrying about death. When his time came, it came—though he'd be damn tough to take down.

"The Nine doesn't need to order your death when you walk right into it." Her shoulders straightened as she tapped the button for the garage level again. "Besides, I don't tell the Nine what to do."

The door slid open and they stepped inside. She took a deep breath as the door closed. "You can't tell me you'd refuse an order from the king to remove my head, Prince. Now can you?"

The temper he'd been controlling for the last several hours bubbled dangerously close to the surface. Grabbing her bicep, he shoved her against the wall of the elevator, leaning his face down. "I'd refuse any order to harm you, Dailtín. A fact you should be well aware of."

Sparks lit her pretty eyes. The woman had no idea how close she was to being forcibly removed from her country.

He fought a snarl. "Besides, you know my king. No way in hell would Dage ever order your death."

The doors slid open again, and she yanked from his grasp, flouncing over to where Kell waited next to three street bikes. Conn pivoted and let out a slow whistle. Two Ducatis and one Suzuki Hayabusa sparkled under the fluorescent lights. Kell stood guard over the Hayabusa as if the black and red beast meant the difference between life and death. Conn hoped to hell it didn't. "Nice bike."

"Nice?" Kell's eyebrow rose. "This was the fastest street bike in existence . . . even before I tweaked her. Now she's incredible."

Conn nodded his head toward the largest Ducati, a streamlined black Superbike. "Adam's?"

"Daire's," Moira said, grabbing a sleek silver helmet off the handle of a red Ducati and swinging her leg over the side. "Scratch her, and he'll kill you." She settled into place, flashing Conn a saucy grin. "Then I won't have to worry about it anymore."

Something thumped hard in Conn's chest. His mate straddled the bike like a natural . . . sleek and dangerous. Sexy as hell. She unclipped her hair and shook out her curls before tugging on the helmet, and he fought a groan. He fought the urge to yank her off and coax her to ride him instead.

Kell slammed a helmet into Conn's gut. Conn frowned. "Thanks." Quick jerks had it over his head and him on the Ducati, revving the engine. She purred to life beneath him, all power, all rumble. Time to meet the folks who wanted him dead.

Light from the moon glinted off sparkling storefronts. Moira bent lower against the bike, allowing the wind to whistle past. She wound through cars, following Kell while Conn protected her back. Although she was riding one of the most powerful vehicles in existence, one embodying true freedom, the sparkle of a pretty cage still narrowed around her. The future ripped her in different directions. The Nine owned destiny, and Connlan claimed fate. Neither were a good fit.

The brand on her hip burned when she turned a corner into the touristy part of town. The light ahead turned yellow and she flicked her wrist, turning it back to green. Her ass tingled as if the vampire behind her caressed it with his gaze. He'd better not be staring at her butt.

She followed Kell into an alley lined with impeccable rubbish bins, double-parking her bike near a dingy metal door. She cut the engine, tearing off the helmet and swinging her leg over the side.

Kell and Conn followed suit. Conn looked good on a motorcycle . . . like a badass from the ancients. His raised eyebrow asked a question she once again couldn't answer. If his instant scowl provided any indication, he was rapidly tiring of the secrets. Damn vamp should've stayed on his own continent.

Kell reached the door first, wiping a hand over the knob. Locks disengaged seconds later.

Moira bit back a smug smile. She was faster.

The door opened inwardly, and the pounding of a new hip-hop song slammed into her. Kell stalked inside.

Conn stopped her, one hand on her arm and the other holding the door open. "Why are we here?"

She doubted he'd believe the Nine met in a nightclub. "Quick meeting with a source. Not important. Why don't you stay with the bikes?"

He released her. "Sure." A gentle nudge to her shoulder had her moving forward. He followed, flanking her back.

She'd known he wouldn't stay outside. Couldn't blame him. She wouldn't have waited in the alley, either. The rush of sweat, smoke, and beer overwhelmed her senses. She peered through the darkness, tracking Kell's progress across a dance floor filled with gyrating bodies.

The pink outline of a squid vibrated with color high on one wall, sending out pulses in time with the band. With a sigh, she maneuvered around some guy dry-humping a brunette against the wall. Two young men tried to stop her movements on the dance floor, flirtatious grins on their faces that quickly disappeared as they looked behind her. She didn't need to turn. Heat rolled off the vampire hotter than the crush of bodies. One poor kid paled until she feared he'd pass out.

A firm hand slapped her ass. "Get me out of here before I hurt someone," Conn growled.

Fire flashed out across her flesh, spiraling higher the constant state of desire she'd been in since he'd arrived. Her temper quickly rose past the desire. Oh, he did not just smack her butt. He was inviting a burning—when she had time.

Throwing elbows, she shoved her way across the dance floor, reaching a dark booth in the rear of the club. Kell sat to one side, keeping his back to the bench and his view open to the crowd. When she arrived, his shoulders relaxed and he faced the interior of the booth.

Moira followed his gaze. "Doctor Pelandrone."

The doctor smiled, shoving thick spectacles up his nose. Wiry black hair curled around his pudgy face, and a reddish hue danced across his leathery skin. He'd been drinking again. A lot. "Moira. Good to see you. Sorry I haven't been in touch lately."

The witch was their chief researcher and a freaking genius with string theory. Unfortunately, he was also half fairy, possibly accounting for his lack of organization—though her money was on the booze. Fairies shouldn't drink.

"I assume you've been busy." It had always bewildered Moira why he owned half of the crazy nightclub. He kept a close eye on his investment, and they always met there. Or maybe it was the free-flowing gin that kept the doctor in his booth when he left his laboratories.

With a smile, she pivoted, allowing Kell to conduct business while she kept an eye on the mix of humans, witches, and shifters in the crowd. Mostly humans tonight.

Conn leaned against the wall. A universe of contained calm inhabited the space around the vampire, as if even noise didn't dare bother him.

Though Moira caught the glances—the shy, the daring, the downright flirtatious glances of women around the bar. Aged eighteen to sixty . . . they all looked. So far, not one shored up enough bravery to approach him. She couldn't blame them. Even with the relaxed pose, danger surrounded him, at home with the deadly glint in his eye. Conn was sexy, but frightening.

Her scowl probably didn't help much. The man was hers. At least in that moment.

Papers shuffled as the doctor slid a file across the Formica. "I did a quick analysis after you called." He rubbed his dark chin. "The transportation is possible, but untraceable."

Conn focused on the doctor, his body tightening. "Who are you trying to trace?"

Kell cut him a glare before turning back to the doctor. "Why not?"

The fairy blanched. "You're talking about hopping dimensions. We can decipher the energy signatures when somebody jumps . . . but once they're out of our dimension, they're gone. Even if they show right back up, we have no way of knowing where they went."

Moira sucked in air, fighting a cough at the body odor assaulting her nostrils. Damn dancers. "Is it possible to transport someone against their will?" She already knew the answer. If Conn hadn't fired his weapon into the abyss, she'd be somewhere else right now.

The doctor shrugged. "I think so. But you'd need to combine string theory and dimensional jumping with some serious power. Concentrated quantum physics. In order to alter the subspace enough to yank someone into a dimensional journey, you'd need some amazing ability and experience."

"Shit." Kell leaned back. "Anything else?"

"Ah, yes. I just spoke with your father, Moira."

"I talked to him yesterday. He's giving the researchers a hand." Her father was a general practitioner and expert in, well, every aspect of medicine. He'd studied for centuries and neurology seemed a favorite. "No news yet."

Conn crossed his arms. "News about what?"

The doctor threw back half a glass of what looked like scotch. His eyes didn't even water when he refocused. "Virus-27."

Kell cut his eyes to Conn. "You didn't think we'd just sit back and await the Realm's researchers, now did you?"

"No." Conn's jaw tightened. "Though I assumed your researchers would want to collaborate with ours."

Moira kept her face stoic. Collaboration depended upon them remaining allies.

"I see." Conn's stoic expression beat hers with pure stubbornness lining his jaw.

"Well then. Let's go report to the council." Kell stood. "Keep your focus on the transportation issue, Doctor. We have enough researchers for now."

The doctor cleared his throat, his gaze darting to Conn and back to Kell. "Well, um, there's more. Google maps show recent, um, mining in Russia."

Kell's shoulders went back. "Did you report to Daire?"

"Yes."

Conn frowned. "The demons are headquartered in Russia. What are they mining?"

Moira forced a shrug. Hopefully the demons weren't mining anything. "Diamonds? We keep an eye on all natural minerals, Conn. You know that." This was a coincidence. No way had someone discovered the witches' weakness.

The mines in Russia had been destroyed centuries ago. Of course, nothing buried stayed that way forever.

Kell nodded. "Daire is on it then. Thanks, Doctor. I'll be in touch." He strode away.

Moira followed her cousin through the bar, more conscious than ever of the daring smiles thrown at her mate. The marking on her hip pounded in time with the beat from the live band—hard, wild, and slightly out of control.

Conn grabbed her arm at the door and lowered his head to brush his lips against her ear. A shiver wandered right down to her toes.

"You're going to tell me what the hell is going on here, Moira." He said the words as a statement.

She heard them as a threat.

They felt like an omen.

Chapter 5

Back on the bike, Moira allowed the smooth ride to calm her thoughts. She angled in and out of cars driving too slowly. Saying a quick chant in her head, she restructured the fuel in her tank, sending the bike careening past Kell.

He scowled as she maneuvered by him. The poor guy had never figured out the correct reconfiguration of the fuel. He'd come close, but she always beat him.

As she left the newer part of town, the shiny lights dimmed, the streets narrowed, and the glass windows looked like stone. She passed the church without slowing, driving another three miles to glide into a narrow lot surrounded on three sides by a crumbling stone fence standing to about eight feet.

Magic raised the hair on her arms. Quantum physics, the application of energy to small matter, protected the area.

Night jasmine filled the air while crickets chirped in the distance. The moon rose high and full in the darkened sky, yet underneath, something rumbled. The wind whispered through Moira's hair, and she shivered.

The men caught up to her and jumped from their bikes. Kell stalked to the north side of the fence and rearranged several of the stones into a pattern of a Celtic knot. Silent as death, the wall parted. Wide shoulders blocked her view of the opening as he paused.

"You've gone far enough, Conn." Kell didn't turn around.

Conn spared her a glance. "I've been invited by the council."

"I'd rather you didn't die on my watch."

Moira nodded. "It would be a terrible thing to do to your old friend." Thank goodness. Someone was finally on her side.

Kell had just disobeyed direct orders by warning Conn. The Nine surely was in trouble when the enforcers doubted its plan.

Conn sighed. "Enough with the drama. I can collect and use Moira's energy. In fact, I've spent a century honing the ability, working with it, making it my own."

A warning skittered down her spine.

Kell exhaled. "I wish I didn't know that." He crossed the first barrier.

Moira stopped Conn from following with a hand against his chest. His heat warmed up to her shoulder. "Last chance to turn back, Conn." She lifted her gaze to meet his. Her two worlds were colliding, and everything she cared about might be crushed. The idea of him dying stole her breath. She tried to shove the fear down, but it resonated in her voice. "Be smart."

His eyes softened and he clapped a hand over hers. Tangling their fingers together, he strode through the opening, tugging her along. "Being smart means we stick together, Moira. The sooner you figure that out, the better for us both." Low and controlled, his tone nevertheless held a ring of determination. "When we reach the veil, will I have time to study it?"

"Yes." Not that staring at the invisible veil would do any good.

The wall slid shut behind them. Lights sprang to life along a wide staircase of tumbled rocks leading down. She allowed Conn to keep her hand as they descended to where Kell waited next to a rock wall in a small square vestibule. He rearranged stones into another intricate knot, and leaned forward until a green light flashed and scanned his eyes. "Kellach 24456 Daisy."

Conn snorted. "Daisy?"

How could she help him survive? Moira cleared her throat. "Daire was mad at Kell when they chose the new passwords." Daisy was the name of a girl they'd both had a crush on as teenagers, centuries ago. She doubted Kell would appreciate that laundry being aired.

The wall parted. Kell strode inside a rectangular room where two hulking soldiers guarded a metal door. Kell removed his gun and placed the weapon in a wicker basket before adding various knives.

Moira followed suit, making sure to engage the safety on her pistol. "No weapons beyond this point." Maybe he'd turn back, now.

The man had prepared for battle. With a shrug, he dumped an impressive array of guns, knives, and stars into the basket. He didn't twitch a muscle as the guards patted him down, though a low growl escaped him when the guard ran his hands over Moira.

She rolled her eyes. "Knock it off."

His deadly gaze remained on the offending guard, who tightened his jaw in a smirk that screamed challenge. He stepped slowly away when he finished frisking her.

Moira shook her head. Their guards were good. But Conn embodied the ultimate soldier.

The door opened inwardly. Marble sconces lit the walls, illuminating powerful oil paintings guiding the way. She followed Kell through, her boots light on the thick red carpet edged with hard stone. "Keep your feet on the red,

Conn—if you want to retain your head." One inch off the scarlet and the walls opened up with weapons.

Conn cleared his throat. "You hung Vicente Voltolini paintings down here." He peered closer to a battle scene from centuries ago. "His entire battle collection."

"Yes." The famous vampire had depicted most of the Realm history until losing his head during the last war with the Kurjans. "He and my aunt Vivienne were . . . close." Moira tugged on Conn's hand, heading down the path. "We're late."

The tunnels ran under the city, a labyrinth of routes. Some led to businesses, some to opportunity, and others to death. She'd learned the way to headquarters a long time ago; she was one of the few with the knowledge. Those who claimed knowledge equaled power truly didn't understand the structure of being in the know. Knowledge equaled danger—pure and simple.

Kell rearranged the final stones against a blank wall, which opened to reveal an empty room surrounded by rock. Finally, he turned his serious gaze on Conn. "You might die."

Conn's lips twitched. "Would you miss me?"

Kell shrugged. "Never has a nonwitch survived the next step."

"Has a mate ever tried?" Conn stared beyond Kell to the harmless-looking room.

Moira grabbed his arm. "Most are too smart to try." Never had anyone but a witch made it through the room. Even a witch with power sometimes hurt afterwards.

Kell scratched his chin. "Dig deep, imagine healing power around you. Go after me and before Moira." He pivoted and stepped into the room, disappearing instantly.

Conn snorted. "That amounted to an 'I love you, man' from anyone else."

Humor didn't touch Moira. "Please don't do this." She'd beg. Anything to keep him alive.

He pivoted, framing her face in his hands. A gentle brush of his lips over hers followed. "Trust me."

She lacked the physical strength to remove him. His familiarity with her powers kept him safe from her magic. Helplessness clogged her throat. She cleared it. "Hold my hand. Don't try to fight the veil's pull, try to use it. Turn the power and make it yours."

He'd mastered her power. For now, anyway. Maybe he'd beat the veil.

Conn frowned. "Kell said to go after him. Alone."

"We usually go alone. There's nothing wrong with going together." She kept her face bland as she told the lie.

Conn stepped near the doorway, his gaze hard on the empty room. "I can feel the tension . . . the change in the air."

"Just wait." He was about to feel more than tension. "Last chance to turn back."

He tightened his hold on her hand, his palm warm and strong. "I'm sorry I didn't come after you sooner, Moira." Then he stepped into the harmless-looking room.

A static wind keened. Holding tight to his mate, Conn fought the urge to cover his ears. The air boiled, rising up around him in gusts of power. Not oxygen. Not hydrogen. But blocks of power more solid than cement.

They beat at him, scraping against skin, bruising his flesh. He tried to turn his head and check on Moira, but the air had thickened too much. Only her hand in his assured him she was there. An invisible brick smashed into his left eyebrow. His head jerked back into a solid wall, bashing his brain against his skull.

Pain clouded his mind.

Anger cleared it.

He dug down, searching inside for peace. Concentrating on the molecules battering him, he tried to alter their formation. The keening rose to an unholy pitch. The blocks sharpened, cutting into his skin.

Goddamn it. Fury roared from his mouth, making no sound.

An edge cut into his throat. His knees weakened. Blocks of nothing kept him standing upright.

A healing balm cascaded up his arm—from Moira's hand holding his. Like silk, the sensation traveled over him, surrounding him. He took a deep breath. The air lightened.

With a rush of energy, he stepped forward.

Into cool silence.

Without taking a breath, he pivoted and reached for her. "Are you all right?"

She nodded, gulping in air. Curls sprung from her head in wild disarray. Rips ruined her shirt and skirt while small cuts bled from exposed skin. "You look like someone put you through a cheese shredder."

He glanced down. His clothes were shredded. Blood trickled from small cuts on his arms. His face ached. "Well. That was fun."

A solid stone wall faced him. Moira pressed her palm and forehead against it, whispering a small chant. The rock slid apart to reveal a massive chamber.

The headquarters of the Council of the Coven Nine.

The focus of the massive room was a raised rock dais complete with table and nine chairs. Tables were set forth before it and two rows of carved seats perched to the left, much like a modern courtroom. Well, except for the raw stone and breath of magic whispering about.

Moira stepped inside and took her place next to Kell behind one table, facing the four present members of the Nine. Conn released her hand to flank her other side.

Vivienne Northwood presided in the center, with Moira's mother to her left, and Grace Sadler, to her right.

Moira's mother and Grace had been council members almost as long as Vivienne, for about a thousand years. A man Conn didn't recognize sat next to Grace.

Moira's mother put hand to her mouth. "Moira. What did you do?"

Conn frowned. They knew he was coming.

"What I needed to do." Moira's voice rang out strong and assured in the chamber.

What the hell did that mean? Conn took a better look at Kell. His clothes appeared just fine and not even a paper cut marred his skin. Surprise had Conn stilling. A rush of anger had his lungs heating. "Don't tell me. You don't walk together through the veil."

"I told you to go alone," Kell muttered. "Not in a millennia would I expect Moira to have just so foolishly endangered her life."

"Shut up, Kell," Moira said.

Conn eyed Vivienne Northcutt. She eyed him back. He cleared his throat. "Councilwoman Northcutt, good to see you."

"And you, Prince. It's a very pleasant surprise that you survived the veil." Her eyes narrowed in calculation.

"Is it?" He'd already considered the ramifications of the Nine knowing he could use magic. If they became enemies, they'd gun for him first. He knew too much about how they worked, how they fought, and now how they shielded themselves. They'd be stupid not to take him out.

"Of course. The king was correct in not doubting your abilities." Menace tinged her smile.

Her politeness shit really annoyed him. He forced a pleasant smile. "Just out of curiosity, what would've happened to my mate had the veil ripped my head off?" His words declared his claim as solidly as if he'd sent a proclamation. Moira was his. Not theirs.

Vivienne folded her hands on the table. "Death has its

own energy, Prince Kayrs. If it had claimed you, Moira would've died as well."

Nothing in the world could've prevented the low, rolling growl that rumbled from his chest.

Chapter 6

Moira ignored the concern in her mother's eyes as well as the condemnation in Viv's. What she couldn't ignore was the warning sound coming from Conn. Her body reacted by flooding with adrenaline. Fight or flight. Unfortunately, at that moment she couldn't do either. "Maybe we should get down to business."

Vivienne cleared her throat. "Very well, though the council would like to speak to you later about your actions, Moira." Said as a polite invitation wrapped in hard spikes.

Moira nodded, then tilted her head in surprise at the fourth person seated behind the large stone desk. Peter Gallagher sat to Grace's side, his light brown eyes sparkling in his handsome face. A new member? She smiled in question at her old friend, wearing quite the wardrobe. She'd never seen the neurologist in a three-piece suit. In the charcoal-gray Armani, he exuded confidence and safety.

"We're trying to remote access Simone and Trevan." Viv tilted her head to where Grace perched over a keyboard, typing furiously. "Simone is in New York and Trevan in Greece, monitoring the demon forces there. For now, Peter Gallagher was sworn in as a member yesterday, filling an unexpected vacancy." Tension wound through the room as if half of the available oxygen disappeared.

Unexpected vacancies meant someone had died. Killing a witch . . . well now, not so easy to do.

"Congratulations," Moira murmured, forcing a smile that made her jaw ache. She and Peter had been friends for nearly a century and both taught at the university. Her father, the most renowned doctor for her people, had taught him. He'd make a fine council member. Too bad the circumstances sucked.

A bell pealed and everyone glanced toward the side wall. With a nod from Viv, a massive screen took shape, forming a picture of a remote chamber similar but much smaller than the main headquarters—located across town. Moira squinted until the screen cleared.

Two soldiers dragged in a struggling man, the top of his feet catching on the tumbled stones as he tried to jerk away. His bald head sported a slight sunburn that swam down his neck to be seen on his large, hairy hands. His pants were torn and blood spray arced across his chest. From the look of his swollen nose, he'd taken a punch. One soldier kicked the man in the back of the leg, and he went down to his knees in the center of the other chamber, facing the camera.

Conn stiffened next to Moira. This wasn't going to be good.

She grabbed his arm. "I think we should wait in the vestibule."

"I don't think so." Low, rough, his voice caught her in the gut and held. "The man is human."

The man threw elbows, attempting to rise. A soldier pressed down on his shoulder, keeping him down.

The prisoner bellowed. "You can't do this. I don't know who the hell you people are—"

"Silence!" Vivienne stood. Fury spun red beneath her angled cheekbones. She glanced at Moira and then Conn, clearing her throat and visibly calming. "Miss Dunne, would you please escort Prince Kayrs to the side chamber? We have some unexpected business to conduct."

"Yes, ma'am." Moira nodded, dread filling her stomach as Conn's shoulders straightened just enough to move the air around them. Her hold tightened on his arm.

He smiled. Then he patted her hand with his large palm. "With all due respect, Councilwoman, I'd rather remain here."

Moira's mother bit back a smile, concentrating on the screen. Viv zeroed in on him like a scavenger spotting a carcass. Her smile rivaled his in terrifying. "I appreciate your curiosity, Prince. But this is an internal coven matter, and we require privacy. Please remove yourself."

The guy on the floor in the other chamber threw out his arms. "I'll remove myself." His voice came through the microphone tinny and high. The soldier clocked him in the back of the head when he struggled to rise again. His palms slapped against the floor as he fell onto his knees again.

Conn kept his gaze on Viv. Regret tipped his lips, while pure intelligence shone from his eyes. "The man is human."

Nothing else needed to be said.

Moira dropped her hand to her side, focusing on the leaders.

"Indeed." Viv's dark eyes flashed, her posture going ramrod straight. She blinked several times. The silence increased until the heavy weight threatened to suffocate them. Without moving a muscle, she glanced at Grace, who slowly shook her head.

Nope. Moira's memory clicked through every coven canon of law . . . dealings with humans were public. If Conn hadn't been invited into the Nine's private headquarters, they could've pled secrecy as to the location. But

Viv had personally invited the liaison to the Realm, and thus the choice to go or stay sat squarely in his hands.

The prisoner spit blood on the floor. "Of course I'm human, you fucking freaks—"

His voice cut off with a flick of Viv's wrist. He grabbed his neck with both hands, his bloodshot eyes bugging out.

Viv attempted to stare Conn down, her jaw clenched, promising retribution. "Well, Prince. Since this man is human, we have no legal reason to request your removal. Yet, as a courtesy, I am asking you to leave while we handle our private business."

Nicely done. Moira had learned early on the power of diplomacy when employed correctly. Viv was a master. Conn had to leave.

"I appreciate the courtesy . . . and truly regret my refusal." Conn took one step forward, his voice echoing from the solid walls. "With all due respect, I choose to remain here."

Son of a bitch. He knew. Moira stiffened. The man knew they were considering withdrawing from the Realm. Yet he'd fought the veil . . . and revealed his powers. The Kayrs had just made a move. Her head swiveled in slow motion to take him in. He'd landed on her continent as a strategic move . . . nothing more. The sharp pain to her heart surprised her. Something to worry about later.

She shook her head. The man had already tipped his hand. He may understand some of their power, but he didn't need to see any more. If he learned anything more, he wouldn't be safe regardless of whether or not their people remained at peace with each other. "Conn." She kept her voice to a soft whisper. "You need to leave."

"No." If fate ever held sound, the tenor resonated in his absolute refusal.

Absolute quiet descended upon the occupants of the massive chamber. Up front, Viv pressed her hands together. "Very well. Connlan Kayrs has chosen to stay and witness the business of the Coven Nine." Her voice implied he'd signed his own death order. She stared through the screen at the man on his knees. "Thomas Willoby. Confess your crimes."

"I ain't done nuthin' wrong." Willoby shrugged the guard's hand off his shoulder. "What are you people? Some crazy devil worshippers?"

Dark amusement lifted Viv's lips. "No. Nice try, though." She reached for a thick manila file, flipping the top open. "Mary Johnson. Betty Maloney. June Frank." Her chin lifted. "Those names mean anything to you?"

"Um, er, no. I don't know what you're talking about."

While he was miles away, Moira could almost smell the stench of fear cascading around him.

"Oh, I think you do." Viv slammed a fist down on the folder. The man on the floor jumped. Dark energy swam along her skin, her eyes morphing all the way to midnight. "You like hurting women, now don't you, Thomas?"

"No, I . . . God. What are you?" Willoby's voice trembled. Sweat coated the front of his shirt.

"God won't help you now." Viv smiled, the sight more frightening than a Halloween ghoul. "See, usually when we find someone like you, we turn them over to the human authorities. Well, we make sure the humans find the trail. But you . . . well, you're special."

"No, I'm not. I'm so sorry. I didn't mean—"

Once again his voice cut off and he grabbed his neck. Viv hadn't even needed to flick her wrist. She had his frequency.

Moira's stomach sank. Conn shouldn't see this. He shouldn't know what they could do . . . what she could do. Viv had cut off the guy's air supply without blinking an eyelash. It was just the beginning.

Viv grabbed a wooden gavel. "You're a rapist, aren't you, Thomas?"

"No, I er—" Willoby choked, his shoulders shuddering. Then he gasped in air. "Yes." He began to sob. "I'm sorry. I need help."

Viv nodded slowly. "I'm here to help you."

"Thank you." He bowed his head.

"June Frank is one of ours, Thomas. She's mated to one of my people." Viv paled. "You hurt her."

"I'm sorry." His shoulders shook with the force of his sobs. "I'll find help and won't hurt anyone else. I promise."

"Good to know." Viv raised her hands high in the air. "So you confess to the rape of the women I've mentioned?"

"Yes."

"Name the others. So we can find them help."

Blubbering, pausing to sniff, he recited a list of names that made Moira's knees weaken. So many names.

Finally, he stopped. "That's all."

"Thank you for your confession," Viv said quietly. She waited until Willoby lifted his head, snorting loudly. Then she held out her hands. "Good-bye."

Willoby half rose on his knees, an unholy screech shooting from him and bouncing through the screen. His body convulsed. Black tar cascaded out of his ears, running down his bare neck.

Conn growled low, shifting to the side, planting his body between Vivienne and Moira.

Willoby lurched forward, rolling to his back and convulsing like a fish thrown from a bowl. Thick, black ink poured from his nostrils, eyes, and wide-open mouth. A toxic film of mist wafted from him.

Moira sucked down bile, fighting the need to turn away. Conn pivoted to face her. His broad shoulders blocked her view of the dead man and the Coven Nine. The pupils in his eyes contracted, allowing the deep green to darken. An unrelenting question lived in their depths bordering on a hard warning. A statement with no words.

She lifted her chin.

He held her gaze as the soldiers dragged Willoby out of the faraway room, leaving a trail of oozing black in the body's wake. Gracefully, too quickly to track, Conn pivoted to face the council.

Moira slid forward to stand on even ground with him. She was the last person who needed to be shielded. Cutting her eyes to the side, she viewed her mate. Gone was the alert anger, the dark warning. He faced the council, a polite smile on his lips, his eyes betraying nothing. If anything, the man looked bored.

Viv pounded with the gavel. "I apologize for that nasty business." The screen went black, returning to stone. "Let's officially call the meeting of the Council of the Coven Nine to order."

Grace tapped the keyboard again. Individual screens rose from the floor to cover the same wall. Simone instantly filled one, the screen casting a slight green tinge to her pale skin and yet somehow enhancing her deep black eyes. She'd pulled her dark curls away from her face, highlighting a worried frown.

The second screen sputtered, and slowly a thin male form took shape. Trevan nodded, his intelligent eyes sparkling with concern.

Viv nodded. "Good. We found you. All right. The meeting is now called to order. First item on the agenda is our missing members."

Simone stepped closer to the camera. "We've lost four

council members within the last year, Mother. Have the enforcers figured out what's going on or not?" Anger sparked her flawless skin a deep red, and fear pinched her full lips.

Vivienne sat and focused on them. "Kell? Moira? What have you discovered?"

A blast of rage slammed into Moira so hard her breath caught. She cut her gaze to Conn, who stood with no expression on his face, shoulders back, stance relaxed. But fury blazed. As his mate, she burned. Maybe she should've informed him about her temporary employment as an enforcer.

Kell clasped his hands behind his back. "Whoever is taking coven members has figured out a way to transport them somewhere. They tried to take Moira earlier."

Her mother gasped, green eyes widening. "Are you all right?"

Moira smiled. "I'm fine, Mother. Truly."

"This is unbelievable, Brigid." Vivienne patted her sister's hand. Her voice rang with authority and power. "How is this possible?"

"We don't know." Kell's jaw hardened. "But since they're now after the Seventh, we need to find out, and quick, to prevent losing her."

"No." Moira straightened her shoulders, ignoring the sudden stiffening of Conn's body. She'd considered the situation carefully and could only find one solution. "Next time, we let them take me. I can find the others." Or at least what happened to them.

In the meantime, she was working on an identification spell to recognize the energy signature of whoever was creating the abyss.

"Hell, no," Conn said, his deep voice echoing around the chamber. "My mate will not be used as bait. With all due respect." His tone hinted respect might be temporary.

Vivienne's eyes flashed. "You're here as a courtesy, Prince Kayrs. Don't forget it."

Conn smiled, slow and sure.

Moira's heart kicked into gear. She placed a quieting hand against his arm.

He quickly covered it with his own. "That leads me to my purpose for being here, Councilwoman Northcutt."

Vivienne's face settled into solicitous lines. "Which would be?"

"Is the Coven Nine planning to withdraw from the Realm?" Conn asked in the polite tone of a bank robber requesting cash.

Dead silence dropped throughout the chamber. Moira tried unsuccessfully to tug her hand from under his, but his bicep flexed, trapping her.

He did not ask that question. He couldn't have asked that question. Did he not just witness a man's organs turn to black tar in his body? "What the hell happened to diplomacy?" she muttered out the side of her mouth.

"It's overrated," he volleyed back.

Only for the fucking Kayrs family. Those men wouldn't know diplomacy if it blew up their homes. Go in fast and hard . . . and screw the consequences. While Moira appreciated the technique, the method threatened to draw a line down the center of her world. She had nowhere to safely land.

Vivienne settled back, her hands clasped on the smooth stone. "Yes."

Surprise grounded Moira in place. Well. Cards on the table then.

Conn nodded. "Why?"

"Why?" A rosy flush crossed Vivienne's face. "The king demanded our people train under yours. We *align* with the Realm. We *do not* answer to it."

"Councilwoman. We're dealing with a new threat, a

new breed of werewolf created by Virus-27. An animal that was formerly a shifter, with all the strength, intelligence, and downright cunning held by shifters." Conn swept a hand out. "No longer are werewolves human converts that die within a year. We all need to train for a new war. Together."

Trevan cleared his throat, the sound echoing oddly through the screen. "I vehemently protest the king's order. Statistically, anytime troops have trained under a new leader, many have transferred allegiance to that leader. King Kayrs knows this."

Conn's smile lacked warmth. "Councilman, while I appreciate your . . . scholarly analysis of the situation, I can assure you, we don't want to steal your soldiers. The king merely wants them properly trained for the new threat."

Moira eyed Trevan. The guy had no clue about training or battlefields.

Vivienne shook her head. "We train alone, Prince. Besides, the king let *humans* know about us—about our world, about our science and genetics. He's lucky he's still breathing." She shuddered as if surprised she'd said the words aloud.

Conn stepped forward. "I'd be very careful with your words, were I you, Councilwoman." His voice lowered to a deadly softness rumbling with power. "Threatening my king is a colossal mistake."

Peter shot to his feet. "Threatening a member of the Nine will get you killed before you breathe another molecule, Kayrs."

Moira yanked her hand free, pressing both palms out. "Whoa. Everyone take a step back. We need each other. The Kurjans are perfecting the virus, the demons are at war with us all, and now some unknown entity is yanking the unwilling through dimensions to God knows where." She sucked in a deep breath. "Everyone relax."

Pete's gaze hardened. "The virus doesn't affect witches, Moira."

"You sure about that?" Conn asked.

"We will be." Vivienne lifted her chin. "The virus attacks the twenty-seventh chromosome of shifters and vampire mates. Probably demon mates, though they won't admit it." She yanked a file up from the floor, flipping it open. "Vampires with their thirty chromosomal pairs seem safe, as do witches with our twenty-nine."

"We don't actually know that." Conn's voice remained level, steady. "The current conclusion of the smartest people on the planet is that the thirtieth chromosome, held only by vampires, Kurjans, and demons, is the one that protects us from the virus. Councilwoman, neither you nor your people have that chromosome."

Moira swallowed. Conn had a point, and a good one. The idea of losing her abilities, of being taken down to a mere human, boiled anger in her gut. The Kurjans needed to be eliminated from the world—for good—which is why she needed to preserve the alliance with the Realm. Regardless of her mating.

Conn settled his stance. "For the record, no humans know about any of us. We've used their expertise to research the genetic ramifications of this virus. They have no idea what they're dealing with."

Moira nodded. "I spoke with Kane Kayrs last week. Along with the king's mate, he's leading the team searching for a cure. They have used well-educated humans to research, but these people are in a different lab, and each is only studying one tiny aspect of the situation. They remain unaware beings other than humans exist." Kane had been matter-of-fact when they'd spoken, and she believed him.

"In addition, Dage *requested* your soldiers for training. He didn't demand anything." Conn clasped his hands behind his back. "If you're concerned about other soldiers discovering your powers . . . well . . . it's too late. I have those powers, and the king is well aware of them."

Moira snapped her teeth together. Did the damn man want the Nine to cut off his head right here and now? "I'm sure the king is discreet."

Peter cleared his throat. "You're an old friend, Moira, and I mean no disrespect. But you're mated to a Kayrs. As an enforcer, the power you're collecting makes you a definite threat. We need to be certain of your allegiance."

It was the last question she wanted to answer. "I took an oath as an enforcer, Peter." The choice to use his first name was deliberate, and brought a tightening to his lips. "While you may not understand that oath, I do." Yeah, She had power. Right now she wanted to prove it to him by turning him into a frog. Not possible, yet the idea calmed her.

Peter sat back, his hands clasped before him on the tablet. "I understand the oath, Moira. Does your mate?"

Conn tightened his hold. "While I haven't read the oath, considering everything you people do is shrouded in secrecy, I assume it's similar to the oath of my soldiers. To give all to the cause."

Viv tapped a pencil on the stone. "Close enough. What if this comes down to war? Moira, there will be no choice for you."

Conn growled low enough only Moira heard. "Should we go to war, Councilwoman, I can assure you my mate would adhere to any vow. She's the most honorable person I know."

Warmth filled Moira's heart. Quite an endorsement from the prince. "Thank you," she murmured softly.

"And you, Connlan?" Brigid spoke up, her head tilted to the side. "You'd align against your mate?"

Moira shuffled her feet. "Mother—"

"No." Conn's voice rang deep and true. "I would not align against my mate." His smile lacked any semblance of humor. "I would, however, take her away from danger, away from you."

Temper and amusement rose in Moira equally. "I believe that's a debate for another day. For now, we need to find the missing coven members."

The lights flared and the two screens went blank.

"Damn it," Vivienne hissed. "What in the hell is wrong with the system?"

Grace shrugged, typing rapidly on a keyboard out of Moira's sight. "We're down again." She rolled dark brown eyes at the leader. "I'll take notes and e-mail them to Trevan and Simone. Let's finish this meeting."

Peter reclaimed his seat. "I'm not convinced we need to send our soldiers to train with the vampires. In addition, last time I checked, the Kurjans and the demons are at war with *the Realm*. If we withdraw, we're no longer at war."

Conn growled low. "You've been discussing the situation with the demons, have you?"

Moira frowned. "Of course not." She focused on her aunt, waiting for Viv to agree.

She remained quiet.

Holy hell. Moira's eyes widened. "You've been in negotiations with the demons? Seriously? They employ the worst mind warfare tactics imaginable. Surely we can't be aligning with them."

"The decisions of the Nine are private, Moira." Vivienne's jaw hardened. "If you'd like to take your rightful place up here and stop playing around with the enforcers, then do it."

"That's enough, Viv." Moira's mother pinned her sister with a glare. "My daughter has been one of the most successful enforcers in history these last thirty years. Don't even think of downplaying her accomplishments."

Yea. Go mom. Moira lifted her chin. "Aligning with the demons is preposterous." Not to mention an incredibly bad decision. The demons screwed with their enemies' brains . . . they destroyed minds. While they might align themselves with the witches for a time, no doubt they'd turn at some point. The mere thought of her abilities in the hands of the demons crawled terror down her spine. "Such an alliance is tantamount to declaring war on the Realm."

"I'm aware of that." Vivienne glanced at Conn and back to Moira. "The Realm is weak. The Kurjans have been preparing for war for centuries, and now the demons have joined in. Not to mention the shifter clans coming after you since the king allowed Caleb Donovan back in the fold."

Moira fought the urge to scream. She understood why Dage let his old friend, who came with numerous allies, back into the Realm. The man had been unjustly blamed for the death of a prophet centuries ago. Ironically enough, Caleb had been claimed by fate as a prophet last year. A fact she'd heard he was denying loudly and often.

Conn rolled his shoulders back. "The Realm isn't weak, Councilwoman. Not by a long shot. While rejoining forces with Caleb angered the demons, as well a few shifting clans, the forces he brought with him strengthened us tenfold."

Moira nodded. Caleb's brother had mated with a lion shifter who'd been betrothed to a demon, angering several clans. He'd been fighting them along with the demons for a century. Currently he had Realm backing. "Let's not forget Caleb is now a prophet for the Realm." A position none of them would dispute.

Vivienne inclined her head. "We are so aware. The Nine must still consider all options." She focused back on the enforcers. "For now, we need to solidify our power base. Kell, you go to Greece and escort Trevan here. Moira, please retrieve your cousin from New York." Viv raised an eyebrow at Conn. "I assume you'll be accompanying her?"

"You assume correct."

Great. Moira frowned. "You want me to leave Ireland?" That didn't make any sense. She eyed her mother, who stared back without expression. A warning set up at the base of Moira's skull. She didn't want to leave her homeland.

Viv grabbed a manila file, tapping it several times. "No. I want you to do your job as an enforcer and escort a member of the Coven Nine here to safety."

Not much leeway there. Moira had Conn, her bitchy cousin, and her irritated aunt to deal with. What else could go wrong?

Chapter 7

The scent of lilac and musty books filled Conn's nostrils as he glanced around Moira's spacious office at the academy. "Do you also need to submit grades at the University of Dublin before we leave town?" His mate taught at both the human university and the witch center of higher learning. He ran his finger over a crystal ornament of a fairy perched in front of books on the shelf. He'd sent the priceless gem to Moira last year when she'd been promoted to full professor at the Quantum academy, a university known only to magic users.

Her shoulders jumped, as if she'd been expecting another question. "No. I turned the human grades in last week." She licked a manila envelope, scrunching her nose afterwards. "Damn glue tastes horrible."

Wheels from her chair squeaked when she pushed back from the alder-wood desk. Anyone in the hallway would know when she was sitting in her chair. Conn needed to teach her more about stealth. "You'd think with all the advancements in computers, we wouldn't need to file a hard copy of grades with the dean." She stood, rolling her eyes.

Conn snorted. "Magic users are notorious for hacking computers. Your dean is smart." Celestial light glinted off the pretty figurine, and he turned toward the night. The shade slats revealed large windows overlooking a quaint courtyard bathed in moonlight. He'd held her hand under the moonlight a century ago as he'd led her away from the festivities—toward destiny.

"Good point." Moira shuffled around two chairs piled high with thick, leather-bound books, her boots clipping across the ancient wooden floor.

He could see her as a scholar. Perhaps later she'd put on glasses and tie her hair up in a bun. A sexy librarian, waiting to be kidnapped—which he pretty much had decided to do. Time to get his mate out of Ireland.

He ran a rough hand through his hair. "The Coven Nine is in trouble." Unsettled, scared, and reacting instead of steering their people.

"I know." Her tone held a note of resigned inevitability. "I'll need to join sooner than I'd planned."

Probably true. Good thing she could do so remotely. Away from whoever was attacking her people. She'd need training against werewolves, although he had no intention of allowing her on the front line. Still, learning defense was a must in their worlds.

"So what other abilities do you possess?" If the woman could turn his spleen into glue, he'd appreciate knowing about it.

She sighed. "I deal in quantum physics, Conn. If something has molecules or waves, I can alter the material state." A frown marred her pretty face as she faced him squarely.

Brave little witch.

"But when altering, I can only choose a state like solid, gas, or liquid. I can't take a destroyed heart and reshape the organ into a working heart. Just into some sort of solid, which wouldn't help at all."

"Too bad."

"Yes." Her tooth bit into the flesh of her bottom lip, making his fangs ache for a taste. "The process is much

easier on humans, of course. You're probably rather safe."
The glint in her eye didn't reassure him. "Besides. You
vamps have plenty of abilities and weapons you don't go
around advertising."

She hadn't quite answered his question.

"I asked what else you could do." The hair on the back
of his neck rose, yanking him from the issue at hand.
"Wait a minute." He grabbed her biceps and shoved her
behind him.

"What the hell are you doing?" she gasped.

An ominous silence filled the corridor outside. He
sniffed the air. Nothing. The silence lay heavy, like a wool
blanket on a summer day. Something waited in the hallway. His gun instantly cooled his hand. "Get down."

Glass shattered. Plastic skipped across the floor. Conn
whirled, grabbing Moira and tucking her face into his
chest, pinning her against the bookshelf. Light flashed,
bright and deadly. His ears rang. More glass shattered and
boots landed hard and loud on the wooden floor.

"Damn it." Conn bent Moira at the waist and shoved
her underneath the desk, pivoting and leaping forward to
take the first body to the ground. Anger ripped through
his system. The flash grenade blurred his vision, but his
knife slashed true. Kurjan blood sprayed across his face,
burning like embers. Strong arms grabbed him, throwing
him into the bookshelf. The door splintered open. Three
more Kurjans swept inside.

They wore all black, with many red medals across their
chests. High ranking. An elite squad. The one in the lead
leveled a large green gun between Conn's eyes. Bright
purple eyes glowed in the monster's stark white face. These
guys deserved to live only in darkness. "Kayrs. It's five
against one. Give us the witch and you won't die today."

Green fire flashed from beneath the desk, the laser bullets turning to lead as they ripped into the leader's face. He crashed to the floor.

Moira jumped to her feet. "Five against two, asshole." She dropped into a slide, knocking the next guy on his ass. Instantly, her knife slashed into its neck, decapitating the monster.

Talk about impressive. Conn jumped for the two Kurjans still standing, ripping the arm off one as his fangs dropped low. The soldier bellowed in pain, silencing as Conn struck into his jugular, taking away part of his neck. A knife cut into Conn's gut, and he grunted, keeping one eye on Moira as he turned his attention on the Kurjan who'd stabbed him. A side kick to the groin and a punch to the monster's face later, he whipped his knife against the enemy's neck. The Kurjan's head rolled to the ground.

Moira battled with the remaining Kurjan, who had size and strength on her. But Conn's mate owned speed and agility. She ducked, slashing with her knife, drawing first blood. The Kurjan landed a lucky punch, connecting with her cheekbone and sending her sprawling.

Conn saw red.

Fury loosed the blood in his veins, allowing adrenaline to course faster. A roar escaped him, and he lunged forward, taking the Kurjan to the floor. The idea of anyone harming Moira, of anyone *daring* to strike out against his woman shattered the chains around the shackled beast inside him. Not only genetics separated vampires from humans. The additional chromosomal pairs comprised enhanced strength of an animalistic nature.

Immortality came with a primitive price.

A pounding clashed inside his skull. His bare hands dug into the bastard's neck, his fingers digging so hard blood sprayed. The need to protect, the primal fury to defend his mate gave him strength beyond the possible.

Purple eyes swirled to red and then black as the Kurjan

struggled, fighting to live. With an animalistic bellow, Conn ripped the head off the body.

Moira darted forward to clutch his arm. Her swollen cheekbone contrasted with her pale face. "Conn. We have to go. More are coming."

She began to dodge into the hall and he stopped her by the scruff of the neck, tugging her behind him. "Stay behind me, Moira." He was first through the door—any door. Always.

He fought the urge to take her hand and dodged into the hallway, swinging his gun one way and then the other. Silence. Light filtered in the broad windows, glinting off the polished oak floorboards. "Come on."

Keeping his back to the wall, he inched toward the exit, his senses on high alert. Nothing moved. If the Kurjans were near, he'd sense them. His mate followed, her breathing even, the gun steady in her grip. They'd have a discussion soon about her current employment, though her training impressed him. Unwanted pride filled his chest.

The outside door remained shut tight. He paused, his senses searching the night. "When I open the door, run for the bikes. *Behind* me." His body would conceal hers as they moved. "If I go down, keep moving."

She snorted. The woman actually snorted.

He'd deal with her later. For now, they needed to run. His shoulder lowered and he twisted the knob, shoving open the heavy maple door and leading with his gun. Their bikes sat at the edge of the curb, sparkling under the full moon. Various vehicles lined the road and music spilled from a bar a block down. The witches hid their school in plain sight. "Run, now."

His torso swung back and forth as he ran down the steps, aiming his gun into the shadows. Nothing moved. A row of hedges lined the brick building. He didn't sense anyone hiding behind them. Quick strides had him across the pillared entryway to the street. Moira threw her leg over her bike and twisted the ignition a second before he did, both forgoing helmets for speed.

"Conn!" she yelled, leaping for him and tackling him to the ground just as a missile hit his motorcycle. *Boom!* The machine sailed into the air and crashed into the front window of a clock shop. Springs, clock faces, and shredded wood flew into the street.

Heat blasted his face. Concrete ripped into his cheek. Cold fury shot the night into focus.

In one fluid movement, he rolled over, lifted Moira, and jumped on the back of her Ducati. "Drive." Folding his larger body around hers, he turned and fired his gun into the alley where the missile originated. He and the Kurjans were about to come to an understanding—as soon as he got his mate to safety. A bellow of pain echoed from the darkness.

Moira kicked the bike loose, turning into the street and punching the power. Bullets pinged across the metal, the small windshield shattered. Conn returned fire. Pain exploded in his rib cage in a blast of five. Lights sped by, music filtering into the distance. Moira dodged into an alley, following it until ripping into traffic at the other end, swerving to avoid a taxi.

A minivan tried to pull into the street. Moira swept her hand out, stalling the vehicle in place. Impressive.

The wind smashed into Conn's face. He lowered his head closer to Moira's neck. Even with the world rushing by, her scent of lilacs surrounded him. Filled him. "Go to the private airport."

She shook her head, curls slamming into his eyes. "Need to get my stuff," she yelled.

He tucked his gun in the back of his pants, reaching around to cover her hands on the bars. Lowering his mouth closer to her ear, he fought the urge to take a bite.

"They'll be waiting. Go to the airport or I'll drive." He did not believe in threats, so when he spoke, he told the truth. Always.

She stiffened. Her head turned, the soft skin of her cheek brushing his mouth. "I smell blood."

Nothing on earth could've prevented the soft kiss he whispered across her smooth skin, even while keeping one eye on the road. Lilacs filled his nose. "Nothing to worry about. 'Tis only a flesh wound." He gave his best Monty Python impression, but the rough cough that followed may have ruined it. The slight shrug she gave relaxed his shoulders—for the moment. When they reached the plane, when they reached safety, boy were they going to talk.

Chapter 8

The private plane leveled off for the long flight to New York. Moira focused across the spacious aisle at Conn barking orders at the king through his phone. Apparently the unexpected attack by the Kurjans created a little anger in the soldier.

She settled back into the sofa, the scent of new leather soothing her. Conn faced her from his own sofa, and a fully stocked bar stood next to a table set for poker. She needed a drink. Or five. The pilots were secluded behind their door, and she hoped they hadn't visited the bar first. She didn't mind flying. Much. But crashing. Well, that made her stomach ache.

Conn clicked off with a growl, taking a moment to study her with those dangerous green eyes. "Are you sure you're unharmed?"

"I'm fine." But she wasn't. The quiet hum of the engines and darkness outside lent an intimacy to the interior she'd like to avoid. Conn's scent of leather and gunpowder permeated the space, sending her pulse jogging and her thighs softening. An inevitable reaction to a vampire mate. "You were shot."

He nodded, ripping off his dark shirt to reveal bullet holes that were already closing. "The bullets fell out on the way." Quick swipes with the shirt had the blood wiped off his cut abdomen.

Moira inhaled deeply. How had she'd forgotten the breadth of his chest? The sheer muscle and strength in that smooth torso? She cleared her throat. "I figured."

His gaze remained on her as if waiting, patient and prepared, to pounce.

They needed to talk, but the words escaped her. After some thought, she gave it a try. "Why did you yell at the king?"

Metallic eyes flashed. "His scouts and informants are pathetic." Conn ran a rough hand through thick hair. "We have a leak. No way it's a coincidence you get attacked by Kurjans the day I show up in Ireland. They found you because of me."

Bollocks. Unease filtered within her already heating blood. "That's probably not exactly true." Only honed strength of will kept her from fidgeting.

Conn lifted his head in the manner of a panther spotting prey. Though identical to hers, his couch seemed a lot smaller. "What do you mean?"

"Ahhh." She was a fighter. As a member of the enforcers, she fought fear every day. Not only fear, but enemy combatants with more experience and devastating weapons. Facing one lone vampire should not create this churning in her stomach. "This wasn't their first attempt." Her voice emerged much softer than she'd intended.

Tension slammed through the enclosed space. "Excuse me?"

His softness exceeded hers in a way that caught the breath in her throat. She forced her hands to remain calmly by her sides. Keeping her face placid, she faced down the vampire.

Sprawled across the aisle, bare to the waist with no

weapons, danger all but surrounded him. Came from him. An irony of fate. True predators blended with their surroundings. The high cheekbones and handsome face masked the most deadly warrior in history.

One she was going to really piss off. "The Kurjans tried to take me on two previous occasions." She waited for the explosion.

None came.

Conn didn't move a muscle, just kept that glittering gaze on her. His lids half lowered. "Say that again."

Oh hell no. The words were hard enough to say the first time. She eyed the back of the plane. A full bathroom and bedroom waited at the rear. No safety there.

"I'm a good fighter, Conn." Damn it. She didn't need to defend herself. His organs were safe as well. Her ability to melt organs so far only worked on humans, probably due to their less complex genetic makeup . . . a fact he didn't need to know.

"What do you expect me to do with this information, Moira?" The innocuous words did nothing to mask the bite behind them.

Shove it up his ass? "Not a damn thing." Anger began to slide through her veins.

He straightened up, leaning forward. "There's the rub, Dailtín. How long have you known me?"

The conversation was beginning to close her throat—too many land mines. "A century." She looked for the trap. Conn wasn't a man to talk. For as long as she'd known him, action had been his mantra.

"How did you think I'd react to your joining the enforcers, taking a vow to give your life for them, coupled with hiding the Kurjan's attack on you?" He cocked his head to the side in curiosity . . . or for a better angle on her jugular. Probably the jugular.

"I didn't give you a thought." The lie nearly caught in

her throat. The brand on her hip flared to life in a flash of pain. "You're at war, Connlan. As the commander of all the Realm soldiers, you have enough responsibilities." She spat the last word out.

One dark eyebrow rose. "Is that what you are, Moira? A responsibility?" Threat existed in each syllable.

She jumped up. The bedroom door probably held a lock. "Yes."

The plane rocked when he slid to his feet, blocking her path to the bedroom. "Then apparently I've ignored my responsibilities long enough."

He loomed over her. She had two choices—either knock him aside or take a step back—and only a split second to decide which one to make. The rational decision was step back and reason with him.

Fuck reason.

She pivoted, kicking him solidly in the shin while dodging forward and shooting her body into his gut in a move guaranteed to throw him over her shoulder.

Except it didn't.

Strong hands gripped her arms and tossed her up in the air—two feet off the ground. Her head missed the top of the plane by a mere inch. She gave a startled yelp, the sound gargling in her throat when he caught her by the biceps, holding her aloft like a limp doll. She lost her breath.

Fury. Pure anger blazed fire through his eyes and a deep crimson spread across his cheekbones. "Your freedom has ended, Brat." He lowered her to her feet and his mouth crashed down on hers. A century ago he'd used persuasion and seduction. Today he took. Raw and demanding, his lips explored while his tongue commanded a kiss that tasted like sin and felt like ownership. Gone were the charming prince and the reasonable mate. In their place stood a predator finally unleashed, playing for keeps.

Lights exploded behind her eyelids. Need ripped

through her body in a force too painful to be called desire. Or even lust. No words could describe the craving that shot fire from every nerve ending. She whimpered, returning his kiss, tangling her tongue with his. A roaring set up in her ears, the brand on her hip scalding with demand. Too much, too much, too much. She lifted her hands and shoved against his chest. Heat filled her palms.

With a soft cry, she wrenched her head away. "Wait." Pain. So much *need* in her body. The only solution to the need held her.

"Wait for what?" Anger still filled his gaze.

Air. She needed air. Filling her lungs, she fought to steady her breath. "Wait." She held out a hand, panic battling with the craving he'd lit. "This is, I mean, this is . . . "

He smiled. The wicked curve of his lips promised sin. "This is inevitable."

She swallowed loudly. "No. I mean, it's been a century. You know. Since . . . " Since her first time. Her only time. The air whished through the vents, and she shivered.

Nimble fingers caressed down her arms. Surprise lifted his eyebrows. "That night was the wildest of my entire life." A too-knowing gaze wandered her face, studying what had to be blazing color. "Oh."

Yeah, oh. She took a tenuous step back.

His eyes softened. Graceful as any panther, he sat down and lifted her to straddle his legs. "Sweetheart. It only hurts the first time."

True. The second, third and even fourth of that night had been incredible. "I know." His legs warmed her inner thighs and she fought the urge to rub against him. "But, well, maybe we should spend time getting to know each other first, this time." Her body howled in protest. Not by any stretch did she consider they'd never lie together again. She had too much need, too much curiosity to walk away without seeing if sex with Conn was as good as she remembered.

"Ah." His smile was lethal. "I have a photographic memory, Moira. I know every inch of you." His palm traveled down her back to tap one finger at the top of her left buttock. Heat flushed along her skin. "For example, right here there's a tiny mark in the shape of a waning moon."

"Yes, but . . ." Focus. She needed to focus.

He leaned in, wandering his lips over her neck. "And, if I nip right here"—his teeth rubbed against her skin— "you make the prettiest sound of need." She groaned, her nipples peaking. She blinked. Once. Twice. A third time. God, she wanted him. Was it fate—the mating mark? Something whispered deep across her mind that it was Connlan. Even if he hadn't marked her, she'd want him. She opened her mouth to say something, anything, and his lips closed over hers.

Vampires burned hotter than any other species. This one burned hotter than most. Heat singed her lips, sending desire sliding through her veins like fresh lava. A shiver wandered down her back, her nerve endings firing in its wake. His lips were firm, his tongue demanding, his hold tight.

She allowed herself to fall into the kiss. Into him, into the wild storm he unleashed.

Tangling her fingers through his hair, she kissed him back, pressing her breasts against his thick chest and her core against his.

Hard. He was so damn hard.

Yet the hands holding her remained gentle. The contrast banished all rational thought. The world fell away. Her skin ignited. Reality, imagination, existence narrowed down to the two of them.

She clutched her fingers, yanking his head back, her gaze on his face. A dark flush covered his high cheekbones, the silver in his eyes more intense than the green. His tongue flicked out to lick his lips and she felt it along her skin.

The craving she'd felt a century ago hadn't been sated through time. If anything, the need had grown. "Is it always like this?"

"Hell, no. Only with you." He dropped his hands to her hips, taking hold and standing. "I'll show you."

Moira wrapped her legs around Conn's hips as he moved toward the bedroom. "Wait. Just wait a minute."

"For what?" His tone implied he was done waiting. He kicked open the door, sliding his mouth along her neck to nip an earlobe.

Her head rolled to the side to allow greater access. "Negotiation." A stupid word, but the only thing that sprang to her fuzzy mind.

He traced the shell of her ear. "Negotiation?"

She gasped. "We're adults, not kids romping for the first time, Conn. We go into this with our eyes wide open."

"I plan to keep my eyes open, Moira." The deep sexy tone of his voice dropped low, and wetness coated her thighs. One quick toss had her bouncing on the bed.

She looked up, her breath caught at the intent in his gaze. Think. She needed to think. "No. I mean, this is only sex. Us releasing some serious tension we've built up. No lifetime commitment—we need to talk about it."

Nimble fingers went to the buttons of his jeans. "I'm finished with talking." His jeans hit the floor. "We've been talking for a while and apparently you haven't been listening."

Naked. Connlan Kayrs stood before her as nude as the day he was born. Male. Aroused. Huge.

She *would not* look at his cock. No way. "Most men are

vulnerable when nude, Conn." The words slipped out before she could think.

He quirked an eyebrow. "Do I look vulnerable to you, Moira?"

"No." She'd forgotten how big he was. Levering up on her knees, she tugged her shirt off. "This is just sex."

He rolled his eyes. Naked and aroused, he still rolled his eyes. "Are you really hitting me with a bullshit statement about this just being sex? I'd assumed I'd allowed you enough time to grow the hell up."

Her temper roared to the surface. She jerked her jeans and panties off. "I am being a grown-up, jackass. This is an adult discussion."

"When did you start waxing? Everything?" His eyes flared with raw heat.

Embarrassment wound through her desire. "It's the modern thing to do." Damn him.

His gaze lingered on her bare skin before wandering up her torso. "Thank God for modern. I like your bra."

Anger nearly choked her. Even so, she felt like an idiot, perched on the bed wearing only a sparkly pink brassiere. Good thing she'd hit the spa last week. "Thanks." She sprang the front clasp loose and tossed the lingerie at his head. See how he liked being off balance.

He snagged the bra out of the air, twirling it around his finger. "I like your breasts better."

She remembered. He'd spent lavish hours on them a century ago.

His fangs dropped low. "Time for a taste."

Chapter 9

The sight of his fangs had her body tensing. Not with fear—with absolute expectation. "You're not listening."

"I listened." He took the one step closer to the bed, eyes darkening as he towered over her. "I'm just not agreeing. I'll keep you safe from any threat out there. But don't think for a moment your body, head, or heart are safe from me. They're mine."

The possessive tone inched her temper and arousal higher. The temper she welcomed, the arousal she'd see a shrink for later. "Not a chance." The words spun out quickly, and even in her state she recognized the thrown gauntlet they were. Of course he'd pick it up. But she failed to anticipate his speed in doing so.

Quick as a thought he grabbed her arm, yanking her flush against his chest. One hand tangled in her thick hair and drew her head back, exposing her pulsing jugular as she perched on her knees on the bed. "Oh sweetheart. I do love your spirit."

Heat. It rolled off the man in waves, engulfing her, making thought difficult. "Thank you."

"Any time." He bit into her bottom lip, the small nip sending a direct line of need to her clit. The warmth of his tongue in soothing the persistent ache made her bite back a groan. His hand tightened, sending erotic tingles of pain along her scalp. "You're it for me, Moira. I'm keeping you."

Right or wrong, she wanted those words. Maybe even needed them. The assurance in them offered the possibility of a future . . . of security. All something she'd worry about later. Her heart thumped hard. "Conn. Show me."

He swooped down, claiming her mouth in a blaze of heat. An unbreakable, nearly brutal kiss turned her knees soft. A tremble worked its way down her spine, a quivering of need beyond fate, beyond the magical, beyond the world she knew so well. A slice of fear cut into the desire, then disappeared as Conn cupped her ass, drawing her closer to his heat. Her belly rubbed against his erection, and she fell back, pulling him with her, both hands clutching his shoulders.

His mouth kept hers as they landed, his hard body over hers, his palms sliding down her sides. One calloused thumb brushed across her marking. Fire flashed out to zap her clit. She broke away from his mouth, hers opening in a silent plea.

Strong movements had her feet clasped at the small of his back, her arms winding around solid muscle to bind him. Her smile felt saucy. "Watch your wishes, Kayrs. Maybe you'll be the one trapped." While she meant the statement as a challenge, as a warning, a hint of truth hung in the air.

His gaze softened as he glanced at her bruised mouth and then back up at her eyes. "You trapped me the first time you said my name." He lowered his head, swirling his heated tongue around one desperate nipple. "I swear, you have the sweetest taste."

Spikes of pleasure careened through her, straight to her core. She gyrated against him. He turned his attention to the other nipple, biting down just enough.

"For the love . . . do something." If he didn't end the torment, her head was going to explode.

He chuckled against her skin, wandering up to nip under her jaw. Grabbing her butt, he plunged inside her with one forceful stroke.

She cried out in shock at his entry, her body tightening, her nostrils flaring as she sucked in air. Pleasure edged with pain, arching her against him. Her thighs gripped his hips, her nails scored his back. So full, so big. A quiver spiraled deep inside her and she paused, frowning. He wasn't moving. It was impossible. But just their being joined sent fire blasting through her. "Conn!" she cried out as she came, huge gusts of pleasure rolling from somewhere indefinable beneath her skin. Somewhere untouchable. The room sheeted white. She shut her eyes, riding the waves. Her nails dug in deeper as the storm overtook her, leaving her helpless as it departed.

He dropped his forehead to hers. "Jesus."

Her eyes opened along with her mouth in amazement. The surrounding particles danced through the air and then narrowed into sharp focus.

He slid out and plunged back in. Then again. "Hold on, sweetheart."

Reality slapped her in the face. The force between them, whether fate or Conn's determination, might be too much for her to beat. She released his back, sliding her hands to his chest to push away. He slammed hard inside her. Pleasure rippled along awakened nerves, and she arched into him with a hiss of demand. She paused, and he plunged again. Sparks shot behind her eyes. She stopped trying to push him away and held on with all the strength she possessed. He drove harder. Faster. Stronger.

A pulsing contraction ripped through her sex, tightening her hold on him. He growled, the hand on her ass leaving bruises, the speed of his thrusts increasing. Their panting breath and the slap of flesh against flesh filled the room.

She fisted both hands in his hair, yanking his mouth down. Her teeth bit into his lips before she slid her tongue inside, determined to find some control as her world spiraled away. He fought her for dominance, his mouth hard on hers, his body pinning hers to the mattress. The kiss was messy, passionate, yet with an underlying sense of safety she'd have to examine later.

He lifted his head. "You make magic work, Moira."

The sweetness in the midst of raw passion flayed her heart. She opened her mouth in confusion, only to snap it shut as he plunged. Hard, fast, and with power, he thrust into her. The tingling inside coiled higher and hotter. She reached for it, clutching onto him, shutting her eyes against the exquisite need. He shifted his angle, brushing over her clit. With a sharp cry, she broke.

His muscles tightened as he came. Collapsing against her, his rapid heartbeat slammed against hers. Almost as if they made sound, the walls she'd erected around her heart crumbled down. Damn it.

Moira awoke to the hum of the air vents in the plane, her back plastered against Conn's front beneath the down comforter. Her entire body ached—though not entirely in a bad way. Her memory hadn't played tricks on her. Sex with Conn was just as explosive and all consuming as she'd remembered.

Lazy, sated, her mind wandered into the past. Into the first time she'd seen him, naked to the waist, throwing a witch across a training field.

"A half-naked vampire. Told you this would be fun," Moira whispered to her sister Darcy as they peered through thick foliage on the southern end of the training area. They'd escaped yet an-

other round of diplomatic meetings to watch the Realm's deadliest soldier teach new moves. She'd been watching Connlan Kayrs all week during the Realm Colloquium held in Ireland. "Maybe he'll shuck his pants, too."

Darcy snickered. "Mother is going to kill us." She turned and eyed the rushing stream behind them, lifting her skirts away from the damp grass. "Let's just not get wet."

"Of course."

Connlan demonstrated a headlock on McPatty's youngest son.

A fluttering set up in Moira's stomach, reminding her of the first time she'd ventured into the rolling sea.

The vampire stood strong, muscles clearly defined and solid in his chest. Even across the distance, the magnificent color of his eyes piqued her curiosity. Rumor had it vampires had two colors for their eyes. She'd probably never see Conn's vampire colors.

Then he'd looked up—directly at her. Stunned by the power in those otherworldly eyes, she caught her breath and stepped back. A protruding branch caught her heel. The rest was inevitable. In a fluff of silk and scattering of leaves, she landed on her arse in the stream, cursing a streak worse than the loudest drunk at Shea's tavern on a Saturday night.

The shock of cold had her muscles going rigid. Smooth rocks lined the stream's bottom, no doubt leaving bruises on her rear. Chilly water rushed around her, instantly soaking her skirts. She pressed down with her palms, slipping on the moss.

"Moira, be quiet." Darcy stepped gingerly over the offending branch, keeping her boots shy of the stream. "I'll lean out . . . you grab my hand."

A twig snapped in warning before a large form yanked brush out of the way. "Allow me." Two strides had Connlan Kayrs in the stream and grasping her by the armpits. He lifted her as if her molecules had been rearranged into air.

As he set her down, pure amusement lifted the corners of his devastating mouth. "You're not dressed for swimming, Miss Dunne."

She stumbled on the uneven ground, seeking balance. He knew her name. Well, her last name. She peered around his hulking body to see men busily training in the field. Thank goodness no one else saw. "How did you see me?"

The smile broadened. "Good eyes. Good ears, too."

Ears? What had she said? Fire rushed into her face. She'd wanted him to remove his pants. Even now, his bare chest beckoned her. What would he taste like? She shook her head. Good thing he couldn't read minds.

"How fortunate." Her tongue felt too large in her mouth. Irritation wandered down her spine.

He smiled at Darcy. "Miss Dunne."

Darcy twittered. She actually twittered. "Prince Kayrs."

The irritation wandered into anger. Moira stepped back. "Thank you for your assistance. You no doubt should return to work." She lifted her chin. The water weighed down her skirts, making it nearly impossible to move.

His eyes sparkled a deeper green than her aunt Viv's climbing ivy. "I'll escort you back to the meeting area."

"No." Panic had her eyes widening to let in more light. She looked akin to a drowned cat. Her mother really would kill her. "Thank you. We'll watch awhile longer."

"I'm not removing my pants." He said it soberly, but his eyes laughed.

How indiscreet. Darcy coughed. Moira sniffed. "I should hope not. But I want to watch the training. Learn the moves." It was the truth.

Darcy rolled her eyes. "Moira, you don't need training. You're the Seventh. When you're on the council, you'll have bodyguards."

"I want to learn to fight." They'd been over it repeatedly. She eyed the vampire. "What do you think?" Maybe he'd teach her.

Kell and Adam always refused, but Daire had seemed open to the possibility.

Conn's gaze wandered over her still warm face, down to her soppy wet boots and back up. "I think you're too pretty to fight."

A tingle set her skin on fire from his traveling gaze. Pleasure warmed her from the compliment, irritation filled her from the dismissal. "Think so, do you?" Holding her palms out, she formed a ball of pulsating plasma. Fate might force her to become a diplomat, but no one should ever underestimate her.

He frowned. "I do think so."

She lifted her hand and blew. The ball swished toward Conn, impacting his chest. He jumped back. A scowl formed grooves in his angled face. "That burned."

The smirk came easily to her face. "Good. At least I know not to underestimate someone."

Fast as an arrow he reached out, grasping her elbows and lifting her until they met eye to eye. "Miss Darcy? What's the Gaelic term for brat?"

"Dailtín." Darcy leaned against a tree, mirth in her voice.

Conn's eyes narrowed, his gaze hard on Moira. "You just earned yourself a nickname. Dailtín."

"I'm not a brat." His easy strength in holding her aloft caused a humming in her belly. A weakness in her knees.

"You're most certainly a brat." His gaze hardened further as one hand lifted to tangle in wet curls. "Don't ever throw blue energy at me again, Moira. You won't like the result."

Any retort stuck like mud in the back of her throat at the look in his eyes, across his sharp face. Her widened eyes searched his for any hint of humor. There was none.

A satisfied glint lit his darkened eyes as he gave one short nod. "I don't threaten, Moira. You'd do well to remember that." Then his mouth was on hers—swift, hard, and removed much too quickly. He set her back on her feet. "I'll see you at the dance tonight." Rocks scattered as he turned on his heel, returning to the training field without a backward glance.

She put a hand to her tingling lips. Something shifted inside her. She wanted a real kiss from the vampire. That night she'd get it.

Moira was jerked back into the present by a hand playing idly up and down her arm, raising goose bumps. Words. She should say some.

Conn nipped her ear. "Are you all right, Dailtín?"

"Fine." She snuggled closer into his warmth. "I was remembering when we met."

"When you fell in the stream." Amusement filled his voice.

"Aye. You kissed me."

"Barely. Yet my world halted on its axis." His breath brushed her skin with heat. "Later that night, when you showed up to the dance in that dress, I almost took you to the floor. In front of everybody."

The dress had been beautiful. "You probably don't even remember the color."

"It was green and it matched your eyes."

Yes, it had. "If you could rewrite our past, would you?" Why she'd ask a question so full of peril had her shaking her head. Of course he would.

"Hell, no. I wouldn't mind smoothing out the present however."

Smoothing her into the role he wanted. Frustration had her clearing her throat. "What do you want from me?"

"I want you to fight for us as strongly as you've been fighting against us." He smoothed the hair away from her cheek and dropped a soft kiss on her neck.

Desire flared back to life. "Why do you pretend there's even an *us*? I mean, we had a one-night encounter a century ago that left us both marked. That doesn't create an *us*." Of course, in his world, it probably did.

"We've been mated for a century."

"We haven't been together, Conn. We haven't been a couple." They hadn't attended weddings, funerals, or parties together.

His hand flexed. "Did you want to be?"

"Sometimes." Naked and satisfied, only the truth belonged between them.

"Me, too." He huffed out a breath. "But I signed the treaty, and you needed time. It was the least I could do." Irritation coated his words. Irritation aimed at himself.

"What do you mean?"

"You were a babe, Moira. A mere twenty-something years old, and I knew it. Yet I took you." His voice lowered in regret.

She stiffened. "You didn't want this." She'd always understood that. Conn wouldn't have bound himself to a witch tied to the Coven Nine if he'd had a choice. The marking had been an accident.

He rolled her over, covering her body with his. "I wanted you. Still do. Always will. If I'd known I'd mark you, I'd have given you time to live first. Time to choose your own path before I yanked you onto mine." Hard and unyielding, his lips molded her mouth to his. His head rose just a fraction. "But make no mistake, I'd have hunted you down when I thought you were ready. You were born to wear my mark."

Heat pricked her skin. "Conn. You need to join the modern times." The secret thrill fluttering in her belly from his possessive tone needed to go away.

"This is about as modern as I get." He smiled, and her flutter sped up. "So, now tell me what Peter was talking about. How are you gaining power by being an enforcer?"

She'd been waiting for him to ask the question. "I can't tell you." The vow she'd made required more than just action. A promise of discretion and confidentiality she had no intention of breaking. "I'm sorry."

The desire to share her world with him caught her unaware. While she was resigned to joining the Nine at some point, for now, she truly enjoyed her job. It'd be nice to share the details with the soldier. But she offered nothing more.

"Interesting. I will discover the truth, you know."

She opened her mouth to argue just as the pilot buzzed through the intercom. "We begin our descent in five minutes, Prince Kayrs."

"Well. I guess we'll table this discussion. For now." Conn sighed, rolling from the bed. "Get dressed, Moira. We need to fetch your cousin before going home."

Sliding to her feet, Moira reached for her bra. Something in his tone provided warning. "Home is Ireland, right?"

He yanked up his jeans. "No. Home is now the west coast of the States. Period."

Great. Let the next battle begin.

Chapter 10

Sometimes being the heir apparent to the Kurjan throne became so boring he wanted to cut his own head off. Kalin lounged in Franco's office, his gaze on the depths of the sea outside the wide expanse of windows. How far underground were they, anyway? A silvery fish swam by every few moments, capturing hidden light to find the way. Quiet and mysterious, the fish kept returning, as if seeking dinner. Silly creature—unaware of the predator watching him.

The Kurjan leader slammed down the phone. "Damn it." Franco swept a broad hand across his desk, knocking papers to dot the ancient hand-knotted Persian rug. "The witch got away. Again." Throwing his reddish hair over his shoulder, he gulped air, his eyes a wild purple, his skin whiter than death. "One of the Kayrs men showed up . . . my source couldn't tell which one." He paced over to lean against the window.

"My guess is Connlan. Considering the witch is his mate." Kalin stretched out long legs. He was only fifteen, but he understood the call of a woman. A different one called to him every other week or so. Of course, they all died.

"More than likely." The Kurjan ruler sat in his desk

chair, regaining control. "Well. I promised my brother a witch to experiment on, and I want that one. Taking a Kayrs mate would cement our place. Even now allies are fleeing from the Realm."

Kalin scratched his head. "That witch is a fighter. She's the Seventh." He appreciated spirit in a woman. Made it more exciting to break her. "The demons must want her even more than we do."

"Yes. But she'll sense them coming. They can't block their brain waves from witches like we can. We should be able to get to her."

"No." Why fixate on that witch? There are many to choose from. Kalin brushed invisible lint off his jeans. "She's with Kayrs now. That means underground and impossible to reach."

"Not if she's an enforcer." Franco flipped open a file on his desk. "I wanted her for several reasons, but you're correct, any witch will do—male or female. It's time for more animal testing on the virus." Yellow teeth flashed in a parody of a grin. "In addition, your uncle Erik has a line on a weakness in the witches."

Erik and Franco were actually his second cousins, but the "uncle" designation just made things easier, and Kalin liked things easy. "What kind of weakness?"

"I don't know yet." Franco shrugged. "But my brother was very excited about it. You know how he gets with new discoveries. Science is everything to him."

"I'd rather be a warrior." Kalin snorted. "It's odd we haven't captured one witch to test the virus on."

Franco hissed. "They're all on guard. Frankly, we've been concentrating on shifters so we could make a werewolf fighting class, and vampire mates . . . well . . . to fuck with them."

"Yes. I'm glad you enjoy the game. Any plans to ally

with the demons or rogue shifter clans to take down the Kayrs family?" Any alliance would need to be temporary. The Kurjans would eventually rule the entire world.

"No." Franco clasped his hands behind his back. "The demons can't be trusted and the shifters are merely frontline soldiers. Just animals. We don't need any of them." He stretched his neck, the vertebrae popping. "We may sit back and let the demons weaken the Realm even further before making our move—once we get the werewolf class under some control."

"I think I'm feeling ready to head out on a raid or two." Capturing a shifter for the experiments might be a fun Saturday night. Before he moved on to vampires and demons. "Getting my hands on a witch might prove exciting as well."

The ruler studied him. "All right. Next time we go on a shifter roundup, you're in. But I'd stay away from witches until you've completed more training. They have weapons you can't foresee."

The warning heightened Kalin's curiosity to find a witch and play. He stretched to his feet, checking his pocket before zipping his leather jacket. His wallet felt light. He'd need to hit the safe on the way out. "Night has finally fallen—I'm heading out for a bit."

"No." Franco straightened his posture. "The plane is down for maintenance and you can't play in my backyard. I like ruling from here . . . nothing can make the locals suspicious. I believe I've been more than clear on this subject."

"You have." Kalin only hunted women away from home. Though why Franco liked the cliffs of Baffin Island in Canada bewildered him. The area screamed remote and chilly. "But I need to get out. Don't worry, I won't hunt tonight." Probably.

"Fine." Franco sighed. "If you hunt, the plane privileges will disappear."

"Whatever." Kalin flashed sharp canines. So might the ruler disappear. He hustled from the office, through the underground fortress, taking the elevator to his new F-10 extended cab waiting on the wet road. No one bothered him on the way.

Thunder rolled overhead as he drove into the small town and parked by the gas station. He pulled a baseball cap from the seat beside him and put it on his head. Colored contacts weren't necessary for his odd green eyes, though he should've darkened his skin some. He would have to stick to places with little light.

He exited the car and tugged the ball cap low, shadowing his face.

The sidewalks were deserted. Clouds opened up, throwing rain against his leather jacket. He hustled down the street, shoving his way into the movie theater. His only intent had been to view a new comedy, but he liked to keep the old man guessing.

He paid for his ticket with his eyes down, grabbing a soda on the way in. The previews had started in the mostly empty room. A couple necked in the front row, the guy's hand under the blonde's shirt . . . probably thinking no one could see them in the dark. Kalin turned to find a seat, then gave a muffled "*oomph*" as an elbow collided with his gut. Popcorn spilled.

Roses. The scent of fresh roses wafted up before pretty blue eyes squinted through the darkness.

A human teenager.

"Sorry. Can't see." She reached out, grabbing his arm with her free hand. "Are you all right?" The soft tone of her voice slid over his skin like lotion.

She barely came to his shoulder. How the heck did she think she'd hurt him? "Yes. Um. Are you all right?"

"Yes." She glanced around, stumbling again. "But I can't see anything."

"I can." His hand moved of its own volition, grasping hers. Small and fragile in his, her skin was softer than butter. He tugged her to the seats, putting her in the second one, taking the aisle seat.

She sat with a relieved sigh. "Thanks, um . . ."

"Kalin." He glanced toward the door. "Are you meeting someone?"

"Nope. I was meeting my friend Joe, but he had to work. I'm Peggy." She tilted a box of popcorn toward him. "Are you meeting anybody?"

"No." How impressive. Most teenaged girls wouldn't venture to a movie by themselves. He shook his head at the popcorn and then realized she couldn't see. Confusion thickened his voice. "No thanks. I don't like popcorn."

She grinned, the flickering lights from the screen dancing across her features. "You're not eating it right." Digging into her purse, she yanked out a box of chocolate-covered caramels to dump into the popcorn. "Now try it."

He did, savoring the taste on his tongue. The salty sweetness spread down his throat, warming him. Finally warming him. "You're right."

The screen began to hitch and shake. The video burned away, and the lights flipped on.

He blinked at the sudden glare, then turned to the side. Pretty. Very pretty. Her brown hair, blue eyes, and balanced features were striking. He sensed her spunk and spirit. "Hi."

Even her smile was cute. "Hi." Then she frowned. "Do you live here?"

"Yes." What was it about her? He hoped the movie came back on—so she wouldn't leave.

"Go to high school?" Her gaze traced his features in an almost physical skimming.

"No. Ah . . . I'm homeschooled." Something heated in his chest. Worry filtered in his brain. He should get out of there. But something kept him firmly in place. He'd never smell another rose without thinking of her stunning smile—or the spark of intelligence in her eyes.

She studied him with her head tilted to the side. God, he hoped he passed for human.

"How old are you?" She scrunched up her face. Her lips were pink and moist.

"Fifteen." He wanted to kiss her. Gently. He didn't think he'd ever kissed a girl gently. "How about you?"

"Seventeen." She glanced at the blank screen. Almost on cue, a voice came over the loudspeaker, announcing technical problems and that they could all get a refund at the front door.

"Shoot. Oh well." She stood, leaning a hand down to help him up. No fear or hesitancy showed in her face. The girl was actually unafraid of him, even though he was twice her size. "So. Want to go bowling?"

His head bobbed up and down.

They walked outside, Peggy chattering about her math class.

How odd it felt to be treated as a normal person by such a fragile female. Even his own people steered clear of him, the air often scented with sulfur and the stench of fear.

She shivered in the cold, and he dropped his jacket over her shoulders, like the guys did on television. Her smile made him feel taller than Franco—which someday he would be.

The rain began to pepper harder. She grabbed his hand, tugging him down the street. "Let's run."

As he wrapped his hand around hers, something shifted inside him. He loosened his hold, careful not to bruise. No hint flowed from her of the possibility she was an enhanced female, a possible mate. No whisper of psychic ability. Yet, as she tangled her small fingers more securely with his, he angled his body to protect her from the rain. He'd follow her anywhere.

Chapter 11

Simone Brightston's New York penthouse screamed sensuality in tones of deep red and purple—much like Moira's, but without the touches of whimsy. Soft light filtered around the apartment, and twinkling lights from the city below filled the sweeping windows. Nighttime had fallen and Moira's senses whispered the moon would be full. She shifted on the velvet couch, hiding a wince at newly discovered intimate muscles.

The council should've sent all three enforcers to retrieve Simone from New York. But no, Moira was facing her cranky cousin all on her own. "What do you mean you're not sure you should leave?"

A delicate shrug lifted Simone's bare shoulder. Her wide sweater slid down both arms. "I have a winter holiday planned. I can still be reached via the net, however."

Moira kept her focus on Simone, ignoring the heat pouring off the vampire sitting next to her. "The Nine has requested your presence at headquarters, and I've been ordered to escort you."

Simone arched a dark eyebrow, pushing thick black hair back. "I'm part of the Nine."

"I understand your job, cousin." What in the hell was going on? The painting behind the couch caught Moira's eye; an early watercolor from Brenna—painted during her teenage years.

Simone followed her gaze, a pretty flush scattering across her face. "I like the colors."

The soft palette contrasted with the rich tones of the rest of the room. Not Simone's taste, but the work held a place of honor.

Interesting.

Running water echoed in the distance and Moira sighed. "You have company?"

"Yes." Not by a tick did Simone's smooth face change. The blush receded. "I'm not vacationing alone."

"Your mother—"

"Irrelevant." Simone's black eyes flashed. "As part of the Nine, I make my own decisions, Moira. A fact you'd understand better if you accepted the invitation to join."

Moira lifted her chin. She doubted Simone would appreciate sitting next to her behind the wide stone bench. "Unlike you, I'm not convinced the missing members are dead. Unless I issue a challenge, there isn't an opening."

"I always thought you'd challenge me." Simone shifted her gaze toward the hallway when the water cut off, returning her focus to Moira with a slight tilt of her head. The words sat as a statement, but the tiniest hint of question hung heavy in the room.

"No." Moira hoped the current beau remained unaware of their world. That's all she needed, more people learning the witches had problems. She hoped the man was a human, one on his way out the door. "We're family, Simone."

"So?"

A fluffy stuffed elephant sat on a cushion by the fireplace—old, yet in excellent condition—a prize they'd won together in a three-legged race during a family festival, decades ago. They'd drawn names, and had done surprisingly well together.

"So, I'm starting to think family holds more meaning than you've let on." Moira wondered how well she knew her cousin.

"I don't understand what you mean." Simone brushed raven dark hair away from her face, her eyes veiled.

Enough of this crap. "I thought you didn't like me." A sad fact Moira had come to terms with years ago, it was one she might reconsider. Simone had always been critical, and downright snotty sometimes. But in New York, she had surrounded herself with reminders of family.

"I'm not sure why. Even so, I wouldn't challenge you for a seat." Moira stared at her cousin. Once challenged, the member could conceded the position or fight for it. Unfortunately, a fight meant one of them would lose all ability to control the elements—to practice magic.

Conn shifted in his seat to look at Moira. "Since your laws are so damn secret, I don't comprehend the protocol here. Do we make her go?"

Simone's smile flashed white teeth in pure warning. "Careful, Kayrs. I might turn you into a chipmunk."

Moira bit her lip against a smile. "This is unprecedented. When the head of the council requests someone's presence, they go. Especially if that head is someone's *mother*." She emphasized the last word with a glare at Simone.

Simone rolled her eyes. "So you're going to tell my mother on me?"

"I'm sure Aunt Viv will notice you're not in Ireland, dumbass."

"You know"—Simone crossed long legs under a filmy black skirt—"that temper of yours might keep you from being an effective member of the Nine."

"Yeah, because us witches are so famous for being cool-headed," Moira retorted.

Conn snorted. "Right. Okay, so we're off, then?"

"No, Conn. We're not off." Moira had a job to do, though she couldn't force a member of the Nine to do something they didn't want to do. The heavy scent of patchouli oil choked the air, making her twitchy.

Simone focused on Conn. "How's your brother?" She had dated the king eons ago. Things had not worked out, and the relationship had ended badly.

"Ah, fine." Conn cut his eyes toward Moira.

She shrugged. Let him deal with that quagmire.

"Good to know." Simone's jaw hardened.

Moira scrambled for a kind thought. "It's nice you've remained friends with Dage, Simone."

They hadn't remained friends. The king had recently taken a mate he appeared to adore.

"Right." Simone's crimson painted lip curled in almost a smile. Light footsteps echoed on the marble tile in the hallway, and she turned toward the sound.

Only long-learned practice kept Moira's jaw from dropping at the man who entered the living room. "Trevan." A member of the Nine for the last five hundred years. "Kellach is looking for you in Greece, as we speak."

"Maybe he should have called first." Trevan smiled, even teeth in an aristocratic face. His dark silk shirt and pants emphasized a long and lean body. His tapered fingers brushed down Simone's hair as he strolled by to take the overstuffed chair next to hers. The scent of expensive cologne permeated the room in layers of lime and ancient wood. "I assume Viv issued the order after communications cut off?"

A blush of pleasure exploded across Simone's high cheekbones from his caress.

"Yes." Moira fought the urge to squirm. Unease tickled

her nape, and the vampire stiffening to attention next to her didn't help.

Trevan steepled his fingers under his chin, his onyx ring flashing in the dim light. "I do wonder about such faulty equipment. In this day and age."

Moira frowned. Surely he wasn't suggesting the members in Ireland left him out on purpose.

Conn cleared his throat. "I find your presence here interesting, Demidov"—although congenial, a thread of warning edged his tone—"considering you failed to mention your location to the Nine during the conference call yesterday."

Trevan's smile didn't reach his dark eyes. "They didn't ask, now did they?"

Moira stilled. Conn was right. Trevan *hadn't* mentioned his location during the meeting. More important was why the council members hadn't zeroed in on his status. Or had they?

Simone plucked an invisible thread off a jeweled pillow. "I thought it prudent to keep my life private, Conn."

Moira's shoulders relaxed. Good explanation. "I understand."

No way would her aunt Viv appreciate her daughter dating Trevan. The guy was five hundred years old, a scholar, not a warrior. He was a genius, but a researcher kept in the back room. One who'd produce excellent results, but lacked social skills—a bit of a wimp.

"Thought you might." Simone smirked, eyeing Conn like a cat with cream. "The world has been privy to your business for far too long."

Wasn't that the freaking truth? Moira plastered on her most sincere smile. While she had no doubt Simone could take care of herself, women in love made mistakes. Even Simone. "This is convenient. We can escort you both to Ireland so the Nine can consolidate and plan."

"I've read your reports with curiosity these last years." Trevan's gaze swept her with interest. "The Seventh as an enforcer. You've grown up quite nicely, little Moira."

Conn showed his teeth. "I have no problem beating the crap out of you, Demidov." Anticipation lit his eyes. "In fact, perhaps I've just discovered our solution. We fight, you lose, and I drop your ass in Ireland before heading home."

Moira hid a smile. What Conn lacked in finesse, he more than made up for in honest threat. A fact Trevan had understood well before goading the vampire.

Interest tipped Trevan's lips. "I would enjoy the fight, Prince." He reached an elegant hand out to cover Simone's, who all but preened in response. "Of course you must promise the king won't retaliate when I burn the skin from your bones with a mere thought." Condescension dripped from each word.

Tempting. Moira fought the thought of allowing the men to actually fight, to let Conn to use his new ability with magic to teach the smug witch a lesson. She cleared her throat. "I hardly think this situation needs to descend to a place of violence, gentlemen." Unless she decided to smack their heads together, of course.

"Oh, I don't know." Simone tapped the three-inch heel of her boot on the tile. "I love a good battle between strong men."

The woman was about to get a good battle between two strong women. Moira drew in air, forcing tension from her body. "We have enough battles going on right now. Our allies should probably keep from turning each other bloody." When in the hell had she become the voice of reason? The mere thought sent irritation shafting down her spine. She was the one with the bad temper. The whole mate business was taking too much work.

Trevan narrowed his gaze. "You think we're still allies

with the Realm, Moira? From my perspective, withdrawal seems imminent."

"That would be a bad move." Conn leaned back, tossing a casual arm around Moira. "If you withdraw, the demons will show up immediately at your door."

"As allies," Simone purred.

Conn chuckled, toying with Moira's curls across her shoulders. "If you truly believe such nonsense, you need serious help. The demons would do anything to harness your power to combine with their mind warfare. Without your consent."

So true. The demons held a serious edge with mind invasion and fought dirty.

Moira tugged a curl free. "Conn's right. They wouldn't work with us; they'd exploit us in a second."

The demons had remained neutralized for the last four hundred years because of the treaty with the Realm. The moment the agreement disintegrated, the witches would enter a new era of danger. While her people had the ability to control brain waves, or what rolled from the body in order to slightly alter perception, the demons attacked the actual minds of enemies—putting in devastating images and misfiring the neurons.

Simone crossed long legs under her tight skirt. "Your basic assumption is incorrect. We're more powerful than the demons." Her eyes glittered a sharp light. "We'd use them."

Conn shifted his substantial weight. "You think you're powerful enough to fight the Realm and the demons, Simone?"

"Yes." Conviction sharpened her gaze.

Moira flashed back to another family picnic where they'd competed in an archery contest. Simone's focus had been absolute. She'd won, even over Daire and Kell.

Trevan leaned forward, his hand still on Simone's. "Of

course, we haven't withdrawn from the Realm. So this discussion is premature. Maybe we should centralize our location and go to Ireland, considering the threats we're dealing with."

Conn nodded. "Good thinking. Speaking of threats, you wouldn't know anything about this odd abyss yanking witches out of their lives, now do you?"

"Of course not," Trevan said. "I assure you, if there's magic involved, we'll solve the problem."

Conn's smile lacked civility. "Until the mystery is solved, watch out for swirling holes trying to eat you, Demidov. I'd hate for you to disappear."

"Right back at you, Prince."

The doorbell rang. Simone frowned. "So much for enjoying my solitude. If a human is selling something, I'm turning him into an ass." With a swish of her skirt, she stood and nearly stomped across the tile.

Conn slowly turned his head toward the door, a frown deepening between his eyes.

The hair on the back of Moira's neck rose.

Simone opened the door. A gasp escaped her. She stumbled back, the color deserting her face.

In a rush of power, Conn leaped over the back of the couch, planting himself between Simone and . . . a demon?

Even in the waning light, the nearly white blond of his hair shone. As tall as Conn, nearly as broad, the demon kept his hands in his pockets, his stance relaxed. Gray eyes peered past Conn. "Simone. Good to see you again." Rough and gravelly, his voice was a sign of the distressed vocal cords of a full-breed demon.

Moira jumped to her feet. Conn held up a hand to stop her. "Stay there."

She didn't see any weapons. But a demon didn't need weapons. She opened her senses. Nothing. Whoever he was, he wasn't trying to mess with their heads. At least not right at that moment.

Simone straightened to her nearly six feet of height. Fire flashed bright and explosive in her eyes. "What the hell do you want?"

The demon's smile held a hard edge. "It's nice to see you too, *Zaychik moy*."

Moira gaped at her cousin. *My bunny?* The Russian endearment spoke of a history. "Who's your friend?"

He smiled perfect white teeth. "Nikolaj Veis. Nick, if you wish."

"How modern of you," Simone muttered. "I believe I asked you a question."

"I wanted to talk," Nick said, frowning at Conn. "Though I hadn't realized you'd acquired a . . . vampire."

"Yeah, we're at war now, aren't we?" Conn's fangs dropped low.

"Indeed we are." Anticipation lit the demon's face. "About time, too. Peace was getting so boring."

"I couldn't agree more." Conn stepped into the demon's space. The air crackled with a tension-filled energy.

Simone cleared her throat. "What did you want to discuss?"

Nick sighed. "I'm not talking in front of a vampire."

Trevan rose gracefully to his feet, sidling to Simone to grasp her arm. "We are not meeting with a demon alone. This is full council business."

Simone scowled. "We're on the council, Trevan. At least hear what he has to say."

Moira shook her head. "Simone, this is a bad idea. We're not leaving you alone with a demon." As an enforcer, her vow dictated she remain in place. There was no way Conn would excuse himself, either.

Simone focused on Nick. "You'll give your word not to attack? That you're here just to talk?"

"Of course." Nick gave a slight bow. "You have my word."

"He'll honor his word." Simone glanced at Moira, her face still pale. "Your mate needs to leave."

Oh, they were so going to have a talk and soon. Moira shook her head.

Simone's phone pealed from her pocket. She answered it and listened for a moment. "Are you serious? When in the world—" Then she put a hand to her forehead. "Ah, Trevan is here. Yes." She shook her head. "Mother, we'll talk about that later."

Nostrils flaring, Simone hung up to glare at the demon. "You spoke with my mother." Anger rolled her vowels into an Irish brogue.

Nick smiled. "It was wonderful to speak with good ole Viv. I think she's mellowed through the years."

Trevan frowned, glancing from Simone to Nick and then back.

"She wants to call a meeting with you." Simone hissed, grabbing a remote and pointing it toward Brenna's painting. A screen dropped from the ceiling. The chambers of the Coven Nine took shape.

Viv stood from the center of the dais. "Good. There you are. I'd like to call this special meeting of the Coven Nine to order. We must deal with the problem in Russia." Her voice came through the screen loud and clear.

She squinted. "Oh. Yes. I'd forgotten Moira would be there. Well, change of plans. Moira, Conn, would you please excuse us?"

Surprise and unease battled for dominance inside Moira. Change of plans? She eyed her mother, whose expression had smoothed to diplomatic lines. "As an enforcer, surely you don't want me to leave two members of our council with a demon."

Viv cleared her throat. "Yes, well. The council has

known Nikolaj Veis for a significant amount of time. We are confident in his assurance of safety today."

"But you're going to talk about Russia . . ." There was no way a demon knew of the mines the witches had destroyed so many years ago. Or of the mineral buried in the land that could annihilate a witch.

The harsh lines in Viv's face guaranteed someone had discovered the mines and found a way to the mineral, even after the witches had demolished the region, basically burying the mines.

Who was this guy everyone seemed to know so well?

Trevan cleared his throat. "Maybe the enforcer should stay. I mean, the Seventh."

Simone cut him a glare. "We'll be fine." Taking a deep breath, she nodded at Moira. "Trust me. We're in no danger." She lifted her head, eyes focusing on the ceiling. Her features wrinkled in puzzlement. "Oh no. That's unfortunate." She turned to face Moira fully. "Do you feel that?"

Sharp nails pricked under Moira's skin. Damn it all to hell. "Yes." Somewhere near, a witch had just screwed up. Air turned to sandpaper along her arms, scraping and demanding. She eyed Conn. "We need to go." Even if the council hadn't ordered that very thing, she needed to go—though she would've left Conn to guard Simone.

Simone rubbed her arms. "Do you need backup, Moira?"

Moira started in surprise. While Simone wasn't an enforcer, she'd probably gained some skills during her long life. The offer though, was unexpected. "No. I appreciate the thought, but Conn should suffice."

Her mate growled, his focus still on the demon.

Moira rolled her eyes. Maybe suffice was a bit of an understatement.

Her boots echoing on the thick tiles, Moira walked toward Conn and grabbed his arm. That close to the demon, a tingle set up along the center of her brain. Just a mild zap. But enough to show serious power—a force being ruthlessly contained.

Nick stepped back.

Moira lifted an eyebrow, tugging Conn out of the penthouse.

The demon strode inside and shut the door.

Conn rubbed his chin. "I don't like this." A scowl turned down his mouth. "Why the hell is the skin on my arms screaming?"

They were in sync.

Moira pulled him down the walkway. "We have a problem."

"Another one?"

Chapter 12

An unnatural silence settled over the Port of New York, devoid of wind or churn of sea. Cargo containers rusted in regimented order. Moira rested her hand against chinked steel. "We're close."

Conn cracked his neck. "I left you in silence the entire drive here so you could meditate. Now you tell me what's going on."

She needed Kell or Daire for backup, that's what was going on. This was her first solo mission as an enforcer, and if the magic sparking through the air provided any indication, she might be out of her league.

"I appreciate the time to meditate." She needed more time. "Basically, there's someone here abusing magic." A whole potful of it.

Conn frowned. "That explains the inactivity on the docks. Why does my skin burn?"

"Because my powers are yours." She shoved back curls from her face. "When someone manipulates subatomic particles to a dramatic degree, the atmosphere changes enough that those of us with the correct genes can feel it like a magnet's pull."

"How do you know they're abusing magic?"

She shrugged. "Sometimes they're not. But to this degree, on the docks of New York, without any prior warning? They don't want us to know something."

"My backup is at least an hour away. How soon did Daire say he could get here?"

Moira drew in a deep breath. "Fifteen minutes. We can wait."

Conn nodded, then lifted his head like a lion catching a scent. He gave a low growl—then a snarl. "We're dealing with more than witches."

An irritant pricked the back of her neck—awareness of a sort. "Kurjans." A witch was working with the Kurjans? So much for waiting for Daire.

"Yes. I sense at least three." Conn leaned closer. "You up to another fight?"

He truly had no idea. "Yes."

Conn reached for his gun at the back of his waist. "Why is a witch messing around on the docks, Moira?"

Unease kept her still. "Ah, I don't know."

Irritation swirled through his dark eyes. "Let's look at this rationally, shall we?"

"I'd rather not."

He lifted an eyebrow. "Something mined in Russia has the enforcers scrambling. And a witch is abusing magic at the *Port of New York*. Now, I'm no Kane Kayrs, but I have to wonder . . . is this witch awaiting a cargo container with something from Russia, maybe shipped from Northern Europe?"

The vamp had a brain. "Quite possibly."

"What's in it?"

"I'm not sure." The lie rolled off her tongue. "We harvest many minerals to use with the elements and practice witchcraft."

"Bullshit." Conn glanced behind him. "The Kurjans are moving in fast."

"Do you think they sense you, too?"

"Probably." He glanced up the twenty-five feet of stacked cargo containers. "They're heading for the dock. Is that where your witch is working?"

"Yes." Working seemed an apt description. "There's a blanket shield over this part of the port." Moira raised her palms to the sky. "Let's put a dent in it, shall we? Get the witch focused on protecting the shield for now." She rearranged oxygen molecules to electricity, shooting up toward the shield.

A pop sounded, and the pounding of the sea became clear. Lightning flashed. Rain began to batter their heads. The witch at the dock held enough power to keep a storm away from the area.

Moira needed help.

Conn placed both hands on the lowest container. "Jump on my back and we'll climb to the top to surprise the Kurjans."

Moira leaped onto his back, tucking her head into his neck and her legs around his hips. Air rushed through her hair. A whisper of thought later, she stood on the top of the three containers. "Vampire speed is so cool."

"They're coming from the north." Gone was her mate. A warrior, all business, all purpose stood in his place. Hard lines cut into the sharp angles of his face, his eyes a dangerous emerald. He grabbed her hand, stalking gracefully across the container to the far edge. "There's your witch."

Salt from the sea coated Moira's face. She peered over the edge to see a woman with long red hair standing next to a twenty-something man with a goatee. Both were witches, but the woman had the power. They waited at the edge of an open berth next to a rumbling semitruck.

Moira squinted her eyes at the dark ocean. Far in the distance a light flickered. "There's the ship."

The witch below swirled her head around, obviously looking for the threat.

Moira smiled. "She knows we're here." Smashing a hole in the shield had been a decent calling card.

Conn stiffened, then pointed to three shadows moving rapidly. "The Kurjans are closing in on the witch." He rubbed his chin. "Either they're too focused to sense a vampire, or they're assuming we're with the witch. Maybe we should wait a minute and see what happens."

The witch below was going to pay. But Moira couldn't allow the Kurjans to take her.

Just then, the witch pivoted, her gaze slamming up. Flashing an angry smile, she formed a green plasma ball.

"Get down," Moira hissed, yanking Conn flat. The ball impacted the side of the top container. Sparks rained into the air and metal scraped against metal as it skidded across the lower container. Halting, the massive load teetered precariously on the edge. Gravity was about to win.

"Damn it." Conn grabbed her, throwing them backwards into the air to flip several times before landing on his feet, yards from the witch. Solid ground. The massive container behind them smashed into the ground with a loud *boom!* He shoved Moira behind him just as the redheaded witch threw another plasma ball.

Moira pushed him to the side. The ball smashed into a crane, sending the metal beast sliding several feet along the wet pavement. High pitched, the screech tortured her eardrums. She swirled air into a ball, throwing it as another glowing weapon was volleyed in their direction. Moira's ball sizzled, then captured the green glow. The energy spit like water being poured over fire. Steam rose and both energies puffed out.

The Kurjans leaped into the clearing, purple gazes taking in the scene.

For a moment, no one moved. Time stopped. Moira panted and blinked the rain out of her eyes. The three groups eyed each other, angled like points of a triangle.

Thunder bellowed from over the sea. Lightning flashed in response.

She centered herself. "I'll take the witches." A tiny part of her didn't want Conn to see her in action. The man would want to jump in. She could handle herself. And if the big men in her life didn't stop trying to shield her, she'd never have any authority—on the council or as an enforcer.

She widened her stance. "By the power of the Coven Nine, you're found guilty of violating Canon 34a and are sentenced accordingly."

The female witch smiled. "My name is Gena McMurphy." A light smattering of greenish electricity began to dance across her arms.

"So?" Moira glanced at the younger male witch. He'd gone pale. Scattered freckles stood out in disarray across his pasty skin. His gaze swiveled between Moira and his friend.

"So, I thought you should know the name of the witch about to harness your power, Seventh." Gena jerked her head at the Kurjans. "We should let the vampire and Kurjans take care of each other."

"Of course." So the witch had heard of Moira. Being the Seventh made her almost royalty.

Lighting zigzagged from high above.

The Kurjan sporting the most medals on his shoulder cleared his throat. "We're just here for the witch." His smile flashed sharp yellow canines. "But we'll take two for the price of one."

Thunder ripped across the sky.

Conn exhaled slowly. Time to even the odds. Why the hell did everyone feel the need to chat? In a rush of speed, he grabbed his gun from his waist and shot the closest Kurjan in the neck. The guy went down.

The second Kurjan bunched and leaped in a fierce

tackle before Conn could get off another shot. They hit the pavement with a boom as loud as the thunder, leaving a vampire-sized dent in the asphalt. Pain cascaded across his shoulders. His gun skidded out of reach. Levering his legs around the Kurjan, Conn swung and reversed their positions. Grabbing his knife from an ankle holster, he cut off the guy's head in one clean slice.

The remaining Kurjan leaped onto Conn's back, knife aimed for the jugular. The guy weighed a ton. Fury rumbled through Conn's chest. He grabbed the soldier's hand, fighting to keep the blade from piercing his skin. From the corner of his eye, he could see Moira battling Gena. Hand to hand. Gena had some moves, but Moira had speed and agility. The male witch angled around behind Moira.

Conn threw an elbow back, connecting with cartilage. Blood spurted, burning his cheek. The Kurjan growled, sinking a fang into Conn's earlobe and yanking.

Pain slashed through his head. The asshole had bitten his earlobe off. Conn snarled, throwing the Kurjan off and jumping to his feet. "You prick." He ignored the blood washing down his neck as he circled the soldier.

Red stained the monster's incisors when he smiled. "I came for a witch and killed a Kayrs. A good day, I think."

Did the Kurjans pass pictures of Conn's family around for fun? How the hell did these guys always identify him? Rain splattered against his face, cooling the blood. "You'll be just another random kill for me. A typical Tuesday, if you will."

The Kurjan charged. Conn grabbed the soldier by the ribs, allowing the momentum to throw them back. Landing hard, he swept his arm out, grabbing his gun. The monster's eyes widened just as Conn swung back and shot him in the ear. "Yeah. Payback's a bitch." He rolled the unconscious enemy off.

Flipping to his feet, he whirled in time to see the male witch grab Moira from behind. The female witch shot forward, slamming her hand against Moira's chest. His mate shrieked. Her entire body went rigid. Rage beat through him harder than the pounding rain. Two strides had him across the asphalt and grabbing the male witch in a headlock. The jerk struggled, then slowly gave in as Conn increased his hold.

"Thanks," Moira muttered as she hit Gena's hand away.

"You got this?" Conn asked.

"Yep."

A groan sounded from behind him. The Kurjan he'd shot was gaining consciousness. "Good. I have two down but not completely." Dragging the male witch, Conn angled his knife and decapitated first one and then the other still breathing Kurjans.

Then he turned to watch his mate.

Moira moved faster than a whisper, leaping forward and taking Gena to the ground. Gena howled in protest. The male witch trembled against him.

The tackled woman fought back, throwing punches. Moira batted the fists out of the way. Then her jaw tightened, and she thrust her palm against the witch's chest.

Conn had taken hearts that way but doubted Moira had the strength to get past the rib cage. The man in his grasp went limp, giving up any pretense of fight.

The witch on the ground shrieked, both hands grabbing Moira's arm. Her eyes went wide in panic. His mate held tight, throwing her head back, closing her eyes. Oxygen popped around them like balloons too full of air. A green glow traveled from the downed witch, up Moira's arms to her chest. Then it disappeared. Inside her?

The wind swept the area, scattering pebbles and the scent of burnt wire. Green mist smoked along the witch's skin, dying out with a whisper. The witch struggled, her body convulsing, then stilling. Her head dropped back to the ground and she went limp.

Moira stood. Green energy flitted along her skin, slowly shifting to electric blue. She turned toward Conn, her eyes deep and fathomless. Jesus. Two steps closer and she placed her hand against the skinny guy's chest. He cried out, his body shuddering. Seconds later, his body sagged and Conn let him fall.

He eyed his mate. "You took their power."

She nodded, shoving curls off her face, sucking in air. Her chest panted with the effort. The line of her neck throbbed. "Yes. Absorbed it." For a witch, losing powers was worse than death.

"Could she have taken yours?"

Moira gave a tired smile, her small body still vibrating. "Maybe." She eyed the young man on the ground. "He'll have at least a century to learn from this mistake. Hopefully he won't make it again."

Conn surveyed the two unconscious witches. "The power can develop again? Someday?"

"Yes."

Conn reached out and grabbed Moira's hand, needing to feel her. Static electricity raced up his arm. "Are you all right?" Taking someone else's power had to hurt, at least a little. Yet another gift the witches had failed to share with the world. Though Moira's ability to fight and adapt impressed him once again.

"Yes." She leaned into him. "Sometimes I need to work off the energy." The words came in short gasps. "Too much power can burn." Her eyelashes fluttered against her skin. Then she was out.

Burn indeed. Conn caught his little mate, wondering what other surprises she held.

Chapter 13

Moira awoke in the plane to the sound of typing. Bubbling energy popped through her veins. She'd taken a lot of power from Gena. Her mate sat across the aisle, pounding his laptop. He sprawled in the seat, and his long fingers were surprisingly agile on the keyboard. Concentrating, he alternated between scowling and nodding. One thing about Conn, he didn't hide his emotions. Part arrogance, part confidence, she got the feeling he disliked wasting time . . . and hiding out wasted time.

She cleared her throat. "Did you tell the king about tonight?"

"Yes." Conn didn't look her way, reading his screen and frowning.

She could've asked him to keep her secret, and for a moment had even considered making the request. But she refused to use him, asking him to be someone he was not. His allegiance to the Realm made him who he was. She understood.

Her mind came fully awake. She sat up in the chair. "Wait. We needed to wait for the shipment."

"Daire showed up right after you passed out. Late to the party, as usual."

Confusion swirled around Moira's head. "He planned

to take Gena into custody?" Someone needed to question the witch.

"Yes."

Relief had her relaxing back into the seat. Daire would get to the truth. "Any news?"

"Yeah. He said the ship didn't come in. So far Gena has not regained consciousness."

"Bollocks." Where the hell was the shipment? "I'm surprised Daire let you take me."

"So am I."

Okay. That couldn't be good. What was the Coven Nine up to?

Conn kept his gaze on the screen. "So. You fight with plasma balls, take another witch's power, and turn organs to mush." The typing continued as he talked. "Can you turn the organs of nonhumans liquid?"

She rubbed her nose. What should she say? "Not yet. I mean, the power grows through the ages. But humans are easy." Maybe she shouldn't let him know his spleen was safe. Oh well, too late. "The enforcers protect the council and are the Nine's front line, as you know—and taking power is the main way we do that." They also helped train the Nine's soldiers for battle, but that was mostly a side job. "We're sent out when someone is abusing quantum physics . . . abusing magic. We, ah, make them stop."

He lifted an eyebrow, leaning forward to peer at his screen. "What other ways do people abuse magic?" Low, a barely perceptible threat hung in his words.

Her body tensed, reacting immediately. "When the humans learned how to split an atom, they created atomic energy . . . a big bomb. Imagine someone screwing with subatomic particles."

"I understand the possibilities but didn't think anyone was stupid enough to try. Or rather, I thought your soldiers had a better grasp on your citizens." Conn sucked in air. "Jesus. They might blow up the entire planet."

"The entire galaxy, more likely." Sometimes morons didn't think before messing around with forces they should avoid. "We also step in when someone is trying to manipulate other beings for profit or gain."

"I see." He closed the laptop, swiveling his chair to face her.

Her thoughts scrambled like a satellite signal gone wrong.

A dark shirt spread across his powerful chest, which tapered to a narrow waist and worn jeans. An inferno swept inside her veins. She traced every contour of his hard face with an attention born of need. His gaze darkened, and he waited her out, letting her drink her fill, not moving.

Awareness filtered through the haze in her head. Patience stood as yet another of his weapons. He held so much control over himself, as well as anything in his way.

As if he'd made the challenge out loud, the need to take him rushed through her. She wanted to be the one woman in the universe who could make him lose that control. The burning fire in her veins from the fight earlier propelled her into action.

With the inherent instinct of a predator, she moved gracefully, dropping to her knees between his legs.

His sharp intake of breath made her bite back a smile. Sage and man filled her nostrils. Slowly, showing him true control, she reached for his belt. Defined abdomen muscles clenched against her knuckles. The buckle released easily, the belt catching on each loop as she drew the leather loose.

He swallowed. Loudly.

Nimble fingers had his jeans unsnapped as she sprang him free. Large, throbbing, and so ready for her. A murmur of appreciation wandered up her throat. How kind of him to go commando. She leaned forward, swiping her tongue across the tip of his cock. Salt and male exploded on her taste buds.

Erotic pain danced along her scalp as his hands dug into her hair. "Moira." Part groan, part plea, he tried to tug her head back.

"No." She shook her head. "I need this, Conn."

With a start, she realized the truth. Many powers fought for dominance inside her. Oh, she'd win. Her natural power would assimilate the other. But for now . . . she needed a release. More than that, she needed Conn. The marking on her hip bone flickered alive, sending tendrils of demand to her clit.

With a groan, he loosened his hold, throwing back his head to smack the seat. Both hands still cupped her scalp, keeping her in place. "Take what you need."

She hummed in appreciation against him, power filling her when he stiffened with a ground-out groan. Books didn't do this justice. Scooting forward, she took more of him in her mouth . . . not even a third of him, yet he breathed heavily, his body tightening.

Conn bit his lip until blood welled in his mouth. Inexperience and determination made for a lethal combination . . . she was going to kill him. His mate's soft licks and adventurous nibbles had his heart thumping so hard he figured a rib or two might break. Not that he gave a flying shit. She could shatter every bone in his body so long as she didn't stop.

The musky scent of her arousal mixed with lilacs and filled his senses. The animal inside him lunged to life, demanding he take her.

Her mouth enclosed his tip and he surged up, choking her. "Sorry." Releasing her hair, he grabbed the armrests, digging in his nails. If the woman wanted to explore, he wouldn't stop her. The wet heat of her mouth remained around him, her jaw relaxing.

She swallowed.

His cock hardened more than he'd thought possible. A roaring filled his ears, his nails rent the leather, and his shoulders shook with the fight to retain control. "Moira, sweetheart. Stop." He didn't mean it. God, he didn't mean it.

She chuckled around him.

That was it.

His control ruptured.

He charged her, knocking her back on her butt. Both hands dug into her jeans, half lifting her and tearing down the sides. The sound spurred him on. Her delicate panties ripped in two.

Flipping her around, he covered her, reaching for her heat. Wet. She was ready. She gave a low laugh, part temptation, part challenge. He gripped her hips and plunged inside her so hard she shot forward, catching herself with her forearms on the rough carpet.

"Conn," she gasped.

He stilled. His balls vibrated with the need to take her. Harder. More.

What the hell was he doing? "Moira." Lush hips filled his palms. His hands shook. "I'm . . ." Stop. He needed to stop. The beast inside him bellowed in protest.

She shoved back against him, her buttocks flush to his groin, her thick heat surrounding him. "Don't stop. Please, don't stop."

At her husky plea, the beast won.

The spongy material of her shirt shredded in his hands. Her skin nearly glowed white in the muted light. Bare, fragile, and so damn soft. He caressed down both sides of her spine, pulsing inside her. She gripped him like a vise, quivering around him. Perfect. She was so fucking perfect his chest hurt.

He slid out and then back in. Blood filled his ears, lilacs

filled his life. His body started to thrust, no longer remotely attached to his brain. Neurons fired uselessly. Wrapped around him, Moira was the only thing in existence. With a growl, he shoved her shoulder down, pushing her face against her forearms.

He wanted her open . . . vulnerable . . . helpless.

The whimper she sobbed sounded like need and demand.

He gave in to the demand, pounding into her. Sensations bombarded him, some hers, some his . . . some beyond them both. His fangs dropped low. Sparks lit down his back to twirl at the base of his spine. Close. He was so close.

Reaching around her, he found her swollen clit. She levered up, her head thrown back, her spine arching, meeting him thrust for thrust.

He tangled his hand in her hair. Pushed her back down. His way—this time, his way. A tightened grip quelled her protest, his palm extending across her scalp to hold her in place. Tight thighs quivered against his as his stance widened, spreading her legs farther. Open. Completely at his mercy.

His other hand clutched her hip, yanking her back to meet every thrust. Her buttocks shook with the force of his momentum, even as she tried to keep up. His tongue swelled with the need for her blood. "Mine." Promise or vow . . . it came from his soul.

She stiffened. Then, with a sigh, her shoulders and thighs relaxed.

Submission. He'd never sought it, he'd never wanted it. Until now.

As his powerful mate submitted of her own free will, she pierced his heart in two, sealing their fate. As if they'd ever had a choice.

The creature inside him, the one he often fought, took

over. He plunged harder, deeper, beyond the physical. She trembled under him. With a pinch to her clit, she broke. A scream of release filled the airplane, her heat squeezing his cock so hard his vision went black.

Waves rippled around him.

Pleasure cascaded from her.

A growl ripped from his soul.

He angled deeper, covering her. Quick as a flash, his fangs pierced her neck. She orgasmed again. Honey and energy flowed into his mouth. His back heated, a hot poker of lust stabbed a centimeter behind his balls. Holding on to everything that mattered in life, he shot forward, keeping her captive. With a roar from the animal within, he came.

Chapter 14

A bulletproof black Hummer met Moira and Conn at the private airport. Ignoring Moira's wild hair and the scent of sex clinging to them, the driver stared straight ahead as he quickly squired them away.

She cleared her throat, tugging on the borrowed shirt Cara had left in the plane. Considering the number of outfits to choose from, Moira wondered just how often a Kayrs mate ended up with shredded jeans. A lingering sadness remained at the loss of her Irish clothing. She liked the hand-sewn perfection of the Irish silks.

Her emotions rioted worse than her hair. Something whispered in the back of her heart that she'd given everything to the vampire on the plane, and of her own volition.

He'd been quiet and thoughtful on the drive, increasing her anxiety. Connlan Kayrs being quiet foretold disaster.

The SUV stopped at a guarded gate of a private community, allowed to pass after the driver flashed a badge. Three streets of luxurious houses lined the way with the ocean at the far end, a lighter colored sea than the one in Ireland.

Conn settled back into the plush leather seat, his gaze on the tumultuous ocean. "We own all the homes in the community and the surrounding land. We have motion, heat, cold, and energy sensors around the perimeter. Our house is in the middle next to Dage's with a gorgeous view of the sea."

"Ah, that's nice." Was this the 1950s? Did the man expect her to plan a Tupperware party or host Bunco? "A subdivision?"

He lifted an eyebrow, a grin threatening on his full lips. "Yes. Now that some of us are taking mates, we need homes. Talen and I've been working on this plan for decades."

"I'm assuming there's an underground headquarters, if necessary?" Genius planning. The rocky cliffs provided ample protection in case of attack. Also, the vampires had shielded themselves from discovery. The Nine's intel hadn't revealed the location.

"Of course. Each home has direct access to headquarters." The driver maneuvered through two more gates sporting armed guards and stopped the SUV before a cultured stone and brick main lodge. "We have offices, meeting rooms, a gym, and a private lab here." Conn jumped out, extending a hand.

She accepted the help, sliding from the vehicle. The nearby ocean sent salt and brine to fill the air—heavier and somehow sweeter than the scent of her ocean at home. Nothing could've prevented the sigh that escaped her.

Conn shut the door and the driver drove off. "Do you want to talk about it?"

She needed time to think before they discussed their future. But the vampire wasn't her only immediate concern. She bit her lip. "Anyone with half a brain knew the second the hundred years expired, you'd be trying to take me from Ireland." Whether he truly wanted her or not, a Kayrs protected his mate. And she was beginning to hope that Conn did want her—a fact that delighted and scared the crap out of her.

"Yes." His arm dropped around her shoulders, providing warmth and a new sense of security.

A sense far too tempting to sink right into with relief.

Even her mother had allowed her to leave the homeland with him. "Yet the council ordered me to your country . . . with you . . . and Daire let you take me from New York."

Conn tugged her toward the solid oak door. "Yeah. I caught that, too." His smile screamed sin. "I don't suppose they thought to make it easy on me as a reward for following the treaty all these years?"

Her own smile felt raw. "The last thing the Nine wants to do is make it easy on you, Connlan."

"I know. Well, I assume the reasoning was twofold. First, this is a clear sign the Nine isn't going to withdraw from the Realm."

She barely kept from shaking her head. Not true. This move might be the first strike in withdrawing from the Realm. "Are you sure?" The man should know by now she'd been raised in a political family and could see past the obvious.

"No. But I thought you might think so."

Her hand on his arm stopped him from opening the door. He pivoted, giving her his full attention.

She lifted her gaze. "I'm not the naïve girl you mated, Conn."

"I know." One gentle knuckle ran down the side of her face. "I've seen you fight, sweetheart."

Warmth filled her at the pride in his masculine voice. "You said the Nine's reasoning might be twofold. What's the second fold?"

"You're the Seventh, Moira. They must want you protected."

The door swung open and a little girl hurled herself at Conn. "Uncle Conn!"

He caught the rushing bundle, swinging the child around to smack loud kisses on her cheek. "I wondered if you'd be the welcoming committee, sweetheart."

The five-year-old levered back, mahogany curls bobbing, and put both tiny hands against his cheeks. "I wanted to see you first before you got all mad." Sparkling blue eyes turned their focus to Moira. "Hi, Aunt Mowra."

What a stunning child. "Hi, Janie. It's wonderful to finally meet you in person." She'd been e-mailing and videoconferencing with her young niece for the last eight months. "Why is Conn going to get mad?" The little psychic owned the future.

The five-year-old smiled, showing a gap in her front teeth. "Not 'cause of you, Auntie. This time, anyways."

The door opened all the way and six and a half feet of hard muscled male stepped into the sun. "Welcome home, Moira." The king extended a dozen yellow and white calla lilies. Their sweet scent hung in the air. He'd tied his thick black hair at the nape, throwing the hard angles of his face into focus.

Pleasure warmed Moira even as a tickle of unease wound through her from the word *home*. She accepted the fragrant flowers, burying her nose before lifting up and forcing a smile. "Thanks, Dage."

Conn tucked Janie against his side. "Why am I about to be angry?"

Dage lifted an eyebrow at his niece. "Someone been predicting the future?"

Janie giggled. "Things gotta happen the way they gotta happen."

"Profound words, little one." Dage gestured them inside a spacious gathering room fronted by floor-to-ceiling windows showcasing the churning gray Pacific Ocean. Couches and chairs sprawled in organized chaos around two pool tables and a massive brick fireplace, reminding

Moira of Kell's dining room. No table for eating, but a lot of area for playing.

"Everyone is off working right now, but we'll have a family get-together later tonight." Dage tugged Janie away from Conn, tossing her in the air before landing her next to Moira. "Show Moira the game room, Janie. Emma should be along to take Moira to the lab soon." His eyes shot warm blue through the intense silver. "I, ah, should apologize now. My mate is rather, er, single-minded in her battle against Virus-27."

Conn couldn't help the chuckle rising in his throat. "That is the understatement of your reign, King." He dropped a kiss on Moira's smooth forehead. "Good luck, sweetheart. You'll be donating some blood for the cause." He rubbed his chin. Maybe he shouldn't have taken any on the plane. Not that he regretted a second of their trip.

Moira frowned.

Janie took her hand with a happy hop. "You're gonna love the new checker set Uncle Conn bought me. When he loses, he has to play tea party and wear an apron. He looks so good in the pink one."

Moira laughed low and husky as Janie continued. "We have a whole room to play games, and there's a television in there to watch movies. Oh, and you gotta see the new classroom my teacher Sarah set up. Sarah came home with Max . . ." Her voice continued down the hall until they took a left turn.

Conn pivoted toward his brother. "Well?"

Dage smiled. "Let's go down to the gym. You haven't seen it yet."

"I designed it." Conn fought irritation and the need to punch his brother in the jaw. "Am I going to hit you?"

Dage shrugged, loping toward the stairwell and jogging down steps. "If you do, I'll hit you back."

Wouldn't be the first time the two of them got into it.

Last time Conn had had to break his own nose three times to fix it right. He followed Dage, fighting unease. He didn't like being separated from his mate. A laughable fact considering they spent the first hundred years of their union on different continents.

Now she was right where he wanted her. A tickle at the back of his neck warned things weren't so easy.

He followed his brother through a doorway leading to a room packed wall-to-wall with tumbling mats, adjacent to the gym. One of many in the community he'd designed. His ire rose at finding Jase and Talen waiting, sprawled on the floor with their backs against the wall.

Talen grinned. "Welcome home." The second oldest and the strategic leader of the Realm, he nevertheless kept in close proximity to his pregnant mate, Cara. The fact that he was downstairs, away from Cara and their daughter Janie, didn't bode well.

"What the hell's going on?" Conn leaned a hand down and yanked Jase to his feet. "What happened to the training schedule?" He'd left Jase in charge of training their men while he'd gone after Moira.

"Nothing. The training is going well." Jase's lips tipped in a smart-ass grin, his maroon eyes remaining serious. An arctic breeze whipped through the room. The youngest of the brothers, Jase harnessed control of the elements in a manner none of them could explain. He scratched his chin. "Kane is in the middle of an experiment right now or he'd be down here to welcome his wayward brother home as well."

Dage cleared his throat. "I'm getting married next month and all my brothers are standing up for me."

Conn raised an eyebrow toward Talen. "Isn't he supposed to ask us?"

Talen stood. "Sometimes he thinks he's the leader."

Dage settled his stance. "I wanted to get the brother

stuff out of the way first, before I had to speak as the king. And *I am* the leader."

This was going to be bad. Conn settled his own stance. "You ready to do the king stuff now?"

"Yes." Dage's silver eyes narrowed. "The war with the demons has heated up. We need to take the front line."

Conn's shoulders relaxed. He'd been expecting the order. While he didn't want to head to the trenches so soon after getting Moira home, he understood the need for him to go. More unease crawled up his back. He hadn't had time to properly train for mind-war with the demons. "I understand. When do I go?"

"You don't." Dage's words hung in the air. "I'm sending Jase."

Chapter 15

The air heated in Conn's lungs. He frowned. "No, you're not." No way in hell was his youngest brother going into a mind-battle with the demons. Jase still carried the scars from fighting and killing when a mere teenager—a fact that plagued the king daily. "My job is on the front lines, Dage."

"I'm aware of that." Dage flicked his gaze to Jase and then back to Conn. "Unfortunately, we have more than one front line going on right now. I need you here."

"No, you don't." He'd hit his brother before, but never when Dage acted as King. This would be a first. "I planned this development. You're protected, as is everyone else here. The greater threat lies in the Baltic States." The demons had centralized their location during the last several decades, and the war needed to go to them.

Jase stepped into danger range. "What about Moira, Conn? What about the swirling vortex of possible pain hunting your mate?"

Conn rounded on his younger brother. They stood eye to eye, both packed hard. Jase had always known how to aim for the jugular. "Fuck you."

Jase smiled. "You're the only one with the ability to utilize quantum physics and practice magic. Even Dage can only use string theory by teleporting." He tucked his hands into the back pockets of faded jeans. But not before Conn saw the purple painted nails on his left hand. Obviously he'd lost to Janie at Go Fish again. "What if this vortex, or whatever it is, hinges on magic? You're it, brother."

The logic in Jase's words slammed Conn's temper even closer to the surface. He had to protect Jase. He couldn't let the demons rip into Jase's mind. His youngest brother should be playing games all the time, having fun and being young. Not facing death or insanity. "Just because you've immobilized your hands doesn't mean I won't hit you."

Jase shrugged. A wall of shimmering ice rippled through the air between them. "Try it."

Conn could. A plasma ball would destroy the wall. But hurting his brother seemed counterproductive to the conversation. "You're forgetting about the magic, asshole."

"Am I?" Arrogance coated Jase's low voice.

Conn flashed back to the time he'd taught his brother to drive their first Model T Ford, which of course, they instantly modified into a beacon of speed. "I like you fine without your mind all warped." He pivoted to face Dage. "How can you order this?"

Blue shot hard spikes within Dage's silver eyes. "Duty's a bitch, Conn."

Emotion turned the king's voice raw in a tone that actually slammed pain through Conn. He struggled to reason with his brother. "My job is to face the biggest threat, and that comes from the demons."

Talen stepped closer. "No. The biggest threat is someone using the ability to take our mates right out from under our noses"—he crossed his arms, his golden gaze narrowing on Dage—"which is why Conn stays here to figure out how to counter them, and I go to the Baltic States."

Jase growled low. The wall of ice shattered. "You know,

this lack of faith is starting to piss me off. Talen, your mate is due to give birth this month. You're useless away from here." He ignored Talen's dropping into a fighting stance. "I may be younger than all of you, but I'm three hundred years old. The elements follow my orders, which will be invaluable against the demons and their mind tricks. I'm going, so deal with it."

Good God, Conn might actually have to beat the crap out of him. Conn turned to face Jase. "What if the demons are the ones controlling the vortex, Jase? Frankly, who the hell knows?" The demons destroyed minds, but maybe they'd learned to harness the dimensions, which was necessary in teleporting.

"Not a chance." Jase yanked his hands out of his jeans to cross his arms. "Vampires are the only species known to teleport, and merely a select few can do so. The Kurjans are genetically similar with their thirty chromosomal pairs, so chances are the Kurjans have developed this talent along with developing the virus that takes our mates back down to human form." He cleared his throat. "Kane and I are the only brothers without mates. The rest of you need to stay close to yours."

"No." Talen's eyes shot green through the gold, guaranteeing his temper would soon blow. "We need to ensure our women are safe, which they are. These women are strong and knew our jobs and duties when agreeing to be our mates."

"Like Cara had a chance to disagree." Jase stepped to the side, closer to Dage.

Humor tipped Talen's upper lip as he mirrored Jase's movement, creating a square of power between the brothers. "I'm sure I asked at some point."

"You can't leave her when she's so close to giving birth." Jase dropped his voice to a softer tone.

Enough. Conn focused on Dage. The king needed to

be convinced. "My mate isn't with child, Dage. She's worked as an enforcer the last few decades and understands the life of a soldier." Probably with more clarity than he'd like. "She's safe here with you." He pressed the advantage when Dage didn't reply. "What if Jase and I go together? With our combined skills, we'd be back in no time."

"I don't need your help," Jase murmured. "And now you've done it." He turned his gaze on Dage.

"I'm going." Dage hardened his jaw. "Your reasons are valid and apply to me more than you. We have three hours to put contingency plans into place before I go."

Irritation battled with anger down Conn's spine. "You can't go."

Dage raised an arrogant brow. "Why the hell not?"

"Because you're the fucking king." A fact his brother would like to forget more often than not. "We have enemies on all fronts, and we need a face as well as a centralized location. You're needed here, Dage. Like it or not." Conn didn't need to turn around to know Talen and Jase nodded in agreement. "Do your job. Let me do mine."

Dage sighed. "You're right. My job is to lead." His lip curled. No doubt he'd rather face all the demons at once than sit in place for the good of the Realm. He turned toward Jase. "You leave for Russia first thing in the morning." The blue shoved silver out of his eyes. "Stay safe and kick ass."

Jase straightened to his full height. "I'll submit a plan within two hours." Without another word, he pivoted and strode from the room.

Conn didn't move when Talen shifted his weight to face Dage alongside him. "He's not ready."

Dage's nostrils flared when he sucked in air. "You both need to go over his plan—look for ways to keep him safe." He ran a rough hand through his hair, the only sign of distress he showed. "If I was somebody else, if we were somebody else . . . I could send a different soldier to lead."

Conn shook his head. "You're not. We're not. As the ruling family, we're the first to go, the first to bleed if necessary." The first to die. He didn't envy his brother in having to send one of them to possible death. How the hell did Dage sleep? Or did he? "Let me go with him."

"No." Lines etched into Dage's face that hadn't existed the year before. "I need you here. Work with Moira, figure out who has learned to force others to teleport. And keep the Nine from withdrawing from the Realm. We have enough enemies."

Indecision kept Conn in place.

Fire leaped into Dage's eyes. "I'm ordering you as your king, Connlan."

Conn met Dage's gaze squarely. He'd do anything for his brothers. He'd taught Jase to fight and had made sure to protect him at all times during the last war—amid blood and carnage. But Dage had taught Conn and had always protected his back. As rulers, as brothers, they needed unity. "I understand." He made his statement, his vow. There'd be no turning back.

Dage focused on Talen. "And you?"

Talen gave a short nod. "We'll come up with a solid battle plan." He rolled his shoulders, heading for the door. "I need to check on Cara and then will give Jase a hand with strategy. We should ask Caleb to go with him."

"Already did." Dage's eye color returned to normal. "Caleb has been fighting the demons for a century, and this will give him more time to deny he's now a prophet." The prophecy mark had appeared on Caleb's neck after Dage had killed one of the three living vampire prophets to save his mate Emma. The prophet had had some crazy idea that Emma and Cara would bring down the Realm.

Talen nodded, then disappeared down the hallway.

"Fair enough." Conn relaxed his shoulders, his gaze remaining on Dage. "The Coven Nine is concerned about their soldiers training under ours—more specifically, Trevan Demidov is concerned their soldiers will follow you and not the Coven Nine."

"All I need is that brainiac arguing philosophy rather than battle strategy. Let's put that guy on the training field." Dage rubbed his chin.

Conn snorted. "Yeah, right. The Nine is also worried about humans finding out about us, as am I. We had a close call not too long ago and Max saved our butts." Not only did the vampires employ humans, but Emma wanted to use their research to help cure diseases, which might open them up for exposure.

"We need the human researchers." Dage shook his head. "We haven't been studying biology the last century like the Kurjans. We need the researchers just for sheer numbers."

Conn didn't like humans anywhere near their genetics. As the king's soldier on the front line, the whole idea made him twitchy. "Emma wants to share our research with human geneticists."

"Emma will keep silent whether she likes it or not." Dage used his king voice.

Conn bit back a grin. As far as he'd noticed, the queen didn't give one hoot about Dage's orders or king voice. "If you say so. My mate is as big a concern as yours right now, if not more so."

"Yes. If the Nine withdraws from the Realm, her first order will be to remove your head. Probably." Dage flashed his teeth in an anticipatory smile. "At least my woman only wants to take action to possibly reveal our entire race. Yours might need to kill you." A deep chuckle rumbled from his chest.

"Very funny." Conn rubbed his five o'clock shadow. He

needed to shave before kissing Moira again. The woman had delicate skin. "What's the plan?"

"Well. The plan with Emma is that I'm monitoring all research and communications with humans. If there's a hint she's about to let our existence go public, I'll shut her down. Virus or not."

Conn did not want to be in the vicinity when that day arrived. "The idea of ending her research will probably result in a bounty on your head."

"True." Dage lifted a shoulder. "Speaking of which, what's your plan with Moira?" The fact the leader of their world deferred to Conn regarding his mate showed trust as a king and loyalty as a brother.

Conn gave a short nod of acknowledgment. "Should the Nine withdraw from the Realm and essentially declare war on us, I have two options. One is to use her, give her false information to misdirect our enemies."

"And the second option. You know, the one you'll actually use?"

Conn appreciated the faith. But if it came down to survival of his people, he'd do what he had to do. "Put her somewhere safe, away from our enemies. Including the Nine."

Dage shook his head. "God, I hope that day never comes."

"As do I."

Chapter 16

Moira waved her hand, sending the blue teddy bear dancing around Janie's head. "Then the Irish princess jumped out of the sea with the emeralds, and King Mullet danced across the sand in pure joy."

Janie giggled, reaching up and grabbing her toy by the feet. "Mr. Mullet would be a good king." She wrapped both arms around the bear. "I love your Irish fairy tales, Aunt Mowra."

The massive vampire leaning against the wall nodded. Max the bodyguard had been very patient during the last two stories. He cleared his throat. "Very good. Okay, that was the last story. I promised your mama I'd take you to her, Janie."

"Okay, Max." Janie rushed forward and hugged Moira. "See ya later."

Moira returned the hug. "You bet." She watched Max lead Janie away before giving a big sigh and wandering away from the toy room. She'd expected Emma to show up, though her friend probably had been delayed in the lab. During the last few months, Moira had stopped worrying about the time difference when she called—Emma was always at work.

Rounding a corner, Moira found a computer center. Excellent. She hustled over to a console near the window, booting up an HP. No password was required, and the system had videoconferencing capabilities—and very strong security. No one would know where she was calling from. Her fingers punched in the right numbers, and she flipped on the camera.

"Moira." Brenna's pretty face came into range, her dark hair pulled back in a ponytail. Just like she'd worn years before, when Moira had taught her to climb a tree. One of the Coven Nine's large conference rooms loomed behind her. "Have wild vampire sex yet?"

Heat flushed Moira's face until her cheeks pounded. "No. God."

Bren's eyes crinkled. The laugher filling them failed to mask the dark circles slashing underneath. "Um. Okay. We'll talk in person. Soon."

"What are you doing at the Coven Nine offices?" Moira leaned closer to the camera. "More important, what's wrong, Bren?"

"I'm here pitching a plan to clean up the East Bay, and nothing's wrong." Brenna bit into her bottom lip, a sure sign she was lying.

"What?" Moira searched her memory. Oh. "You haven't heard about your application for the Quantum Academy." She waved her hand in the air. "Don't even worry about that. You'll be accepted."

"I wasn't." Brenna's jaw tightened, just like their father's when giving bad news. "But it's no big deal. Really."

Fire licked down the back of Moira's neck. "What do you mean you weren't accepted?" She'd taught Brenna magic since the girl had taken her first steps. "You're excellent at quantum physics." A mistake had been made.

Brenna eyed the corner of her computer, her gaze dropping. "The form letter just thanked me for the application, said the school is competitive . . . blah, blah, blah." She rubbed her nose. "Seriously. Not a big deal."

The breath in Moira's lungs heated. "Those bastards! Don't you worry about a thing. The second I get back—"

"No." Brenna's gaze pierced the camera. "You will not fix this. They don't want me, Moira." Determination settled hard across her delicate features. "Sometimes we all forget. But . . ."

She was the eighth sister. An unheard-of anomaly . . . one many people regarded with fear.

"How absolutely stupid. We'll start our own university." Not a bad idea, actually. Moira would send her resignation along with a big "Bugger off" the second she got off the line. If they thought they could treat her baby sister like this, they were nuts.

Brenna laughed. "Right. When you're not enforcing our laws or having crazy vampire-monkey sex . . . sure you'll find time to start a college."

"Vampire-monkey sex?" Moira snorted.

"Yep. That's how I imagine it." Brenna wiggled her eyebrows, reaching for a stack of papers to wave in front of the camera. "The plans for treating the homeless in the south. I'll e-mail the time line to you . . . the Coven Nine already has my first draft."

"Thanks." Her sister always planned ahead. "Um, how are things going with the Nine?"

Delight lifted the corners of Brenna's eyes. "You mean since you reported Trevan being in New York with Simone?"

"Yes. How did that go over?"

"Like a fart in church." Bren leaned closer to the screen. "The guy's a weakling. I mean, yuck." She straightened, glancing to the side. "Did you know Simone got hot and heavy with a demon? Centuries ago?"

Interesting. "I'm not sure, but I think he showed up at her house." While there was an uneasy alliance between demons and witches, they certainly steered clear of each other socially. "At least the demon who arrived seemed to know her."

"Bizarre." Bren's eyes sparkled with the thrill of gossip. "I heard Mom tell Aunt Viv at least Simone wasn't with a demon any more. That must've been from before you were born, right?"

Moira shrugged. "This is the first I've heard about it." Simone sure liked to walk on the dark side. "What happened with Simone and the demon? I mean, was it Nick Veis?"

"I don't know. Aunt Viv said something about Simone committing emotional suicide when it comes to males." Bren stiffened, jerking her head to the side. "So, ah, that's the status on the homeless."

Female voices echoed behind her, and their mother peered down to the camera. "Are you calling the Nine or just your mother?" The smile lifted her lips, but the dark circles under her eyes rivaled Brenna's.

Grace Sadler elbowed Brigid out of the way. "Hello, Moira. How's it going with the vampire?" She perched red cats-eyed glasses atop her sunshine-colored hair, wiggling her arched eyebrows. "Are you playing somewhere tropical?" Although several hundred years old, Grace could give any model alive a run for her money. She'd dated her share of vampires and had yet to settle down.

Brigid nudged Grace to the side. "Stop harassing my daughter, Grace. We need to double-check the security on this server before Moira tells us where she is." Her eyes, a darker green than Moira's, flashed bright with concern.

"Why?" Moira adjusted the camera to better view both women.

Brigid shrugged. "Safety. Whoever is yanking people out of their spaces must first know their location. It's like when a vampire teleports . . . the few who do. They have to know where they're going first. They don't just shoot themselves out into the world."

Realization slapped Moira hard. "So that's why you wanted me out of the country—where you knew Conn would hide me." Anger and hurt lowered her voice.

Her mother flushed. "Yes, initially that was my plan. I know you're an excellent enforcer, but you're still my daughter." She rubbed a hand across her eyes, then leaned down to type quickly. "Okay . . . this line is secure . . . we can talk. The family is safe, but you're the Seventh. Whoever's after us has already tried for you."

"I have a job to do." At least until the dreaded day she joined the council. Why couldn't anyone understand that fact?

"Yes." Brigid sighed. "Whether you like it or not, keeping yourself safe is what the Nine wants from you right now. Ah, and, in addition, I want to send Brenna to you to protect."

Moira's heart stopped. She opened her mouth but words refused to find sound. A rushing filled her ears.

Brenna rolled her eyes. "Not going to happen." She typed, her concentration trained downward. "I have a pretty good battle plan set up against the demons. I was hoping you'd give it to Dage"—her Celtic pendant dangled in front of the viewfinder—"assuming we're not aligning with the demons, of course." Her smile lacked humor while her eyes sparked irritation. "The e-mail should be incoming."

It didn't make any sense for her mother to want to send Brenna to her. The Nine protected their own. "They don't want to send you here." Moira's mind raced as she faced her mother. "Do you?"

Sorrow filled Brigid's eyes. "No."

"You said that because you want my location." Moira's voice cracked as she suddenly understood. "That's why the

Nine sent me to fetch Simone. You knew Conn would bring me here." To the king's headquarters. "You set this up so I could infiltrate their compound, and you didn't even have the courtesy to tell me!"

Brenna sat back, fire lighting her eyes. "What is going on?" Her gaze hardened. "The world is going to hell. The Nine is in an uproar over the missing members, my economic council is trying to figure out how to keep people from starving, and something's up with the local shifters. Yet, you're all not saying anything."

Moira's mind spun. "The Nine has withdrawn from the Realm." Conn now had a bounty on his head. For all intents and purposes, she was a bounty hunter employed by the Coven Nine. Duty was about to rip her to shreds.

Grace slid an arm around Brigid's shoulders. "We've only taken a preliminary vote, Moira. The official one isn't until tonight, so you have some time."

"Time for what?" Time to plan how to destroy the Realm from the inside? To plan a way to take Conn's head . . . as if she could?

He'd been fighting for three hundred years longer than she had. His experience outdid hers, by far. The man trusted her. Well, he probably trusted her. The only time he let down his guard with her was . . . when naked. She might have given her pledge to the Nine, but she hadn't given her soul.

It was coming down to more than what she wanted to do for a living. The decisions she faced would determine who she became.

"The demons will want Janie. As do the Kurjans, and anyone aligning with them." She faced her mother, ignoring Grace. "Putting the Kayrs family in danger threatens that child, that little girl, Mother."

"I know." Brigid's lips trembled. "We're meeting again tonight, Moira. I'm doing what I can."

Her mother would vote against withdrawal. From the tightening of Grace's jaw, she'd probably vote in favor. Simone and Trevan, probably in favor. That left Peter and Viv. If they voted against, there would be a tie. "I'll join the Coven Nine to avoid war." She glanced to the side where Brenna sat, her face frozen. "Go through the canons to see if there's any way to avoid this."

Brenna nodded. "I will. Withdrawing from the Realm is a huge mistake." She frowned, straightening and wrinkling her nose. "What is that smell?"

Grace dropped her glasses into place on her nose, biting her lip. "I don't know. Is something on fire?"

"Smells like ozone," Brigid murmured, glancing around.

Ozone? Panic ripped through Moira. "Get out of there. Get out, now!" She leaped to her feet, knocking the computer mouse to the floor.

"What—" Brenna started, then gasped. Her head swiveled around toward a mass of air beginning to swirl. Papers billowed up. A chair crashed against a far wall.

"Get down!" Brigid yelled, grabbing Brenna and ducking out of camera range.

Moira's heart pounded against her ribs. She clutched both hands to the desk. "Grace, get down!"

Grace swiveled toward the side, her glasses flying off her face. She bounced to run. The swirling vortex shot forward, enclosing her like a winter coat. Crying out, her eyes wide in panic, she reached for the computer. As if the air had a mouth, it swallowed.

Grace disappeared.

Moira clapped her hand over her lips. Oh God. She had to get home. "Mom! Brenna?" She leaned closer to the computer, squinting to see. Papers and what looked like a stapler settled hard on the table.

Brenna stood, pulling Brigid up. Armed guards ran into camera range. Brigid angled toward the camera, her face stark white, her eyes wide. "Stay where you are, Moira. The Nine needs to handle this. Don't do anything until you hear from me. We'll be in touch." The computer went dark.

Moira backed away. The Nine? At this point it was the Five. She needed to hurry home and help. She whirled when the door opened and Conn stalked inside. "I have to get out of here."

He reached her in two strides. Broad hands ran down her arms, spreading warmth through her limbs. He captured her gaze, concern bracketing his mouth with harsh lines. "What's wrong?"

"I was on a conference with my mother. They took Grace." Fear exploded in Moira's chest. The room fuzzed. She swayed. Conn kept her upright, his hold gentle and solid. Then fury coated her vision red. They were working through the council members one by one. Her mother or aunt would be next. "The bastards." Temper shot heat up her spine, making her fingers tingle. Electricity sparked blue along her skin like a match to oil.

Conn hissed, releasing her to clench and unclench his burned hands. "Control it, sweetheart."

A haze descended across her eyes. They'd taken another member of the Nine—through some damn portal. The earth rumbled in shared anger. She lifted her hands, palms out. "I need to go. Now."

"No." Conn grabbed her again, shaking her words to a stop. "Right now you're secure. You will remain so."

She shoved him. Hard. He didn't move. "I'm an enforcer. Someone just kidnapped a member of the Nine." But they wanted her. She knew they did. More important, if she left headquarters, Conn could relocate his family without her knowledge. If she were taken, no matter what happened, the Kayrs family would be safe. Then she wouldn't have to choose between her loyalty to her people and her loyalty to Conn. Besides, she had a job to do. "I'm not going to let you keep me here when I could be actively searching for the bastards taking my people."

"We'll send our best troops. I'll even go if you want. You need to stay here."

"You're not listening to me." Moira fought the urge to burn Conn again.

He studied her face, his gaze hard. "I'm listening. I'm just not agreeing. Deal with it." His cell phone buzzed, and he flipped the screen open to read. With a raised eyebrow, he closed the device, tucking the cell in his pocket.

Moira eyed the door. "I need to get home and assist the council, Conn." If she had to burn him to a cinder, she would.

He shut his eyes for a brief second before opening them, his jaw setting. "You're not going anywhere, Moira. The text message was from Dage. Your aunt just requested assistance from the Realm in protecting you." Raw determination hardened his jaw. "This is a good thing. Either way, you're staying here until I deal with this threat."

She took a step away. Her aunt wanted her to remain with the Kayrs family in case the Nine withdrew—so she was in place to betray them. Nobody had the right to tell her to stay. "Who the hell do you think you are?" Anger returned so fast her breath caught. "More important, who the hell do you think I am?"

His shoulders went back. "You're my mate."

The freaking vampire truly didn't understand her. "So what? I have a job to do."

Triumph glittered in his eyes. "I understand. The leader of the council, your boss, ordered you to stay here until we figure out what's going on."

"No." Her voice shook she was so furious. "My aunt ordered The Seventh to stay here in a blanket of safety." Or as a Trojan horse. "I'm an enforcer."

He cocked his head to the side. "Either way, you work for the Nine, Moira."

The man was correct. She gave one short nod. "I quit. Now get out of my way so I can fly to Ireland and tell Viv that in person. My choice is to go forward on my own." Being an enforcer had fit her on all fronts. She'd miss her job, but no way would she let anyone dictate her life. Destiny had made her the seventh sister of the seventh sister, which gave her powers beyond those shared by the Nine. She hadn't even begun to tap into the energy she could harness.

"Good. We'll e-mail your letter of resignation." Conn folded his arms.

Her jaw ached as she clenched her teeth together. "I don't answer to you any more than the council, Conn. Get the fuck out of my way."

His eyes sparked. "Do you really think I'm going to let you put yourself in a danger the Nine can't even quantify?"

"Think you can stop me?" She summoned her own energy, gasping at the heat through her lungs. A ball of energy began to form above her left palm.

Faster than she'd have imagined possible, Conn shot forward and lifted her by the elbows, laying her down on an empty table. Her shoulders hit with a dull thunk. Hovering over her, he leaned down, his breath heated against her lips. "We already played that game, Dailtín. I'd rather not go there again."

Her body flushed hot with desire while her mind sparked with fury. She gave a muffled shriek, levering her legs to kick him solidly in the stomach. He huffed an irritated "*oof*," but didn't move, a light of male intent filling his eyes along with a translucent green she'd never seen.

Determination filled Moira. He wanted to play, did he?

Scissoring her legs, she clasped his chest, twisting sideways and throwing him to the floor. He landed with a snarl.

Leaping, she dropped onto his stomach, angling one knee toward his balls and an elbow against his jugular. A keyboard bounced off the table, landing next to him.

He smiled.

She stilled.

Her eyes widened. Instinct forced her to press harder against his neck.

He flung a hand under her knee while grabbing her arm. Smooth reflexes had him lifting her away. "Whoever taught you to fight should be shot." Her ass hit the floor. Seconds later he covered her head to toe.

The enforcers had taught her. "I'm a good fighter, Conn." The heat of his body contrasted with the chill of the wooden floor in a way that sped up her heartbeat. Her body urged her to wrap her legs around his waist, but pure stubbornness had her slapping both palms against his ears.

He huffed out air, grabbing her wrists and extending them above her head. "You are such a brat." He settled into her. "As a fighter, you're fast and strike well. The second you pause, you'd better hold a weapon in your hand."

Her nipples pebbled against his chest. "You're right." When strength came into play, she didn't stand a chance with someone his size. Energy crackled along her arms. "I do hold a weapon."

"Excellent." He pressed his hardened groin against her.

She fought the need to rub along his length. "Get off me."

"Why would I do that?" His free hand roamed down the side of her body to clasp her ass and tug her into male hardness. "This is where I like you."

Forget subtlety or suggestion. The man always said just what he wanted. "Too bad."

His dark eyebrows shot up. "Bet I could change your mind."

The heat filling her pores guaranteed he could. Her body clamored for his. The branding on her hip pounded with painful need. But the situation called for them to come to some sort of agreement. "I'm not the person you envision for your mate, Conn. I'm an enforcer."

"As such, you have your orders." He scowled. "Sometimes our jobs require more of us than they should." His hand tightened on her butt. A rock-hard erection pressed against her flesh, and she fought a whimper. "Believe me, Moira. I understand how frustrating it is to be stuck underground in safety when there's a fight going on. I understand the need to be at the front and protect those you love."

He said love. Of course, he was talking about his brothers, but still her heart jumped. "You do a good job protecting your family. Keep doing so, but I need to go."

"Just what do you think you are?" His gaze dropped to her mouth, which actually tingled in response.

"A mate."

"That's family, darlin'. Like it or not." He wet his lips, and she fought a groan. "Our world starts right here. You and me. Everything else spirals out . . . my people, your people, friends, and enemies."

"You make it sound so simple." She took a deep breath. "What if it came down to your king or me? Say you had to choose, and only one of us would survive?"

"I'm choosing not to engage in silly riddles, Moira. We chart our own destinies, and I'll keep my choices from narrowing to you or my king. You should know that." He partially lifted her off the floor, sliding her along his length.

Her nipples pebbled. Arrogance and faith in his own abilities made up the vampire. She appreciated the qualities, though they infuriated her at the same time. "I hope you're right."

They probably shouldn't be rolling around on the floor of the public computer room. Anyone might walk inside.

Something vibrated in his pocket against her, and she jumped in surprise. Conn chuckled, releasing her wrists to yank out the cell phone and press it to his cheek. "I'm busy." His entire body stiffened as he listened. "I'll be right there." Rolling to his feet, he tugged Moira up.

Gentle fingers brushed curls off her face. He leaned in with a hard kiss. "The demons attacked a clan of feline shifters in Alaska, taking hostages. They're members of the Realm and I need to go."

"Let me come." She'd never fought with demons. Magic should help.

"No." Conn stepped back. "I gave my word to your aunt to keep you safe, darlin'. You're a lot like Dage. He hates the mantle of his position, too."

With two long strides, Conn opened the door. "Soldiers will be here in a minute to take you to headquarters. If we're raiding, our mates are underground. You might as well explore. You're going to be there a while."

Then, he was gone.

Chapter 17

Janie clutched her teddy bear closer to her chest, her eyes drooping. Mr. Mullet wasn't doing a good job of keeping her awake. They were snuggled underground again . . . where the earth sometimes whispered to her. Pony pictures drawed by Uncle Dage covered her bedroom walls, and a pretty dollhouse Uncle Conn had made sat in the corner. Her mama whistled in the other room, sewing socks for the baby . . . but they looked more like orange holders. She really couldn't sew.

Janie needed to stay awake until her daddy came home . . . he and her uncles had hurried off to fight again, and she had a bad feeling. The kind of feeling she got after eating too much cotton candy and too many hotdogs.

Soon enough she found herself wandering along a wide golf course just like the one a pony had played on during her favorite television show last week. With a shrug, she gave into the dream. Might as well make the grass purple, and the trees made of licorice. Yum. Even the air smelled yummy.

Where in the world was Zane? Her best friend, her only friend since she left home, they met in dreams. When they both slept. She searched the area . . . then found him. Her laughter echoed across the distance, where he stood in a big sand trap made of . . . what was that? Oh no. Cotton candy.

He smiled, jumping out of the pink mess. But his smile didn't seem right. His pretty green eyes didn't smile, too.

She ran, meeting him near a shiny flag blowing in the wind. "What's wrong?"

He lifted a dark eyebrow like her daddy did. Then he dropped to sit so she wouldn't have to look up. Zane turned eleven a while ago . . . and grew way taller than her. It wasn't fun being only five years old. She sat next to him, biting her lip. "What's wrong?"

"I have to move." He rubbed his jaw, sadness coming off him.

"Oh." She patted his big hand on the purple grass. "I just moved, too. You might like your new home."

"No." He shook his head, sending long dark hair flying. "My father, we don't know where he is. His unit has disappeared."

Janie's chest ached. Zane's daddy worked as a soldier with the vampires, fighting against the bad Kurjans. "Maybe they're hiding out to catch all of the bad guys. Your daddy will be home soon, Zane." Please let Zane's daddy be all right. She remembered how scary it was living without a daddy . . . she didn't have one until Talen showed up. Now she had him. The world was safer with him.

"I hope so." Zane's smile seemed lopsided. "Until he returns, we're going to live with my mother's people. Her family."

Janie didn't ask where his mama's family lived. They'd agreed a long time ago not to tell. Well, Zane said they needed to keep secrets, just in case. So she didn't ask. "Do you like her family?"

He shrugged. "They train as hard as my people, so that'll be good. I'll keep training."

Her head ached. Sometimes she saw the future, but she didn't get to choose when. Even stuff she didn't understand had rules. She didn't like rules. "Do you have to move far away?" Okay. She really wondered where Zane lived.

He shook his head. "How is Mr. Mullet?"

She'd described her bear, a present from Aunt Emma, to him once, but had never been able to bring Mr. Mullet into a dream. "He's good. I asked him to keep me awake, but he didn't." She eyed the tops of the trees turning a sunny yellow. "I'm not sure why I can't bring him into the dream. Honest, I don't think he wants to come." She'd brought other goodies to show Zane, and she always wore the horseshoe necklace he'd given her for her last birthday.

"Perhaps bears don't like dreams."

"Yeah." She'd been wondering about something. "I saw a movie last week with vampires as the bad guys."

He frowned. "A scary movie?"

"Kind of." She had a television in her room and couldn't sleep that night. Her mama didn't know she'd watched it. "They had big fangs and drank blood."

"Oh." Zane rubbed his hands on his jeans.

"Do you have fangs?"

"Yes. Got them last year." He opened his mouth and his side teeth lowered down. Sharp and white, they could cause a big owie.

"Do they hurt?" She wanted to touch one, but didn't think Zane would like her fingers in his mouth.

"No." The teeth went back into his mouth. "Though it took a while to get used to them. I kept cutting my lip." He grinned.

Janie snorted. "That's funny. But you drink blood, right?" Yuck.

He shrugged. "Well, humans need blood when they get hurt, and you give them that with needles. So yeah, when we are injured and need blood, we just get it faster because we can use our fangs."

"In the movie, the vampires needed blood to live 'cause they couldn't make their own. So they fed on people."

"Don't believe movies, Janie. We make our own blood, as do you. Though, our blood will heal a human because of the extra stuff in it." Zane stood, holding down a hand to help her up. "I need to go right now, and it may be a while until I have a chance to fully sleep and dream. For some reason, it takes me longer to get into this world than it does you."

Janie pushed her lip out. "You'll be back, right?"

"I will. For now, my brothers need help, and my mother is worried. I need to take care of them."

Janie nodded, standing and squeezing his hand. "You're my best friend, Zane. Forever." In fact, someday they were going to save the world. Probably. Well, if things went the right way in life.

"You're my best friend too, Janie Belle." He'd given her the name the first time they met, saying "Janet Isabella" sounded too grown up for his new buddy. "No matter what happens, remember that, okay?" He blocked out the dream sun, and she fought a shiver. It was good they were on the same side.

"I'll remember." She let him go, watching him walk down the purple grass until disappearing.

A tickle made her neck itch. She sighed. It had been at least six months since Kalin tried to get into her dreams. Kalin was a Kurjan, a bad boy, and someday he and Zane were gonna fight. She wanted them all to be friends. A nice girl would try hard to be Kalin's friend.

She let him inside her dream.

He'd gotten even taller. She tilted her head, letting him walk across the grass toward her. The Kurjans had pasty white skin, either purple or red eyes, and reddish or black-red hair. But Kalin's eyes were green, his skin not totally pasty, and his hair black with red tips. Usually.

She waited until he got closer. "What happened to your hair?" It was all black with no red. It matched his lips and . . . yep. His fingernails. "You look like one of those scary people on the grownup channel."

He smiled, flashing sharp teeth. "Yeah. I dyed my hair." As he came closer, the smell of salty ocean came with him. Weird that she never smelled Zane in a dream. He probably smelled like something really good.

Kalin shrugged. "Yeah. It's pissing my people off."

"Huh." Janie shuffled her feet. "You said *pissing*." Bad boys said bad words. Though for some reason, the black lipstick made him seem less scary than last time.

"Um. Sorry." He dropped right where Zane had sat. "How are things?"

She frowned, sitting a small distance away. "Okay. How are you?"

He twirled a pocketknife in his hands. "Confused. I mean, I've always accepted my destiny—to rule the Kurjans, then the world. But . . . I don't know." He flicked the blade open. "Everyone is afraid of me, and it's not like I can talk to anyone."

Boy teenagers were weird. Even Kurjan ones. He was what, fifteen now? "You can talk to me."

"Thank you." He closed the blade, shoving it in the pants pocket of his skinny black jeans. Just like the teenagers wore on television. "I figured you're the only one I can talk to. Thanks for letting me in the dream."

"Do you wanna be friends?" If they became friends, then Kalin and Zane would be friends, and they would end the war.

Kalin shrugged. "I don't know. Friends are new to me."

Janie sat up straighter. "You found a friend, Kalin?" This might be so good. If Kalin made a friend, he'd want more.

She'd had lots of friends in preschool before they moved. It was fun having lots of friends. Some would want to play games; others would dress up with her in princess costumes. Now she was a real princess. But she missed her friends.

A slight pink covered Kalin's face. "I think so. I mean, she's kind of a friend."

Oh. Kalin found a girlfriend. Janie fought the urge to sing about Kalin in a tree. He wouldn't like that. "What's her name?"

"Peggy." Kalin grabbed a pebble off the green, throwing it into the sand trap. "She's human."

"You should give her flowers." Janie had watched a TV show last week where the boy picked daisies and gave them to a girl with a broken leg. "Or candy."

Kalin ran his palm along the short, springy grass. "I guess. I mean, I probably should clear the field first. We've been talking on the phone a lot. She likes the Goth look, but she has these other friends, guys . . . and I was thinking . . ."

Janie gasped. "You can't kill them, Kalin. Not if you want Peggy to like you."

He glanced up, his green eyes swirling with red sparks. "Sure I can. I mean, if you love someone, you want them to really know you, right?"

"Well, yeah." Janie frowned. "But you've never killed anyone yet, right? So you don't need to start."

He blinked. Twice. "No. I haven't killed, but I will. We are at war, Janie. I'm a soldier." He rubbed his chin, exactly like Zane had done. Must be a boy thing. "She thinks I'm this kind of dangerous guy she met at the movies one night. She has no idea who I am."

"You can be who you want. Be someone she'll like." Be someone who wants to end the war. For the first real time,

Janie figured they had a chance to fix everything. "Sometimes it's what we mean to do that matters." She sighed.

How could she put this in boy words? "When I went to preschool, a girl named Melanie brung a cool pencil—blue with pink dots. I super-duper wanted it. She left it on the table one day, and I thought about taking it." Janie's face got hot. She probably shouldn't tell Kalin this. "But I didn't . . . and I was happy I didn't. I could've and nobody would've caught me, but stealing is bad. I was good."

Kalin frowned. "So you're saying even though I can end these guys, if I choose to not to do that, I've become a better person?"

"Sure, and then you'd prove you're a better person. So next time the decision will be easier." Hopefully. This teenage stuff confused her. "You want Peggy to know the real you."

"Interesting."

"So, uh, do you have fangs?" She wondered if his were like Zane's.

Kalin tilted his head to the side and opened his mouth. His fangs shot out, sharp and clean.

"Do you drink blood?" The idea still seemed icky.

"Yes." His teeth went back to normal. "Though only if I'm hurt."

She'd gotten a paper cut last week and tasted the blood. But she didn't like it. "What does blood taste like to you?"

He shrugged. "Depends on whose blood I'm drinking. If someone eats a bunch of candy, their blood is sweeter. Everyone's different."

"Oh." She bet her mama's blood tasted like chocolate.

Kalin stood, reaching a hand to help Janie up.

She took his offer and slid her hand into his. It was big like Zane's, but not as warm. "Thanks."

She let go once on her feet.

Kalin smiled. "Any time. Thanks for listening, Janie." He turned to stroll off the green without a backward glance.

Kalin woke himself from the dream with a start, wondering if the little genius was on to something. Why in the world had he lied to her? Of course he'd killed. Many times, usually women he hunted. For some reason, he hadn't wanted Janie to know. He stretched in the bed.

Cold. Even with heaters, a chill always wound through his room built into the rocks underground. Probably because the ocean fronted the rock cliffs. So many fathoms down it became freezing. "Lights." They flicked on, and he rolled from the bed, missing the bright colors and warmth of Janie's dream world.

How bizarre that his future enemy was his only friend.

His feet curled into a thick Persian rug he'd stolen from a woman he'd killed in Kansas. She'd been a redhead who owned an antique store. He liked to take a gift, something to help him remember his women. Usually he took smaller trinkets, but the richness of the rug called to him. He'd had to lug it to the private plane he had waiting. Franco didn't care if Kalin killed, just insisted he do so away from headquarters, so Kalin always had a plane waiting.

He shrugged, his gaze landing on pictures scattered across the rock wall. "Hello, Peggy."

The stunning teenager filled every photograph in different scenes, in different clothes. The night pictures he'd taken himself, plus a few during cloudy days when she'd hurried into school, unaware of his vigil. He'd hired a local delinquent to take pictures during the sunny days, since the sun would fry his skin from his body. Hundreds of pictures. Of course, Kalin had broken the moron's neck after delivery. He certainly didn't want Peggy to think he was stalking her. He merely wanted pictures.

After bowling that first night, they'd slid easily into

friendship. He'd made a mistake revealing his real age. Should've said he was older. Although she thought him too young to date, something about him intrigued her. Women were like moths . . . the flame attracted them. He was different from boys at her school—homeschooled, yet dangerous.

Soon, very soon he'd make his move. Kiss her, take her to a hotel for the night. The night they'd held hands, running through the rain had almost killed him. His jeans had been so tight he thought he'd explode. The girl was sexy as hell. He'd gotten plenty of experience the last couple years. Sure, those women weren't willing, but he'd still learned. He'd please Peggy.

The center picture was his favorite. He had taken it at the bowling alley with his cell phone. She smiled at him and actually posed. Her sparkling blue eyes filled with life, and her shiny brown hair billowed around her shoulders.

Interesting. Kalin had never put it together before, but Peggy looked like Janie. Same coloring. Same delicate bone structure.

He threw on sweats and thick socks, yawning and wandering through his quarters to Franco's private office. No need to knock. He'd one day rule their nation . . . and he didn't knock. The leader stood dressed in his soldier's black and red uniform by the wall of windows showcasing deep-sea life. It was dark, merciless, and absent of fish.

"Franco." Kalin dropped into a leather chair that chilled his skin further. His father had owned fish in a pretty tank. Nobody owned the fish outside the windows—those that were nowhere to be seen at the moment. What would his father have thought about Peggy? Too bad Talen had murdered him. Now Kalin would never know.

Franco turned, his purple eyes swirling. At seven feet tall, the man held grace in spades. "You look ridiculous."

Kalin shrugged. "The black paint makes it easier for me

to walk among humans." So he could spend more time with Peggy. Show her that fifteen was old enough for her.

"I wish you'd get your head back in the game." Franco scowled. "You haven't even read my brother's newest report about the chances of turning Virus-27 airborne."

"Won't that endanger Kurjan mates?" Kalin yawned again, scratching his belly. Man, he needed more sleep. Sadness filtered through him that he couldn't mate Peggy. The idea made his groin harden. He dreamt about her ruling with him—once he cured her of that independent streak. He couldn't mate her, and not just because she wasn't an enhanced female. Fate held other plans for him. Peggy would make a nice companion on the side.

"Possibly." Franco shrugged. "Hopefully Erik will come up with an antidote. If not, well, you understand the final plan."

"Yep. Though I plan on killing Talen Kayrs long before that." Kalin stretched his neck. "The bastard killed my father . . . and his head is mine." His father had taken Cara Kayrs, and Talen had retaliated. He wondered if he should hide the fact that he intended to kill Talen from Janie?

"Of course." Franco turned back toward the silent sea.

"If my father had lived, he'd have passed the reins to me." Would Kalin need to kill Franco to take his rightful place? Intriguing thought.

"Your father was as ambitious as he was foolhardy. He would not have easily given up ruling." Franco swirled around, power filling his eyes. "Why is this in your mind? Apparently you just want to screw around with humans and have stopped dedicating yourself to training."

The smile sliding across Kalin's lips failed to keep his fangs from dropping. "I'm dedicated, and you know it." He cocked his head to the side. "You're correct that ambition ruled my father. To be honest, I'm not sure he'd ever have turned over control." At some point in time, leadership would've come down to a fight to the death.

Franco shrugged. "True. We have many years to plan each other's deaths, Kalin. At some point, I may want to step down. My immediate plans are a bit more narrow in focus."

Interesting. "What plans?" Something tickled the base of Kalin's neck. What motivated Franco if not power?

"Irrelevant."

No. Knowledge equaled power, a lesson Kalin learned early on. He clicked through facts. "Oh yeah. The Prophet Lily?"

"Don't you worry about Lily. I'm making plans as we speak." Franco licked his lips.

Kalin leaned forward in his chair. Wait a minute. "The virus. Please don't tell me you came up with this whole virus plan to free Lily from her dead mate." The virus took a vampire mate down to human again . . . hopefully . . . so she could be remated. Kurjans only got one mate. One living mate, that was.

Franco snorted. "Don't be silly. Freeing Lily to mate again is a fortunate by-product of the virus. Of course, I made sure the waiter infected her last year."

The dark flush crossing Franco's face made Kalin bite back a grin. "Well now. Good luck with her." She'd lost her mate centuries ago, but had only contracted the virus recently. "How odd the virus actually allows women the chance to leave a mating match. We're following the humans." What was next? No-fault divorce laws?

Franco growled. "Mind your own business. I do wish you'd hurry up and desert your current phase. Take off the black lipstick . . . and return to killing people."

Kalin stretched to his feet and sauntered toward the door. "I'll see what I can do."

Chapter 18

April in Alaska was like the dead of winter anywhere else in the States. Conn adjusted his earpiece, tugging the bulletproof vest down farther. Bruised clouds hung low, sending spirals of mist to the ground. Even so, majestic pine trees dotted through, providing more cover for the men preparing to strike.

"The plan is solid"—he stomped snow off his boots—"for this unexpected situation." Jordan Pride, the head of the feline nation, stood next to Conn. Jordan had been staying at headquarters to plan strategy against a couple rogue clans still after the Prophet Caleb because he'd supported his brother when the man married a shifter who'd been betrothed to a demon. Just one of the lame reasons Caleb had been exiled until last year.

Jordan tied thick blond hair back at the nape. "Yes. The demon attack against one of my clans is a surprise move." His tawny eyes flared hot. "They're trying to splinter support for the Realm."

If so, the demons didn't know Jordan very well. The situation just pissed him off.

Conn eyed Jase. What a fine time to make sure his brother was ready to fight the demons. Fortune was smiling. Well, not for the captured shifters. He turned his attention toward Dage, biting back a growl. "I just finished lecturing my mate and holding you up as an example of a leader who understood staying behind and sacrificing for the greater good."

Dage loosened the securing straps of several knives along his vest, anticipation flashing bright in his eyes. "That probably backfired."

"Yes. The woman is on edge, even more than usual." Instinct whispered across his mind that all hell was about to break loose.

Dage nodded. "The Nine took a preliminary vote last night to withdraw from the Realm. If they do so, their first action will be to put Moira to work."

Everything in Conn stilled. He'd learned long ago not to question Dage's inside sources. "She won't betray us, Dage."

"So she'll betray her family?" Dage smacked a clip into a glowing green gun.

"No." If Conn knew his mate, she'd figure out a way to please them all, possibly getting herself killed in the process. "How preliminary?"

"Probably very, considering another member of the Nine was taken." Dage rolled his neck. "Keep your head in this game right now, Conn. We'll deal with the rest later."

A rumble rolled across the earpiece lines and Talen's irritated voice belted through. "If you ladies are finished with chat time, do you think we could blow this place to hell?" The demon compound stood set against the Shelton Mountains, more than likely extending deep into the earth.

"The taking of hostages is a new tactic for the demons." Conn released the safety on his gun. "We can only hope they're unaware they kidnapped the mate of a pride member away from home." Upon learning of the raid, the man had immediately zeroed in on his mate's location. Feline mates could track each other anywhere in the world, as could vampire mates. A fact that had saved Cara and Emma when Talen had tracked Cara after a Kurjan kidnapping.

Dage gave a short nod. "Jase, take the lead."

Jase had developed a daring and intricate plan on the helicopter ride. He clicked on. "Conn, set the charges. Talen, head to the west side behind him." Grabbing his gun, he nodded to his team of three, which included the king. "The front door is ours."

Conn hefted the bag of C-4 and ran through the night, dodging branches and creating a new path. He'd wanted to flank Jase, but maybe it was time to let the youngest brother stand on his own.

One demon guard stood in Conn's way. With a strong arm around the neck, he snapped hard and tossed the body to the ground. A broken neck wouldn't kill the guy, but it would take some time to mend. Three more bodies littered the forest floor by the time Conn reached the side of the metal building. The final one managed to give a strangled cry into his communicator before losing his head. That soldier wouldn't recover.

The air shimmered around Conn. Blackness coated his brain like spilled oil. He stopped, put his back against the rough bark of a pine and sucked in air. The bite centered him. "The demons know we're here."

Images slammed through his mind—fire, death, pain. Shards of imaginary glass ripped across his skull and behind his eyes.

Cold air filled his lungs, and he forced the images into a box. Then he flicked the box to hell. Ramming shields around his mind, he allowed the soldier fate had created to rise to the surface. All intent, all strategy, he jogged forward, no longer feeling the press of energy into his brain. Single-mindedness protected him in his quest to destroy.

He reached the building. Spacing the charges in metal grooves, he hustled behind a stand of trees and yanked out the detonator. "Charges set on the east side."

"At your mark," Jase said.

"We're in place," Talen said, his voice low with purpose.

Conn pressed the red button. A loud boom echoed. Oxygen swooshed through the forest, drawn to the blaze of fire lighting up the remote area. Metal ripped into pieces, spiraling up into the air to land against trees and the slight snow with the hiss of heat on ice. Grabbing his other gun, he ran full bore into the melee.

Scalding heat blistered his face. He fired from a low crouch, sending three demons down. He needed to take their heads to kill them, but for now, down would do. Jase crashed through the front, bullets spraying in a sweeping motion. Fire blazed bright and hot, smoke filled the room. Bodies dropped until only the vampire teams remained.

Conn cut his eyes to Talen. "Too easy."

An alarm blared with a high shriek, swirling red lights springing to life. Jase nodded to one of his men, who knelt and aimed a modified rocket launcher toward the rear of the holding. "Get down."

The missile exploded from the end of the weapon, tearing into the quartz and sending pieces flying. Conn ducked his head, shards cutting into his vest before dropping to the floor. His ears rang. "Talen, any heat signatures?" He lifted up. A massive hole penetrated the rock, revealing an elevator shaft and a set of emergency stairs leading down. Excellent shot.

Talen yanked the heat reader out of his pocket. "Yes. Underground . . . three meters. Several signatures, but they flow together shielded by rock. I can't tell how many."

Jase shot forward. "Talen and Conn, scale down. Use the cables." He paused at the stairs. "Dage, Jordan, you're with me."

Conn ripped his flashlight out of a pocket, secured it to his gun, and pointed it down into the tunnel. Rough cable scraped against his leather gloves when he grabbed on. He looked at Talen. "Count to five, then follow."

When Talen nodded, Conn scaled down the tunnel. His boots soon clomped against a closed door. "Team two, take the first level."

Hand over hand he scaled down until reaching a second landing. "Talen, take level two."

A longer distance kept the darkness pressing around him until his boots landed on the top of the elevator. Last floor. Reporting his position, he yanked a knife loose to cut into the escape hatch on top.

Static crackled over the line. "We're in a myriad of tunnels, lots of dark images slamming through our brains. The demons must be close," Jase muttered. "The tunnels head away from your locations. Everyone check in—three-minute intervals."

Conn ripped open the hatch and dropped into the elevator, wincing as the carriage rocked. Sliding his knife through the door, he wrenched the sides open. Gun in hand, he leaned out and swept the area, aiming bullets into the necks of two guards. One got off a shot that ripped into Conn's vest. His ribs bellowed in pain.

Demons. The two lay on the ground, silver haired, dressed all in black, sparkling medallions on their lapels signaling their low rank. Crouching, Conn decapitated both, his mind quickly shutting out the smell of blood and death. He rose to his feet, his gaze on the heavy metal door they'd guarded from this small vestibule. "Two demons down. I'm heading into another area."

Firefights exploded across the communication lines. "We've been engaged," Jase yelled, the sound of his rushing breath causing Conn to still. The line went dead.

"Talen, report," Conn ordered.

Nothing. Only silence. The demons had found a way to jam the communications. Well, he had faith in his brothers and a job to do. Setting a charge at the door, he dodged into the elevator. The bomb exploded. Debris flew by and the earth rumbled a protest. His gun swung right and left as he sprang into the hall and through the doorway, shoulders relaxing at the series of cells on each side.

Most were empty, but five panther shifters huddled bruised and bloody in the last one. Their hair was streaked a unique blond, black, and brown and was matted with blood. They'd fought hard. Two males and three females hurried forward.

There was a time females were protected during war, regardless of the species. The thought of Moira being taken filled Conn with rage. He had to shove the fury down to clear his mind and help these people. The tallest male clasped his broken arm against his ribs, his catlike eyes narrowed in pain. "They want Pride. Is he here?"

Conn jerked. "The demons want Jordan? Why?" That didn't make any sense. Unless the demons had joined forces with the Kurjans and wanted to collect shifters to turn into werewolves. Weres became the ultimate, disposable soldiers who mindlessly obeyed a master. He didn't see a demon-Kurjan alliance working, considering demons believed Kurjans to be lower than dogs on the evolutionary scale. Nice pets but not really necessary. "How many of you survived the raid?" He set two charges against the lock.

"This is it." The male growled, nodding to the others to step back and cover their heads. "The rest are dead."

Anger rolled through Conn. The demons should've stayed out of the war. "Fire in the hole." He stood out of the way, until the small charge blew and the door flew open.

The shifters hustled out, gazes sweeping the hallway.

Conn gestured toward the doorway. "We'll have to scale up the walls where reinforcements await." Along with a medical team.

The leader stopped, turning to face him. A weapon sat comfortably in his hand, which he levered at Conn's neck. "I guess you'll have to do this time, Prince." Three darts shot out, piercing Conn's jugular. A haze descended over his eyes. With a growl of pure rage, he leaped forward, his fingers digging into the panther's neck.

They went down hard onto stone. Nausea swirled in Conn's gut. His ears rang. Blindness consumed him. With his last breath, he'd kill this fucker. Images of Moira, of Janie, and his family flashed through his mind as he ripped the panther's head off.

A woman cried out. "Robert!"

Two more sharp needles pierced Conn's flesh. He dropped to the side, his shoulder denting the rock. Strong arms grabbed him under the armpits, dragging him into the cell. "You'd be smarter to cut off my head," he slurred, his head rolling to the side. His arms weighed more than he'd thought possible. He chuckled like he was drunk.

"He's heavy," the remaining male hissed. "I told Robert we shouldn't break his arm just for show. Open the door in the back of the cell. We're running out of time."

One of the shifters tore the earpiece out of Conn's ear. The small device pinged against a metal bar in the far distance.

"Good throw. Too bad I'm going to kill you," he garbled out.

"Why isn't he out cold? We shot him full of enough tranq to take down a buffalo," a female said, her nails digging into his ankles. "Throw him in the cart. We can roll the bastard to the helicopter."

"Don't wanna fly." Conn kicked out, but his leg moved like he sat under sand. A crack filled the silence, and he let a smile loose. Guess he hurt the bitch. Thoughts filtered across his brain, most tinged with a sparkly green. What the hell had they given him?

"You asshole." She dropped his feet, kicking him hard in the thigh.

The scent of fresh blood made his stomach rumble. He forced out a laugh. "Not my type, lady." Moira. Moira was his type. She'd kicked him, too. Why were people always kicking him? Maybe he should buy her a ring. Moira. Buy Moira a ring. Not the animal swearing at him.

The female kicked him again, connecting with his ankle. He jerked back to the present, still unable to see. "Gonna kill you. Fillet like a fish." Moira liked salmon, always had. He had a great baked salmon dish he wanted to cook for her. "Like to cook."

Under water. Was he underwater? Someone lifted him, dropping him face first into a rusted container. Pain scraped nails across his cheekbone. He began to roll, his stomach lurching. Darkness claimed him until agony ripped through his head. An eternity later, the back of his scalp slammed against a floor again, the humming of a motor vibrating his body. Helicopter?

The world spun as they lifted into the air. Rage tried to wind through the confusion in Conn's brain. With a roar, he kicked out as hard as he could, connecting with bone and flesh. A furious bellow filled the night, weakening into nothingness. Had he kicked someone out the door?

Sharp needles pierced his arm. He fell into sleep.

Chapter 19

Moira needed a diversion to get the hell out of the Kayrs fortress. She couldn't betray Conn or bring danger to Janie's doorstep. But she couldn't turn her back on family and the Nine, either. Her mind clicked through battle plans as she sat back in the folding chair, stretching her shoulders. Even while calculating her odds, she fought a grin as the Queen of the Realm exploded in temper.

"This is bullshit." Emma Paulsen, soon to be Kayrs, slammed a beaker down in the well-appointed lab. Test tubes lined the cement counter, along with a bunch of machines busy bleeping and spitting out data. The scent of bleach and cleanser ruled the room. "They go off to fight, and we're stuck underground not anywhere near the stuff I need at the lab." Her amazing blue eyes flashed in equal parts anger and fear.

"They'll be fine, Emma." Her sister Cara rubbed a very pregnant belly from a lush office chair, the luxurious recliner out of place in the stark lab, but obviously provided for her comfort. She surveyed a row of drawers with eyes the exact color of Emma's. "Any idea where Kane keeps his candy stash down here?" The drawers slid open without a hitch, and Cara sighed each time she slammed one shut. "I know he has chocolate somewhere."

Moira fought a chill at the cool air being pumped

through the vents, homesickness nearly swamping her. Brenna loved chocolate. Darcy would rather have caramel. They'd gone to blows over a Snickers once.

"Why isn't Kane in here working with you?" Maybe she could get him to help her out. Or at least trick him somehow. Of course, considering the guy was probably the smartest sentient being on the planet, the chances of that were slim. Rumor had it he could fight, and well.

Emma let out an elegant sniff. Wisps of black hair dropped out of the knot on top of her head to frame her narrow face as she smacked a manila file folder against her leg. "The oh-so-powerful Kayrs brother is working aboveground in the lab I need to be in. You know, the one with the vents allowing us to experiment with different elements?"

"Ah," Moira glanced at the row of beakers lining a shelf running a length of the counter. "You understand you're the queen and have to be protected at all costs, right?" If the woman thought the vampire nation would let her be in any danger, she was crazy. Not to mention that she was mated to Dage, probably one of the most protective mates on the planet.

Emma pivoted slowly, her lab coat whispering against her denim-clad legs. "Is that right?"

Uh-oh. "Well, I mean . . ."

The queen raised a dark eyebrow. "Well, using your logic, you're mated to a prince, Moira. Surely that means you need to be kept blanketed in safety at all times, too." The queen used sarcasm like a pro.

There had to be a good way to say this. "I'm trained, Emma. I mean, I'm an enforcer."

"What makes you think I can't fight?" Emma put both hands on her hips. "Not only do I kick ass, I can teleport. For the love of Pete, the king's abilities are mine. Almost."

Interesting. "That happened quickly. Well then, yeah.

You're right." Moira shrugged, eyeing the door. "I tried to get out when Conn left, but the security in this place is outrageous." She'd have to take out a vampire or seven to escape, and she would. "Do you know where the armory is?"

Cara laughed. "Yes. But, we're not letting you shoot your way out, Moira. Not until the guys get back, at least."

Although Moira had just spent the last half hour on the phone with her mother being ordered to stay in place, she'd find the armory on her own. The assurances that the Nine's soldiers had gone after Grace hadn't relieved her . . . considering no one knew where to look. Moira eyed her new friend. "So how's the babe? Ready to make his appearance?"

Cara bit her lip. "Yes. He kicks like crazy." A smile lit her stunning face. "It's nice knowing he has to be a boy since vampires only make boys. I painted his room green. Talen wanted blue, but the green reminded me of his eyes when he gets, ah, irritated." She rubbed her belly. "I'd like to get a sonogram and make sure the baby is fine." Her gaze focused on Moira. "Can you visualize a witch in the womb or are they protected from sight as well?"

"Sonograms only work on humans." The rest of the species on earth created too strong a shield for developing babies. Moira shrugged. "You're an empath. You feel how the babe is doing."

"Yeah, I do." A smaller smile flirted with Cara's lips. "He gives me a strong sense of peace, much like Janie did at this point. The boy is fine. Stubborn, like Talen." She closed her eyes, pursing her lips. Irritation flashed across her pale skin when her eyelids popped open. "The stupid virus—I can't reach Talen."

Emma peered into a microscope, her voice muffled. "He'd shield from you during the fight, anyway." She straightened, leaning sideways and scribbling notes in a chart. "My psychic abilities have focused solely on the virus lately. I wish I could aim the visions into the future where I want." She glanced over her shoulder, focusing on Moira. "Can you sense Conn?"

"No." Moira fought a frown. "We've worked so hard to shield each other the last century since we were living our own lives. I'm not sure if we'll be able to speak telepathically like you do. Or even if we can track each other." That would be convenient right now.

"You won't know unless you try." Cara leaned toward the counter, sliding open a drawer. With a triumphant "a-ha," she yanked out a candy bar.

Moira mentally listed the supplies most likely found in the lab. Brute strength wouldn't free her, but altering matter on a subatomic level might. Nothing like magic to blow a hole in a wall. "So, how's the progress on the virus coming?"

"That's what I'd like to hear." A woman swept into the room, blond hair cascading down her back and tawny eyes flashing. She held a large notebook in one hand.

"Moira, this is Katie Smith, our local friendly lion shifter." Emma tilted her head. "Katie, this is Moira, Conn's mate."

Katie held out a hand and smiled. "Hi. You saved Cara's baby months ago."

Moira shook. "No, not really. I merely helped Emma alter the matter in her cure to negate the catalyst." The Kurjans had created a catalyst that sped up the progression of the virus and Cara had been infected. Emma and Moira had neutralized the catalyst, thus slowing progression—but they hadn't altered the actual virus.

"Yes, you did." Cara licked chocolate off her fingers. "A debt I'll never be able to repay."

"You already made me an aunt with Janie, and now I

have a nephew on the way. We're even." Moira wondered what other types of candy Kane hid. She'd love a piece of butterscotch. Then she faltered. "I mean, well, I'm not married—"

"No stuttering here, girlfriend." Cara smiled, reaching for another candy bar. "Believe me, as a Kayrs mate, I get it. Confusion is a way of life."

Moira let out a relieved laugh. "Yes. Ah, thanks."

Katie shuffled her feet. The scent of wild orchids mixed with Cajun spices wafted around. "So, anything new with the virus?"

Midnight black hair flew when Emma shook her head. "The antivirals we've been experimenting with slow down the progression almost to a standstill. While the eight pills a day are a pain, at least they're giving us some time to find a complete cure."

Katie frowned, gliding toward the counter. "Are we doing more tests on the catalyst today?"

Moira lifted her head. "Are you a scientist, too?" Maybe the lion shifter would help her escape.

"No." Katie sighed. "I take notes. Emma does experiments, and I write stuff down. So helpful."

"You are helpful, Katie. And yes, we're doing more research on the catalyst today." Emma grabbed another file and nodded toward a row of syringes filled with golden liquid. "I thought we'd blend some with the werewolf blood Kane obtained, and mix in the HIV drugs used to treat humans."

"Are these normal doses or are we super dosing again today?" Katie asked.

"Normal doses," Emma said.

"Good. I do appreciate being able to help. At least I see what's going on." Katie nodded, placing her notebook next to the shots. "How did my blood tests come out from yesterday?"

Emma grabbed a blue file and flipped the top open to read. "Your tests were good. No change in the progression of the virus, which means the handful of pills you're taking every day is actually doing some good." She flipped the file shut, smiling. "We're buying time."

Katie shook her head. "I stopped taking the medication a month ago. Yet the virus is doing nothing."

Emma slammed down the file. "You stopped taking your pills? Katie, you're killing me."

Moira bit her lip. "Ah, you have the virus?" At Katie's nod, she continued, "Why stop taking the medication?"

"I can't shift." Shivering pain coated Katie's voice. "The second they infected me, I lost the ability to shift into a lion." Tears filled her bourbon colored eyes. "My friend, Maggie, is a wolf shifter and she was infected with the virus and the catalyst. Every month during a full moon she fights the need to turn into a werewolf, and turns into a wolf instead. She can still shift."

Moira had heard the Kurjans were trying to create a slave werewolf class, which would be stronger and live longer than humans turned werewolves. "I thought three cycles of a full moon and someone infected became a werewolf for good." Of course, that was only when a werewolf bit a human. Having shifters turn into werewolves was a whole new mess.

Katie nodded. "Yeah. We waited three full moons, thinking if Maggie beat them all, she'd be cured. Instead, she has to fight the urge every full moon." Emotion swirled through Katie's eyes. "Maggie can still shift into a wolf . . . at least once a month."

"So. There have actually been documented cases of shifters being infected." Moira wondered what else the leaders of the Realm had kept under wraps. She needed to notify the Coven Nine. "Since Maggie is a wolf shifter and you're a lion shifter, you might react differently to the virus." Shifters were canine, feline, or multi—those who could shift into any animal except canine or feline.

Emma huffed out a breath. "I've told Katie that repeatedly. We have no idea how the virus will continue to affect her. Hopefully the bug will be neutralized and go away, similar to a common cold." She slid the file into a drawer. "We think maybe the catalyst in Maggie's system is what allowed the virus to progress to the point of where she had to shift." A frown marred the queen's face. "But again, we don't know anything for sure, Katie. Quitting the medicine could be a huge mistake for you."

"Then I should take this all the way." Katie moved too fast for anyone to react. With impressive reflexes, she grabbed a syringe, shoving the needle into her arm and pressing the stopper. The shimmering liquid slid through the needle, leaving an empty threat behind.

Cara clapped her hands over her mouth. "Oh my God."

Emma dropped her pencil, her face sheeting white. "Katie. What did you just do?" She rushed forward, grabbing and turning Katie's arm to view the protruding needle.

"Don't worry. I've been doing my research on the catalyst and know how much to take." The lioness shrugged, removing the syringe and dropping the shot into a metal trash can. "I'm done waiting. Either this thing helps me shift again, or it kills me."

"You don't need to worry about the catalyst." Cara shoved herself to her feet, struggling with the last couple inches. The chair released her with a groan. She steadied herself with a hand on the counter. "Jordan is going to kill you."

Katie grabbed a rolling chair and dropped onto the seat, freeing herself from Emma. "The man keeps offering to mate with me. He thinks it might bring back my shifting ability."

"Mating might work," Emma hissed. "I'd rather experiment with Jordan than place poison in your veins." She
paced back and forth, her hand running through her hair.
"I can't believe you did this." Her gaze darted around the
counter. "I have nothing. There's *nothing* to inject you with
to counteract what you just did." She whirled on Katie,
her hands in the air. "I would've recommended mating
with Jordan as an experiment before you did something
like this."

A wry smile lifted Katie's lips. "First of all, the leader of
the entire feline world can't mate with someone unable to
shift." She shrugged. "Old-fashioned and probably wrong,
but you all know it's true."

Moira straightened. They had to be talking about Jordan Pride. She'd met the dangerous lion on several occasions. The man seemed to possess an abundance of honor
and duty. Would he mate out of duty? Somehow, based on
her knowledge of the passionate natures of shifters, she
doubted it.

"Jordan is capable of making his own decisions. He can
mate whoever he wants." Cara lifted her chin. "He offered, and I think you should've said yes. Considering
you love the man." Her hand trembled against her stomach.

Katie flushed pink. "Yeah, well, he never showed an
ounce of interest until deciding I needed saving. Sacrificing himself is merely one reason he's such a good leader."

Moira barely kept herself from nodding. She wouldn't
mate a guy who was trying to do her a favor. It was one
of the reasons she'd kept her distance from Conn all those
years. He'd stay with her out of duty. She wanted more.
Needed more. Tears pressured the back of her eyelids.
Sadness settled like a dead weight in her stomach. What if
he hadn't marked her that night? Would they have found
something together . . . on their own? Regretting such a

thing was silly, yet she couldn't help but wish they'd had a chance.

Katie dabbed at the blood still welling on her arm. "How long until this thing kicks in?"

Emma huffed out in irritation. "We don't know. Infection took a day with Cara, but she's human. This might take years with you." If possible, the queen paled further. Her hand went to her head. "Damn vision coming." She swayed and only Moira's quick movements kept her from falling to the floor.

She grabbed the queen under the armpits, faltering and assisting her to the stone floor. Pressing Emma against the cupboards to prevent her from pitching forward, Moira balanced her friend with hands against her shoulders. "What's wrong?"

Tears filled Emma's eyes. Her face pinched in pain. "It's Conn. He's gone."

The clouds opened up, beating them with rain turning to ice as it dropped. Dage Kayrs used his boot to roll the man over, a frown on his face. He left a size sixteen muddy print in the guy's side. "Panther." He sniffed the air, his gut beginning to clench. "I smell Conn. This guy grappled with Conn." It looked like the shifter had been tossed down a mountain. Or out a helicopter. Dage had heard the bird lift, but had been wrestling with two demons at the time.

The downed panther didn't move, his breath shallow, his nose smashed nearly flat.

Jordan Pride sprinted over, his lip twisted into a snarl. A gash bled across his left cheekbone. "That's Robert Wright, a soldier for the clan."

The clan leader knelt, running his gaze over the injured man. "Wright, hold on. We have a medical team coming." Jordan frowned. "I smell Conn all over him." Glancing around, he studied the smoldering building, the bodies of a few demons littering the ground, as well as their wounded. A low growl escaped. "We didn't meet enough resistance to warrant a fight, Dage."

"This was a trap." Dage fought to rein his temper. They'd fought about ten demons, all woefully undertrained. Newbies. But they'd managed to mess with his mind to the point a cloud still slowed his thought processes. "Yeah, and I'm thinking your shifter friends were in on the plan." Otherwise none of this made sense. Where were the captured shifters? Why had Conn fought with this guy?

Jase jogged up, wiping blood off his forehead. "I found a dead shifter three stories down, with Conn's scent all over him." He tossed a dart with black feathers for Dage to catch. "Several of these littered the floor—and I found a tunnel leading outside. The pine needles and grass were crushed, probably by the helicopter we heard."

"They drugged him?" They would have needed a boatload of tranquilizers . . . and a changing mixture to keep him down. Dage gave a short nod to a medic rushing forward with a kit and pointed to Wright. "Wake him up."

The medic's eyebrow rose in his dark face, but he knelt and conducted a brief examination. The wind whipped hair into his mouth, and he spit out the strands. "If I inject him with adrenaline, he may die."

Jordan growled, fury digging into the lines of his face. "Will he have a chance to talk first?"

The medic cut his gaze to Dage and back. "He might have a few minutes, but I can't guarantee it." Flipping open his pack, he grabbed a syringe, shielding it from the elements with his body. "Shifters are tough to kill, but they can die by internal bleeding if the injuries are great enough." He ran his fingers over what appeared to be broken ribs. "I'd say the injuries are life-threatening here. We need to get him to the hospital in Canada."

"We're going to need more hospitals," Jordan murmured.

"Already in the works." Dage had ordered the creation of new medical facilities the second the Kurjans had declared war. "I purchased the real estate decades ago and have been earmarking funds for construction as well as scholarships for medical training." He'd doubled the order for hospitals when the demons had joined in the war. Now it appeared some of the shifter allies he thought he'd had were coming after him. If the witches withdrew from the Realm, he was screwed. For one second he flashed back to the last war centuries ago, when his parents had been killed and he'd needed to step up. He'd thought the pain and difficulty had been because of his youth.

He was wrong.

Men hustled around, collecting the wounded. "What should I do?" the medic asked, wiping rain off his forehead.

Jordan dropped into a crouch. The rain mingled with the spattered blood, turning his blond hair a matted red. "Inject him."

At Dage's nod, the medic plunged a syringe into the cat's chest. Wright gasped, his entire body clenching, and then relaxing. "What—" He opened blood-filled eyes, blinking to focus. Vibrations from his pain shimmered in the air.

Jordan lowered his face. "Where did they take Connlan Kayrs?" He placed one hand against Wright's ribs.

The medic opened his mouth to object, and Dage jerked his head toward the burning building. "We have injured over by the tree line. Go help." The vampire took one last hard look at Wright, grabbed his kit, and hurried off. Dage settled his stance, letting Jordan handle his man, who was obviously too weak to shift.

Wright's eyes widened. He coughed, the rattle spitting clotted blood out his mouth. He blinked against the rain.

Jordan pressed down. "Tell me or I swear to God, I'm going to yank each rib out of you one at a time." His voice lowered to a guttural rumble sounding more animal than man.

Wright bellowed in pain, his shoulders spasming and scattering pine needles. "I . . . fuck you," he gasped, his legs kicking out.

Jordan dug his fingers in, and Wright shrieked, the sound like death a day late. Grabbing the panther's hair and yanking back, Jordan lowered his face to an inch away. "That was nothing. My knife comes out next. Where is Kayrs?"

Wright's eyes fluttered, his shoulders relaxed. "Dunno," he slurred, smiling blood covered canines. "Wouldn't tell us. Just get you, get on helicopter."

Smart. Dage crossed his arms. "Whoever planned this figured you wouldn't make it, Robert. Not a lot of faith in you."

Jordan leaned back. "You planned this to trap me? Why?"

Wright coughed, sending blood flying. "We know"—he gasped out—"you're mating a werewolf. And . . . Caleb."

"Caleb?" Dage dropped to his haunches to better hear. "Your clan isn't one that has fought with Caleb over the years for supporting his brother."

Jordan snarled. "Katie's not a werewolf, you prick. She has a virus."

Wright closed his eyes. "Realm's weak. Time to take over." His head trembling, his eyes slowly opened to focus on Jordan. "You're weak. Marcus is strong." His lids fluttered shut. One rattling exhale whooshed out of his lungs, and his body relaxed in death.

Jordan stood, turning his back on the panther. "Marcus Paltrow, the head of the clan." He waved an arm at his enforcers. "I'll get the word out . . . we'll find Conn." Pivoting, he jogged over to confer with his men.

Dage tapped his ear communicator.

"Did you save the shifters?" Kane said by way of answer, the typing of computer keys ticking across the line.

"It was a trap. They wanted Jordan and took Conn."

The typing stopped. Kane exhaled slowly, giving Dage his full attention.

"Marcus Paltrow engineered the trap. Find him."

"On it." Kane clicked off.

Neither of them said what couldn't be said. If the shifters had wanted Jordan, Conn would be more of a liability than asset. Dage surveyed the medics patching up his men.

Jase cleared his throat. "They could've killed him in the tunnels."

An explosion of energy ripped through Dage's system, so he kept his face bland. "The group was supposed to get Jordan, failed, so they took who they could. I'm assuming their leader will create a plan."

Jase cocked an eyebrow in direct contrast to the hand clenching and unclenching at his side. "A plan? Dage, we're talking about Conn, the greatest soldier ever born. He won't break."

Dread slid down Dage's trachea to settle in his gut. "No. *Breaking* Conn won't be the point." Dage waited until Jase's eyes widened with realization, then raw fury. "Exactly."

"They wouldn't."

"Sure they would. Publicly decapitating the most powerful soldier ever born to the Realm? How weak would we look?"

If Conn died, the ensuring war would coat the earth in

blood. Not to mention what it'd do to Dage personally—as well as to his brothers. "Thinking as a king, the move would be bold and send a message."

"And thinking as a brother?" Jase asked, no longer wiping the shredding rain off his face.

Power coiled inside Dage, careening to shoot out. Force of will, tenuous and fading, shoved it down. "As a brother, I'd unleash hell." He believed in mercy. And right or wrong, he believed in vengeance. The two rarely existed during the same span of time. If the shifters beheaded his brother, mercy would cease to exist.

"Have faith in Conn, Dage."

"I do." If he didn't, he'd be ripping through the shifting clans for answers, not caring who he hurt. He eyed Jordan talking to his enforcers. "Sounds like the shifting clans are as unsettled as the Realm right now." The world was exploding.

Talen raced up, smashing wet pine needles into the snow.

Dage centered himself. "Report."

Talen tucked a knife into his pocket. "We've cleared the entire facility. Five demons down, the rest made it out the back as the first charge blew." He glanced down at the dead shifter. "Counting this guy, two dead shifters, neither Jordan's. We have three wounded, not seriously." Emerald overtook the gold in Talen's dangerous eyes. "And my brother is gone."

Chapter 20

Moira settled Emma on the smooth rock floor of the underground lab. "Is there any water?"

Katie rushed over and grabbed a bottle from the refrigerator, unscrewing the cap and handing it to the trembling queen.

Emma took a deep swallow, pressing her hand to her head. "Damn migraines." She opened her eyes, squinting into the light.

"What did you see?" Moira dropped to her haunches. Two of her sisters were psychic, but they didn't react in pain. Maybe vampire mates had a tougher time of it—though current science hinted enhanced humans were distant cousins to the witches. Fear swirled in her abdomen. "How is Conn hurt?"

Emma shuddered out a sigh. "I don't know. He went down . . . and pain cut into my leg. Then everything went black."

A roaring filled Moira's ears. Panic stopped her breath. Oh God. Not Conn.

The door swept open. Moira leaped up, pivoting to protect the queen. Kane Kayrs stood in the doorway, dressed in all black, his thick dark hair ruffled and his eyes an angry dark violet. His gaze dropped to Emma. "Vision?"

"Yes." Emma pushed to her feet, her hands trembling as she gripped the counter. "I saw Conn go down, but not much afterwards. He seemed, well, fuzzy."

"The shifters drugged him." Kane tilted his head toward the desk. "Migraine medicine is stashed in the top drawer for you. Just in case." He surveyed the room, his gaze landing on Moira. "Conn's your mate. I need you to reach out and find his location."

Moira swallowed hard. Fear threatened to overwhelm her senses. Light blue energy flickered on her arms. "We've spent the last century shielding ourselves from each other, Kane. I don't have a sense of Conn."

Fury at herself ripped along her spine at the time she'd wasted. Why had she waited for Conn to show up in Ireland? She could've sought him out—made it work between them. Then she could've been a link between the witches and the Realm . . . so there wouldn't be a movement to withdraw. Oh God. She loved the vampire.

Kane nodded. "I understand. Come with me, I have an idea." He pivoted on his heel, heavy footsteps echoing down the hall.

She'd do anything. Moira raised both eyebrows at the empty doorway. "Please tell me he isn't going to suck my brain out or something." The combined scents of bleach and lemon cleanser from the lab rolled a large pit in her stomach. Or maybe that was from fear and helplessness.

Emma snorted. "If Kane thought that would get him results, he'd take your whole head." She placed a hand on Moira's arm. "I'm sure Conn's all right. He's a fighter, Moira."

"I know." He'd been hurt, according to Emma. Who could get close enough to injure Conn? Moira sighed. "No matter how calm and logical Kane is, he can't get into my head." Even if she agreed to let him, her shields had strength of their own. And as an enforcer, she could kick serious ass. She'd figure out a way to get Conn back.

Cara glided closer, her hand over her belly. "Kane isn't anything near calm. He's furious." She pursed her lips. "Fighting serious guilt. Probably thinks he could've helped had he gone on the raid, instead of continuing to work on the virus." She paled and bent at the waist. "Ow. The kid's a kicker." Straightening, she rubbed her side. "Do you want me to come with you? An empath might help."

Warmth flowed through Moira. She had friends. Well, almost family. "No. I can do this." She strode toward the door. "Thanks, though." Sconces lit the rock walls of the hallway as she took the direction Kane had taken, not surprised to find him waiting for her outside an open doorway. "What's in there?"

"My humble abode." Kane gestured her inside.

She swept by him, realizing her head barely reached the top of his chest. For some reason she'd never noticed his size . . . always concentrating on his big brain. The Kayrs size. She'd always appreciated Conn's hulking size. What if he was hurt? The tinkling of water over rocks stopped her tormented thoughts, and she surveyed the peaceful room. "This place is all Zen."

Kane shut the door, stalking around a wide leather couch to survey his space. "Yeah. When I'm down here, I like to relax."

A deep screen showed a tranquil lake on a spring day. Dark furnishings and soft lighting lent coziness to the living room, much like her father's study. Maleness permeated the space with a heavy sense of safety, like that she felt at Daire's hunting lodge on the southern coast of Ireland. Rich oil paintings of fantasy scenes adorned the walls. "I figured you'd go more for the modern glass and steel look."

Kane patted the back of an overstuffed chair. "I spend

enough time around glass and chrome in the lab. Now
stop being nervous and come sit down."

Just because her hands were sweating and butterflies on
crack winged through her stomach didn't mean she was
nervous. Taking a deep breath, because the room smelled
like cinnamon and vanilla and not because her lungs
ached, she skirted the sofa and dropped into the chair.

Kane grabbed the matching chair and shifted it to the
side so they could sit face-to-face. He sat and held out
both hands. "Put your palms on mine."

Bugger. Moira wiped her hands on her jeans, reaching
out to place them over Kane's much bigger ones. Her
hands shook. "What now?"

Slap! Kane flipped his hands over and smacked hers in a
game as old as time. "I win."

Moira jerked away. Surprised humor rippled through
her and she coughed a laugh. "Very funny."

Kane sat back, amusement flitting across his angled face.
He had the same stubborn jaw as Conn, but his cheekbones seemed higher, even sharper. "You need to relax."

He was right. She took several deep breaths, forcing her
shoulders to lower and her hands to steady. Mates should
be able to communicate telepathically, but she sucked as a
mate. "Okay. What now?" Conn couldn't be really hurt.

"How about we try some deep relaxation techniques?"

She'd rather hit something. "I'm not sure I can be hyp-
notized, Kane."

"No worries. Let's work on relaxing. Open your mind
up a little to seek out Conn. A trial experiment to attempt
a connection."

Well, she'd heard of worse ideas. "If I do this, will you
help me get back aboveground?" She needed to be on the
front lines, yet truly didn't want to raid the armory and
have to shoot her way out of the king's headquarters. But
she would.

"No."

He could've at least considered the option. Moira sighed. "What should I do?"

"I want you to close your eyes and concentrate on your breathing. Good air in, bad air out." Kane's voice softened. "Start with your toes, relaxing and letting all tension ebb away. Move up to your calves, working on your legs, hips, ribs, heart and so on until you get to your head."

She'd meditated before. Kane was rushing this, probably in a hurry to find his brother. So was she. "Conn knows how to manipulate matter with energy," she murmured, concentrating on her breath and allowing stress to flow away from her skin.

"I know."

Her eyelids flipped open. "Did you teach him?"

A smile threatened. "Ah, no. He tried to teach me. Burned the crap out of my eyebrows." Kane settled into the leather. "Something about the process escaped me."

Yeah, a high intelligence wasn't enough. "Altering matter with energy takes more than studying quantum physics, Kane. You need to *feel* the change as much as think it." She glanced around. Even in the comfortable room, the heaviness of the rock above pressed down.

"I don't comprehend 'feeling.' Logic and thought . . . that's what matters." Kane studied her, reaching and pressing the button on a remote. The screen shifted from the lake to a full moon, the light leaping from the wall. A deep forest spread out beneath the sky, the trees so thick they blurred into one long, free form.

Moira's eyes misted. "How did you know?"

"You're a witch." He ran a hand through his hair, leaving it ruffled. "I don't understand the power you get from the moon, but so long as you believe it's there, we'll use it."

The glimmering body seemed to draw Moira in, offering a comfort of sorts. Her arms grew weightless, as if she floated an inch under a lake's surface. "Some argue the moon has feminine energy, which explains most female witches being stronger than males. Some, not all. Lunar power does exist—just look at the influence of the moon on the tides." Speaking of influence, her head rolled back against the cushion. "What did you do?"

"Nothing. You relaxed yourself. Nicely done." A rustle sounded and the scent of male and smoldering amber wafted around her. "Now close your eyes and picture Conn."

Conn filled her head. Green eyes, powerful shoulders, smart-assed grin. Connlan Kayrs shoved every other thought to hell. The look in his eye as he'd taken her on the plane shot through her memories, speeding up her heart rate. She pulled in air to fill her chest, forcing her body to stay calm. "I found him."

"Okay. Now reach out to him."

She tried. As if calling someone on a cell phone, she sent a question through time, through space to find him—a cosmic hello. Magic swirled around her brain along with science. Yet she couldn't accept the thought of speaking into someone else's mind. How was it possible? Well . . . waves carried light, they carried sound . . . cell phones worked with radio waves. Thought waves, especially those coming from power, certainly made sense. Maybe she could do this.

"Stop thinking. Try and find Conn." Kane failed to mask the bite in his words. "While I can't figure out how, there's no denying the fact my mated brothers can speak telepathically with their mates. So do so."

Moira dug her nails into the leather. "I am trying." Accepting the possibility of telepathing her thoughts into Conn's stubborn head equaled a huge leap of faith for her. "Now stop interrupting me." Damn Kayrs brothers. Bossy,

each and every one of them. Something she'd complain to
Conn about when he arrived home.

She allowed the earth to warm her feet. *Conn?* His
name echoed around her head, but nothing came back.
No images, no feelings, not even a vague sense. Irritated,
she opened her eyes and caught Kane without his mask
on. He quickly yanked down a veil to shield the anger and
urgency filling his eyes. Calm interest remained.

She tugged her neck to the side, popping out the tension. "You're concerned."

"Yes." He rubbed his chin. "If whoever took Conn is
smart, and we have to assume they are, considering they
succeeded, they'll know to kill him."

"Why?" Her voice cracked. A fear she'd kept at bay
clenched her stomach.

"If they don't, they'll die. Conn will make sure of it." A
matter-of-fact tone rode Kane's words, but the air around
him tensed.

What if they kept Conn drugged? He had to be alive.
As his mate, wouldn't she at least be able to sense if he
stopped living? Her gaze landed on a crystal figurine of a
frog glinting in the muted light, perched haphazardly on
the side table. She grabbed it, the coolness comforting her
palms. "Are you attached to this?"

"No." Kane leaned back in the thick chair, his arms on
the rests. Tension radiated from him, scattering waves
and disrupting the peace of the room. "Some woman I
dated in the seventies threw that at my head when she
dumped me." The vampire shrugged. "Apparently I was a
toad who couldn't commit."

Moira frowned. "Why keep it?"

"Why not?"

Indeed. Well, if he wasn't attached to the little bugger,
maybe she could center herself better. Perching the frog

on her palm, Moira tilted her head to probe into the shine. Particles swam before her eyes, morphing out and in, assuming the form of the amphibian, then free forming into a ball. The glow dimmed as she dug deeper, going for the subatomic particles, seeing them, feeling them. Focusing a gentle wave, she cascaded energy throughout, scattering them to vibrate in a different configuration.

Light shimmered, expressed in particles and waves. A glow centered around the ball, crackling with her energy. She tossed the circle to her other hand, allowing the light to shift from white to blue and back to white. Joy in the creating, in the altering of matter to energy warmed her.

She sent out a message to Conn.

Pain slammed into her solar plexus. She cried out, drawing her stomach in, dropping the ball. The energy burned a hole in the antique rug, whishing out to nothingness. She jerked her head into the cushions. "He hurts. So bad. Ribs, neck, well . . . everywhere." Tears stabbed behind her eyes.

"Focus, Moira." Kane leaned forward, his hands cupping her knees. Heat flowed from his palms. "Where is he? What do you see?"

Nothing. She didn't see a damn thing. Pain ripped along her spine. *Conn?*

Moira? While faint, his voice filtered across her consciousness.

Yes. Where are you? Open your eyes.

Can't. Swollen shut. Love you.

Pain exploded in her head. Then nothing. Whatever connection they'd found disappeared.

She scrubbed away tears. "He's hurt. No clear vision, doesn't know where he is." He said he loved her. "I think he fell unconscious at the end because everything went dark." Conn passed out. He wasn't dead. "I didn't feel a knife at his neck or anything like that." Her voice quivered, and she cleared her throat as she wondered who she was trying to convince—Kane or herself?

Kane wiped a rough hand across his mouth, his eyes shifting to black. Vampires had dual-colored eyes; the tertiary color emerged only in times of great emotion. She'd wondered what Kane's color would be. Now she wished she didn't know. "Did you smell anything?"

She lifted her chin, shutting her eyes. "Blood and dirt."

"Hear anything?"

"The drip of water . . . like on stone. An echo, something hollow."

"Feel anything but pain?" Kane continued to shoot questions at her, not giving her a chance to stop and think.

"Rope against my wrists, hands high above." They were torturing him. Rage ripped through her system, the need to draw blood filming a haze over her vision. She'd find them. And she'd rip their heads off.

"See anything?"

"No. Just darkness." Moira leaped to her feet. "We need to go. We have to go and find him. *Now!*" She may be confused as hell about the man, but nobody tortured her mate.

Chapter 21

Conn concentrated on his left femur, mentally shoving the bone back into place. Except it didn't move. The smell of earth and raw flesh filled his senses. His flesh. Water dripped somewhere in the distance, teasing him. He needed a drink.

Water would do.

Blood would do better.

He'd lost most of his. While losing all blood wouldn't kill a vampire, it'd destroy his brain, and he'd live forever in a vegetative state. He trusted his brothers to cut his head off at that point.

Conn blinked, sending any healing force he owned to reduce the swelling around his eyes. Neurons fired with pain from every cell in his body. The steel corded ropes cut into his wrists as he hung from the ceiling. A shiny, new lock kept the ropes attached to rings in the ceiling of the cell. Ten feet wide, eleven feet deep, it had a dirt floor and one exit. Exposed rebar stuck out of solid walls where they'd built his cage into the rock. Smart. Most walls he'd plow through, but not a mountain.

The bars appeared to be steel and the door his only escape. He was aboveground, the enclosure dug into rock. A cell designed to hold Jordan, and currently trapping Conn.

His bare toes curled into the dust, his heels inches up. His shirt and most of his pants were shredded from hits with spiked metal bats.

A light haze wandered through his mind, and he shook his head to clear his thinking. The assholes had used him for target practice from safely on the other side of the bars. They'd aimed darts loaded with drugs at the space between his eyes.

And waited for the sedative to take effect before entering with weapons. Smart bastards.

Moira had called into his head. Even with pain catching the breath in his throat, pleasure fought through. For seconds, she'd been with him. His mate. Then she was gone. Hours ago, possibly a whole day. Too bad he couldn't show her where they kept him. An hour's flight, maybe two from where he'd raided the demon's holding—might be in any direction. More light filtered through his pupils. Ah, good. He visualized bouncing gold healing cells to the mangled tissue, which relaxed across his brow. His focus sharpened. The blood in his veins attacked the drugs, learning to metabolize the sedative faster.

A spiked bat rested against the thick-planked wall outside his cell in another small, empty room with a door. Was this the only area built into the rock? Exposed bulbs hung from cords nailed into the rough ceilings, illuminating him enough for his captors to see when they swung the bats. Two metal folding chairs rested next to the weapon still dripping with his blood.

The door skidded open through the dirt. Marcus shoved his way inside, pivoting to force it closed. The bottom caught several times on the way. A strap held yet another dart gun over his shoulder.

Conn curled a lip. "Some moron cut the door too long."

Marcus stilled, turning around. "Apparently not all of the darts hit the mark." He shrugged, kicking a chair open and dropping down. His nearly yellow gaze flicked over Conn.

The vampire stared back.

Like most cats, Marcus preferred light, loose clothing in khaki and linen.

Conn would appreciate the red staining the guy's duds more if it hadn't been his own blood. "You know, I dated a woman centuries ago who wore her hair in a braid like that." What kind of a guy French braided his hair?

Marcus lifted one shoulder. "Yes, well, I kept getting your blood in it. The woman I'm dating *now* braided it for me." Mainly black with red tints, the mane showed the cat's genetics. Pure panther.

"So what's your endgame here, Marcus?" Torture hadn't gleaned the location of the Realm's new headquarters from Conn. He'd lose his head before giving up his family.

Marcus sniffed his feline nose, rubbing thick hair along his dark jaw line. "I want Jordan."

"You're not his type."

Something lurked in the panther's eyes . . . rage went deeper than political gain.

"Why do you want him so badly? His death won't guarantee you leadership of the pride." In fact, there were several lions, panthers, and cougs more likely to take over for Jordan if the lion fell.

The cat's shoulders went back. His chest puffed out. His eyes flicked green. "Let's just say I owe him."

Interesting. Conn's thoughts sped up to normal. The drugs faded away like mist after a storm and he began to think clearly. Who was Marcus? Panther clan . . . answered to Jordan . . . Marcus Paltrow. Yeah, that was the guy's name. Conn had met the shifter at the Realm Colloquium last year.

The dripping water continued, swelling Conn's tongue.

His fangs lowered. Time to piss this guy off. "You don't stand a chance against Jordan. I've known Pride for centuries. He'd rip your head off and then go hunting breakfast while whistling." Though it'd be severely off-key. Pride had no ear for tune.

Marcus leaped to his feet, a mottled red filling his face. "Bullshit. I could kick Pride's ass in a second. God knows the bastard deserves it. After . . ."

Conn frowned, his memories slamming back. "Dating. You said the woman you're dating braided your hair." A small panther with sharp little teeth had stood by Marcus' side during the colloquium. "What happened to your mate?"

Electricity crackled against the panther's skin as he wavered, his face shimmering, desperate fury filling his eyes. If the prick shifted, at that distance the blast would break every bone in Conn's body.

Marcus bared his teeth, clenching his jaw until the skin rolled up into layers. With a shudder, he relaxed. "They turned her human. She killed herself."

Conn clenched his wrists. "She was infected with the virus? When?"

"At the colloquium." Marcus raised the gun and fired a dart into Conn's neck. "Jordan Pride *ordered* us to attend, to give a show of support for the Realm. The bastard knew the virus was out there . . . he knew we exposed ourselves."

The dart stung for a mere second. Conn's system handled the sedative, absorbing the drug into his tissues. He let his eyelids droop. "Why didn't you tell us? We've been working on a cure."

"I don't trust you." Marcus hissed the words, firing again. "You've allowed Caleb back in. You've failed to protect your own mates from the Kurjan virus. The demons are after you."

Ah, the demons. "Yes. Yet you're working with them." The demons as a whole considered shifters tantamount to talented pets. Just slightly above humans. A demon mated a shifter once in a blue moon, but it was rare, and all the more cause for insult when Caleb's brother mated a shifter betrothed to a demon. "Are you a demon's pet, Marcus?"

The panther scowled. "You're a shortsighted idiot, Kayrs. The demons agreed to assist us with this little trap, in exchange for seeing you folks in action. My guess is they're coming up with battle plans . . ."

Conn's sneer drooped. "They sent newbies . . . untrained soldiers to report back. They didn't care if you succeeded, asshole."

Marcus caressed his gun, his gaze assessing. "I didn't get Pride, thus I didn't succeed. The lion's time will come. He'll pay for what he did to my people."

Another mate had been infected and the bastard hadn't even contacted them. Conn forced his shoulders to slump and his words to slur. "Who else, Marcus? Who else did they get?"

The cat studied him for a moment, rage and pain flickering in his eyes. "They got five from my clan. I haven't heard of any others." He shrugged the gun off his shoulder to lean against the wall. "Two are females, who lost the ability to shift."

Conn barely kept his head from jerking up. Drugged. He needed to appear drugged. "Any males infected?" The virus didn't infect vampires, all whom were male and had more chromosomal pairs than every other race except for demons. The scientists believed that was what protected them from the virus. They'd been waiting for confirmation that the virus infected male shifters.

"Three males." Marcus gripped the bars with whitened knuckles. "And guess what, Kayrs?" His voice lowered to a hiss. "They didn't lose the ability to shift. Sure, the moon had to be full. They shifted into something that . . ." The color drained from his angular face. A snarl ripped from his throat. "We had to kill them all."

Jesus. The Kurjans might be successful in creating a werewolf slave class from shifters.

"So going after Jordan isn't a political move. You want revenge." Conn understood. If someone killed Moira, he'd burn the earth dry for vengeance. But he'd go after the right people, the ones at fault.

"Turning against the Realm won't help you find justice." He concentrated, and his femur popped back into place.

"Sure it will." Marcus smiled. "I know about you, Kayrs, and your great friendship with Jordan Pride. His buddy, his comrade in war, dying in his place? This will kill him." Marcus cracked his knuckles. "Taking you out serves revenge and my political agenda. Good thing you showed up in that tunnel."

A vehicle rumbled by outside. Men's voices echoed in the distance. Ah. Conn's senses were returning. But man, he needed blood.

The door shoved open again, catching at several points and scattering dirt. Metal glinted from a tripod as a teenager quickly set a video camera on top, his movements smooth and economical. He took a moment to glare over his shoulder, his eyes full of hate, his features a younger version of Marcus'. "We're gonna make you truly immortal, vampire scum."

Even annoyed, empathy for the boy slid through Conn. He'd lost his mother when a mere twenty years old, and the wound still cut deep. He doubted the surly teenager would appreciate the sympathy, though, and wondered if the kid had streaked his hair a bright blue and pierced his nose, chin, and ears before his mother died. Adrenaline began to pump through Conn's meager amount of blood.

Marcus jerked his head toward the door. "Tell Roland to bring in the blowtorch."

With another venomous glare, the teenager loped away.

"Your son?" Conn asked.

"Yes." Marcus fiddled with the camera until a green light blinked.

"I'm surprised you'd let him witness you torturing someone." Jase had been thrust into war at the age of fifteen, and it had been a mistake. Kids should be protected from life.

"He deserves vengeance." Marcus grabbed the gun in one hand, levering the barrel toward Conn's chest. "I can't broadcast your death in real time, as the king would trace our location. But I can video the removal of your head for the entire Realm to enjoy."

"You'll die before I do, Marcus." Conn's head lolled on his shoulders as he formulated a plan. He was getting tired of pretending to be drugged. When the hell was Marcus going to make a move?

"Even if you didn't, my brothers would spend their last breath hunting you down like the vermin you are, taking turns slicing the skin from your body." Not to mention his mate. Moira would track the bastard as well. Pride filled him along with unease. While the woman was trained, she lacked the physical strength to really fight. Good thing she made her own weapons with energy.

"Your brothers are weak." Marcus kicked the chair out of the way. "Even the Coven Nine is aligning with the demons against you, which means the end. For the Kayrs lineage at least." He angled the tripod closer to the bars. "First I'm going to beat you bloody. Well, bloodier. Then I plan to start you on fire. Finally, we'll slice your head off. Everyone will see the weakness of the Realm." Grabbing the gun, he fired three darts into Conn's abs.

Conn let out a fake snarl and jerked against his restraints, turning to face the back wall and sagging down.

"Damn it," Marcus huffed. "Kayrs, turn around. I need your agony to be seen."

Conn let out a low groan, his body staying lax.

The bars rattled and the earthy scent of panther wafted closer. The air swished around Conn, and pain immediately exploded at the base of his spine. He hadn't expected Marcus to swing the bat. Three more hits came in rapid succession, the metal spikes ripping flesh from his bones. Half of his remaining kidney ripped apart, staying attached to the bat.

No more. With a growl that came from beyond his soul, Conn twisted around, kicking the bat and pulling himself up high enough to clap his knees to Marcus' neck. The bat slammed against the rock wall with a vibrating hum. Marcus bellowed in protest. Conn balanced himself with the steel ropes and his prey's body.

He levered back, tightening his knees harder against the panther's jugular, ignoring the shards of pain shooting through his internal organs.

Marcus grabbed for Conn's thighs, his face turning purple, his mouth opening to gasp for air. His fingertips dug in, seeking release. A shimmering glowed along his skin.

Conn twisted, anger hazing his vision. "You start to shift and I'll break your neck." He needed to keep the guy alive to get out of there safely. "Give me the key."

Marcus' cheeks billowed out like those of a fish in a cartoon. He clenched his hand into a fist, pummeling Conn's battered thigh. Shredded tendons and destroyed muscles screamed in agony. With a quick jerk, Marcus reached for his back pocket, swinging up and plunging a double-edged knife into Conn's knee. Tissue and muscle opened up like a sardine can.

Fire cascaded through his leg. He roared, his nervous system igniting to fight. A twist of his hips snapped the panther's neck. Marcus dropped to the ground with a dull thud.

Don't feel. Think. Conn spit out blood, his mind roiling, his gut clenching. Moira's pretty green eyes flashed into his head. Dizziness swamped him. The bastard had pierced his femoral artery. Blood he couldn't afford to lose washed down his leg. Sparkling dots scattered across his vision.

Conn? Where the hell are you? Feminine, not so sweet, Moira's voice whispered through his consciousness. Insistent, demanding and . . . concerned.

Dunno. His head rolled to the side for real. *Need a snack.*

You can snack on me when you return. Her voice strengthened. They were getting better at telepathics. *Look around. What do you see?*

The urgency in her tone centered him. His eyes snapped open. *Hold on, Dailtín.* This was going to fucking hurt. Shoving pain away from the surface, he grabbed the steel ropes, swinging his head back and his legs into the air, bending at the knees. The knife handle smacked into his hand. His low growl of pain competed with the shrieking one he kept inside.

Biting his lip, he rotated his hold, yanking the knife out. His breath caught in his gut. His heart may have stopped. He was unable to control his legs. They dropped back to the ground, one foot landing on the dead shifter's chest. Pain hurled through Conn and he sucked the waves in. Rode them. Welcomed them until they ebbed. Time wasn't his friend. Someone would come looking for Marcus soon.

His wrist rotated, and he shoved the blade into the lock, twisting until scraps of metal fell onto his face. He jabbed the blade up harder. The lock released with a snap. Sparks flew as the rope unraveled. Like a newborn foal, he dropped to his knees into a pool of his own blood, prickles detonating along his neck and shoulders.

Conn? Where the hell are you? Moira snapped words into his head like a drill sergeant counting push-ups. Jesus. He was half-dead here. Shouldn't the woman be whispering sweet nothings into his brain . . . cajoling him to return to her?

Hold your horses. Eyeing Marcus with distaste, Conn grabbed the shifter by the shoulders. His fangs shot down, and he dug them into the panther's neck, drinking deep, allowing the nutrient-rich liquid to balm his insides, if not his outside yet.

A jolt of power washed through his body. His connection with Moira snapped closed. Damn. He actually felt bereft.

Energy filtered up Conn's spine, even as he tossed the shifter away. The spicy taste of panther, especially male, lingered on his tongue. He needed a mint. Taking a deep breath, sending healing cells to the worst of his wounds, he patted Marcus down.

Oh yeah. Conn slid a cell phone from the shifter's back pocket, flipped it open, and dialed.

"Kayrs." Only someone who knew Dage well would recognize the stress and fury riding under the king's low tone.

"Kayrs28877." Conn gave the ALL RIGHT code and edged out of the cell, grabbing the metal bat in his free hand. He shook off the remains of his kidney to the ground. Into the phone he growled, "Miss me?"

Two beats of silence. "Are you gone?" Rapid typing echoed across the line.

"Funny. Don't know where I am, could probably use backup." Even with the panther's blood, the wound in his leg still bled. Not as bad, but it sure wasn't closing. His vision still wavered. Maybe he wasn't as immune to the drugs as he'd hoped.

"We're tracing your location now." Dage's tone rose slightly and his footsteps pounded across the distance. "I'll teleport when we get a lock and the others will meet us via air." He paused, the sound of a belt hitting the floor.

"No. I don't know what I'm facing." Conn shook his head. Dage could teleport, but no metal or weapons of any kind could arrive with him. "Come by helicopter, scout the area." He grasped the doorknob, slowly twisting.

"No." Dage used his king voice. "Do I need to bring Talen?"

"No." Teleporting together would greatly weaken Dage. "If you're showing up, I need you in top form." Conn didn't argue further. Nothing on earth would keep his brother away. King or not.

Tugging the door open an inch, Conn set his stance and eyed the silent room beyond.

Movement sounded through the phone, and Talen's voice rose over the typing of keys. "He's here." Tapping echoed. "Compound in the Rocky Mountains, thirty minutes from Denver." The cocking of a gun overrode the keyboard. "There's one building dug into the mountain . . . guarded by three men outside."

Relief filled Conn. At least they knew where he was.

His relief quickly slid to dread as he scouted his escape route. "Ah, you need to stay away." His eyesight had returned to the point that he could decipher laser triggers set throughout. A keypad protruded from the wall next to his head. If a blast hit just right, it might blow him to pieces. "The place is wired tight—the room I'm in and probably the outside, too. Tell Moira—"

"Tell her yourself," Dage growled. "Talen, bring up the building in infrared."

Ah, Dage's new toy. "That won't help me at this point.

I'm going to blow the place, and hope the explosion sends me sky-high and not to hell." Conn tried to contact Moira directly, but only static met his attempt. If he lived through this, they really needed to work on that skill.

"That's a stupid idea," Dage muttered.

From behind Conn.

Conn whirled around, his eyes wide. "You stupid idiot. You could've put yourself down right in the middle of the laser zone."

An outside door opened, the daylight making the red beams disappear. A shifter entered on the other side of the room, his eyes going wide at Conn in the doorway. He yelled a warning, pivoting and running back out. "Blow the building! Blow the building!"

A rumble filled the earth.

The explosives detonated.

Heat flashed through the space.

The world burned.

Chapter 22

"Who the hell do you think you are?" Conn grabbed the King of the Realm and shoved him against the wall of the strategy room in the Oregon headquarters. Fury burned him hotter than the inferno they'd just wisped through. The scent of scalded hair assaulted his nostrils. They'd barely made it.

Dage knocked him back, his normally bronze face pale. "Get off me. You weigh a ton to transport." He kept the wall up with his shoulders, sagging against it. The fire had singed the side of his shirt, and raw, red skin rippled across one hard forearm in a burn deep enough to showcase white bone. His eyes blazed a furious blue. Never a good sign.

"You're the *king*." When the hell would the man realize that? Conn's heartbeat slowed to a normal pace. Pain flared back to life. He shifted his weight to his good leg, striving for nonchalance.

Talen shrugged out of a bulletproof vest from behind a thick table scattered with battle plans. "You both need a vein." His jaw was set, his hair tied back. His older brother had been preparing for a fight.

"My blood's better." Jase replaced the safety on his gun, placing the weapon on the table. He yanked up a shirt-sleeve to bare his wrist.

Kane snorted. "No, it's not."

Conn held Dage's gaze, anger spiraling higher when his brother lifted an eyebrow in challenge.

The king cleared his throat. "You want to fight about it?" Anticipation tipped his upper lip. "I'll wait until you've recovered, of course." He cut his eyes to Conn's still bleeding leg, tracking several other injuries in his perusal back to Conn's face.

Asshole. When was he going to realize his life meant more? Conn allowed a slow smile to cross his face. "No, I don't want to fight. But I'm telling Emma you did."

Dage's nostrils flared. "You wouldn't."

"I would." Conn took a second to appreciate the quickly veiled panic in his brother's eyes, then dust mites danced across his vision. "What the hell?" He swayed. "Crap." Then, darkness.

Moira settled into the overstuffed chair, her gaze on the half-naked warrior on the bed. Their bed. The bedroom held the scent of sage and gunpowder, the hand-woven Irish rug matching the down comforter. Three oil paintings lined the wall, all midnight scenes of her homeland showcasing a full moon. He'd decorated the room with her in mind.

They'd hurt him. Fury burned along her skin, crackling with an audible pop. Raw wounds dotted his chest and abdomen, no longer bleeding but swollen with angry bruises. Jase had shoved his wrist in Conn's unconscious mouth, so at least he'd gotten some blood to heal.

"Moira." His voice rumbled her name, his incredible eyes opening. "Lose the anger, Brat. I need happy thoughts."

She couldn't help the smile. What a smart-ass. "You think you're in my head now, do you?" He bunched to sit up, and she jumped toward the bed, pressing down on the unwounded part of his chest. "Oh no, you don't."

His hands encircled her wrists. A gleam filled his eyes. With a sharp tug, he landed her on top of him. "Hello."

She scrambled to sit up, away from his injuries. Anger burned right to desire. He'd played her. "You're hurt, damn it."

One dark eyebrow rose in that arrogant face. "You said I could snack on you."

Well, the man had needed blood. She nodded, trying to tug one wrist free.

"Nope." Tightening his hold, he lifted his hands above his head, tugging her flat against him, chest to chest. "Hmmm. Very nice."

Moira fought the flush trying to heat her face, her nipples pebbling against his heat. A warming began to hum in her core. "Conn, you're injured." Her voice emerged breathless and much too weak.

"So be gentle with me," he murmured, his lips wandering across her jaw to torture her earlobe. "Skin like the softest of thoughts. Smooth as my mother's Irish porcelain." He nipped, the small bite flaring her marking to life. "Yet so much prettier." He dropped his head back down, his gaze caressing her face. "You're the prettiest thing I've seen in my three hundred plus years, Dailtín."

The sincerity, the simmering desire in his tone flared her need to life. Emotion she neither wanted nor needed pricked tears at the back of her eyes. "I hate that they hurt you, Conn." While she batted the tears away, they survived thick and full in her voice.

His gaze softened. "Ah, darlin'. I'm fine." The hold on her wrists loosened, and he brushed the curls off her face.

"No you're not. The doctor examined you while you were out." For over an hour. "You lost most of your liver and both kidneys." How hard they must've hit him to cause such internal damage. Rage and helplessness commingled until she felt small. So small.

"Moira. Livers and kidneys grow back. Give me a couple days and I'll be good as new, ready to chase down the entire clan. I'm healing as we speak."

Vulnerability kept her immobile. He'd been hurt, yet she needed comforting. "This . . . you . . ." Confusion had her biting her lip.

Understanding lightened his eyes. "It's all right. You don't always have to be so damn strong." One broad hand caressed from her shoulder down to her hip in one smooth stroke. Soothing. Kindness and understanding in such a deadly package.

The tears won the internal battle, escaping to slide down her cheeks. She didn't know any way but the truth. And the truth was scaring her to death. "I'm not weak, Conn."

He tugged her to straddle him. "No, you're not."

A slight shift of his hips had her atop his groin, safely away from his abdominal wounds. She wiped tears off her face, refusing to roll her eyes. Safety didn't exist when Connlan Kayrs had a plan.

His fingers tightened, keeping her hips in place. "What are you so afraid of, Moira?"

"Losing myself." The words emerged soft and fast, so much truth in them she caught her breath.

"Maybe you'll find yourself." His eyes closed.

"The Nine is considering withdrawing from the Realm." There. She'd said it.

"I know. They had a preliminary vote before Grace was kidnapped."

Surprise shot through her followed by a smoldering hint of temper. "You sound as if you're discussing the weather." He'd known. Yet he hadn't said a word.

"Just the facts."

"So what's your plan here, Conn? You know my job."

"No plan. For now, the Nine is scrambling and can't make a cohesive decision."

He was wrong. The Nine could withdraw should the present members vote to do so. "What does that mean?"

"We hold tight until they make a decision. When they do, then I'll neutralize you if necessary." His voice slurred on the second part of his statement. "Make no mistake, you and I remain solid even if the rest of the world blows up. We start at that point, then move outward." He inhaled through his nose. "We might have to table this philosophical discussion." A cut on his right shoulder mended shut.

She'd kick his ass for the neutralizing threat later when he was feeling better. "You still need blood." Rumor had it hers was magical.

A smile threatened his full lips. "Is that an offer?"

She thought about it. Need flitted along her nerve endings. "Yes."

His eyes flipped open, shooting silver through the green. "Well, now." Slow as a summer dream, he slid one arm behind his head. "I accept."

Even injured, even exhausted, the man held an edge that whispered a warning. Most predators did. Her thighs warmed, a sensation she welcomed much easier than the vise squeezing her heart. "You want my neck?"

His lids half closed. "No," he murmured very softly. "I want all of you, Moira." A deep breath lifted her to settle back in place. "For now, your neck would be enjoyable." Twin fangs dropped low.

A guttural growl escaped him and she shivered. Fighting the urge to clear her throat, fighting the need to run, she gingerly set her hands on either side of his wide shoulders and leaned down. He threaded his free hand through her hair, tightening his hold and turning her head to the side.

Something natural, something feminine in her sighed, relaxing. He had her. And deep down, where certainty lived, she knew he wasn't letting go.

His rough tongue rasped from her collarbone to the underside of her jaw. A quiver swept her skin, followed by a blast of heat. She pressed down against him, core to core, softness to his hardness. He was hard. For her.

Her eyes rolled back in her head. The tiniest of whimpers escaped. "Please."

As if he'd been waiting, he struck. Deep and fast, he gave no quarter, drinking. Taking. Owning. His hold tightened. A rumble filled his chest, an animal appeased.

She arched, her body tinder, his mouth a match. Thoughts faded like old memories, worries fled as if chased. Nothing in reality, nothing in imagination, could compare to the sensation of her mate taking her blood. Her limbs softened, yet she shared power with him. Power flowing from him bolstered her. Energy, raw and pure.

Elemental.

Primitive.

Everlasting.

Sharp fangs retracted and he laved the wound, sealing it. A deep sigh escaped him. "Damn, woman." His lids drifted shut. The hand in her hair loosened, and he tugged her to his side, rolling to tuck her in. His breath evened out in deep sleep.

She sucked in air, vulnerability skating through her. The man had taken more than her blood. Very few, if any, people could handle Connlan Kayrs. She wasn't one of them. Her back to his heated front, the temptation to sink into him, into his vision of the world, was almost too much to deny. Even worse, a part of her, a much larger part than she liked, wanted to please him. Wanted to make his world true.

It was that thought that had her sliding off the bed and running for the door.

She made it to the corridor, her eyes darting for the nearest exit in the rock walls. She had to get out of there, flee to the surface. The hour had to be close to midnight. The moon beckoned. Her boots echoed against the stone floor as she ran, finding the stairwell. Two steps inside and she collided with a chest that might as well have been a rock wall.

An "*oof*" escaped her as she bounced back. Only the quickest of reflexes helped the king grab her arms, keeping her from slamming into the metal door behind her.

Like a rabbit in a snare, she struggled, panting.

He released her, stepping back. "Moira." Acceptance and understanding filtered across the king's face. "Feeling trapped, are we?"

"Yes." She gulped, trying to stem the panic rippling under her skin.

Dage studied her, a slight smile hovering on his lips. "Want to fight?"

"Fight?" The King of the Realm wanted to fight with her?

"Sure." The smile erupted, a gleam in his eye. "We have the best sparring mats around. Kell has trained you, no?"

Yeah. Till she bled from the ears. "Maybe a little."

The king had dimples.

Interesting.

He grasped her arm, all but tugging her down the stairs to the next level, which he opened onto a massive gym complete with tumbling mats. He shut the door. "Whenever I'm feeling the weight of this life, I hit something, usually Conn." Cheerful anticipation lit the king's words. "So. Gloves, knives, what?"

Emotion rose hard and fast within her. "Nothing. We fight free-form." The need to hit overwhelmed her. He may be trying to help, but the vampire was about to get his ass kicked.

Chapter 23

Kalin nursed his soda in the worn booth at the hopping diner, hunkered down in his new bomber jacket. He fought the urge to scratch his face. The makeup adding color to his skin itched. High school students wandered around, some playing pool, others darts. A cool hangout, although they didn't serve blood.

Even there, he was cold. As soon as the scientists figured out a gene therapy so his people could venture into the sun, Kalin would move somewhere hot and learn to surf—while taking over the world, of course.

A trio of giggling girls at a corner table threw flirty glances his way. Sophomores most likely, wearing low-cut shirts they'd probably covered with sweatshirts when leaving their safe homes. Sparkly makeup coated their faces. One could pass for a clown. He fought a grin. If the twits had any idea what he could do to them. What he wanted to do to them.

The stench of burnt hamburger formed a bad taste in his mouth. Why anyone would eat there was beyond him.

The glass door opened, tinkling with a small bell. Peggy glided inside, brushing her hair back. Somehow the room warmed. He straightened in his seat, throwing out his chest.

She spotted him, waving and winding through a group

of boys playing darts to drop into the booth across the table. Most people, even warriors centuries older than he, faltered and gathered their strength when approaching him. Not Peggy. She moved forward like she had nothing to fear, like he was safe. The idea of protecting her from the cruelties of the world heated his skin.

Her unique scent of roses filtered toward him, making his heart thump faster. She smiled. "Hi. Sorry I'm late. I had to help close the store." She worked part-time for her parent's outdoor sports store and knew everything about fly-fishing.

"Hi." His gaze dropped to the light blue letterman's jacket hanging on her small frame. The male scent of sweat and cologne assaulted his nostrils. A prickle messed with the back of his neck. "Whose jacket?"

She blushed, running a hand along the frayed collar. "Joe Neilson. You know, the quarterback I told you about?" Her smile revealed perfect white teeth, shinier than the purest pearl. "He finally asked me out."

Fire rushed through Kalin so fast his breath caught. She'd mentioned the boy, but just in passing. He was a friend who studied with her sometimes. "I hadn't realized you liked him." What the fuck had Kalin been doing here? He'd wanted to court her slowly.

She shrugged, her pretty blue eyes lighting up. "I've had a crush on him for a while." As if sensing his distress, she reached across and grabbed his hand. "I'm so glad we're friends, Kalin. Even though you're two years younger than me, you mean a lot to me." She patted his knuckles, the world lighting up with her smile. "In fact, I've been tutoring a sophomore I think you might like."

He'd been the dark guy, too young, yet the guy who had made Joe take notice. Kalin flashed his teeth.

Peggy jerked back, her eyes widening. He closed his mouth, and she gave a startled giggle. Shaking her head, she obviously ignored whatever instincts the gods had given her. "Are you all right?"

"Yeah." He leaned back, smoothing on a small grin. Reality clicked into place with sharp cracks. Betrayal ripped down his spine, soothing in an odd way. Oh, it hurt. And temper wanted to open wide jaws and kill everyone in the diner. But . . . he settled into himself. His skin fit again. "In fact, I was on the phone earlier with a girl who I think is my future."

"Really?" Peggy waved at the group of girls in the corner. A vein fluttered in her neck, proving she wasn't quite reassured. Prey did have some basic instinct for survival. "What's her name?"

"Janie. She lives in the States." Enough of this. He relaxed, the weight of destiny no longer pressing. "So. You leave for your trip late tonight, right?"

"Yes." Peggy gave a happy hop in the seat, her smile relaxing as she turned to face him. She'd reassured herself of her safety.

Silly human girl.

"I'm going to visit my aunt and uncle in Omaha . . . I'm taking the red-eye. It'll be a fun two weeks of relaxing and helping on the farm. I love the farm." She frowned, creating cute lines on the sides of her eyes. "I'll miss you, though."

Not as much as she'd miss Joe, apparently. "I'll miss you too." Kalin's brain began calculating plans.

She glanced at her watch. "Oh. I'm supposed to meet Joe for yogurt." Her frown wasn't as cute. "Do you, ah, want to come?"

"No." Kalin stood, stretching a hand to help her up. Her skin felt smooth in his palm. Was she smooth all over? "I need to get home. But you have a great time."

He walked her out, turning to head in the opposite direction to jump in his truck. Anger tasted like acid in his throat. Something under his rib cage echoed with a pain he'd never felt . . . dull and devastating. His cell phone rang, nearly freezing his ear off when he lifted it, and he growled.

"Kalin. Where are you?" Franco asked over the sound of papers being shuffled.

"On my way home. I want the plane ready now . . . we're going to Omaha." He clicked off, a smile on his face, heat filling his pores. Yeah. Janie was right. Peggy needed to meet the real Kalin.

Moira's feet danced on the thick grappling mats covering the floor of an entire room, the padding made just to kick butt. The adjoining room held weights, exercise machines, and punching bags. The scent of pine cleanser and sweat seemed embedded in the mats. She focused on the king. "I feel kind of funny kicking the crap out of you."

His smile held too much anticipation for her peace of mind. "I appreciate the sentiment. I've never sparred with a witch before." A dark T-shirt failed to conceal the tight muscles of his chest, and his loose sweats showed toned thighs. "It'd be an honor if you didn't hold back. Give me what you've got."

Good plan. She needed to hit him hard and fast. Leaping for him, her knees landed on either side of his head, clapping tight, as she swung her torso down between his legs and clasped the back of his knees. Gravity assisted her in dropping the king face-first toward the mat. She whipped through and landed on his shoulder blades, one knee to the nape of his neck.

He chuckled, the side of his mouth smashed, his palms against the floor. "That was awesome." Powerful muscles bunched. Dage lifted into a handstand, sending her winging across the room like ice cream on a spoon during a food fight.

She tucked and landed, rolling to her feet. "Nice move."

"Thanks." He eyed her knees, maneuvering closer. "So, when Conn and I spar, we talk about stuff. Like why we're pissed at life."

"I'm not pissed at life." She slid, swinging her legs out to knock him flat.

He jumped, knocking her down and landing with feet on either side of her hips. Then he dropped to his knees, both hands pinning her shoulders. "Who are you pissed at?"

Swiveling at the waist, she swung her legs to scissor around the king, yanking him to the side. His head hit the floor with a dull thump. "Fate and destiny. I'm so tired of fighting them." Releasing him, she somersaulted backwards to her feet.

Dage back flipped to stand. "Perhaps you should stop fighting *against* everything and start fighting *for* something."

"Showoff. You think I should fight for Conn."

"Of course for Conn. Go for the life you want with him." Dage's metallic eyes filled with understanding. "The war is getting worse. We have enemies on every front . . . some who used to be our friends. Pick a path, Moira."

A path? "How easy you make it seem." Irritation formed a crackling ball of energy before her, and she cupped it with her right hand.

He lifted an eyebrow. "Actually, duty totally sucks. I hate being here, putting on a calm face when I'd rather be smashing someone's head in." His tennis shoes left deep indents in the mat as he opened his stance, arms spread out at the side. "Besides, I understand what a pain Conn is. Bossy, so sure he needs to jump in front of us all."

Her eyes widened, letting in more light. "Exactly. I'm seriously trained. I don't need anyone leaping to catch a bullet for me."

"He loves you, Moira." Deep and sure, the king struck the ultimate blow.

She faltered. The energy webbed in her hand. "No. The marking surprised us both. I'm a duty."

Dage threw back his head and laughed. "No, sweetheart. You're a pain in the ass. Conn can handle any duty. You now . . . you're another story. He wants you happy. He wants you safe. I strongly suggest you figure out a way to help him achieve both . . . while still following your own path in life."

The energy pulsed a bright blue, sending shards of adrenaline through her blood. Why did everyone think she had the gift of compromise? Because she was the Seventh? "I have neither the patience nor desire to do so."

"Then you'll lose"— Dage shrugged—"which seems absolutely foolhardy . . . considering you love him with everything you are." His legs bunched, shoes dancing on the mat. "You're both stubborn, smart, and damn good at your jobs. You'll either make a great team or you'll kill each other."

The king didn't miss a thing.

"You're such an asshole." She gulped back air. Probably not something one should call the King of the Realm.

He nodded, his smile broadening. "Not the first time I've been called that, Moira." He rubbed the back of his neck. "I, ah, don't think you see him. Not really."

What the hell did that mean? "I see him." Awake or asleep, she'd always seen Conn.

"No." Dage sighed, his gaze transfixed on the energy. "I don't think you understand the meaning of this last century. How difficult it was for him to remain here, to stay away from the one woman created just for him. To stay away . . . from you."

"He signed a treaty." Even as she said the words, she knew the absurdity in them. Connlan Kayrs cared little for treaties—if at all. "I needed the time." She'd had to train in the land of her people by the experts.

"I know," Dage said softly. "But Conn needed you. He's the ultimate soldier . . . and he couldn't protect or defend the woman he loves—for a hundred years. He rarely sleeps, and I've seen him smile more in the last week than the last five decades. Even though he's been tortured to a point that his organs need to rebuild."

Her heart thudded. Hard. The glow shifted to a darker blue in her hand. Deep and true. "I know."

Dage cracked his knuckles. "I, ah, I couldn't have done it. Couldn't have stayed away this long. But Conn . . . he sacrificed for what you needed." The king sauntered over and grabbed a towel off the floor to wipe his forehead.

Yeah. But, what now?

She tried not to be insulted the king turned his back on her and the energy weapon. Must mean he trusted her to play fair. She struggled to focus on the discussion. "If Conn had learned I trained as an enforcer, he wouldn't have waited so long." The soldier would've rushed to Ireland to drag her to safety. Of course, there she was, safely ensconced underground.

"No, nothing would've kept my brother from Ireland had he discovered your new vocation." A gleam shone from the king's eyes. He threw the towel down, sauntering back into place, centering his stance. "Though you impressed the heck out of him in New York."

Moira grinned. "That's nice to hear." Maybe since Conn had seen her in action, he'd better understand her need to continue with the enforcers. "So your suggestion is to, what? I mean, you have advice, right?" The guy seemed wise. He should have something helpful to say.

"You owe Conn."

Her head jerked up. "Excuse me?"

"You owe him. He sacrificed for a century, now you

need to find out a way to let him be true to his idea of a mate . . . while still following your own fate." Dage widened his stance. "You're a smart woman, Moira. Figure it out."

She thought she'd found an enlightened Kayrs man. Instinct whispered the king wasn't above manipulation to keep the turbulent waters from messing with his family. In which, of course, he now included her.

"You're all stuck in the Stone Age."

"You sound like Emma."

"Your mate is a smart woman." Moira drew air in, allowing the energy to strengthen. "I figured you'd want to discuss, ah, the Nine's plans to withdraw from the Realm." Try to talk her over to his side.

"Hell no." A smile threatened on Dage's full lips. "If the Nine withdraws, you're in a horrible position, darlin'. Nothing you can do about it."

"But I'll be a threat to you." To his entire world.

"Yes, but you're family. I won't hurt you." Dage's gaze softened. "Besides, Conn handles most of my threats. He'll make sure none of us get hurt, at least from the Nine's withdrawal."

"What the heck does that mean?" While Conn wouldn't hurt her, he was the ultimate soldier. What would he do?

"I think it'd be better if we didn't push him to that point, Moira. Just a thought." The king's eyes flicked blue through the silver. "Enough talking." A muscle ticced along his neck, and he eyed the energy ball. "Throw."

She didn't need a second order. Yanking her arm back, she belted the energy toward Dage. The ball careened, whacking him square in the chest, shoving him back two feet. A delighted smile lit his face as he peered down, the energy crackling along his front. The smell of burning fabric choked out the air.

He sighed. "Extinguish." The energy snuffed out like

the oxygen had been killed. His shirt lay in burnt tatters, exposing an intricate tattoo wandering across the left side of his chest and over his shoulder. The Kayrs marking in big picture.

"That was very cool. But, I couldn't let you burn me. That would piss Emma off to no end." He scrubbed his ribs as if in sudden thought. "Very cool."

The door shoved open and Katie stomped inside, shoving hair out of her eyes. She skidded to a stop. "Ah, sorry. I came to meditate."

Jordan stalked in right behind her, a scowl on his face. His multicolored hair streamed around his angled face. The guy even looked like a lion in human form, anger dancing on his skin. "We need to talk. I mean now."

Dage glanced from one to the other. "Well, then." He stepped forward and took Moira's arm. "You go ahead. My sister-in-law and I are going to have a contest to see who can kick a punching bag more times in five minutes." His grip tightened, and she chose not to argue.

Katie huffed out air. "Thanks." Had the king and Conn's mate been sparring? She'd never seen a witch spar. Dage's shirt had been burned right off his body. Maybe Moira would grapple with her later.

The door closed behind the king, and Katie pivoted to face Jordan.

His growl was entirely too realistic. "What the hell do you mean you're not coming home with me tomorrow?"

The word *home* nearly made Katie's knees buckle. Her home would never be with the leader of the lions. Not unless she could get her shifting abilities back. "I'm staying here. With Emma and Cara." She needed to remain close to the scientists who would cure her—especially now.

"Why?" Jordan tugged on his denim shirt, his dark jeans showcasing strong legs. He hadn't run in two days, and the energy rolled off him in waves. As did his scent of cinnamon and oak. Wild, like the man himself.

Although miles underground, she knew the moon was rising high and strong. Something inside her screamed. Her muscles vibrated down her flanks, making even her butt twitch. "I injected myself with the catalyst."

Jordan paled. "You. Did. What?" He staggered back a step, pure shock filling his tawny eyes.

Oxygen filled her lungs when she inhaled deeply. Not much in life scared her. The head of the lion clans stood at least a foot taller than her, with muscles earned by running and working his ranch. Jordan in full temper would scare anyone. "You heard me."

Color slid under his skin, enhancing the dark hollows below his cheekbones. His roar reached every corner in the room. "Why?" His hands clenched at his sides, as if he didn't trust himself not to choke her.

She took a step back. Although she'd known him nearly her entire life, she'd never seen such a look on his face. "I need to shift, Jordan. I can't live like this. The catalyst sped up the virus in Maggie's blood—so she can shift."

His multicolored hair flew as he shook his head. "She's a wolf shifter. We don't fucking know how you'll react." Two steps and his hands clamped around her forearms. "I said I'd mate you."

She yanked back, anger shoving fear to hell. "Thanks for the pity offer. I'm not mating out of charity, you arrogant ass." She'd loved him forever. But she wasn't a charity case. "I'm not stupid. I know about the political problems you're facing with the clans because of me and my . . . condition." Pain made the words taste like gristle on her tongue. "Besides, there's no guarantee that would work. Then you'd be mated not only to someone you don't love, but to someone who couldn't shift. Maybe couldn't give you little rulers to raise."

She sucked in air. Something demanded her attention. Immediately. Agony slashed into her abdomen. Clutching her stomach, she doubled over. Need. A hunger so harsh she couldn't breathe. "Jordan."

She felt a soothing balm, a necessary healing. The moon. But a shadow lurked—thick shadow—dark and compelling. It bellowed for her. "Outside. Please, take me outside."

"Goddamn it." Jordan shot a hand through his hair, pacing toward the wall. Catlike reflexes shot his fist into the padding. The protective covering split, sending white tufts flying.

A sparkling of colors danced in her vision, her tears morphing the shades like in a kaleidoscope. Her knees hit the floor. The rock ceiling pounded above her. The moon. She needed light. Pain reached the level of sound, a screaming filling her head. Her palm slid forward on the uneven mat, her head bowed. Agony made her gasp. "Please."

Two paces had Jordan swinging her into his arms. Quick strides had them in the hallway and then running up the stairs to the top level. His boots pounded the concrete, the sound echoing throughout the stairwell. The air grew lighter the farther up they went. "How can you possibly think I don't care for you?"

Her head swung around, need filling every pore. The calling got louder. Needles sprang up under her skin, slashing through, each filled with poison. She stiffened in Jordan's grasp. "Hurry."

His growl promised retribution. Yanking the stairwell door open, he ran toward two guards manning the outside elevator.

One held out a hand to stop him. "Wait—"

"Open the damn door," Jordan bellowed.

The first guard jerked his head back, his gaze widening.

Then he nodded, pushing the button. He tapped his ear-piece. "Chalton, get Dage."

Jordan jumped inside the cart, his breathing heavy against her cheek as Katie struggled to stay focused. She needed the moon. Was she going to change into a were-wolf? Terror made her turn her face into Jordan's strength as a soft sob escaped. Her limbs tingled with fire.

"You'll be all right." Jordan tucked his head around her, hurrying out of the elevator onto a rough cliff cut into the rock. The sea tumbled below, sending up the moist scent of salt. National forest protected the land around them. He laid her down on the smooth rock, allowing the moon to bathe her. Dropping to a crouch, he kept vigil.

Peace. Katie relaxed, her body going limp. She lifted her face to the moon—soft light, creating healing energy. Par-ticles of the light washed over her skin, balming. Sooth-ing. Protecting.

She closed her eyes and searched for the lioness inside her. Time to come out. A sputtering filled her ears, much like a car engine refusing to ignite. She tried harder. Her shoulders tensed. Was there still a lioness inside her? She lifted her head and howled to the useless moon.

High above, hidden behind a shield of trees . . . some-thing howled back.

Jordan leaped to his feet. "What the hell was that?"

She felt it. A craving . . . a need. Dark, hungry, it wanted to reach her. It wailed, the consonants almost rolling into her name. She sat up. "He wants me." A shiver shook her entire body. Whatever sought her didn't want to chat. Hunger all but rode the airwaves down. Blood. The howler thirsted for her blood.

The elevator opened and Dage ran outside. "Emma told me. The catalyst."

Katie rose to her knees, her eyelids heavy but the moon surrounding her in safety. Her head tilted, instinctively searching. Fear scented the air. Not hers. Not Jordan's. The creature above . . . even while it hunted, it feared.

What? Her?

Jordan grabbed her shoulders, hauling her up. She sagged against him. Sadness encased her limbs in heaviness. "The shot didn't work. No werewolf, no lioness. I'm the same." She refused to let tears fall. Later, when she was alone in her bed . . . then she'd cry. "Let's go back downstairs." Away from the monster trying to ram into her pores.

The howling increased, skittering unease down her spine. Pins pricked at her brain . . . some type of message. Darkness, longing, and a demand. She shoved it out, sliding shields into place, protecting her mind. Wind whipped clouds across the sky, a whistle competing with the keening from above.

Dage looked up. His jaw tightened, his eyes shifting blue through the silver.

Katie leaned into Jordan's strength as she watched the king. Sometimes she forgot he wasn't human.

He wore diplomacy and kindness like a shield. Every once in a while the animal within reared up, more deadly because of its unwilling slumber. He ignored her perusal. "Suit up, Jordan. Sounds like we're going hunting."

Katie trudged into the elevator. "He's a werewolf. Strong. I sensed him." Now she could sense beasts. Though she wasn't one of them.

She wasn't anything.

Chapter 24

Moira stretched her neck, limping into Conn's quarters. The door shut behind her. The living room sofa whispered an invitation for her to sit and watch one of the many movies stacked on the shelves built into the walls. Squinting, she studied the titles. *My Freckled Pony. Springtime Puppies go to Hollywood. The Pink Fairy.* Apparently Janie and Uncle Conn spent time together watching movies.

There were also adult comedies and dramas on a higher shelf. Before choosing, she took a closer look around. The man had built a pretty cage.

Dage had been right. Beating the heck out of a punching bag had put things in perspective. She didn't belong in a cage. Conn would have to see her abilities, and her need to fight.

She eased toward the small kitchen to grab a sports drink. The king hoarded his like gold and wouldn't share after their time in the gym. Not like she couldn't find him another grape drink somewhere as a replacement—if he *had* shared.

The fridge was disorganized. Quick movements had the shelves righted in no time by color and size. She grabbed an apple juice from the refrigerator and turned, her heart dropping at the warrior standing in the doorway to the sleeping quarters. "Conn."

He lounged against the doorframe, loose sweats perched low on masculine hips, his chest bare and covered in bruises. But no open wounds. Broad hands finger-combed his wet hair away from his face, allowing the ends to almost reach his shoulders. She liked that he'd grown it out . . . the bad-boy look fit him well. "Moira."

She cleared her throat. The brand on her hip warmed. "So, uh, how are you feeling?"

His chin lowered, his focus absolute. On her. He shoved off from the wall. She gulped a swallow. Heat flushed through her, in direct contrast to the chill at her back. Her mouth opened, but nothing emerged.

Smooth, slow, he prowled into the kitchen. She'd seen many animals, many warriors. Not one came close to Connlan Kayrs. In grace or menace.

Her muscles tensed . . . adrenaline slid inside her veins like heated honey. Her panties soaked. Invisible bonds tied her in place, trapping her in his hypnotic hold.

He drew in oxygen, his nostrils flaring, a dark flush spiraling across his high cheekbones. "I can smell you. Lilacs and woman." Then he was within touching distance.

Her lungs grew heavy. The air thickened. She opened her eyes wide, allowing more light and range of view to reach her brain—like any prey facing a predator. "I can smell you, too." Male. Her chest rose slowly, visibly as she tried to force air inside.

He cocked his head to the side, placed his index finger against her neck to run down and across one diamond-hard nipple. Her knees weakened. He licked his lips. "I never had much self-control in the kitchen." His smile flashed, his gaze on her breasts. "Whatever smells so good, I need a taste."

She swallowed. Loudly. "Ah . . ."

His lids lowered to half-mast. He glanced behind her to the organized shelves. "What is up with the obsessive food organization?"

The quiet question hinted at an intimacy she wanted to avoid.

She shrugged. "When I was little, I ate a bunch of Aunt Viv's prunes that had been altered to look like plums. My sisters knew and didn't tell me what they were. They acted like prunes, though. I was so sick." Oh, but she'd gotten her revenge on Darcy. Knowing what natural herbs could cause hives had come in very handy. "So I learned to organize by color and size so it didn't happen again."

"Ah." He tugged her forward, shutting the door before pushing her back against the smooth surface. Both hands went to her waist, smoothing under her shirt, sliding up to cup her breasts. Fire licked along her skin. Nothing in the world could've kept her from pressing forward, filling his palms and allowing shards of pleasure to shoot to her core. Her head fell back against the stainless steel.

"I love a good snack in the afternoon." He stepped into her, his mouth dropping to nuzzle the hollow of her neck. "I think I'll start my snack here." Low, slumbering, his voice vibrated against her flesh.

One strong thigh slid between her legs, sliding up, forcing her to ride him. Her moan rose to a plea. "Conn—"

Like the curtain in a theatre, he s raised her shirt and sports bra up over her head. "We've never gone slow, Moira."

Her eyes eased open. The dark desire on his face made her gasp. Then crave. Slow wasn't how she wanted him. Too dangerous. She grabbed his head, yanking it down to hers and nipping his bottom lip. His hands tightened their hold.

He levered back, pinning her nipples between thumb and forefingers. "I said slow. Release my hair."

She clutched harder, narrowing her gaze.

He pinched.

Pain shot straight to her clit. She gasped, her hold loosening.

His eyes darkened. "Let. Go. Moira." Slightly, imperceptibly, his hold tightened on her swollen nipples. When she didn't comply, he increased the pressure.

With a moan, she untangled her fingers, dropping her hands to her sides. He held her captive, confused. She didn't know whether to jerk back . . . or ask for more.

"Oh, baby girl, the things I'm going to teach you." Keeping her gaze, he rolled her nipples, tightening his hold until she nearly panted. His slow smile promised something dark. Something forbidden. Something she wanted.

Warmth from his mouth quickly replaced his fingers, suckling her right breast. A mewling filled her head. She bit her lip to stop the sound. He chuckled, the vibrations nearly sending her over the edge. So much wet heat engulfed her smarting nipple she rubbed against his thigh, seeking something.

His leg deserted her. "Not yet." Dropping to his knees, he tugged off her sweats and thong. "Ah. So pretty." Slowly, way too slowly, he inched forward, planting one gentle kiss on her mound.

Her hips jerked as if she'd been electrocuted. Desire splintered into a thousand pieces to shoot through her body. Her hands dropped to clutch the top of his shoulders, her head rested against the cool appliance. Clever fingers parted her, and his tongue went to work. Fast, soft, devastating, he kept her on the edge until the only thing that existed was his mouth. Until two fingers entered her, searching, stretching. He found the hidden bundle of nerves . . . and the universe exploded.

She rode his fingers, pressed against his mouth, and cried

out his name. The pleasure filled her so completely reality became a dream. With a sigh, she came down, her entire body having the strength of a drunken fairy. Conn gave one last kiss across the marking on her hip and stood.

He yanked off his sweats. Strong hands grabbed her butt, lifting her. She wrapped her legs around his hips. A step forward and he impaled her.

The cool fridge supported her back while he began to thrust. She grasped his chest. "Are you strong enough to do this?" A spiraling deep inside threatened to steal her concentration.

"Yes." His fangs dropped low. With a quick strike, he claimed her neck.

His moan outdid hers as blood flowed between them, healing and strong. She could feel the change in him, like a lit fuse sparking through his veins to heal. A dam broke dead center of her chest. A concrete barrier inside her, designed to keep the floodwaters back . . . crumbled from the force of emotion hurtling from him.

His hips thrust harder, taking her higher. She clung on, desperate to jump into the abyss. The slap of flesh against flesh drowned out their harsh breathing.

Sensation wrapped around her, all emotion, all intent. His entire body vibrated against her. Trapping her. His fangs withdrew. Rough, his tongue laved the wound. She tilted her head to allow for better access.

He bit.

The orgasm ripped through her, shutting down her brain. Pleasure, pain, and so much sensation commingled until she could only hold on, chanting his name. His speed increased, along with his strength. He released her neck. With a growl, feeling like love against her skin, and resonating like ownership in her heart, he came.

Chapter 25

It had taken all night. Although underground at head-quarters, Kalin could sense the sun rising in the sky above. So dangerous. So tempting.

He stepped out of the shower, kicking his clothes to the side. Wrapping a towel around his waist, he frowned at the long line of scratches down his torso. Peggy's attack had surprised him. The girl had more fight in her than he'd hoped. Not that her spirit had done her any good.

He lumbered down the hall to his bedroom, stopping short at the leader sitting in a reading chair. "Franco."

Franco nodded, tossing aside the worn copy of Machia-velli's *The Art of War*. "I take it your trip to Omaha went well?"

"Yes. Very." Kalin dropped the towel, reaching to tug on some sweats. Nudity had never concerned him over-much. "We flew low and didn't file a flight plan, so there will be no record of the trip."

Franco's silver eyebrows rose over his deep purple eyes. "I see you got rid of the black polish and lipstick."

"I'm out of that phase." Kalin shrugged. No more pre-tending to be human. The species was prey for a reason.

"So, there won't be any repercussions from your jour-ney?" Franco's stark white face tightened.

Kalin couldn't wait until he ruled the world and didn't

have to hide. "No. The girl was from here, which is why I waited until she reached Nebraska. I took her at the airport, and believe me, no one saw." The surprised look on her face had been priceless. And when she'd met the real him, well now. "She had a rather high tolerance for pain." Impressed the hell out of him. For nearly two seconds he'd considered keeping her.

Franco rolled his eyes, standing and strolling for the door. "I'll monitor the Omaha news just in case. When will she be found?"

"Soon." He'd dumped her behind a nightclub near the garbage. Where she deserved.

Silly girl giving up the life he could've given her. He'd like to go after that loser Joe, but would have to wait. Coincidence wasn't his friend. Joe's turn would come, and with it enough pain to make the sadness still lingering in Kalin's solar plexus fade away.

The laptop dinged on the sturdy desk he'd taken from a woman in Georgia the year before. She'd even tasted like peaches, crying in a thick accent. Kalin sauntered forward, clicking keys. "Erik is calling. They put him through to here."

Franco strode toward the computer. "Bring him up."

Erik filled the screen, his curly red hair sticking out in every direction. "Where's my witch?"

"Nice to see you too, brother." Franco clasped both hands behind his back. "We don't have a witch yet. Why don't you get your own?"

Crimson eyes flashed.

Kalin swallowed. Sure, his people had odd colors. But red hair and red eyes? The guy even creeped him out. "I'll go get you a witch, Erik." He'd never taken a witch. Might be a decent challenge for him.

Erik clicked his tongue loudly. "How nice of you, Kalin."

"No." Franco pressed a heavy hand down on Kalin's shoulder. "We'll find you a witch. What about your misgivings?" Low, rolling, Franco's tone issued threat.

Kalin stiffened, glancing from Franco to his brother. "What misgivings?"

Erik straightened his lab coat, tucking a silver pen into the breast pocket. "Any airborne virus will affect all mates, even our own. I merely noted we need an inoculation before we mutate the virus to mass contaminate—which is still far in the future . . . and taking longer since you can't seem to acquire a witch."

"Why Erik. I had no idea you thought to find yourself a mate." Franco curled his lip, condescension dripping from each word.

Kalin shrugged the hand off his shoulder. He'd heard the rumors about Erik and didn't give a damn. The guy could like men, goats, or monkeys for all he cared, so long as he did his job. "How is it going with the captured shifters?"

"Well." Erik glared at his brother and leaned to the side, flipping open a manila folder. "After infecting several felines at the colloquium last year, we kidnapped a few wolf shifters and have injected them. The females react faster than the males, as we suspected."

Figured. A virus equaled weakness. Of course the females succumbed first. "Any luck with enslaving them?" Kalin asked.

"Not yet." Erik squinted, frowning. "The virus takes them down to werewolf form, but with more of a . . . backbone . . . so to speak, than a normal human werewolf." He cleared his throat, tossing aside the folder. "Keep in mind, gentlemen, these constitute our first trials with the virus. The plan is long term."

Maybe that part of the plan would take a while. In fact, every psychic vibe Kalin had inherited from his deceased mother bellowed that nothing would happen until Janie came of age. Janie was truly the catalyst for the future, and he didn't need their oracles spouting predictions to know that fact. For now, other concerns occupied his mind. "What about the gene manipulation therapy?"

"We're researching several viable solutions." Erik nodded to someone off camera. "Your I.Q. is too high to measure, Kalin. Why don't you put that big brain to work and come help me with the research?"

Being stuck underground in some lab sounded like hell. "I need to keep training. My talents lie in battle." A fact Kalin had learned early. The need to hit and destroy sometimes turned his blood on fire. Hunting and stalking his prey calmed him so he could at least get some sleep. "My father's sword adorns the wall above my bed." Sharp, deadly, and shining in the meager light, the weapon would someday take off Talen Kayrs' head. Kalin even slumbered under the mantle of death.

"So long as you're keeping up your studies while learning how to hit things, I'll keep up the research on light manipulation therapy." Erik rolled his eyes. "Why you're in such a hurry to venture into the sun, I'll never know. I have to go." Without another word, the screen went dark.

"Kalin." Franco kept his gaze on the dead screen. "My brother might be a genius, but never forget he's weak."

"Of course." Kalin doubted being gay led to weakness. "Though whether or not he mates is of no concern to me."

"My concerns are broader than his sickness." Franco pivoted, heading for the door. "Erik enjoys philosophy and believes himself a modern intellectual. Always watch the smart ones." Franco paused at the doorway. "It's good to have you back." Then he headed down the hallway.

Kalin's gaze shifted to the wall of Peggy's pictures. "It's good to be back." Reaching for the center photograph, he ripped it in two. She'd confused him, a fact she'd paid dearly for. "Even sobbing, begging for your life, you were pretty."

With a sigh, he reached for the rest of the pictures. They no longer belonged.

Chapter 26

"You cut his head off." Conn scratched his chin, his gaze on the still form of the dead werewolf. The very dead werewolf.

Dage had placed the head near the body on the gurney of the autopsy room before fetching his mate. He stood next to her now, handing her a wickedly sharp syringe. She took it in her blue-gloved hands, inserting the needle into the beast's arm.

Jordan shrugged, his stance set against the concrete floor. A long, jagged scratch marred the right side of his face. Apparently it had been quite the fight. "Talen decapitated him, I didn't. Katie sensed him. She knew he was there, said when the beast died, something moved through her."

Conn fought a chill at the words.

Maybe the coldness came from the autopsy room they'd set up in anticipation of catching a were. The monster sprawled across the slab, coarse black hair covering every surface. Its snout appeared narrower than usual, not quite canine. Defined muscles lay under the heavy fur, showing he'd once had power.

Conn glanced at Emma as she drew blood from the animal's hairy arm. "How soon will you get the results?"

She stood, tapping the deep red blood in the syringe. "With the new equipment Kane tweaked, we should have an answer in a few hours." She frowned, her blue eyes sparking. "If we shared the technological advances with humans, several diseases might be cured." Tossing her hair over her lab coat with a shake of her head, she aimed for the door. "Something we'll discuss in detail once I determine whether this werewolf began as a human or a shifter."

Dage prowled after her. "I look forward to the discussion, love." Tipping his head back to take a deep gulp of his ever-present grape energy drink, he glanced over his shoulder. "Conn, Talen wants to meet in the third-floor conference room in fifteen minutes. You, too, Jordan." His footsteps echoed down the hallway.

Jordan nodded. Fierce brown eyes flicked toward the werewolf's head. "He wanted Katie. He sensed Katie." It had guaranteed the beast would lose his head.

Every once in a while Conn forgot about the killer lurking behind Jordan's easy smile. "The werewolf put up a good fight." Dage had reported it as an intelligent fight, different from a normal one.

"Yes." Jordan glanced down, frowning at a long gash across his knuckles. He stretched his hand, opening and closing his fingers, allowing claws to emerge. "I haven't apologized for what happened with Marcus. My people, my fault."

"No." Conn's fangs emerged, pricking his lip to draw blood. "They caught me. My head wasn't in the game . . . for obvious reasons." A snarl wanted loose and he shoved it down, taking control of the beast inside him for the moment. He was better than the decapitated monster sprawled on the table. He could think and plan.

"Women." Jordan's claws retracted, his mellow tone belied by the frozen fury on his face—powerful and animalistic, even in human form. "What are you going to do with yours?"

Conn wanted to respond with amusement. He searched, but the weight in his gut kept him somber. "I don't know. She's gifted . . . and driven. Even with her powers, she's not, well . . ."

"One of us." Jordan tucked his hands in his jeans pockets. "She may fight, she may even kill in battle. But the things we've done, even for the better good—"

"Yes." Conn spoke softly, tearing his gaze from the remembered knowledge he saw in Jordan's. "We were at war, we did what we had to do." A mantra he'd repeated to himself on more than one dark night. "Do you ever ask yourself if the end justified the means?"

The people he'd killed, murdered really—Kurjans, shifters, enemy combatants—had needed to die for the war to end three hundred years ago. He'd killed coldly and without mercy, ensuring Dage could broker the treaty. Ensuring the people who wanted war to continue wouldn't be at the table.

"No." Jordan's voice lowered to a tone hinting he lied to them both. "It's too late for that question." Most people didn't realize the congenial leader of the feline nation had been as vicious and frequent an assassin as Conn in the last war.

"You're right." The chill in the room came from death, not air in the vents. The discussion held no place in this century. "What's your plan with Katie?"

The lion's snarl held frustration. "She's so young."

Conn barked out a laugh, lacking in humor. "Been there. I wouldn't wait a century, my friend. It's too long." He glanced at the man he'd bonded with over battle tactics and duty so long ago. They weren't brothers, but they were close. "She loves you."

"She's a child with a crush." Lines of frustration cut into the lion's face. "I had hoped to give her time, but now she's vulnerable . . . and we're at war again."

So that was it. "Our mates don't need to see what we do, Jordan." Conn hadn't been ordered to kill again. Yet. When he went, Moira would stay home. "The burden stays on our shoulders, not theirs."

"Perhaps." Jordan stretched his neck. "Katie needs to remain here while Emma figures out a way to deal with the catalyst now in her blood." His words thickened on the last. "I'd stay, but I have a nation to clean up. Marcus was only the beginning."

Yeah. Jordan needed to get the felines under control. "The sooner your people are solid, the better. At least, before the Bane's Council comes for our heads." The Bane's Council hunted and killed werewolves, and the vampires hadn't exactly been forthcoming about the infected wolf shifter being hidden on Jordan's ranch.

"I know. By now I thought we'd have found Maggie's people, but no luck. Perhaps she was alone." Jordan shrugged, pivoting for the door. "In my mind, she's a wolf, not a werewolf."

The Bane's Council wouldn't see it that way.

Silence descended as the lion took his leave. Conn inhaled, filling his lungs. Bleach and death commingled in a scent that crawled like spiders over his skin. The urge to fight, the urge to protect the life he wanted, swirled through his blood until his shoulders snapped straight. The monster on the gurney was the beginning, and he knew it. He also knew, without question, what Emma's test would reveal. He sensed the truth.

This was no ordinary werewolf. Its legs hung off the metal edge, its muscle tone beyond that of a normal animal. Well over eight feet, even in death, power suffused the were. After Emma concluded her tests, he'd have to notify the Bane's Council. Right or wrong, he wouldn't report Maggie's existence.

Conn stepped closer, peering down at the animal. "The

only question I have is whether you were lion, wolf, or multi." Wait. He had a second question. How in the hell had Katie sensed the beast?

His soldier's mind whipped battle plans into place. If Katie had a gift, he'd use it. Even if he had to go through Jordan Pride.

War sucked.

Moira edged down the hallway toward a gathering room at the opposite end of the elevator. She desperately needed an Irish whiskey. Stomping around the corner, she stopped in her tracks at Katie huddled in a captain's chair, her somber gaze on the flickering light of a television showing all static. The low buzz filled the room along with the smoky scent of despair.

Taking a breath, Moira flicked her wrist and the television shut off. Pivoting, she dropped into a deep leather chair the color of Brenna's gray eyes. An oddity, since the rest of the sisters had green eyes. Bren's eyes had created a family joke. Her father raised his eyebrows at any man in the vicinity with gray eyes, always sending her mother into peals of laughter. "Katie. Can I help?"

Katie jerked, her gaze swinging away from the blank screen. "Not unless you can cure the virus." Red and swollen, the rims of her eyes made Moira blink in reaction.

"Ah, no. We've tried for the last eight months." To alter a cure enough to bind to the necessary chromosomes was possible, but they needed a physical concoction first. "Emma found the right concoction of drugs to counteract *the catalyst* in a pregnant mate . . . and I assume she'll start looking for a way to attack the catalyst in your blood. If you'll let her."

"No. I made my decision."

Yeah. Moira figured. "Well, then she'll find a drug or

drugs to fight the virus as a whole." Someday, with hard work . . . and luck.

Katie sighed. "When? I mean, look how long AIDS research has been going on for humans. They haven't found a cure."

Moira narrowed her focus, searching beyond the scattering brain waves cascading off Katie. Dark and discombobulated, the rhythm changed in speed and frequency. "Wow. You have a lot going on there." All waves held set patterns . . . which she then altered to seek a different result. She had no idea how to alter Katie's.

"Checking out my screwed-up aura?"

"Kind of." Moira leaned forward, frowning at the shades of brown and gray in the waves. "Want me to try and reorganize the waves?" Such an attempt may be a seriously bad idea—sometimes waves and particles exploded. "There's a definite risk."

Katie shrugged, her eyes dull. "Go for it. I don't care."

"All right." Moira rested her hands on her knees, palms up. She reached past the layers of brown, pleased to find a sparkling green flickering. "So. Tell me about Jordan." The green flared to life, then sputtered.

"He rescued me from a foster dad with a gun. Jim Bob. Moron." Katie wiggled in her seat, sending the fragments spiraling. "I was four, and shifted by accident. Had no idea I was a feline shifter. Jim Bob chased me into the woods. Jordan intercepted him."

Moira needed the green to return. The emerald tones seemed more in tune with Katie's natural state. "So he saved you. Quite the hero." There it was. She dug into the scattering, trying to thicken the pattern like the homemade quilt Darcy had made for her bed at the cottage.

"Yes. Turns out my parents had been part of his pride, but moved to the city and lost touch. They died in a car accident. I don't remember them." Sadness filtered through the words, while natural baby blue specks wound through Katie's waves—a normal color for regret.

"So Jordan raised you?" Every time Moira used his name, Katie's natural colors shone brighter, but the grays and browns continued to dominate.

"No. My mother is a member of his pride. She adopted me." Love filled the air. Strong red and pinks joined the green. The browns remained static.

A low hum of pain centered between Moira's ears. A warning. The air crackled. "Now isn't the time." She withdrew, sliding away from the subatomic particles to the surface of life. "I'm sorry. The competing forces going on within you need to battle it out . . . then possibly we can alter the energy."

Katie nodded, her somber expression remaining the same. "I figured. When the moon rose, the competition began . . . almost as if my brain was being separated into two distinct shapes. The process doesn't hurt, oddly enough." She tucked her legs under her. "You know what I miss?" Soft, low, she spoke almost as if she were alone in the room.

"What?"

"The colors"—Katie glanced up, their gazes meeting— "when I shift. Everything brightens and sparkles . . . and I can see the colors inside the colors. Like you do."

"Yes." Moira nodded, her heart aching. Losing that ability would cripple her. "I'm so sorry, Katie." Though reaching out and fighting was the solution.

A deep breath lifted Katie's chest. Her eyes cleared. "Yes, well. Outside when the beast howled, I felt him. I *knew* where he hid." She shrugged, a dark smile revealing smooth teeth. "Such knowledge might come in handy."

Moira sat back. The furious anticipation filling the lioness's eyes sent a chill down her spine. "Maybe." She stood. Emma was busy dealing with the werewolf, but Moira hoped Cara had a second to brainstorm. "We're going to figure this out." At Kate's quiet nod, Moira turned and hustled from the room. Something told her time was running out for her new friend.

She wound through the underground abyss, coming to Cara's quarters and knocking on the outside of the steel door, her knuckles protesting. A bomb couldn't open the door. But a very pregnant, flushed woman could.

Surprise caught Moira's breath. "Are you feeling all right?" She grasped Cara's arms, turning her toward the sofa. The smell of gardenias comforted her, a row of them lined up on a shelf across the room. Brenna loved gardenias. When the hell was she going to get her sister to safety?

"I'm fine." Cara rubbed her belly, waddling to sit down. "The baby is playing soccer inside me, that's all." She stretched her neck, drawing in air, smoothing hair away from her face. "Talen said they caught a were?"

"Yeah. Conn hurried off to get a look at the beast. Katie said she sensed him."

Cara's face pinched. "I wish she hadn't injected herself with the catalyst." Her eyes widened. "Hey, do you think you're able to create a spell and slow the progression?"

Moira shrugged, settling into the leather cushions. The color exactly matched her sofa in Dublin and a pang of homesickness hit her. "I doubt it. With you, the spell combined with Emma's concoction did the trick, and we can't guarantee the same thing would work with Katie." The hormones in Cara's body from the pregnancy had to have played a serious part—maybe the only part that mattered. Moira schooled her face into a thoughtful gaze.

Cara rolled her eyes. "Please. Don't ever play poker with Katie." A sigh escaped her as she arched her back, frowning. "This kid has some power." She frowned. "I know the hormones from gestating a vampire baby have protected me from the virus progressing too fast."

"What happens when he's born?" Moira didn't want to ask, but obviously the Kayrs women were educated scientists. Certainly, they'd thought of asking.

"We don't know." Cara bit her lip. "The regimen of medication seems to help, but as with any new illness, all we have is trial and error."

That's all they had in life, as far as Moira was concerned. She glanced around the small quarters, smiling at the sheer amount of greenery. Multiple shades of green adorned thin leaves, fat leaves, even furry leaves. "Talen prepared the place with you in mind."

Cara's smile flashed a dimple, and she pointed to a gorgeous drawing of Janie hanging on the wall. "Yeah, and Dage sketches pictures of us for the walls—the king is seriously talented. You should see his pictures of Emma."

Moira returned the grin. "I know. He's sent me sketches of the family for years."

A beep sounded on the laptop across the room. Cara pushed to her feet, wandering over and pressing a button. "What's up, Chalton?"

A face appeared, male and vampire. Soldier. "I have a secured call for Moira and heard she's with you." Even as he spoke, the rapid typing of keys and buzzing of machines continued uninterrupted.

Moira stood, adrenaline shooting her to the computer. "I'm here." Who'd be calling her? Nobody but the Nine knew where she was; she hadn't even told Brenna.

Chalton disappeared and Kell took shape, his black eyes sparking with anger. "When did you last talk to Brenna?"

Moira's knees buckled, and she fell into the office chair by the desk. The painting of an electric blue fantasy scene Bren had painted last year adorned the wall behind Kell. He was sitting in Brenna's living room. "Why?" she whispered, leaning closer to his face so he could reassure her Brenna was fine.

Male voices echoed from behind him. "I came to pick her up. She's not here."

There was more. There had to be. "And?"

Kell exhaled, running a hand through his thick hair. "The place is trashed. There's blood."

The sound that escaped Moira may have been a plea. She barely registered Cara's reassuring hand dropping to her shoulder. "How much blood?"

"Enough." Movement flashed behind him. "When they tried to take you, remember the mess it created?"

"Yes." Her mind spun back to the breaking glass, the papers flying all over—the sheer power coming from the abyss. "But no blood. I mean, I didn't get cut or anything." Glass could've injured Brenna before she was taken. If Kell was back in Ireland, all hell had broken loose. "Why are you home?"

His eyes hardened in an already hard face. "I came home last night to force the Nine into seclusion. Whether they like it or not."

Moira nodded. The enforcers would do their job to protect the council regardless of repercussions. "Did you?"

"Yes." A storm moved through Kell's gray eyes. "My sense is someone was here. They came here to take Bren." His jaw set in cold rage.

Moira frowned. "If it wasn't whoever's taking the Nine, who was it?" Could the Kurjans have taken Brenna? To what gain?

Most men would've shrugged. Kell remained still. "Demons, Kurjans, shifters? To force the Nine into compliance." Not by a twitch did his facial expression change. "Vampires?"

Fire swept through Moira. "The Realm isn't playing dirty, Kell."

His lip curled. "The Realm always plays dirty, sweetheart. That's why we align with them." He glanced around her, studying. "Why do you think you're with them?"

She frowned. "I know why I'm here." She now held knowledge about the Realm's research into the virus as well as the current location of their secret headquarters.

Kell nodded. "Exactly. Not for a second does anyone think the Realm will take out a Kayrs mate."

In other words, she was safe. While the vampires may try to detain her, they'd never harm her. She could broadcast her location to the world easily. What a chance Conn had taken in bringing her to his home. "I won't betray Conn."

Kell's eyes flickered. "You'll do what's necessary to protect the Nine, Moira."

She'd been warned. The day she'd joined as an enforcer, Kell had personally cautioned her about the possible sacrifices. Based on the look in his eyes, he remembered. He'd been growly her entire life. "You're truly an asshole, cousin."

His smile lacked any semblance of humor. "You're not the first to say that."

"Conn wouldn't have taken Brenna." Not without telling her, anyway.

"You sure about that?" Doubt filled Kell's eyes.

Moira's mind spun. Was she? Allowing Kell to keep her gaze, she centered herself. Life was about choices, and it was time she made one. She either trusted Conn or she didn't.

"I'm sure." Steel filled her voice, and gumption filled her spine. Her shoulders snapped back. "You either trust me or you don't, Kell Gideon."

His eyebrow lifted. The man hated his middle name. "Good enough." He glanced down, and the slow pecking of two-finger typing filled the silence. "I'm searching for

Simone and Trevan right now. They're no longer in New York, but I think they're still in the States. When I find them, you need to go get them." He stopped typing. "Secure them at Realm headquarters, since you trust your mate so much."

"No." Not a word her cousin heard often—if ever. "I'm going to find Brenna." Moira kept her voice steady, though inside she was screaming. The idea of Bren out there being tortured or even worse . . .

"Really? How're you going to do that, cousin?" Like always, Kell showed no emotion. Not even curiosity.

Anger mixed with unease in her stomach. "I don't have a plan yet." She was closer to Brenna than anyone else and needed to figure it out.

"A neighbor heard noise last night. She convinced herself it was the television because things quieted down quickly." Kell glanced off to the right and gave a short nod. "So Brenna has probably been gone for about eight hours, possibly ten."

She might be anywhere in the world. "Brenna's strong."

Fire flashed in his eyes. Finally. An emotion. "She's twenty years old, Moira. She's too young to be strong."

"You underestimate her." They all did. Not just because she was the baby, but because so many had viewed her with suspicion bordering on the superstitious. An eighth sister was truly unheard of. So the family had gathered around to protect and defend her. "We've all trained her. She's smart." More than likely smarter than the rest of them.

"Yes. She's smart." Kell's mask drew back into place. "So are you. I'll call you the second I have a lead on your sister. Until then, I need you to secure Simone and the prick she's dating."

Well now. "What's your problem with Councilman Demidov?"

Kell's left eyelid twitched. "My problem with Demidov is he shields himself with paper and statistics . . . completely ignoring the real world. I don't approve of my cousin seeing him. Simone needs someone stronger."

"Simone can take care of herself."

"You've only known her a century, if that, Moira. You may not understand everything." Kell stood and light glinted off the myriad of guns and knives tucked into his vest. He leaned down. "I'll send you their location as soon as it comes in. We're heading your way. Until then, do your job."

The screen went black.

Well! The arrogance of the man. Nothing on earth would allow Moira to admit she might have trouble getting out of headquarters. She was an enforcer, damn it.

She stood, her mind spinning as she faced Cara. "As soon as the intel arrives, I need to go fetch my cousin." And the asshole. But she needed to reach out and find her sister immediately.

Cara pursed her lips. "Your best recourse is to take Conn with you. It may be your only recourse."

"You're right." Moira ran a hand through her hair. "I hope he has a strategy to hunt down Brenna." She'd take all the help she could get.

Cara rubbed a palm down her arm. "Your sister will be all right, Moira." Worry lined the woman's face.

Moira nodded. "She has to be." Guilt swamped her so quickly she swayed. She should've forced Brenna to head to the States with her . . . the vampires would have kept her safe.

Cara frowned, her gaze over Moira's shoulder. "What—"

Energy whipped into Moira's back. Heat ripped along her skin. Fear had her jumping around. "Oh God." Fear morphed into terror as she widened her stance, protecting the pregnant woman. "Get down now! Get behind the couch."

The air shimmered, opening into a dark abyss. An ear-shattering shriek careened forth. She stepped back, spreading her arms to keep the energy from Cara. The kitchen cupboards opened as if yanked by angry hands. Cups spilled out to shatter against the floor. Papers swept from the desk, swirling in the air to slap into her chest.

How the hell had they found her? Adrenaline spiked through her blood. "Run, Cara!"

Cara grabbed her from behind, yanking her toward the door. "We'll both run," she yelled over the roar.

With a whoosh of sound, the swirling mass darted forward.

Chapter 27

Moira sent out a shrieking call for help . . . bellowing Conn's name. Focus. She needed to focus to save Cara. Grabbing a pillow, she flung it into the abyss. Male laughter, deep and long, came back.

Moira pivoted, bunching to tackle Cara to the ground. A roaring surrounded her, surrounded them, enclosing them in a gust of energy.

Everything went black.

Silence slammed noise down.

Pain ripped into Moira's nerve endings.

The force would kill them both. Drawing inward, Moira focused power to spiral through her body. A powerful group of protective cells gathered in her imagination, and she projected an umbrella of safety outward, hoping she caught Cara in the net. Her energy would combat the invisible knives trying to rip them apart.

Claustrophobia trapped panic in her throat. Nothingness replaced the dark. Was she in a vacuum? Where was Cara? God. The baby.

She tried to reach out. She tried to scream.

Nothing.

Sound returned first. Too loud, too harsh. A male voice roared in triumph. A female murmured at a softer frequency. Light zipped back with agonizing sharpness—too fast and too much.

As if her brain was a motherboard under electrical attack, it shut down. A zap echoed between her ears.

Peace swallowed her in gentle darkness.

Conn reached the door in unison with Talen, both throwing shoulders into the sealed barrier. Shards flew as the metal crashed in, bouncing off a table and knocking three potted plants to the ground. Dirt spilled across the floor, mingling with broken glass, pillow stuffing, and papers.

Talen ran through the destroyed living room toward the bedroom, bellowing his mate's name.

Conn surveyed the damage, his heartbeat roaring in his ears. He lifted his nose to sniff. No blood. He didn't smell blood. How had they found Moira?

Talen rushed out of the bedroom, his eyes an angry green lacking any gold. "What happened? How in the hell did they find us? Who the hell took them?" Raw fury coated his face.

Dage ran into the room. "Chalton put a call in to Moira from Kell. We're trying to reach him now."

Conn turned almost in slow motion to face his brother. "Moira cried out for help at the last second." The terror-filled shriek filling his head had nearly dropped him to the ground.

Dage lifted an eyebrow, sliding a cell phone to his ear. "Kell. It's Dage. Moira and Cara were just ripped out of our headquarters." His jaw tightened as he listened. "How?" His voice dropped further. "Apparently when you called in, you were hijacked."

Words were spoken on the other end.

"I don't know how. But make no mistake. If we don't

find them, I'm coming after you." He listened, then blinked hard. "Okay. You have an hour to locate them. This is witchcraft . . . you figure it out."

The phone clicked shut. "Brenna was taken last night. That's why he called Moira."

Conn fought the beast inside to remain calm. He needed to plan. "Okay. If they were teleported out of here, whoever was pulling strings had to be certain of their location, right?"

Dage nodded. "Without a doubt. I can only teleport *to* a location, so if I'm seeking someone, I have to know where they are. This new ability to teleport people against their will has to work the same way. You just can't find people in the universe. It's the location. Somehow, this asshole found ours."

"Kell's transmission." Talen leaned down to rescue a potted fern, placing the plant on the sofa table before striding toward the door. "Let's suit up."

Moira stretched awake, an odd ringing in her ears. Memories crashed in and she shot to her feet. Pain slashed into her head. She closed her eyes in protest. Swaying, she pressed both palms against her temples. She would not throw up.

Silence echoed around her. The musky scent of earth filled her nostrils. Slowly, she opened her eyes.

Metal bars came into view.

And an empty room beyond.

Fuzzy. The world was fuzzy. In confusion, she surveyed the cell, glancing behind her. "Cara!" Moira darted forward, reaching the bed and the unconscious woman. She pushed hair off Cara's forehead. The woman was too pale. The baby was too still.

They needed to get out of there. She glanced around. Metal bars evenly spaced lined the twenty-by-thirty cell containing a bed with what appeared to be an attached bath. The outside room was about the same size. The floor was concrete and a dark rock made up the walls. A basement of some sort.

She focused on the bars, seeing the subatomic particles, imagining them altering.

Nothing happened. The particles remained in solid state.

Damn it. Transporting had diminished her strength. But maybe she had enough left for an inquiry spell not requiring the manipulation of particles. A force had pulled them through. She might be able to determine who'd taken them by doing a simple analysis of the energy.

Visualizing the energy signature, she spread her palms out toward the far wall. Oxygen swirled into wind. The individual energy molecules sparked gold. She panted, fighting to keep the spell going. The effort weighed down her arms. Digging deep, struggling to keep focus, she forced the molecules into the shape of a man. His face flashed, then disappeared.

"Trevan?" Her arms dropped to her sides. Son of a bitch. She'd seen Trevan's face.

The outside door opened. "You called my name?" The witch strolled into the room, a smile on his intelligent face.

"You heard me?" She'd barely whispered it.

"Sure. The room has microphones that transmit outside. Just in case. Very impressive spell you just managed to concoct." He tilted his head toward Cara. "I think she's all right. You even kept her safe through the transport. Nicely done, Seventh."

The approval in his voice made her gag. "If you've harmed her, there's not a place on earth you'll be able to hide from Talen Kayrs." Moira faced him squarely.

Trevan lifted a shoulder. "I'd worry more about yourself, were I you."

"You're right. I'll be the one to kill you."

He leaned against the far wall, a smile on his face, flashing an onyx ring as he gestured. "I knew you'd be the one. That you'd survive."

His words entered her brain as if traveling through cotton.

She shook her head against the fuzziness. Cara needed help. Moira focused again on the bars, throwing all her energy into altering them.

Nothing happened.

"The revealing spell you just did will be your last. Frankly, I'm not sure how you pulled that off." Trevan wiped invisible dirt off his black silk shirt. "The walls are phanakite."

Dread caught her breath in her throat, but she kept her face placid. "That's fitting." Phanakite was a rare mineral deriving its name from the Greek word *deceiver* since it was often mistaken for quartz. The hard mineral also rendered quantum physics manipulation impossible. A fact her people had managed to keep secret from the rest of the world for the past thousands of years. "You planned ahead, Councilman Demidov."

"Yes, I did." He gave an exaggerated sigh. "Though you almost hijacked my shipment in New York. Shame on you, Seventh."

His intelligence had turned to pure arrogance. Nobody had seen it coming.

"So it was you mining in Russia, not the demons. Then you shipped it here." Calling him a traitor wasn't bad enough. There had to be a more insulting word.

"Yes. You wouldn't believe how difficult it was to get to the mineral—old Viv did a great job eons ago burying those mines. But . . . I'm better than she is." He rubbed his shoulder, the arrogance settling hard on his face. "I had hoped to use the phanakite to get cooperation from the council members. Unfortunately, you're the first to survive the journey through dimensions."

Pain exploded in her solar plexus. The missing council members were dead? "You killed them?"

"No." He pushed away from the wall like a graceful puma. "Their lack of skill killed them. They could've survived transporting, but they didn't."

Fear squeezed her lungs. Oh God. "Brenna?" Moira rushed forward, wrapping her fingers around the cold metal. Her sister couldn't be dead. Kell said someone had taken her, not that she had been transported.

Trevan's smile belonged on an anaconda. "Sweet little Brenna. So sad." Manicured fingers tapped in numbers on a mounted security pad. Locks disengaged with smooth rolling plunks. The door of the outside room opened, and he swept through.

The bolts reengaged . . . slamming home with finality.

Every cell in Moira's body froze. Brenna was alive. She had to be. Her disappearance didn't match the pattern of missing Coven Nine members. Trevan was just messing with her. She called out to her mate. *Conn?*

No response. She wasn't surprised. Her entire body felt like it had been short-circuited from the journey.

A groan came from behind Moira. She whirled, rushing to sit by Cara's side.

Cara's eyes fluttered open. "Ouch."

"Are you all right?" Moira helped her friend to a seated position on the rough wool blanket.

"No." Cara frowned, scooting back to rest against the mineral enriched wall. "I'm so fucking sick of people yanking me through dimensions."

"Ah." Moira dropped her gaze to Cara's protruding stomach. "Not your first time, huh?"

"No." Cara rubbed her hands along her belly. "Once with Emma and once with Dage. Those times nothing hurt."

"Yeah. Transporting the unwilling seems to cause pain." Moira rose, eyeing the far door. "Can you contact Talen? We may need help getting out of here, wherever we are."

"No," Cara sighed. "I haven't been able to communicate with him since contracting the virus. But you can do your witch thing, right? I mean, unlock the door or whatever?"

"Witch thing?" Moira's lips twitched.

"Yeah. Rearrange the particles and freeze the lock. Or something."

"No." Moira turned around to face her friend. "The process of teleporting us here messed with my energy." She had taken an oath to protect the secret that might take them down, at any cost. No matter how much she trusted Cara, Moira couldn't talk about the walls.

"That makes sense." Cara rose unsteadily to her feet. "I don't feel well." Water whooshed out of her skirt to splash against the floor. "Holy crap."

"Oh God." Moira grabbed her, setting her down on the bed. "Okay. What does that mean? I mean, does that mean . . ."

"Yes." Cara wrinkled her face in pain, clutching her stomach. "Of course it does. What else could go wrong? We might as well be trapped in an elevator. You know . . . just in time for labor." The woman was babbling.

Moira didn't know a thing about delivering a baby. Especially in a basement. Or cave. Or wherever the hell they were. "Deep breaths. Take deep breaths."

Cara batted her away. "Go figure out how to get us out of here. You're the Seventh, for cripes' sakes."

The cranky woman now in labor had a point. The locks

sprang open on the outside door, and Moira swirled around to block Cara with her body. A woman's laughing chuckle wafted inside. "Trevan, where in the world are we going? We're late for our reservations."

Simone. Fire ripped up Moira's spine. No way had Trevan been able to rip people through time and space without help. If it was the last thing she did, she'd end her cousin's life.

Simone's voice became louder. "What do you have down here protected by three coded entries?"

Trevan entered, tugging her inside. The woman's long skirts swished against the dusty cement. She staggered, losing her smile. Her dark eyes widened on Moira. "What have you done?" she gasped.

Trevan smiled like a nerd with a crush. "Well now. I've secured the Seventh as well as a Kayrs mate. I told you brains and not brawn would lead the world, darling. This is our chance." He tugged Simone back against him, securing an arm around her waist and lowering his mouth to her ear, his focus remaining on Moira. "This is our moment, Simone."

Simone's porcelain pure skin paled to translucence. Her gaze met Moira's. Shock, understanding, and then finally acceptance filtered through her black eyes. "How secure are they?"

"Very. Besides the three locked doors, the walls are phanakite." His mouth wandered down Simone's neck in a lover's caress.

Simone closed her eyes, swallowing loudly. "So they're helpless."

"Yes." Trevan rose up to smile broadly. "The Kurjans will fetch them later, securing our treaty with them."

The Kurjans had been trying for a witch to experiment on all year. Moira frowned at her cousin. "You didn't realize your lover was killing off the Coven Nine?"

Simone's hands clenched in fists. "No. Are they dead?"

Trevan shrugged, shifting Simone. "Unfortunately. None of them were strong enough to make the trip. Until Moira." Approval coated his voice as he gave a short nod.

Cara groaned low behind Moira.

Trevan's eyes widened. "She's not in labor."

"She is." Moira lifted her chin. "I really don't want to be you right now, Trevan." Talen would rip the man apart with his bare hands. That is, if he could find the witch. She eyed her pale cousin. So Simone hadn't known. "I'm sorry. I thought you were working with him."

"No." Simone inhaled, glancing down at her long skirt and sparkling tank top.

Trevan tugged her harder against him. "I wanted to surprise you, darling. Did I?"

"Yes," Simone whispered.

"You want to lead, don't you? You're pleased?" Trevan asked.

Simone straightened her shoulders. "Of course, sweetheart. You know we were meant to run the council." She eyed the door. "It appears you've thought of everything. There's no way for them to escape."

Trevan preened like a rabid bird. "I knew you'd be pleased."

"Oh, I am." Simone relaxed against her lover, her voice lowering to a purr. "Though the sooner they're gone, the better. Ah, when will we be rid of them?" While she sounded sexy as hell, her face remained stoic, her concentration on Moira.

Trevan tugged her head back, caressing his mouth down her profile, his gaze thoughtful. She closed her eyes, leaning into him, sighing. He chuckled. "The Kurjans will arrive tonight."

Simone smiled. "Excellent."

Moira frowned. Maybe Simone could get Trevan to talk. "Ask him about Brenna, Simone."

Her eyes flashed opened. "Brenna?" She stilled. "What about Brenna?"

Trevan released her, sliding toward the door. "We'll discuss this upstairs, Simone."

Simone half turned, her hands going to her hips. "What do you mean? You didn't try to take Brenna, did you?"

"If I did?" Challenge lifted his chin. "Sometimes sacrifices need to be made to get where we want to in life. You understand that, correct?"

"Yes. I understand that." Simone's shoulders slumped.

"You love me, right?" Triumph turned Trevan's face from an intelligent mask to something reprehensible.

Simone sighed. "Yes. I do." Her glance cut to Moira and back. "But apparently I don't know you very well."

His chuckle filled the ominous room. "We'll have to work on that. For now, you need to make sure you understand and accept your path." While congenial, his tone held certain threat.

"I do." Simone straightened her shoulders. "I always have." She turned toward Moira. "You might want to get ready to face that destiny you're so proud of." Her elegant sniff echoed around the cage. "Let's go, Trevan."

He smiled, turning to punch in his code.

With a breath of sound, Simone was on him. She hit him full in the back, knocking his face into the door. A crunch echoed. Blood sprayed. Her bare arm snaked around his neck and she jerked tight, her knees clasping his rib cage.

Trevan turned with a dark roar, slamming backward into the wall. Simone's shoulders hit hard, nearly dislodging her. She cried out in pain, her eyes flashing as she struggled to keep her hold.

"Dig your knees in harder, Simone," Moira urged. Could the woman fight? Kell had trained her at some point, hadn't he? "Good. Now cut off his air supply. Crush his Adam's apple if you can."

Blood dripped down Trevan's furious face. An animalistic growl escaped through his bared teeth. Grabbing Simone's hair, he gave a sharp yank, pulling her over his shoulder. She landed on her feet, staggering. She struggled furiously, but he pulled back an arm and punched her in the jaw. She sagged, her hands rising weakly.

He hit her again.

"Stop it!" Moira hissed. "Let her go, you asshole."

He lowered his face to Simone's, raw fury etched in every line. "You little bitch. Did you really think you could beat me?"

"Didn't see as I had a choice," Simone slurred. "Not enough time to plan."

Moira stomach rolled. Simone was right. It was their only chance to escape before Trevan relocked all the doors. "Let her go, Trevan. Taking the head of the Nine's daughter will get you killed for sure. Aunt Viv can rip the skin right off your body, and you know it."

Trevan swallowed, then he yanked a gun from behind his pressed trousers. "Well now. I guess the Kurjans get two witches and a Kayrs mate." He jammed the barrel to Simone's temple. "Step away from the bars, Moira."

Dragging Simone across the room, he waited until Moira backed up. He kept the nearly unconscious woman in front of him, unlocked the door, and threw her inside.

Moira caught her cousin, easing her to the floor.

"I'm sorry," Simone murmured. Then she passed out.

Chapter 28

Moira smoothed Simone's hair back from her already purpling face. "I think her cheekbone is broken."

Cara struggled to swing her legs over the edge of the bed, reaching for Simone's arms. "That's not all he broke." She grimaced, tugging the unconscious woman up. "Her heart pretty much shattered the second she walked in the room. Set her up here."

With a grunt, Moira lifted Simone to the bed, resting her back against the wall. She slumped down, her long black hair falling over her face. "Sometimes I forget you're an empath."

"So do I." Cara scooted over, sucking in air. "Just so you know. Not for one second did she plan to go along with him."

"Yeah." Moira had known that from Simone's first shocked look. "She took the only chance she had to knock him out and get us free." Unfortunately, now Moira had two women needing her to rescue them. She frowned, vaguely remembering she had heard a woman when they'd arrived. "If Simone hasn't been helping Trevan, who has?"

Cara clutched her stomach, curling into a ball. A low moan escaped her. The smoky scent of pain filled the air. Brain waves, or maybe life waves, cascaded off her in shades of blue and green. "Um. This baby's coming."

Panic had Moira rising to her feet. "Make him stop." The words emerged before she could bite her lip.

Cara gave a strangled laugh. "You know he's Talen's son, right? If he wants out . . ."

Of course. Another stubborn Kayrs male. She wished she could communicate with them. "Oh. Okay. Um, lie back and I'll, uh, take a look." Whatever force had whipped them there must've started labor.

Simone groaned awake, smoothing a hand over her left cheekbone. "Trevan's an asshole."

Moira huffed out a laugh. "I'm worried he broke your face."

"Feels like it." Simone blinked twice, focusing on Cara cringing at the end of the bed. "Ah, you're not . . ." She tugged herself to her feet, getting out of the way. Her heeled boots slid through the water and her arms wind-milled as she regained her balance. "Ug."

"Yeah." Cara stretched out, her eyes wide in panic as she kicked her underwear across the cell. "I can't do this. I mean, I really can't do this. A vampire baby for goodness sakes. I need Talen."

Moira needed Talen, too. She shared a panicked look with Simone.

Simone cleared her throat, spreading her hands out. "This is fine. I lived on a farm once."

"A farm?" Cara nearly shrieked.

"Yes." Simone rubbed her palms together. "Trust me. So long as the little vamp doesn't bite you on the way out . . ."

"What?" Cara did shriek this time. "Talen said the fangs didn't come in until they were around ten years old."

Simone snorted, dropping to her knees at the edge of the bed. "That's true." She rolled up Cara's skirt. "I was just kidding. Okay, let's take some deep breaths here."

"Funny. Very funny." Cara threw an arm over her eyes. Pain vibrated from her in waves. "This hurts."

"Go see if there are towels in the bathroom," Simone murmured to her cousin.

Moira ran inside the bathroom, flinging open a cupboard and yanking out two white towels smelling of a spring breeze. Clean. Good. She hustled back, towels in hand. "Got them."

Fear clogged her throat. Cara had the virus and needed a doctor. The woman was in a weakened condition. What if she died the second the babe came out? What if the baby had problems?

"Ah, we don't have much time here. This baby wants out." Simone placed one towel over Cara's bent knees. "Moira, I need you to pin my hair back."

Moira scanned the cell, panic jerking her movements. She spotted the black cord holding Simone's Celtic knot pendant around her cousin's neck. She had the exact same one. A while back, Kell purchased birthday presents for all his cousins in bulk, doling the same pendant out all year. They'd given him a hard time, but really, the guy had tried. With a sob, she unlatched Simone's cord, winding it through her hair to secure. "There you go."

"Thanks." Simone took a deep breath. "Okay. Now we're just going to breathe deep and focus."

Focusing took minutes. Then an hour. Then two more hours. Moira jerked with each contraction as Cara's entire body went rigid and she moaned. Then, when each pain subsided, Moira sagged against the wall in relief.

Finally, Simone settled the towel more securely across Cara's knees. "Cara, it's time to push."

"No. God no." Cara's body trembled. "I'm not pushing. He's staying in until Talen gets here." Terror filled the woman's voice.

Moira bent down, her face next to Cara's. "Your babe needs to breathe, Cara. Push him out so he can. I promise you it'll be all right." They couldn't let the baby die. Or Cara for that matter.

Tears filled Cara's eyes. "You promise?"

"Yes." How she'd keep such a promise, she didn't know. But she would.

Simone grabbed a towel to place on the bed. "I think he's ready. With the next contraction, bear down."

Cara nodded, sweat pooling on her forehead. "Simone? I'm sorry about Trevan."

A sad smile lit Simone's battered face. "Thank you. No worries, he's not the first mistake I've made."

Cara stiffened, groaning. "I'm sorry . . . about Dage . . . too."

Simone glanced up. "Oh, I didn't mean the king. We weren't in love." She rolled her eyes. "Though I would've made a hell of a queen."

Moira frowned. Who had hurt Simone in the past? Was it the mysterious demon?

Simone drew in a deep breath. "I, ah, wasn't very graceful when we met at the colloquium. Sorry."

Cara hissed out. "No worries. It had to be weird seeing your ex with someone else."

"Yes, well." Simone placed a hand on Cara's stomach. "I'm often the most beautiful woman in the room. It pisses me off when not everyone notices."

Moira grinned, smoothing Cara's hair off her face. "I've always admired your keen sense of self-awareness, Simone." She sobered, realizing the truth in the statement. Whatever faults Simone possessed, she accepted and discussed them freely. "I shouldn't have thought for one second you would align against the Nine."

"You know what I don't like about you, Moira?" Simone kept her gaze under the towel.

"The fact that I'm the Seventh?"

"No. The fact that you're the Seventh and can tell everyone to kiss your ass . . . yet you don't. You're worried about being the right Seventh, of doing what you should. Stop sniveling. Step up and be the Seventh, whatever the hell that means."

The statement held enough truth to make Moira's temper raise its head. "What, are we bonding now?"

Simone glanced up with a smile. "God help the world. We are."

Cara gave a strangled cry, her body going rigid. "Enough bonding. Here he comes." She clutched onto Moira's hand with white knuckles. "Oh my God, this hurts." A contraction rippled down her stomach. "Talen?" She gasped, half sitting up. "I can hear him." She shut her eyes, concentrating. "Somehow, through the baby, I can reach Talen."

"You can reach your mate telepathically?" Simone's head snapped up. "Tell him we're in the Cascade mountains in California. And to bring help."

Most people didn't know about the vampires' ability to telepathically reach their mates. Moira shut her eyes, searching for Conn. Nothing. She tried again. Only breezy silence met her call. She flipped her lids open. "I can't reach Conn." Cara's gift must be because of the labor, because the baby was coming. Or maybe through the baby. "Does Talen know where we are?"

Cara bit her lip, lifting her body off the bed, her face contorting in pain. "Yes," she panted. "They're on the way." Her hold tightened on Moira. "I've got to push."

"Here he is," Simone said in a hushed voice. "One more push. Come on, Cara. One more."

With a high-pitched yelp, Cara bore down. A scream escaped her. Simone reached forward, grabbing the baby. She swaddled him, wiping him clean. Moira's eyes misted over. Just then, the babe opened his mouth and gave one short, irritated cry.

Cara laughed, tears streaming down her face. "Sounds pissy just like Talen." She reached out, taking the baby and holding him close. Her face fell. "I can't reach Talen anymore." She uncovered her son, checking him over. "That's okay. Daddy will be here soon."

Moira focused on the newest Kayrs, ignoring whatever Simone was doing under the towel. The baby looked just like his father. High forehead, tons of black hair, strong features with sizzling, metallic gray eyes. She gasped at the vampire colors. "Look at those eyes." The babe focused on her, reaching out with one chubby hand. "Are babies supposed to focus this fast?"

"No." Cara tried to smooth wild hair back from his little face. "But he's a vampire and Talen's son, so who the heck knows." She nuzzled his cheek, one hand supporting his head. "Ten fingers, ten toes, no fangs." Her smile lit her face. "He's perfect."

Simone tossed the second towel into the bathroom. Her smile made her appear even more beautiful, if that was possible. "He is perfect." She raised both eyebrows. "His eyes. Very unusual."

Cara turned the babe to face her. "Talen's eyes turn metallic when he's, ah, emotional."

Simone shook her head. "I'm sure. The vampire colors don't usually show up until puberty. I wonder if that stunning gray is his normal color. Intriguing." She hustled into the bathroom and the sound of running water echoed. She emerged, drying her hands on yet another clean towel. Apparently Trevan had prepared for an extended stay. "So. What now?"

Chapter 29

Conn fought to keep his face stoic as the helicopter banked hard to the right. His bones had healed, but the internal organ damage shot shards of pain through his nerve endings. He settled next to Jase, closing his eyes, forcing all sensation into a box. Dage and Talen took up the front seat, while Jordan and Kane followed in two more low-flying Black Hawks.

The sun lowered in the west, bright rays of reds and golds reflecting inside the vehicle. Jase tapped keys on his laptop. "Are you sure you're up to this, Conn?"

"Yes." Conn sought his mate, scowling when there was no response.

Jase nodded. "I've brought up Trevan's place in the Cascade Mountains. He's prepared for us."

Conn opened his eyes, glancing at the screen. "The house stands in the center of about twenty-five acres. At first glance, I see land mines, external traps, and sensors. Thirty guards, teams of three sweeping the perimeter." He'd kill them all. "The house is shielded—I can't lock on any heat signatures." Chances were Trevan stashed the women in the basement, somewhere secure. He shut his eyes again, searching. "I can't contact my mate." Anger mixed with an unfamiliar fear in his gut. Why couldn't he reach her?

Jase frowned. "How do you contain a witch?"

You knock her out or kill her. "I don't know." The heaviness of the weapons arranged throughout his vest centered Conn. "Demidov is a dead man."

Dage banked the copter in a sharp left turn. "I assume yanking an unwilling person through dimensions and time to land somewhere else would short-circuit anyone's abilities. Even a witch." His silver eyes shone with pure shards of vampire blue. "Demidov doesn't have long to live. But I need him alive for now."

"He dies."

"Not until we figure out how he's transporting people against their will." Dage glanced out the window. "Then you can kill him."

"No promises." Conn settled back into the seat. The only question would be who got to the witch first, Talen or Conn. "If Cara's hurt, you won't be able to stop Talen." None of them would. Conn wouldn't even try.

"I know." Dage's knuckles went white on the controls.

Conn fought the dread in his gut. Cara was pregnant . . . being forced to travel dimensions couldn't be good for her or the baby. His nephew. She'd only had seconds to communicate with Talen . . . because the baby was coming.

Talen's growl came through his earpiece. "Kell just checked in. There was an advanced tracker on Brenna's computer. That's how Trevan zeroed in on Moira's position before taking them."

Cold. His brother's voice was low and cold . . . a tone Conn had never heard from him before. Learning his mate had reached labor while being held captive had almost sent the vampire over the edge. "Moira's the Seventh, Talen. She's strong and smart and incredibly gifted. She'll protect Cara and your babe." As he spoke the words, Conn realized the absolute truth in them. His woman was a fighter, and a damn good one. She knew her job.

He'd better do his. "All right. I want four teams. We hit them from the north and the east. Dage, drop Talen and me on the roof of the house. You go make sure the soldiers don't close in on us." Conn needed to have Talen's back and keep the man from getting killed with his focus so completely on his mate.

"Got it," Dage said.

Conn flashed his teeth. He liked keeping the king close in any battle situation, considering he'd never let his king fall. Much less his brother. "Stay safe, King." He wasn't looking forward to the day when he and Talen put their feet down and told Dage he couldn't go into battle. At least not while the war was heating up and their friends were turning into enemies. The king had to be protected at all costs.

Dage lifted an eyebrow. "Good luck with that."

"Stay out of my head." Prick.

"Sorry. Your thoughts are screaming." Dage banked left. "On the ground in three minutes."

Jase tucked the laptop under the seat, sliding open the side door. Conn followed suit, his gaze tracking the pattern of trails winding through the pine trees below. He'd memorized the layout of land mines, as well as the last soldier positions. The wind whipped into his face, carrying the scent of pine and spruce. "Keep in mind the power necessary to forcibly transport members of the Coven Nine. Demidov is probably working with someone." He glanced at Jase. "I want a storm. Massive, powerful, and dangerous. As big as you can make it."

Jase's eyes lit up in anticipation. "Hurricane or snowballs the size of basketballs?"

"Hail. Sharp and deadly." Loud enough to cover their movements through the forest.

"No problem." Jase leaned out the opening, holding the bar. "But you know I can't easily turn it off if I make a storm that size."

"I know." An issue Conn would deal with later. For now, they needed the cover.

Missiles shot from the earth. Dage evaded, swooping in toward the roof of the sprawling house as the other two helicopters returned fire. "Get ready."

Conn grabbed the doorframe, leaning out. When the copter perched about ten feet from the roof, he jumped. He landed in unison with lightning rippling across the sky. Clouds formed out of nowhere, throwing hail the size of basketballs. Damn, Jase was good.

A dark form caught Conn's vision, and Talen slammed boots on the angled shingles, snagging the pitch to hold on. "Let's get this bastard." His eyes glowed unearthly in the night.

"Yep." Conn straightened, running along the top and arriving at a skylight. What kind of arrogant moron kept a skylight in a house holding hostages? "This guy isn't expecting us. Must be planning to move the women fast." No need for stealth. The world was lighting up with fire behind him. Jumping up, he smashed his feet into the glass, falling through to the room below.

He landed in a crouch . . . in a master bathroom. The plush carpet was an emerald green matching his mate's pretty eyes. The reminder of her made his fangs lengthen, his body vibrate as the animal wanted loose. The animal needed to protect and defend his mate. Quiet surrounded him.

Talen dropped down, scanning the area. "Dage wants him alive." Angry and annoyed, his tone came out through obvious fangs.

Conn rose, grabbing his gun from his waistband. "What are the chances of that?"

"Zero." Talen kicked open the door. "Where is everybody?"

The moron really hadn't expected them. "The guards

are outside fighting . . . Trevan must have an escape route. We need to hurry." The visible heat signatures had held bulk as well as weapons, so the women must be underground. If they were still there. Dread and fear set up in Conn's gut, and he ruthlessly shoved them aside.

Priceless watercolors lined the hallway, reminding Conn of his mother's fanciest parlor. He swept side to side with his gun, hurrying toward the stairs and running down to a sprawling living area with a huge stone fireplace. Explosions echoed in the distance.

He turned the corner, heading down another set of stairs to a playroom with pool tables, arcade games, and a bar. A warning tickled at the base of his neck. "Back."

Talen whipped back around the corner just as gunfire erupted. Watercolors exploded, pieces of glass shattering. Dropping to his knees, Conn emerged from safety, firing toward the bar. Talen followed suit, aiming at the men behind the pool tables. One shrieked in pain.

Conn's bullets aimed true, taking out two men with glowing green guns behind the bar. Bottles shattered. The scent of bourbon and scotch permeated the air . . . along with blood. With a roar, Talen leaped over the pool table, his knife in hand. Red arced across the window, spraying like a rainbow of death. When Talen rose and turned, gone was his brother. In his place stood vengeance.

Giving a short nod, Conn pivoted and rushed toward another flight of stairs. Down. He'd keep going down until he found his woman.

A whisper of her reached out. The hint of lilacs. A savage wildness consumed him. Taking his mate out of safety and away from him pissed off the soldier inside him. Almost as much as the action challenged the animal lurking even deeper.

She was his.

The soldier easily, almost too willingly, gave over to the

predator. Gone was reason, gone was mercy. Anyone else standing between him and his mate would die. Slow, fast, he no longer cared. Their time would end.

With a snarl, the animal rose in dominance, pure instinct taking over.

Talen swept the area, turning his focus and aim to a thick oak door set to the side. Conn nodded, putting his boot to it. The door slammed open to reveal wide cement steps leading down. He hated basements. "Down."

The metal door slid open and Trevan rushed inside to slam it shut. Moira grabbed the bars with both hands, shielding Cara and the babe from his sight. She forced a smile. "So. Guess we have company." Though dim, the sound of gunfire could be heard in the distance. Even stronger, the sense of Conn drew nearer. She may not be able to get into his head yet, but his fury sent out vibrations.

Trevan pivoted to her, his eyes wild. "How the hell did they find you?" He gestured toward the walls. "No way you could send a message."

He didn't know about Cara's ability to reach her mate. A closely guarded secret, and one Moira had kept through the years. "I'm more powerful than you think, dumbass."

A beep sounded from his pocket and he yanked out a phone to read a message. Fury swept across his face in clotted red. "The outer door has been breached. The locks will slow them down some, but they'll eventually make it inside here." His smile chilled her blood. The gun he pulled from his waistband heated her right back up.

"You going to shoot me, Trevan?" Not for a second did she believe he'd kill his bargaining chip.

"No." He took two steps forward and slid to the side, pointing the weapon.

The shot echoed around the small room.

"No," Moira screamed, leaping to shield Cara and the babe in unison with Simone.

The bullet hit the new mother, throwing her back against the wall. Blood sprayed out, catching Moira across the face. A vicious roar split the night from the other side of the door. Moira leaped forward, her hands going to the wound in Cara's right shoulder—three inches from the babe's head.

Cara's mouth dropped open. She paled to white cardboard, her blue eyes cutting to Trevan. "Talen will kill you." Her hand cupped her child's head, caressing when he started to whimper.

Moira took the towel Simone had grabbed, pressing hard against the bullet hole. "Cara. Focus, hon. You're going into shock." Rage shot through her. Talen wouldn't get a chance to kill Trevan. She glared over her shoulder. "What the hell are you thinking?" Who could actually shoot at a woman holding her newborn? What kind of a monster was he?

Simone dropped to her knees by the bed. "Cara, let me hold the baby so we can take a look at your injury." Tremors shook her voice.

"No." Cara tightened her hold on the baby, tears gathering in her eyes. Shock had her pupils dilating.

Trevan stepped up to the bars, the gun pointed at Cara's head. Moira nodded to Simone, who placed her hands on the towel to stem the bleeding.

Then Moira stood and turned, shielding. "Why?"

Trevan leveled the weapon between her eyes, reaching to the side wall and punching in a code. The bars swung open. "Come here. Make one move and I'll shoot the baby."

Anger threatened to still her legs. But outside, next to

him, she had more of a chance to get the weapon. She needed to get his focus off Cara. So Moira stepped lightly toward him, training moves filtering through her thoughts. He grabbed her hair and yanked her to his side, shutting the door, pressing her back to his front. Cold metal pressed against her temple.

Leather slid around her neck.

Weakness assaulted her limbs. Her blood slowed. A tingling set up in her extremities.

He whipped her around, clinking something into place. She reached up, her eyes widening at the cold lock. "What the hell?" Her eyelids fluttered. A lump of dread settled hard in her stomach. Oh God, it couldn't be.

Trevan smiled. "Phanakite. A collar just for you, bitch."

With a low cry, she dug her nails into the leather, her fingers burning. Leather mixed with phanakite. Against her jugular, against her flesh. She tugged. Nothing. Her muscles went lax. It couldn't touch her skin like this. She might never recover. Tears poked her eyes, and she forced them back.

Trevan punched in another code, and the far wall opened to reveal a passageway. He turned toward the cell. "Simone. I had hoped things would be different." Then he grabbed Moira's arm and tugged her through. The door slid shut, and lights strung along the ceiling flickered to life. He shoved her into the passenger seat of a golf cart. "Well now. I guess contingency plans are always a good idea, right, Seventh?"

Her mind twirled. She clutched the fabric seat, trying to keep her balance. "Why did you shoot Cara?" The words emerged slow and slurred.

He pressed the pedal, sending the cart flying forward through the tunnels. "Whatever Kayrs shows up will stop and make sure she and the babe are all right. I just bought us some time."

Moira struggled to keep upright. Damp earth filled her nostrils. Lights flashed by, and she blinked. She swayed.

Trevan clapped a hand around her arm. "Don't go falling out, now. Your body will adjust to the collar. You won't get any strength back, but you should be able to sit upright soon." His voice echoed from far away.

She lost track of time. Or maybe reality. Finally they came to the end of the tunnel. Trevan jumped out and yanked open a worn door. Snow and wind bombarded inside, and Moira turned her head to the side, shutting her eyes. So cold. Slowly, her thoughts began to organize.

Trevan grabbed her hair, tugging her off the seat.

She protested as he pulled her into the swirling storm. A sprawling hill lay to the right, trees and rock ahead. Atop the hill stood a large warming hut. Hail pelted her, leaving bruises. But the pain centered her. Until she tripped over a rock, smashing to the ground. Her hands stopped her fall, shredding from brittle pinecones. Cold, she was so cold. Trevan tightened his hold on her hair, dragging her along an overgrown trail into the forest.

The knees of her jeans shredded. She stumbled to her feet, yanking her head away. The wind nearly knocked her over. She should run.

Trevan grabbed the front of her blouse and forced her through the trees. A rocky cliff stood before them. He reached out, slid his hand across the rock, and a keypad appeared.

Dizziness swamped Moira. The stones moved. Crap. An elevator? Her mind wanted to fight. Her body wanted to sleep for weeks. "Take the collar off, Trevan." She staggered inside the elevator, reaching out to steady herself against the walls.

"No." The door slid shut. The lift began to rise. "Your mate won't find the elevator, Moira. We'll be safe at the top while waiting for my people."

Nobody would see the lift. But Conn would scale the mountain to rescue her. None of it was making sense. The collar muddled everything.

The lift halted and the doors slid open. Mother Nature smashed her way inside. The squeal from the wind pierced Moira's eardrums. She cringed back when Trevan clasped her hand, but he dragged her into the storm unhampered, as if she had no strength.

Hail pelted them during the short trek from rock to cabin. With a sigh of relief, Trevan pushed open the door and propelled her inside.

Chapter 30

Trevan shoved Moira against the wall of the cabin, casting a worried glance at the hail battering the window. "This storm is unbelievable." Quick motions had her handcuffed to iron rings set into the rough wooden planks.

She looked around for a weapon. Shelves held gloves, goggles, and hand warmers. The walls were bare, and unbleached pine spread across the floors. A broken board from the floor would make an excellent weapon. A closed door stood to the north, probably to a bathroom. "Your helicopter isn't going to make it here, asshole." Moira struggled to keep her neck upright. The collar seemed to be dragging energy right out of her skin.

Trevan tightened his jaw. "Sure it is. The landing spot is next to this warming hut. We always meet transportation right here."

A tingling set up at the base of her neck. She focused on the closed interior door. An energy, one barely measurable, pulsated in the next room. Something familiar. "Who's in there?"

His eyes lightened. "You truly have power, Seventh." He strode over to the door, ripping it open and revealing a bathroom. Reaching inside, he grabbed something and yanked.

Moira cried out as her sister tumbled out. "Brenna!" Thank God. Relief threatened to steal whatever strength Moira had left. Tears gathered, wanting to fall.

Brenna shook her head, her eyes fluttering before opening. Frayed rope bound her hands and feet. Duct tape covered her mouth. She wore a matching, sparkling collar around her neck. Her dark eyes widened on her sister before she scowled.

Trevan grabbed her hair and dragged her next to Moira, handcuffing her to the wall. "I left her in the bathroom— wasn't sure how long we'd be." Flashing a wide smile, he ripped off the tape.

"Ouchgoddamityoufucking prick," Brenna hissed. Angry motions had her tossing strands out of her face. "I am so going to kill you. First I'm going to take your skin, then I'm concentrating on your liver. You think my aunt is scary—"

Trevan backhanded her, slamming her head back into the oak.

Brenna gasped. "Now that just hurt, Trevan."

Moira struggled against the cuffs, feeling like sand had swallowed her limbs. She'd kill him. She'd take his liver out and eat it. "How did he get you here, Bren?"

"Two of his guys dropped by. I let them right in." Self-disgust curled Brenna's lip. "We fought, and I woke up on a plane coming to this palace. He brought me to keep you in control, the dumbass. How did you get here?"

"Transported. Prick." Moira stared into the darkness outside the wide window. Anger rose at her helplessness. "Take this collar off and fight me like a man, Trevan." She could take him one-on-one. Using a device made of phanakite violated every oath he'd ever taken.

"No." He frowned at his cuticles. "I bruised my hand on your cousin's face already." His tongue darted out to wet his lips. "Quite a surprise, that one. Thought I knew Simone."

"Guess you don't understand women." Brenna rested her head against the wall.

He shrugged. "I wouldn't say that. Besides, Simone was a temporary distraction. One I now regret."

Moira kept her body still, forcing boredom into her tone. "Right. Considering you already have a woman." She had heard a female voice . . . who the hell was it?

"Nice try." Trevan inched closer to the window. "I promised my lady protection and unfortunately am unable to satisfy your curiosity."

Moira's feet began to tingle, her hands going numb. The collar needed to be removed, and fast. "I suggest you make a run for it now, Trevan. My mate will be here soon."

"I'm counting on Connlan making an appearance. My people will arrive in due time, and we'll arrange an alternate meeting point with the Kurjans." Trevan grinned, flipping open a cell phone to speak. "That helicopter needs to land on the roof within thirty minutes, or I'll kill you and your entire family. Everyone you've ever known, in fact." He listened and then nodded. "I thought you'd see things my way. Are the sharpshooters in position? Good."

Nausea competed with dread in Moira's stomach. "You'd truly hand me over to the Kurjans? Knowing they want a witch to experiment on?"

"I need an alliance with them to take over the Nine." He punched a code into a keypad on the wall, and the hill below them lit, illuminating the pelting hail. Wind beat against the sides, shaking the rafters. "Ladies, I believe we're about to have some fun while we wait."

Moira's eyes fluttered, and she bit down on her lip. The pain helped her focus. "What have you done?"

Trevan rubbed his hands together. "We're against solid

rock with a sheer cliff on the other side. This hill, this sweet-looking hill, is the only way to reach you, Moira. I assume we'll see your mate shortly."

The gods continued to hail missiles at the ground, and Moira forced a smile. "Your sharpshooters can't see through that muck. They can't find my mate."

Though was he all right? Conn's internal injuries hadn't had time to heal, and the skirmish below had sounded bloody.

"They can spot him well enough, don't you worry." Trevan placed one hand against the window. "Besides, bullets are the least of your boy's worries."

"Conn will find land mines and traps," Brenna whispered. "Don't worry, Moira."

Trevan shook his head. "The land mines are set too far down to be sensed. While they won't kill like normal, they'll certainly injure and slow a vampire—which is all I need for my shooters to take him down long enough so we can cut his head off."

Moira shared a worried look with her sister. The plan wasn't bad. Conn's injuries would slow him down, and the blast from a land mine wouldn't help. Not to mention carefully aimed bullets.

"How could you turn your back on everything you've vowed to protect?" Moira asked.

Trevan turned, both dark eyebrows raised. "Why would I protect a council that won't grow? We're the most powerful species on this planet, yet we follow the vampires' lead and chase down our own . . . for doing what comes naturally." Two steps and his face lowered close to hers. "Deep down, we all know this. How else could I have spun the king's training request so easily?"

The bastard had set them all up from the beginning. "So you weren't concerned the king wanted our soldiers."

Trevan shrugged. "Don't know, don't care. Maybe the

king had ulterior motives, maybe he didn't. But the Coven Nine was all too ready to dig in their feet about training our own soldiers."

She shook her head. "This is treason."

"Treason is a matter of perspective." His gaze dropped to her lips and back up. "How many of your own have you taken down, *Enforcer*? For practicing magic?"

His minty breath made her stomach roll. "That wasn't magic. That was the manipulation of matter to harm. The laws exist for a reason." So the whole damn planet didn't blow up.

"Laws change along with leadership." With a dark gleam in his eye, he placed a kiss on her lips.

She bared her teeth and snapped.

He darted back, barely missing her sharp bite. Regret flashed across his handsome face. "I'm sorry I won't get a chance to break you, Seventh." With a shrug, he sidled back to the window. "I guess the Kurjans get all the fun this time."

"Do they know?" As hard as she tried, she couldn't keep the tremor from her voice. "Did you tell them about the phanakite?" Having the witches' biggest weakness become public knowledge was frightful. The repercussions were unfathomable.

"No." Trevan's breath fogged the glass. "My lady talked me out of that. Guess you owe her."

Apparently his woman was a whole lot smarter than he was. No way the Kurjans wouldn't turn that kind of information against him. "Tell me who she is so I can properly thank her."

He laughed. "Well, while the Kurjans are ripping through your genetics, I'll have some fun with your little sister here." His autocratic head tilted toward Brenna. "I'll still need leverage with the Coven Nine. For a while."

Brenna bared her teeth, and a gray vein appeared along

her smooth forehead. Her eyes were bloodshot. "I'm going to boil your heart to mush inside your body."

While Moira appreciated the sentiment, the fact her sister's skin was becoming translucent from the collar clutched fear in her throat.

Trevan squinted into the night and then straightened his shoulders. "Looks like it's showtime."

Moira followed his gaze, her stomach clenching hard. A spotlight highlighted a large form at the bottom of the hill, his dark clothing a contrast to the white hammering hail. She sucked in air, using every ounce of her energy to throw thoughts into his mind. *Stop, damn it.*

Why? Conn's voice came through low and furious.

She opened herself up wider. Pain slashed into her sides. His kidneys were not ready for battle. *Sharpshooters and land mines. They're too far down to be sensed.*

Stay tight, mate. I'll set one off and discern the layout from that point.

That's stupid. She mentally raised her voice to a shriek. *You'll blow yourself up.*

Relax, woman. The dark form bunched and began climbing the hill in a zigzag pattern. *How badly are you injured?* Concern melded with pain in his voice.

I'm not hurt. Just shackled to the wall and contained. So is Brenna. Boy, was she going to have to explain that one.

Is Brenna injured?

No. Bruised, pissed, and shackled.

Why can't you use magic to break the shackles? He grunted, pain exploding in his solar plexus. The figure came closer.

I'll explain later. Was that your lung? The man couldn't run without a lung. His internal injuries were worse than even the doctor had realized.

Think so. Need to concentrate now. See you in a minute.

She opened her mouth to protest. Vampires could die by beheading, and vary rarely, from losing all their blood.

That wouldn't kill them instantly, but they'd go brain dead with no hope of recovery. How much blood had Conn already lost?

An explosion rose above the storm. Fire billowed up from the ground followed by a sharp boom.

Trevan jumped once, tightening his hand in a fist. "Finally. A damn mine."

Terror slammed Moira's heart against her ribs. She peered out the window, forcing tears back. The hail had turned to snow, mingling with smoke from the explosion. Spotlights shifted to land on a figure lying prone. Conn.

He rolled to the side and staggered to his feet. His head lifted. The silver of his eyes shone through the night, focusing on her.

Moira struggled against the handcuffs, turning her wrists raw. Pain reached to her fingertips. "You're a dead man, Trevan. Run now. But it won't do you any good."

About halfway down the hill, Conn's head swiveled one way and the other.

Brenna gave a weak laugh. "He's on to you, Trevan. He'll decipher the configuration now."

Land mines, especially modified ones, needed to be buried in a pattern so they didn't set each other off.

Trevan nodded. "Yes." He lifted the phone to his ear, pressing a button. Three breaths later, he said, "Shoot him."

"No!" Moira cried out, reaching for Conn in her head. Nothing but static filled her mind. Either her terror or his injuries were keeping them from communicating. Nausea gagged her. The numbness in her extremities had gotten worse. She eyed Brenna. "Are you going numb?" she mouthed.

"Hours ago," Brenna whispered.

Moira bit her lip again to try and retain some clarity. The small pain didn't help. What kind of damage might the collars do if left on too long? As far as she knew, once a witch was away from exposure, their powers returned. But most witches hadn't spent time with the mineral touching their skin. "We'll be all right." Desperation had her yanking at the restraints, nearly pulling her shoulder out of joint. She needed to get free and help Conn.

Shots rang out. He fell. More shots cascaded in quick succession. He struggled to his feet, staggering closer, and closer.

"Fire!" Trevan yelled into the phone.

A rapid volley of bullets fired through the air from high in the tree line. Conn's body jerked with each one. Moira gasped at every impact, her body clenching. So much damage. He dropped to his knees. Pivoting, he turned and fired into the trees. A bellow echoed when someone crashed down.

More flashes of fire lit the tops of the trees. There were too many shooters for Conn to get them all.

"Stop them, Trevan. Please." She wasn't a woman who begged. But this time, she would.

"Not a chance, Seventh." Smug satisfaction coated Trevan's smooth voice.

Rage burned so fast through Moira her tears heated. "I don't know when. I don't know how. But someday, I'm going to rip your heart out of your body." She said it as a threat, felt it as a vow.

He turned slowly, his eyes darkening, his face paling. "Well then. Let's hope the Kurjans arrive before I decide you're an actual danger to me."

Oh, he understood the threat. "I'm the Seventh, Trevan. Don't you ever forget it." As if she could protect Conn with her eyesight alone, she searched for him through the falling snow. Spotlights lit the area, keeping him visible.

He stumbled to his feet, leaving a river of red on the ground.

God. He'd lost too much blood.

Flashes of fire cascaded from the trees. More bullets impacted him. His body shuddered. Yet he stepped forward.

So brave. Her mate. Love was too pale an idea to describe what flew through her. Power, destiny, fate commingled in an inferno that had her head snapping back. Gathering her strength, pretending she had more than she felt, she sent every ounce of her power careening through the air. Sent all the power of the Seventh, all the power of a mate, to help him. For one second, she believed she was stronger than phanakite. Stronger than her enemies. More powerful than death.

Conn shot to his feet. His chest expanded. His shoulders snapped back, his head up, his chin down—ready to charge.

A light pierced down from high above. A dark form swimming among the clouds. A helicopter.

Oh God. Trevan's backup.

Trevan puffed out his chest. "Apparently our ride has arrived, ladies." He pivoted to watch the scene outside where Conn had stopped to stare up at the circling beast. "Well, I guess we could wait for a couple moments as they blow your mate to miniature particles, Moira." His exhale scattered fog across the window. "Even you won't be able to reassemble him."

Pain and fear rippled through her so fast her knees buckled. She'd sent everything she had to Conn, and it wasn't enough.

The rapid smattering of gunfire filled the night, flashes of orange coming from the nearly silent helicopter. The spray careened into the tree line, igniting the tops of the fir trees into a billowing mass of fire. Into the tree line! A spotlight captured the beast, illuminating Jase as he leaned out, firing into the forest.

Almost in slow motion, Moira turned her head toward the hill. Conn came running at them full bore, his chin down, his gaze on her.

Trevan jumped back, yanking a gun from his waistband. He levered, aiming for her mate.

With a flash of speed and the shattering of glass, Connlan Kayrs leaped through the window.

Chapter 31

Conn landed hard, glass shattering under his thick
boots. Rage destroyed the strategic training he'd developed over centuries. Raw fury shoved temperance out
of his heart. And fear, fear for the woman he loved, well
now. That sent any humanity he may have owned straight
to hell.

His hand clenched around Trevan's throat before the
man could get off one more shot. A careless swipe of his
arm had the witch's gun skittering across the floor.

Bleeding, nearly destroyed, working with half a demolished heart, Conn lifted his enemy with one hand, slamming the bastard down on the ground with all the force
the universe contained.

Demidov's skull exploded like a melon.

The animal Conn had become let loose with a growl.
He squeezed harder, ripping the head right off the already
dead body. Then he flung it out the window.

Rising, his fangs elongated, blood cascading down his
cheeks, Conn searched for his mate. She leaned weakly
against the wall, her hands shackled, her eyes huge pools
of green in an entirely too pale face.

His legs grew heavy as he stumbled toward her, the blood
deserting his body, his veins going dry. The last thing in

this world he'd do was free her. Enamel flew when he gritted his teeth and reached for the shackles.

"Conn." Her pretty eyes filled with tears. "Take off the collar. Please take off the collar." Her voice came out breathy. Weak.

He frowned, wrapping his hand around the small lock until it crumbled into pieces. His fingers shook as he undid the binding, sliding the black leather off her neck. Sparkles lined it. Quartz?

She released more of a sigh than a breath. Her lashes fluttered while he unclasped the cuffs around her wrists. Two seconds later she reached for Brenna's collar.

Conn growled. He hadn't seen Brenna. She'd been right there, and yet, he'd only seen Moira. His mate. He reached for Brenna's restraints, releasing her wrists as Moira threw the collar across the room. Brenna sagged to a crouch, deep gasps of air coming from her, her hand trembling as she pushed back her hair.

The room swayed. Or maybe that was him. A roaring filled his ears. Moira reached for him, her hands on his biceps.

Wood dented when his knees hit the floor.

The outside door splintered open, and he half turned to shield his mate.

Jase jumped inside, already ripping his wrist open with sharp fangs. "Here." He shoved the wound toward Conn's mouth.

The scent of blood filled Conn's nostrils. Animalistic need filled his growl. He lunged for Jase's arm, sinking his fangs deep. Drinking. Power shot into his mouth, into his veins. Straight to his heart, which most needed to heal. He released his hold, trying to force his canines out.

Jase shoved his vein in harder. "Take more. I don't need it."

Dage leaped through the door, his gaze taking in the

entire scene. With two quick strides, he lifted Brenna off the floor, tearing the tape off her ankles. "Trevan's reinforcements are coming. Get to the helicopter."

Moira staggered forward, grabbing one of Conn's arms as Jase latched on to the other, hefting him up. Together, they assisted the half-conscious soldier outside. The helicopter's blades threw snow and pinecones at them like small missiles. Pain smashed into her face, her heart beating too fast against her ribs.

Even after drinking from Jase, Conn left a wide trail of blood through the snow. Yet he put each foot in front of the other, his head down, most of his weight leaning toward his brother.

Where did he get such strength? As his mate, she could feel the pounding pain ripping like tendrils of death through his tissues, through his organs. And yet, he moved—with a pure force of will.

"Not leaving you alone in this world," he growled out, low and soft. Too soft.

"I love you." The words came from nowhere near her brain. Maybe not even her heart. From somewhere deeper. Not exactly the wine and roses moment.

"I know. Get in the helicopter." He released her to sag against Jase, waiting until she was safely inside before pulling his large body in next to her. Jase flanked him, facing outside, his gun aimed into the darkness.

Dage placed Brenna in the copilot's seat, jumped into his own, and snapped buttons on the ceiling to life. "Hold on, everybody. Jase, get ready."

The bird lifted in the air. Jase grabbed a grenade from his cargo pants, yanked the pin out with his teeth, and side armed the weapon through the mashed window into the hut. "Bye, Trevan."

The helicopter cleared the area just before a massive explosion blew the wooden sides of the cabin in all four directions. Fire rolled into the sky, followed by dark smoke. Heat sheeted across the windshield.

Moira reached for Conn's hand resting on his thigh. He flipped his palm around, tangling his fingers with hers. Holding on. "Are you all right, Dailtín?" he murmured.

"Yes." Hell no. Trevan had used a phanakite collar on her and Brenna. Weakness still threatened to steal her breath. She was discombobulated. Hopefully her mate wouldn't catch on. She didn't have time to go and rest in some hospital. "I need to get to Ireland, Connlan." She stiffened, expecting a fight.

"I know." Conn opened his eyes. "What's the plan, Dage?"

Dage banked left, heading toward Trevan's main house and descending. Fire lit the trees on every side. "Talen took Cara and the baby for medical help. Kane and Jase will stay here and go through the rest of Trevan's holdings, make sure we didn't miss anything or anybody." The helicopter touched down with a slight bump, sending wafts of snow into the air. "I have a plane prepared for you to escort the members of the Nine as well as Moira and Brenna to Ireland. The Coven Nine is waiting." Grim and angry, the king's voice promised the meeting wouldn't be pleasant.

Jase jumped out, nodding at Kane near the other helicopter.

Moira frowned. "You said *members* of the Coven Nine."

"Yes." Dage tilted his head toward where Kane assisted two women from the back seat. "Simone and Grace."

Moira gasped. "Grace is alive?" Trevan had said Moira was the first survivor of his transporting kidnapping plan. Lying bastard.

"Yes." Dage pressed a couple buttons on the console.

"We found her in a closet, wounded, with some weird collar around her neck." His eyes met Moira's in the mirror. "Looked like quartz, and I'm assuming an explanation will be forthcoming soon."

The king assumed wrong. Moira struggled to slide open her door. Conn tightened his hold. "Stay still, sweetheart." While his head rested against the seat and his eyes remained closed, the command held bite. Her mate was regaining his strength. Well, that was probably good.

She turned her focus through the open doorway on his other side, where Kane assisted Grace and Simone toward the craft. Grace's pale face held a myriad of fresh purple bruises. Her long scarlet skirt brushed the dirty snow, turning the bottom into a sooty mess. A circular green tinge marred her neck.

Moira grabbed her throat, scrubbing the skin.

"You have a green mark," Conn said, not moving.

How long would the color last? Moira reached across Conn to help Simone into the helicopter. "Are you all right?"

Simone nodded, quickly wincing. "Yes, just a small headache. Cara will be fine. Talen shoved his vampire vein into her mouth immediately."

Moira sighed. "I assume Talen is beyond grateful you tried to jump in front of her and take the bullet?" The realization hit that she didn't know her cousin at all. Simone hadn't given a second thought to forfeiting her life for Cara's or the babe's.

"I wasn't fast enough." Simone sighed, resting back, her pose similar to Conn's. "I want to go home." She scooted in farther to allow room for Grace, whose hands were visibly trembling. Kane shut the door behind her, slapping the outside twice before jogging to safety.

Dage pulled back on the throttle and they lifted into the

air. Blinking lights from the controls flicked across his strong profile. Brenna snuggled down in the copilot's seat. "Wake me when we arrive at the plane," she whispered.

Moira fought her own eyelids closing. The phanakite collar had truly drained her. But sleep seemed an unwise luxury. She needed to get her thoughts in order before meeting with the council. As Conn's breathing evened out next to her, she glanced across the bench at Grace. "How did you survive the transporting?"

The councilwoman waved bruised knuckles in the air. Apparently she'd fought back. "I'm not sure. I imagined a safety bubble around myself, and suddenly a light pierced the darkness." She gingerly fingered her neck. "He gave me a collar." Her deep blue eyes widened and she angled toward Moira. "Is Trevan really dead?"

"Yes." Moira kept her face bland. The man may have been a councilmember, but she felt nothing at his death. He'd turned his back on all of them.

Grace put a fist to her mouth. "Good." Tears filled her eyes, and she turned away to the storm outside her window.

Moira lacked the energy to comfort. Her eyelids closed and she snuggled closer to her mate. Maybe she'd relax her eyes for a moment. While her body went limp in exhaustion, her mind spun.

She was missing something.

Before she could figure out what it was, the helicopter touched down. The snow had given way to a light smattering of rain across the tarmac. The battle-weary group exited the vehicle almost in slow motion, staggering, limping, and stumbling into the jet already humming with power and ready to go.

The main cabin held eight thick leather chairs facing a wide screen. Dage gently placed Brenna in one, sliding it open to form a bed and grabbing blankets from an over-

head bin to tuck her in. Simone assisted Grace and then
grabbed her own place. Moira leaned against the side, her
mind spinning. Tired. So damn tired.

Dage stalked back toward them. His fangs shot out, and
he ripped into his wrist. The musky scent of blood filled
the space.

Conn opened his mouth to protest, and Dage pinned
him to the wall with a forearm to the neck. The entire
plane rocked with the force of their powerful bodies. His
wrist smacked against Conn's lips. "Take some blood or
I'm going to kill you."

Moira backed out of the way.

Conn's eyes swirled silver, then narrowed. He bit down,
amusement lighting his face at Dage's harsh intake of
breath. A healthy flush worked across his cheekbones. His
nostrils flared when he finished drinking.

Dage released him. "Moira. Do you need blood?"

Moira started in surprise. She felt pretty woozy. Her
throat ached like she had a horrible cold. But combining
vampire blood with whatever reaction she'd had from the
collar seemed risky. "No. But thanks."

"All right." The king pivoted. "Conn, take your mate
to the back bedroom. You both have twelve hours to rest.
I expect your heart and at least one lung healed by the
time you set down. I'll secure headquarters and then call
in during the meeting with the Nine. Good luck." He
slammed the door shut and jogged down the steps to the
tarmac.

A thick hand tugged Moira past the bathroom to the
bedroom. The one they'd shared last time. Even exhausted, heat flowed through her to pool in her abdomen.

Conn chuckled. "I'm not saying I couldn't satisfy you,
sweetheart. Though we should sleep a bit first." He tugged
off his clothing.

She rolled her eyes, crawling over the bed to flop
against the pillows. Quick motions had her boots kicked
off and thumping on the floor. "Good plan." She shivered
in her wet jeans, snuggling deeper down.

A T-shirt landed next to her head. "You're wet, Dailtín.
Change your clothes or I'll do it for you." Thunks
sounded as weapons hit the floor.

The thought was tempting, but the guy needed to heal.
Without opening her eyes, she shimmied out of her jeans
and shirt, tugging on the clean shirt. The bed dipped, and
Conn rolled her under the covers, his muscled body
warming her. "Sleep. We'll talk later."

The comment should worry her, but at the moment,
she was too tired to be concerned. She'd figure everything
out when her brain kicked in. Willing her mind to relax,
sending calming thoughts to her body, she counted Conn's
even breaths. He was out. Pain radiated from him, along
with the tingle of healing. The king's blood probably held
some serious power. The extra power Conn gained as her
mate should finish the healing process.

She counted sheep. She counted vampires. Then she
counted the challenges to her relationship. That took the
longest.

A soft knock on the door had her lifting up. "Come in,"
she whispered. Her mate didn't move.

The door slid open on a whisper of sound, the hall light
outlining Brenna. She tiptoed inside, sliding the door
closed with a soft click. Light steps had her around the bed
and snuggling next to her sister. "Is he healing?"

"Yes." Moira scooted over to make more room on the
pillow. Her body was already pressed against the hard rock
of her mate. "You should be sleeping." She kept her voice
to the same soft whisper used by her sister.

"Can't sleep." Brenna tugged her hair free. "My throat
hurts. I feel weak." She clasped her hands on her stomach,

extending her legs with a sigh. "I think . . . well, I don't know . . ."

"Think what?"

"Trevan forced something down my throat—a liquid. I think maybe . . ."

Dread slammed hard into Moira's gut. "Liquid phanakite?"

"I don't know." Brenna sighed. "Was probably just a tranquilizer. We'll worry about that later. Right now, something more timely is bothering me."

"What might that be?" Moira had her own suspicions, but Brenna could solve a puzzle faster than anyone she'd ever met.

"A couple things. First, well, the king isn't stupid."

"I know." Moira turned on her side toward Brenna. She reached out, winding her fingers through her sister's, reassuring them both. "We can't do anything about his knowledge."

"He'll discover what phanakite does. The secret is out." Brenna cuddled closer.

"Yes. But Dage won't hurt our people." Probably.

Brenna tightened her hold. "I have two labs working on a countermeasure to the mineral."

Moira started. "You do?"

"Of course. Secrets may last a long time, but never forever. We've been arrogant to think so."

Pride filled Moira. "You're a smart woman, Bren. Any luck?"

"Nope. So far, nothing. But I will find a defense against that crap." Brenna's voice crackled, her throat probably as sore as Moira's. "I have another concern."

"Grace." Moira tried to swallow and ease some of the pain.

"Yes. She's dressed in a gorgeous designer skirt and top. Not exactly prisoner garb."

"True." Moira catalogued her last image of the council-woman. "Trevan was a freak. He may have dressed her like that on purpose the last few days."

"I know." Brenna sighed. "And her face is seriously bruised."

"New bruises." Moira tucked her hand under her cheek. "Very fresh. Almost like she received them the last hour. When the vampires attacked."

"She could've smashed her face into a wall a few times before putting the collar on her own neck." Brenna's voice turned thoughtful. "But I can't imagine forcing that mineral on your own skin. No way."

"I heard a woman's voice when I first arrived." Accusing a member of the Coven Nine of betraying them held certain threat. "My guess is Grace was working with Trevan." How had she missed this?

"We have no proof." Brenna sighed. "None at all."

"I know." That left Moira with only one option. "I'll take care of it."

Seconds ticked by. Brenna stiffened next to her. "You can't. Even normally I'd talk you out of it. But now, feeling so weak. You don't have the strength."

Moira shrugged. "Sometimes fate doesn't give us a choice, Bren." It appeared she was about to meet hers. Or lose herself trying.

Chapter 32

Rather than the mystical mist of the Coven Nine's underground headquarters intriguing him, this time the damn place just pissed him off. Conn fought to control his scowl, standing before the remaining members of the Nine. His mate stood next to him and only Kell's presence on her other side kept him from positioning her behind him. Brenna stood next to Kell.

The veil had been easier to cross. Conn had gone through it alone, and he'd kept his weapons this time.

Moira, Brenna, and Conn stood before the Nine somewhat presentable, having stopped at the penthouses for showers and clean clothing before arriving at headquarters and crossing the veil.

The Coven leaders sat in their places behind the massive stone platform in various displays of disarray. Purpling bruises marred Grace and Simone's faces. Dark circles cut into the cheeks of Moira's mother, and her aunt didn't look much better. Even the newest member, Gallagher, frowned so hard his head had to hurt. The empty four seats along the side screamed trouble and war.

No way was Conn leaving Moira there . . . where they couldn't protect their own.

A screen lit the far wall and Dage took shape.

Vivienne's eyes flashed a scarlet hue. "Trevan is dead?" Her hand swept the desk, nearly dislodging a Starbucks cup. The incongruity between the modern coffee and the ancient tomb failed to lighten Conn's mood.

Dage cleared his throat. "By my orders, your councilman is dead."

"I killed him." Conn remained in place. The king was not taking the fall. "I ripped his head off his body with my hands. After he took my mate."

Dage stiffened.

Too bad. If the Nine wanted to take someone down, it'd be Conn. Not that he'd go down easy. And he had a sneaky suspicion his too-quiet mate would jump in and fight on his behalf. Warmth filtered through him . . . though his kidneys still ached.

"Yes, well." Vivienne cleared her throat. "While I appreciate the need to protect a mate, the Nine has a right to deal with our own members. Much as you hold the power to rule your people, King."

Dage nodded. "Yes. If there had been time, and if we weren't in battle, we would've turned Demidov over to you." He rubbed his chin. "Unfortunately, there wasn't time."

Vivienne nodded. "I understand." She glanced at the other members of the Nine. "If the vampires would excuse us, I believe we have some issues to discuss."

"Like the phanakite?" Dage asked very softly.

Gasps filled the chamber. Vivienne sat up straighter, her dark hair swishing forward over her Chanel suit. "How long have you known?"

"Three hours. Since my lab called with results on one of the collars." The king cut his gaze to Moira's neck and then back to the raised dais. "Your secret, of course, is safe with us." Diplomatic words, yet they sealed the treaty between vampires and witches for all time. The witches couldn't afford to withdraw from the Realm, now that Dage held such a weapon.

"That's kind of you, King." Vivienne's jaw tightened so hard her teeth must've ached. "Good thing we're allies, now, isn't it?"

"The Realm will always consider the Coven Nine and its followers our friends, Councilwoman Northcutt."

Conn shuffled his feet. Dage spun the bullshit with the best of them.

The relief flowing from his mate eased Conn's shoulders. Moira's sister peered around Kell's broad chest, her gaze sending some kind of message. What the hell was going on?

Moira stiffened up, as if gathering courage. Before she could speak, Vivienne narrowed in on her. "So. We have four vacancies on the Nine, Moira."

"Yes, ma'am." Moira took a step forward.

Conn growled low, pleased when she stilled. She'd stay right by his side, damn it.

Her head lifted even higher. "On that note, I'd like to challenge Grace Sadler to her seat on the Nine."

Viv half rose. Moira's mother leaned forward, her hand going to her throat. Simone smiled, slow and somehow nearly sweet. Peter frowned.

Grace paled, her eyes flashing almost black. "What is the meaning of this? We have four vacant seats. You don't need mine." Fury washed red across her battered face, quickly disappearing as the witch struggled for control. The bruises failed to mask the blonde's stunning beauty.

"Yet I want yours." Moira allowed her voice to lower in the way Conn's always did when he issued a threat. Quite effective, that.

Pride filled him. The woman learned fast and well. His heart thrummed as she widened her stance in the dark jeans, her combat boots finding purchase.

He cocked his head to the side. "Moira." His voice stayed low. Only the twitch of her hair indicated she heard him. "I'm not sure I like where this is going."

She glanced over her shoulder. "I guarantee you won't." Then she refocused on the Nine.

He bit back a grin. Such an impressive spirit.

Yet the woman had been injured, and held captive by a mineral that drained her resources. She further depleted herself by sending him as much power as she could muster, when he most needed it. She wasn't prepared to do battle . . . and if the energy swirling around the room provided any indication, a fight was coming.

Brigid cleared her throat, her gaze thoughtful on her seventh daughter. "Moira? Why Grace?"

Conn stepped forward. Not by a hair did she acknowledge his support, turning her focus on Councilwoman Sadler. "She was working with Trevan."

Vivienne stood. "You've acquired proof of this accusation?" Her voice echoed throughout the chamber with anger and incredulousness.

"No direct proof. But I'm right." Moira straightened her shoulders further, her gaze never leaving Grace's. "And Grace knows it."

Grace snarled a smile. "You're crazy, Seventh. You don't hold proof because there isn't any. He kept me locked up with a collar, too. My skin is bruised, too. When the time came, the vampires rescued me just like you." She smoothed her hair back into the tight bun she'd donned earlier. "I think you were more affected by the ordeal than you believe."

"Thanks for the concern." Moira took another step closer to the dais. "Your bruises are too recent and your green strip not nearly as thick or deep as Brenna's. Yet you were taken first."

All gazes turned toward the councilwoman flushing a

mottled red. "Your accusations are unfounded, and as you admitted, you lack evidence."

Moira smiled. "I'm not asking for your resignation. Nor am I directing the matter to the enforcers." She reached down and carefully rolled up one sleeve of her dark shirt. "What I am doing is challenging you for your seat. As such, I need neither proof nor foundation." Finished, she quickly rolled the other. "Either step down, or prepare to get your ass kicked."

Her mother leaned forward. "Moira. Make very sure you know what you're doing."

The concern from Brigid made the area on the back of Conn's scalp itch. Grace stood, a shimmer of dark warning dancing on her skin. "I've been on the Nine for nearly a thousand years, you irritating chit. I have more power in my left hand than you do in your entire body."

"Well then." Moira's hands relaxed to rest by her sides. "I take it you accept the challenge."

Grace whirled to face Brigid. "Talk to your daughter. I'll destroy her."

Brigid glanced at Moira and then back to Grace. The moments ticked by. Brigid's shoulders lifted. "My daughter knows what she's doing. I suggest you step down and give the enforcers time to investigate you. This path, you'll lose everything."

Moira's stance didn't alter in the slightest. But Conn felt the wave of relief and strength that shot from her when Brigid backed her play. He was feeling anything but relief. The dents and scars littering the ancient rock walls now made sense—incredible damage from fighting with quantum physics. The thought that such a weapon would be turned on his mate rolled something dangerous to heat in his gut. In his soul.

"King Kayrs, thank you for joining us today." Vivienne exhaled loudly.

Dage nodded. "Of course. I'll be in touch regarding the training schedules for your soldiers." The screen went dark.

Viv paused, her gaze remaining on the blank wall. "I don't recall agreeing to that." She shook her head, turning to face Grace. "We'll worry about training later. For now . . . Grace Sadler, you have been challenged for your seat by Moira Dunne. Do you accept said challenge or do you wish to terminate your involvement with the Coven Nine?"

Grace's eyes flashed black, and her chin lifted with an anticipatory smile. "I accept said challenge."

Conn began to step forward, stopped by his mate's hand on his arm. Concern flowed through him as he stared down at her. She kept her gaze straight ahead, her eyes clear, her shoulders calm.

Vivienne nodded. "So be it." She grabbed a thick scroll from under the desk, leaned down, and began scribbling. Finally, she lifted her head, gesturing toward the row of seats made out of rock. "Those here shall sit in witness of the proclamation as we set the rules."

Kell and Brenna immediately crossed the room and took their places in what Conn considered a jury box. Who knew the witches acted according to early Roman law?

Moira half turned toward Conn.

He shook his head. "No."

Amusement lit her eyes along with her small laugh. "No choice for you, Kayrs. Time to trust."

Trust, his ass. He didn't like the idea of her agreeing to fight . . . no matter that he'd be right next to her.

"I need to formalize my challenge." She ran both hands up his arms to clutch his biceps. "We value our traditions, too. Please go sit as witness as we set the time and date."

Conn frowned. "I'd prefer to stand right here."

She closed her eyes, taking a deep breath. "I love you, Connlan Kayrs. You're going to have to learn to trust me. This is the time when we talk. Later, well, later I'll fight her." Moira's lids flipped open, revealing a darker green than he'd ever seen. Deep, mysterious, powerful.

His heart thrummed. The blood heated in his veins. Raw desire nearly crippled him. "Moira." All sound faded away. The other people in the room disappeared. For one second, she was the only thing in his entire universe.

A flush crept along her skin. Ancient power crackled through the air. She released him. "Let's get this over with. We can argue about the actual fight later. For now, just the words need to be said."

Everything in him vibrated with the right to stand in front of her. With rough hands, he grabbed her and crushed his mouth to hers. So many feelings, so many plans. He took, his lips unrelenting on hers, his tongue sweeping her mouth. *Mine.* Only when she shuddered against him, her body submitting to his, did he release her. He steadied her until she could meet his gaze. "I'll sit and witness the actual words, Dailtín. No promises when the time comes to fight."

Knowing the witches, they planned these things down to the last second . . . and he had months, maybe years, to properly train her.

She smiled. "Fair enough."

Conn pivoted on his heel, stalking over to drop into a chair next to Kell. It squeaked under his weight.

Vivienne raised both hands in the air. "The Coven Nine acknowledges the challenge and acceptance. A fight for the coven seat shall commence." Reaching for a burnished teakwood gavel, she lifted it, and crashed it down on the stone desk with a resounding *crack!*

Without warning, a shimmering wall of power rose up between all spectators and the two witches vying for the seat. Conn jumped to his feet with a growl of outrage, fists smashing into the wall. A zap of electricity knocked him back into his chair. Fury ripped through him so fast his breath heated. The wall curved, extending to cover the council members as well.

Brenna cleared her throat. "Coven law dictates when a challenge is accepted, the fight commences immediately."

He turned on her. "Moira knew this?"

Brenna paled, the green around her neck nearly glowing against her skin. "Yes. The divider is absolute and ancient—put in place so we can't jump in and help. There are often family members fighting for a seat on the Nine."

Conn turned to study the shield. The opaque surface shimmered and moved as if alive. His mate stood facing him, an apology in her eyes. The woman had known and lied to him. "Moira."

Brenna sighed. "She can't see or hear you, Conn. You need to sit down. There's no way inside."

Conn growled, moving as close to the wall as he could get without risking electrocution. His eyes were on Moira as she turned to face a witch centuries more experienced. His mate filled his vision, yet the chamber hoarded all sound. She'd fooled him. Fury at her and fear for her sent adrenaline and fire shooting through his veins.

She'd better survive this so he could kill her.

Chapter 33

A sense of finality echoed when the wall rose to the ceiling. The myriads of locks, physical and mystical, clinked as they slammed home. Moira shivered. Conn let off so much heat. With his retreat, cold slithered around. She glanced at where he sat, seeing only a large wall of rock. No light or sound came from behind the barrier.

Grace threw back her head and laughed. "Conn seemed to help you out there by the casual way he went and sat down, Seventh. Your mate will most likely go looking for your cousin when this is over." She smacked her lips together, the sound echoing through the silent room.

"My cousin follows coven law."

"I plan on making your man my pet when we're finished here." Grace sauntered around the wide desk and down the stairs to lean against the opposite wall. "Seeing him beg might be the highlight of my year."

Moira raised an eyebrow. "That is a man who doesn't beg."

Grace lifted a slender shoulder. "We'll see. He should be quite grateful for the dutiful, boring, weak mate I send back to him." Static electricity crackled along her arms, lifting tendrils of hair that had escaped the bun. "No more magic, no more enforcing for you, little Moira."

Moira planted her feet securely on the worn stone of the floor. "That would be a problem, considering most men dislike boring women, Grace. Take you and Trevan for example." She centered herself, searching for the power inside. "I mean, there had to be a reason the man moved on to Simone."

Graced hissed out breath. "That was nothing . . . just part of the plan. We wanted to use Simone to bring down Vivienne."

"No, not true." Moira forced a sly smile. "He was dumping you for Simone, without a question. Told her the full truth, asked her to help him lead the council. Only after she refused his offer did he throw her in a cell . . . and return to you."

Sparks flew from Grace's fingertips. "You're so young. We used Simone as a pawn and would've kept her to take down her mother. She was a temporary infatuation to Trevan. I've been with him for years. We've been *planning* to take over the Nine for decades."

"So you're telling the truth now, are you?" Moira circled to the left, eyeing the energy crackling across the woman's skin.

"Why not?" Grace shrugged, moving to the right, keeping pace. "The witnesses can only see . . . not hear. No one will believe you after I take your powers. It'll be just you being a poor loser."

"Faking your own death—now that was brilliant." Moira shook her head. "My guess is Trevan thought of that one . . . I wonder if he actually planned to kill you and keep Simone."

"You're not smart enough to mess with my head." Grace held her hands out a foot apart, orange light zinging between them. Static electricity crackled in the air.

Buggering orange light? Who the hell harnessed orange? Moira had seen blue, forms of purple, even some deep green. But never orange. She eyed the electricity.

Grace laughed. "A millennia provides a few extra powers, Seventh. Guess you should've waited your turn through the centuries."

Moira lifted her gaze from Grace's hand while allowing a small smile to curve her lips. "I am the Seventh, Grace. I don't need extra powers. I have more than you can fathom."

But did she? Sure she'd taken down many a witch misusing their power, but never anyone as old as Grace. Or as powerful.

"We're about to find out. But I can tell you . . . power grows through age. You know that. You're barely a foal out of the stall." Grace widened her hands, allowing the energy to grow into a pulsating, sunlike ball.

"Maybe." With her mind, Moira shaped plasma into a ball at chest level, keeping her arms relaxed. The round form pounded, electric blue sizzling with audible pops. "Not only am I the Seventh, I'm a Kayrs mate. You're delusional if you think I don't get power from Connlan." Her ball grew bigger, drawing particles from the surrounding air. "I'm giving you one chance here, Grace. Drop the fight, go out the door, and confess."

Grace sighed. "Okay." Her shoulders slumped. Then she pivoted and threw the ball at Moira's head.

Moira ducked. Tips of her hair lit on fire. The ball ripped into the door, leaving a popcorn bowl–size dent in it. With a growl, she patted her hair to extinguish the fire. Bunching her legs, she jumped, side-kicking the blue energy toward Grace. Faster than normal light, it careened.

The witch dropped, rolling to the side and back up to her feet. Explosive energy smashed into the wall.

Grace's hair straggled into her face, and she jerked the

leather holder out of her sagging bun. Thick blond hair tumbled down. "I'm going to enjoy this." A glowing softball appeared in her hand, and she threw it with a quick release of muscle.

Moira leaped sideways, only to be hit with another ball right in the leg. Agony burned through her skin.

With a cry, she went down.

In rapid succession, Grace belted ball after ball at her, ripping fiery pain wherever they landed.

The magical wall between them and the witnesses cracked, reshaping with a hiss.

Did Conn do that? Something told her he had . . . his strength was unbelievable. Moira growled in pain and rolled to her knees. She swiped her hands toward the floor. A wall of pulsating blue shot up.

Grace continued to throw, the orange balls plopping into the shield, wavering and dropping harmlessly to burn the stone floor. Her eyes widened, and anger curled her lip.

Moira stood, her chin down, fury ripping through her system. Pulling both arms back, palms out, she shoved air toward the shield. "Attack."

Like air hitting water, the protection coiled, gathered, and shot forward. The mass engulfed Grace like a hunting net, swallowing her in opaque energy and tying tight at her feet. She struggled, her mouth open in a silent scream.

Her eyes shifted to black. She shut them, stretching her neck, struggling to raise her hands. The enclosure webbed and wavered. Her skin glowed, her hair stood on end. Tightening her face, she pressed her palms together. With a crunch of a contained explosion, the shield morphed from blue to white.

It shattered.

Shards of sharpened energy ripped through the room. One pierced Moira's upper arm, digging deep. Blood welled. A second shot into her boot, far enough to cut her ankle. Pain cascaded from both entry points. She reached up and yanked the energy free of her bicep. Spent, the white turned to dust in her hand. Her intact boot pressed down and forced the projectile out of her other foot. "Nice."

Grace smiled, panting slightly. "We're merely getting started."

A burst of energy slammed into Moira's back, sending her sprawling across the hard floor. Her palms scraped against tiny pebbles, and her head bounced back on her neck. Heat licked her skin, the scent of burned fabric assaulted her nostrils. "Damn it. This is one of my favorite shirts." She leaped to her feet, keeping her face calm. Fear threatened to wind through her fury.

Grace could create energy from a distant point, and direct it without being near. Moira hadn't learned that trick. She needed to keep her back against the walls.

Grace puckered her lips. "Oops. Not enough power to create multiple energies from different graphic points, Seventh?"

"No." Moira calculated her options. She needed an advantage. A tickle set up at the base of her skull. A whisper. *You know more than witchcraft.*

Her muscles stilled. She eyed the stone barrier. Power pounded behind it. Conn was correct. She'd been limiting herself. Concentrating on the floor underneath Grace, she visualized the molecules, the atomic particles, and beyond to the sub level. She mentally slid them out of alignment.

An oval of black tar encircled Grace's feet. The witch cried out, her body struggling to move while her legs stayed still. The thick liquid skimmed past her ankles, heading for her knees. She flung both hands down. The tar hardened.

With a growl, she blinked and the material shattered.

Her eyes flew open, and she took two steps toward Moira. "Very nice. But not good enough."

Moira shot forward in a bunching tackle, catching Grace around the waist. The women hit the ground hard. A ringing set up in Moira's ears, and her stomach clenched. Grayness danced across her vision. Tired. She was so tired.

Summoning will, she pulled back a fist and punched Grace in the nose. Blood cascaded down the blonde's face. A hiss of pain blew from her lips.

Grace grabbed Moira's hair, yanking her down to the side. A knee to Moira's rib cage exploded stars behind her closed eyelids. She gasped in pain. Weakness weighed down her limbs.

Damn it, brat. You wanted to fight. Now fucking fight. Conn's voice echoed with anger and determination.

Her limbs tingled. Her mind cooled. She rolled to her feet, palms out and shoulders back.

Grace spun the other way, pushing up, tossing bloody hair over her shoulder. Her eyes turned a fathomless black. Orange flames licked along her skin.

Moira took a deep breath. She opened her senses and drew in power from the stone, the oxygen, the light—and from Conn. Opening her heart, she yanked his energy into her body. Electric blue danced before her eyes, along her flesh. Her vision sharpened until she could see past the subatomic particles. Little universes in little universes.

The world disappeared. The sound of Grace panting for breath faded into nothingness. Moira became the center. Of everything.

She placed her hands together in the symbol of a prayer. Then she opened them, palms out, facing Grace.

Grace snarled, blood dripping over her lips. A ball of orange shimmered out of nothing to surround her, pulsing with anger, sharp spikes rippling along the edges. With a grim smile, Grace shot the mass at Moira.

Moira swept her arms to the side. Blue energy leaped forward, ripping into the orange, heat zapping around the room. Ozone choked the space. The earth rumbled. Sound billowed to deafening and lights flashed to blinding. So much sensation slammed into her at once, she wavered. Pain cascaded under her skin. Over her muscle. Like a river of needles.

She sucked it in, let the agony ebb and then fade to nothing. The energies continued to battle, blue and orange melding until a dingy brown morphed in the center of the chamber. Gathering her courage, shoring her strength, Moira bunched her muscles and leaped into the mass, straight at Grace.

Time stalled. Reality became a dream as pain ripped into her flesh, shredding her eardrums with an unholy screech.

Her heart stopped.

Her brain liquefied.

Then air.

She landed on the other side, calling on Conn's strength. A high kick to Grace's face sent the woman to the floor. Moira skidded on her knees toward her prey, her arm out, her concentration absolute. Her palm clapped down hard on Grace's chest.

Power. Energy. Darkness. Moira pulled, drawing them in, fighting with forces beyond comprehension.

Grace's eyes widened, and she grabbed Moira's wrist. She snarled, yanking back, trying to dislodge the younger witch.

Moira shook her head, centered herself. "I. Am. The. Seventh." She tightened her hold, reaching deep inside her enemy for all knowledge, all power. With one last burst of energy, she took everything Grace had. Stars exploded in front of her eyes. Her heart swelled with too much to handle. With a gasp, Moira fell back.

Conn reached her first.

The members of the Nine stood.

Moira's limbs jerked. Livid energy ripped along her skin. She was overdosing on power. Cold, hard power. A quaking set up in her ankles and rippled to her head.

"Give me some," Conn murmured, gathering her up, nearly enclosing her with his body.

She parted her lips, her teeth chattering. "Too much."

He nodded, lowering his mouth to hers.

Warmth spread through her, shooting heat to combat the chilling cold. She moaned, leaning closer, letting fire slide along the ice. His tongue swept inside, bringing peace and safety. His nostrils flared as he drew in power, those amazing eyes turning nearly black. He blinked twice . . . and lifted his head.

Moira took a deep breath. Her body still trembled, but the powers had balanced, the energy working to form a cohesive whole. With Conn's help, she staggered to her feet to face the Coven Nine. Then she stepped toward the dais—on her own.

Grace remained prone on the stone floor, passed out cold. The guards would soon arrive to take her for medical attention.

Vivienne clapped the gavel on the stone. The resounding smack echoed around the chamber. "The challenge is done. Moira Dunne, you are the victor. Welcome to the Coven Nine."

Moira relaxed her shoulders, fighting to keep her hands from shaking. "Thank you, Councilwoman Northcutt. Pursuant to Canon 2.4 of the Nine, I hereby transfer my seat on the council to my sister, Brenna Dunne."

Brenna gasped. "What are you doing?"

Moira turned toward her sister, trying to stop her head from spinning off her neck. "You're the better choice, Bren."

"I am not. You're the Seventh." Brenna's dark eyes flashed with concern. "I haven't even been to university yet."

"I know." Moira stepped toward her sister, reaching out to clasp her hands. "You've studied everything from economics to physics and you truly care about the job. You'll be an excellent council member. I'm an enforcer, sis." Her powers as the Seventh were needed on the front line, but maybe someday she would join Brenna up there.

"Well then." Vivienne sucked in air, her eyes widening. Quiet filled the chamber. Many of their people considered Brenna a threat, an unknown anomaly. Viv straightened her shoulders and tapped the gavel against her hand, bringing the attention back to the dais. "Brenna Dunne. Do you accept?"

Brenna glanced at her sister, then up to where their mother stood, a smile on her face and love filling her eyes. "I accept." Her head up, she glided around the dais and took Grace's vacated seat.

Tears of pride pricked the back of Moira's eyes. She ruthlessly battled them down. The Nine had issues. She may have just caused more problems for her baby sister than she'd hoped. But she had faith. As she returned to normal, her senses came alive. And with them the realization that her battles had just begun for the evening.

Anger, concern, and determination cascaded off her mate in waves. She eyed him.

He reached out and manacled one large hand around her bicep. "Moira. Now we talk."

"No." She kept her voice low, her stance casual. "I have work to do, Conn." For the love of all holiness, she'd just taken down a member of the Nine.

He lowered his head to an inch of hers, uncaring of the others in the room. "The most important aspect of everything is right here, right now between us." Determination and unbendable will formed every line in his body. "Move your ass or I'll move it for you."

The unstable energy inside her sprang to life. She lifted her chin, squarely meeting his gaze. "You think you could?" Did he have any idea what taking Grace's powers had done to her?

His eyes flicked black and then green. Midnight blue crackled on his arms. Energy. "Yes."

Her mouth dropped open at the metamorphosis before her. Power and particles forming something new . . . a vampire with the gift. When he tightened his hold and strode toward the door, she had no choice but to follow.

Chapter 34

Moira preceded Conn inside her apartment, the energy still buzzing through her system. She needed time to assimilate what she'd taken from Grace . . . beating Kell's punching bag next door held certain appeal.

Conn shut the door, leaning against it with a dull thud. She turned to face him, forcing a gasp back down her throat. His eyes were black—fathomless and deep. She bit her lip. "I know your eyes change color from green to silver . . . have they ever turned black before?"

"No." His voice lowered to a hoarse rumble. Scary, yet sexy as hell. "I assume once I absorb this energy I'll return to normal." The gaze he used to travel her length and back up scalded rather than smoldered.

"That's how the transfer usually works." The marking at her hip flared to life. She forgot all about Kell's training room. "You know. There are ways to burn off the energy." Some of it, anyway.

"Are there, now?" Conn asked very softly.

Her calves bunched to run as instinct recognized the predator fixing his sights on her. Desire held her in place. "I believe you wanted to talk?"

His stillness reminded her of the split second before lighting struck . . . when the air charged and the world stopped breathing. Not by a whisper did he twitch or respond. He just waited.

She suddenly understood why prey froze when scenting danger. There had to be movement to know which way to run. "So, uh, you're kind of mad, huh?"

His gaze remained steady.

She eyed the several feet to her bedroom and the door that locked. The air changed, swirled with tension, providing warning. Yet Conn hadn't shifted a muscle.

Irritation blew out on her sigh. "Fine. I tricked you. Sorry." She scowled, taking a step toward him. "Coven law is Coven law, and I had to fight Grace alone. You wouldn't have taken your seat in the box had I told you the truth."

"That's irrelevant." Finally he spoke. Low, soft, and way too deadly.

"Irrelevant?" She put her hands on her hips. "No, it isn't."

"Yes, it is." His calmness made her tremble. "I've repeatedly explained that we come first. You and I. Loyalty and truth. Period."

"I understand, but you wouldn't have stepped aside."

"You're not listening. I don't give a damn about the repercussions. About the end result of any situation. What matters is us. The truth." He pushed away from the door, washing the scent of sage and gunpowder over her. "Even if you believe without a doubt that you won't like the results, you tell me the truth, Brat."

Exasperation made heat rise in her face. "Then we would've gotten in a big fight, Conn."

"I don't care. We don't need to agree. But I won't tolerate tricks or lies. You know that." He reached out and enclosed her biceps with strong hands.

The word *tolerate* made her want to punch him. They may have mated a century ago, but she'd grown with the times. She lifted her chin. "Trust goes both ways, Connlan."

The heat from his palms speared to her abdomen, peaking her nipples on the way.

"You're right." He lowered his face to an inch of hers. "Not once have I tricked or lied to you, Dailtín. So understand this. As my mate, you don't want to live in a world where I don't trust you."

The unsteady energy within her pores ignited with her temper. "Is that a threat?"

His gaze narrowed. "I don't threaten. Ever." Black fire danced on his skin, melding blue and green.

What kind of power did the combining energies give him? Her body vibrated with the need to move. To burn off some energy. She struggled to concentrate, to clear her mind. "I'm so tired of everyone telling me what to do."

His irritated snort filled the entryway. "Stop whining and take a chance, Moira."

She saw red. "Whining? What the hell? I do take chances, Conn. I take a chance every time I go out and enforce our laws. The chance of losing my powers, the chance of losing the opportunity to someday lead the council." He had no clue what he was talking about.

"No." The mocking glint in his eye was going to get him singed beyond recognition. "You're the Seventh, darlin', and you have no problem using those abilities. Taking them, doing what you're meant to do. Enforce." He moved closer with the grace of any animal at home in his own skin. "The only unexpected, the only true chance you need to take, is . . . me."

As truth went, the statement rang true.

"You've been in love with who you thought I'd be for a century." Her chin lifted. She wasn't just the Seventh. Or the Seventh they'd all envisioned. What if he couldn't stand who she truly ended up to be?

"No. I've been in love with *you*."

At his words, something eased inside her. A harsh fear she hadn't realized she harbored. The man didn't lie. For good or bad, for now and the future, he wanted the real her. Whoever she turned out to be.

Time for her to go for what she truly wanted. "I choose you, Connlan." He'd always offered her everything he had, everything he was—the light and the dark. "We're going to fight." The idea of a peaceful existence made her want to sigh—the possibility of it made her want to laugh. "You had better like working with explosives."

His slow smile filled her with warmth. "The strongest steel is forged in the hottest fires, Moira. A fact I've always understood."

God, loved him. Leaping forward, she caught her knees on his hips, her lips on his. He bore the brunt of her attack easily, both hands cupping her ass. Energy crackled with audible pops between them, around them. She dug her fingers into his thick hair, delving deep, her tongue sweeping inside his mouth, her core against his.

Flame roared through her too hot to be considered passion, too desperate to be considered need. Hunger. Raw and absolute, it opened its jaws and consumed. Good and bad, darkness and light, fate and free will . . . all ceased to exist. The world narrowed to her mouth on his, her body absorbing his heat.

A rumble hung in the distance . . . a shifting of the earth. Of the universe. She heard the warning, she *felt* the change . . . but passion enslaved her. "More. God. More," she mumbled, reaching down to rip his shirt over his head.

A low moan escaped her as she pressed a kiss on his pounding jugular, tracing his heated skin down to his collarbone to nip. Prickles of pain swept her scalp as he knotted a hand in her hair and jerked her face back to his. Any restraint he may have owned disappeared, leaving strength and demand in its place. Gone was the gentleness he always seemed to aim for, deserting him along with his control.

Her shirt hit the floor along with her bra. His free hand was everywhere, jerking her clothing away, claiming her flesh with a heated palm. The dark flush across his face should've provided warning. Need mixed with determination, and absolute power bracketed hard lines on either side of his mouth, making him look more like a vengeful god than an earthly soldier. She'd given him her choice, and he'd accepted. He was beyond this world. His expression showed he wanted her . . . and nothing would keep him from having her.

She shivered at the knowledge.

Cool air brushed her shoulder blades. Moving. They were moving. He kissed her again, growling against her, taking control, taking over. She forgot all about movement or fear. Her back hit the softness of her bed. She had a second to breathe as he shed his clothing.

He leaped forward, caging her, the meddling energies dancing on his skin. Her nerve endings fired, fighting the burn, then accepting the heat. His mouth sought her nipple, scalding hot. He flicked. She cried out, the pleasure beyond imagination.

Running her hands down his smooth back, she marveled at the strength. His palms glided down her sides, tracing each rib. His mouth wandered up her chest, over her collarbone to nip at the underside of her jaw—gentle and passionate.

His mouth found hers. Firm, possessive, his tongue explored while his body pinned hers to the bed.

Desire, love, fate all combined into a pure need. "Now, Conn."

With one hard thrust, he plunged inside her. The growl he gave was all animal, all claiming.

She arched her back at the invasion, shock opening her

eyes wide. Nerves flared to life in need, and she clutched his ass, wrapping her legs around his hips. His eyes were still black, and she tried to focus, tried to be concerned. But then he started to move, to pound, to take her somewhere nowhere near her bedroom.

The world sheeted white.

All sound disappeared.

She clung onto his shoulders, her nails digging, fighting to stay tethered to earth. Reality spun away. The elements commingled around them in pure energy. Light zapped around the room, whistling through the air.

His mouth dropped to trace her ear, his fang nipping her lobe.

Pleasure cut hard and deep, stamping her for all time. The race to the pinnacle was more important than breathing, than living. A craving set up in every pore as he lifted her hips from the bed, hammering into her with a force born of true need. Life or death. The beginning and the end.

She struggled against the crest, against the unknown for one second, teetering on the brink of the unfathomable, instinct screaming there was no way back.

With a sob from beyond her soul, she broke.

The world exploded. Her insides blew apart with a pleasure so intense her mind shattered, the only possibility of survival existing in Conn's strong hands holding her against his body. She clung, riding the waves, allowing the energy between them to seep into her flesh, into her existence. She convulsed around him, forcing a growl from his mouth as he came, his entire body rigid.

Seconds, minutes, maybe lifetimes later, he relaxed his hold, resting against her.

She gave a weak push. "Ug. Heavy."

"Sorry," he murmured, flopping to his side, deep breaths panting from his smooth chest.

She snorted a soft laugh. The sweat on her skin and on his dried with the air. At least she wasn't the only one whose world just blew up. She glanced around. Her entire room was demolished. The curtains hung drunkenly from a destroyed curtain rod, her jewelry looked like a spoiled child had flung the collection to the floor and the smooth walls held dents. "Holy crap."

Conn chuckled, rolling to face her. His amazing eyes had returned to their deep green color. Relief nearly swamped her. Then he spoke. "Ah. Let me check something." He pushed her gently to her side, his hand caressing her left buttock.

A flare of pain made her catch her breath. "Ow. Knock it off." She rolled back over.

He twisted his lip, puzzlement drawing his brows down. "I, ah, I marked you, darlin'."

"I know." Even now, the marking on the front of her hip pulsed with need. But . . . "Wait. Why does my ass burn?" Oh no he didn't. Twisting her neck, she looked over her shoulder. "Another marking? How?"

"Ah, I don't know. It's never happened before." He smiled, pleasure softening his hard face. "Perhaps because we've been apart for so long . . . more likely from the weird energy we took from a member of the Nine. Probably won't happen again."

Pleasure swamped her anew. "It means a new start. One we choose." Just in case, she'd make sure his hands stayed away from her face during sex for the next century.

He yanked the covers over them, drawing her into his body. "So. How are you feeling?"

She took inventory and snuggled her butt into his groin. "Better. That was a heck of a way to burn off energy." Her fingers plucked at the comforter as she sought the right words. "With the demons being angry we didn't align with them, Daire will need to cover the Baltic States for a while."

"That makes sense. We're sending Jase . . . maybe we should send them together." Conn ran a broad hand down her arm to tangle his fingers with hers, his heated chest warming her spine. "Does that mean you'll want the U.S. territory?"

She stiffened. "Well, yes. Are you saying my being an enforcer is all right with you now?"

His exhale blew her hair forward. "*All right* doesn't quite fit. But I do understand your need to protect your people . . . and you're good at it." His soft kiss against her head melted her. "I love you, Moira. Asking you to be someone you're not, I wouldn't do. Besides, I'm excellent backup. And now that I have all this witch energy, I'd make a hell of an enforcer."

She laughed, relief relaxing her muscles. "You lead the Realm soldiers, Conn. That's plenty."

"I already told you I'm a multitasker." He tugged her to her back, covering her with his body. "You don't go out without me, Dailtín." Soft, sated, his expression still held no small amount of determination.

Damn compromise. "Yeah. We fight well together." Talk about an understatement. She smiled. He understood her . . . and would let her follow her own path. "I love you, Connlan."

His smile went wide. "I love you, too. So how about we get married at the chapel where I first saw you? Tomorrow?"

Married? "Well, I guess it's time. I mean, since we courted for a century." Her next smart retort was cut off by his lips on hers. She kissed him back, sliding into fate or maybe destiny. Either way, it was one she chose.

Epilogue

Safe in the underground lab in Oregon, Emma Kayrs slammed her hands onto her hips, facing the King of the Realm. Irritation kept her from jumping into his arms in welcome. "You went off to battle again."

Surprise flashed in his silver eyes. "Of course."

She lifted both eyebrows. "Excuse me?"

"That's my job, love." He cocked his head at the machines hurriedly spitting out data. "What have you found?"

"Oh no." He was not going to distract her by talking about science. "I know your job. Leading doesn't include putting yourself on the front line." He wouldn't be the stubborn vampire she adored if he had allowed anyone else to face danger for him. And she loved the sweet picture he'd sketched of her sleeping that he'd left on the nightstand for her. But still.

Lethal charm flashed with his smile. "I'll be more careful next time I fight." Two strides had him in her space and grabbing her arms. His lips took hers with a rush of power . . . and need.

She fell into his kiss with a soft sigh. When he lifted his head, she had to blink several times to regain focus. "So, ah, welcome back. I found a wedding dress."

Pleasure darkened his eyes. "Did you, now?"

A shiver of want wandered down her spine. "Yes. It's very pretty."

"I'm sure it's nothing compared to you." He brushed hair back from her face. "Anyhow, you won't be wearing anything for long." Lethal charm lifted his lips.

Desire warmed her abdomen. "You're sweet, King." Focus. She needed to focus. "Are we all right with the Coven Nine?"

"Yes, solid." He rubbed his palms along her arms, sending tingles through every nerve in her body. "I have Simone reaching out to the demons now. She seems to think there's some unrest in the demon ranks. We'll see."

Interesting. If the demons fought each other, then they couldn't fight the vampires. Emma glanced at the humming machines. "The werewolf you caught was a panther shifter . . . male." The first male nonhuman werewolf they'd found.

Dage sighed. "I'm sorry to hear that." His gaze narrowed on her face. "Have you slept?"

She tried unsuccessfully to take a step back. "Ah, well . . . kind of—" She yelped as the world tilted and she found herself over his shoulder. "What the hell?"

"You need sleep." He caressed her rear. "But first, let's go for a swim, love."

In another section of headquarters, Cara Kayrs leaned back against the headboard deep in the earth, her family surrounding her. A bandage covered the side of her neck, although the wound had already healed—thanks to a good dose of Talen's blood. Soft light cascaded from a bedside lamp, illuminating a spotted white Anne plant surrounded by several budding African violets on the antique dresser. Fresh oxygen pumped into the air from the vents and the natural plants.

Janie snuggled close, the baby slept peacefully on Cara's

chest, and her mate ran his fingers through her hair as she rested on his shoulder. She inhaled a deep breath, tempted to yank her empathic shields into place. "Would you relax? I'm fine."

Talen growled low and quiet, stretching his long legs out on the huge bed. "You took a bullet right after giving birth. After being kidnapped from what should've been a secured location." His hold tightened, emotion slamming off him in waves. "I'm never leaving your side again."

Oh, for the love of Pete. "Then I'll end up beheading you." She tried to joke, but thought she might actually be serious.

"Humph." He sighed. "Conn ripped Demidov's head off." Irritation tinged the words. "I wanted to finish him."

Cara wasn't sorry the witch had died. "What do you think is going to happen with the Coven Nine? Will Moira need to join?"

"She doesn't seem to want to join. Which is good, because I don't think Conn would let her right now . . . too much unrest in Ireland." Talen settled Cara more comfortably across his broad chest, reaching over to cup his son's sleeping head. "We need to name this little man, don't you think?" His voice lowered in wonder. "He's big, even for a Kayrs babe."

Cara smiled into the darkness. "I thought . . . maybe . . . Garrett Talen Kayrs."

Talen exhaled. "After my father and myself." He placed a gentle kiss on the top of her head. "I wondered if you wanted to give him Paulsen as a middle name."

She hadn't even considered Paulsen. "No. My last name is Kayrs, as Emma's will be soon." Oh crap, what about Janie? Janie's father had died before her birth, and Cara had given her the Paulsen name.

Talen reached easily into her mind. "No worries, mate. I care little about the human legal system but figured you still might. I'm drawing up papers to legally change Janie's last name to mine. I guess they're adoption papers. Though she's my daughter whether or not some damn paper says so."

Cara's bones melted along with her heart. "We should talk to Janie."

"I asked Janie." His breath brushed her hair with warmth. In fact, huge rolling waves of heat cascaded off the vampire

"You did?" Cara shifted her gaze to her sleeping daughter. "What did she say?"

Talen chuckled. "She raised one eyebrow at me . . . you know, like Dage does?"

"Dage does, huh?" Cara mused. Every single Kayrs man had the gift. With Talen, it usually meant he was irritated with something Cara had done . . . often involving danger of some sort. "What did she say?"

"Well, she lifted her tiny little chin and said her last name had always been Kayrs. That I could even ask her preschool teacher Miss Kimmie from last year because that's what Janie put on her papers." He shifted. "Speaking of which, I'm concerned."

Cara stilled. "About Janie?"

"We're relocating a few military families here, vampire and shifter. So she has some kids to play with. Our girl may be the key to the future, but she needs a decent childhood. The chance to be a kid."

Cara shut her eyes, emotion all but choking her. The man truly did love them. Completely. "You're sweet, Talen."

His growl made her smile. "I most certainly am not." Against her shoulder, his heart beat steadily. For her. "We took Janie away from friends and school. When I, ah . . ."

"When you kidnapped us?" Thank God.

"When I took you, and you saved me." He nuzzled her hair. "I hadn't realized I was only half alive until you showed me warmth."

For a warrior, the man held charm. "I love you, Talen."

"I love you too, mate."

Janie fought a grin at the talking, snuggling even closer to her mama. Life was good. Her baby brother finally showed up, and everyone was okay. Well, kind of. Aunt Katie might get a new job hunting werewolves, and Uncle Jordan was gonna be mad. Aunt Mowra needed to learn how to let Uncle Conn help sometimes, or he'd put her underground again. Auntie Emma was going to punch Uncle Dage in the face. He really wasn't gonna like that. And Mama. Well, Mama still had the sickness. But it was moving slow and there was time to fix it.

But for now, Janie needed to check in with Zane, so she let sleep come.

The dream started in the middle of a sunny day . . .

Janie wandered through a forest with leaves bigger than her daddy's hands. Big, furry, and green. Lime green. Maybe they really existed somewhere. Maybe not.

The dirt trail crunched under her new tennis shoes, so she imagined peppermint candy lined the way. Up ahead a bunch of rocks tumbled next to the side of a mountain.

Kalin sat on one, swinging his leg back and forth.

Her tummy hurt. Like it did after she ate too much popcorn.

She sucked in air that didn't smell like peppermint. But her chin lifted like her mama's always did, and she kept moving until she stood in front of him. "I didn't think you'd be back."

"I found my path." He wore faded jeans and a shiny

green shirt that matched his eyes. The black nails and lipstick were gone. The red tips on his black hair shone in
the sun, somehow brighter than before. His jaw looked
hard, and his shoulders looked wide.

"You picked wrong." If Kalin had chosen the right
way, he wouldn't have barged into her dream. Now they
couldn't ever be friends. She wouldn't cry in front of him,
though. No matter what he said, she wouldn't cry.

He shrugged. "You tried to help me, I know you did.
But sometimes fate decides. Like with the scorpion."

She wrinkled her nose. "What scorpion?" The weird
crawlers with the poisoned pinchers kind of freaked her
out. She and Aunt Emma had watched a show on them a
while ago.

"Every scorpion." Kalin studied her, looking for something.

What, she didn't know.

"You're probably too young. It's the story about the
scorpion and the frog. The old parable."

"What's a para . . . para . . . ?" She hated it when other
people knew more stuff than she did.

"Parable. It's a story." Even while making her sad, his
voice stayed gentle. Almost as if he didn't have a choice in
this life, and neither did she. He was wrong. "An old story.
Do you want to hear it?"

No. "Okay."

He patted the rock beside him, and she lifted her chin
higher. No way was she sitting by him if he decided to be
bad again.

His smile flashed really sharp teeth. "One day there was
a terrifying flood. A dangerous flood that threatened the
entire world. It swept through a valley, and a scorpion
and frog got stuck on the side of a rushing river. A mean-
looking stork waited on the other side, probably wanting
to eat the poor frog."

Her lip began to shake and she bit it. Somehow she knew the frog wasn't going to have a good day. "What did they do?"

"The scorpion asked for a ride across the river, and in exchange promised to protect the frog from the stork. Of course, the frog was scared, but he wanted to survive." Kalin grabbed a blade of grass from the rock, twirling it through his fingers. He had a pretty voice. Already deep, and he seemed older than fifteen.

Old enough to change his life. "We all want to survive." Her voice came out sad, but she couldn't help it.

He nodded. "Yes. We do. So, the frog let the scorpion jump on his back, and he started to swim. About halfway across, the scorpion lashed out and stung the frog."

Something inside her ached. Right where her heart was. "Why?"

Kalin raised his dark eyebrows. "That's what the frog asked, because now they were both going to die. You know what the scorpion said?"

"No," Janie whispered. "What did he say?"

"The scorpion said, 'because that's my nature.' " Kalin threw the blade of grass onto the ground. "And they both died."

They didn't have to. They could've swum to the other side and both lived. Maybe even changed the way everyone lived. "I don't like your story."

Kalin shrugged. "Probably not. But you know who I am in the story, Janie?"

She drew in air, glad trees stood nearby. Even in dreams, she liked nature near, just like her mama. "Yes, Kalin, I do."

"Good." He jumped off the rock.

She stayed still. "You're the stork."

His head jerked back, surprise filling his eyes. "The stork?"

"Yes. Nobody knows what the stork is gonna do. He

can do the right thing, and save them all." Or he could watch them drown.

Kalin rubbed his chin, surprise turning to thoughtfulness. "You're going to be a fascinating woman someday, Janie." He glanced toward the forest and shrugged. "I look forward to proving you wrong. I'm not the stork."

Janie followed his gaze, nearly taking a step back at the boy striding out of the trees. Zane. But not completely Zane. He'd grown taller, his black hair cut short, a purple bruise down his chin. Anger swirled in the deep green of his eyes. Something scary swirled around him.

Kalin stepped closer to her. "Well. If it isn't the frog."

At the moment Zane looked more like a scorpion. He'd dressed in all black, even his big boots.

Janie clasped her hands together. "I've missed you. Where have you been?"

He didn't look at her, just kept his gaze on Kalin. "Leave now."

"Or what?"

"I'll kick your ass."

Janie barely kept from gasping. Zane never swore. At least not in front of her. He was eleven, yet was as tall as Kalin already. And as big in the shoulders. She searched for something to get him to look at her. "Kalin told me the story of the scorpion and the frog."

Zane's eyelids lowered a little bit, making him seem more dangerous. "She's too young for that story."

Kalin laughed. "I figured she should know the players, Zane. Who we all are." He took three strides toward the edge of the rocks. "I suppose you think you're the scorpion?"

Zane shook his head before Kalin finished his sentence. "Nope. Not even close."

Kalin threw back his head and laughed, quickly disappearing behind the rocks.

Janie waited until he'd left the dream before turning toward Zane. "Where have you been?"

He shrugged. "Training. I told you I'd be busy." Finally he looked at her.

"What happened to your face?"

"My mother's people train harder than my father's." Zane stretched his neck. "Why did you let Kalin in your dream?"

"I didn't. He sat on the rocks when I got here." She'd stopped being so careful about keeping her dreams private. "I talked to him before and thought he had changed." Unlike the scorpion.

Zane shook his head. "Kalin isn't going to change."

"Are you?" The words came out before she could think.

"No." The word was soft, but Zane's eyes looked hard. "It's you and me, Janie Belle. No matter what I have to do . . . I promise it'll be you and me. We're gonna fix it all."

She reached forward and took his hand. "Do you want me to come find you?" Everyone called her smart. A smart girl would figure out a way.

"No." Zane's smile finally showed up. The fun one she loved. "Not right now. When the time comes, I'll find you."

"You promise?" She wished she could hurry up and grow, so they could fix the world.

His smile faded. "I promise, Janie Belle."

She grinned wider. "'Cause you're the scorpion?"

He shook his head. Very slowly. "No, Belle. I'm the flood."

Did you miss the first two books in Rebecca's DARK PROTECTORS series?

Fated

Marry Me . . .

Cara Paulsen does not give up easily. A scientist and a single mother, she's used to fighting for what she wants, keeping a cool head, and doing whatever it takes to protect her daughter Janie. But "whatever it takes" has never before included a shotgun wedding to a dangerous-looking stranger with an attitude problem . . .

. . . Or Else

Sure, the mysterious Talen says that he's there to protect Cara and Janie. He also says that he's a three-hundred-year-old vampire. Of course, the way he touches her, Cara might actually believe he's had that long to practice . . .

Claimed

A Daring Rescue

Emma Paulsen is a geneticist driven by science. But she's also a psychic, so when a dark, good-hearted vampire frees her from the clutches of the evil Kurjans, she realizes he must be the man who's been haunting her dreams. But with a virus threatening vampires' mates, Emma may discover a whole new meaning of "lovesick." . . .

A Deadly Decision

As King of the Realm, Dage Kayrs has learned to practice diplomacy. Still, it's taken three hundred years to find his mate, so he'll stop at nothing to protect her—even if it means turning his back on his own kind. . . .

Printed in Great Britain
by Amazon

22910193R00199